THE FUTURE KING

LOGRES

VOLUME ONE: BOOK ONE

M. L. MACKWORTH-PRAED

Copyright © 2015 M. L. Mackworth-Praed

M. L. Mackworth-Praed asserts the moral right to be identified as the author of this work.

ISBN-13: 978-1516827244
ISBN-10: 1516827244

This novel is entirely a work of fiction. The names, characters and incidents portrayed in it are the work of the author's imagination. Any resemblance to actual persons, living or dead, events or localities is entirely coincidental.

Any reference to historical persons in this novel is for the benefit of the narrative and is entirely for fictional purposes.

All rights reserved.
This book or any portion thereof may not be reproduced or used in any manner whatsoever without the express written permission of the author except for the use of brief quotations in a book review.

For Kristof

Gwenhwyfar

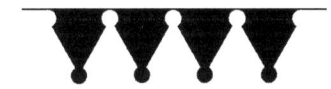

She always liked to watch the rain.

The pregnant clouds split open to douse the earth below, cleansing the air with fresh scents that leaked through the gap in the passenger window. She inhaled deeply and bit the skin away from her fingernails, the smell of leather upholstery sickly as it mingled with the damp. Past the pane of glass, distorted by racing droplets, figures hurried towards swinging doors. The familiar clipping of boots caught her attention. Her mother strode towards the car under the protection of a designer handbag.

'This will be good for you, Gwen.' A short hard slam of the car door, and her mother was adjusting herself in the driver's seat. 'You'll see. I'd have loved the chance to go to a new school. Make new friends, meet new people…' The keys were implanted into the ignition with surgical precision. 'Besides, it's all set. Your father's starting his new job today. Here. I got you your timetable.' The sheet of paper hovered between them until her mother abandoned it in her lap. 'Everything's arranged. You just need to go and find 44B. The receptionist said it was upstairs.'

Gwenhwyfar examined the alien sheet. The paper scraped over her half-polished nail. 'Where upstairs?'

'Oh, I don't know. You'll just have to ask someone. I'm supposed to be at the hairdresser's at half past nine.' Her mother smiled briskly as she released the handbrake. 'It'll be fine, trust me. Just be yourself.'

With one kiss on the cheek Gwenhwyfar clambered out of the car into the rain, tugging at her new skirt in a conscious effort to make it longer. Her mother offered a wave with a flick of her short blonde hair as the four-by-four glided over the soaked tarmac. Gwenhwyfar turned to the building with the bitter rain pricking her skin. The windows gaped at her until she pushed her way through the stiff double doors. A shrill bell sounded as the morning rush greeted her.

'No pushing in the corridors, Miss Knight!' someone proclaimed, his voice straining to be heard above the din. 'Miss Morte! Miss Woods! I said no pushing in the corridors!'

Gwenhwyfar stumbled as the students barged past her. The teacher shouted again, but the culprits were already halfway down the corridor, sauntering along as a tight-knit trio. Gwenhwyfar consulted her soggy timetable. The teacher hurried by. This was her chance.

'Excuse me—!' The thin man seemed to deliberately walk faster as she attempted to gain on him, her short legs hindering her progress. 'Sir? I was wondering—'

They nearly collided. He looked straight over her head at first, but eventually his eyes found their way down to hers.

'Sorry,' Gwenhwyfar stammered, 'but could you tell me where room 44B is?'

He didn't quite seem to hear.

'Forty-four B? It's upstairs, but I don't know where.'

The teacher's shoulders snapped back like the wings of a bird in landing. 'Ah yes! You must be the new student. Gwenhwyfar?'

She always had to correct people. 'Gwen.'

'That's right, of course! Gwen.' He pointed a bony finger after the three girls. 'Just take the second staircase; then go left. It's at the end of the corridor by the toilets. Can't miss it.' He sent her a brief smile that might have been reassuring had he not used it as an excuse to vacate her company. As he left, an onslaught of students streamed past her. Doing her best to ignore the curious attention she found herself receiving, she made a beeline for the second staircase, at the end of the whitewashed hall.

Logres wasn't as charming as her old school. It felt bare and clinical and had thin discoloured carpets. She wondered why her parents had chosen it for her, but guessed it was for convenience. It was within walking distance of their ugly new townhouse, a large building misplaced in a small cul-de-sac in the suburbs of Surrey.

She scaled the stairs far too soon for her liking. Forty-four B was dingy and poorly lit, with the once-white walls now yellowed to cream. Tables were clustered, not in rows, and as various friend groups claimed their seats she realised that there was nowhere she could sit that wasn't in plain view of the rest of the class. Quickly she chose the only empty table. A blonde girl on the table nearest to hers eyed her; then whispered with friends. The three girls who had pushed into her strode into the room. Gwenhwyfar's stomach dropped the moment their eyes homed in on her.

'You're in my seat,' was the comment that she got, her first student-to-student contact of the day. 'Move.'

Miss Knight watched her with contempt, her bag strap choked in one hand and her blazer pocket distended with the other. Her lapel was crested with the standing sword and rearing dragon of Logres. Miss Morte and Miss Woods took up positions behind her, like actresses trained to stand on their mark. Both had tried to mimic Miss Knight's every characteristic, from her carefully applied smoky eyeliner, to the arrangement of her brown hair into a self-conscious and meticulous bun.

Miss Knight swooped closer. 'Do you not speak English or something—?' Her supporting actresses giggled. 'You—are—in—my—seat. *Move.*'

'Sorry, I didn't know.' As soon as Gwenhwyfar vacated the chair, Miss Knight was sitting in it, checking her appearance in a pocket mirror. Miss Morte and Miss Woods followed suit, using the fourth chair as a bag dump.

It was the whispering blonde girl who came to her rescue. 'Hey!' she called. 'Come sit with us!' As Gwenhwyfar edged towards them the blonde girl scooted over and offered half her seat. 'You're the new girl, aren't you?' She was petite, perhaps a little taller than Gwenhwyfar, and had blue eyes with arching, scrupulously plucked eyebrows. The blush in her cheeks was a powdery rose pink. 'I'm Emily, and this is Hattie and Charlotte.' The two offered a friendly smile. Hattie was almost as blonde as Emily, while Charlotte's defining characteristic seemed to be the overuse of black mascara.

'I'm Gwen. Thanks for letting me sit with you.' She hunched her back as they had done earlier, and immediately all three girls bent towards her curiously. 'So what's her problem, then?'

'Viola's?' Emily lowered her voice. 'She's just angry with the world because her dad ran off with another man.' Hattie and Charlotte sniggered as Gwenhwyfar failed to conceal her surprise. 'She still lives with him, though. Him and his boyfriend.'

'I was in the cafeteria the other day, and I heard Rhea saying some pretty nasty stuff about Emily,' Hattie murmured. 'She said that she was a snob.'

This was news to Emily. Her outraged gasp was proof enough of that. 'She didn't!'

'She did. *And* she was spreading rumours that you were secretly going out with Gavin.'

Emily's disgust only seemed to magnify at this horrific news. 'Eww! Gavin who?'

'You know! Gavin Miles. The one who always hangs around with Tom and people.'

Gwenhwyfar looked to Viola Knight's table. The three girls were touching up their make up. 'Sorry, but which one's Rhea?'

Charlotte nodded in the direction of Miss Morte. 'The fat one: with the squashed nose. The one with long hair is Rebecca. *She* accused Emily of prank-calling her sister, and got her into a huge fight about it. I mean, if Emily *had* prank-called her sister, why would she have left her name?'

Gwenhwyfar inspected the two. Rhea looked no fatter than Rebecca, and in all honesty, neither of them seemed bigger than Charlotte herself.

'I heard Rhea left that message and just pretended it was me, because she thinks some guy she likes fancies me,' Emily smirked, glancing to the other table again. 'How pathetic is that?'

'Pretty pathetic,' Hattie agreed. Gwenhwyfar hadn't noticed that a teacher had entered the room, and was trying to get the class to quieten down. 'Then again, you can hardly blame her. No guy could possibly like her. She's *vile*!'

'Viola doesn't even like them.' Emily was sitting straight now, inspecting her perfectly painted nails for blemishes. 'She just lets them follow her around for her own amusement. I mean it's not like you ever see her with them at lunchtime—'

'Emily Rose, I said quiet!' The shock of being scolded hit home for a moment, but then the three girls were snickering again.

'Sorry miss,' apologised Emily, though the smile quirking her pink lips told Gwenhwyfar that she wasn't. Rhea and Rebecca were glaring at their table with suspicion, trying to pick up the tail ends of the conversation that had obviously been about them.

Registration was quick, though Gwenhwyfar had enough time to scan the room and learn a few names. She picked out Morgan Faye, a milk-skinned, doe-eyed girl with chestnut curls. There was a moment of horror when the teacher, Miss Ray, singled her out as new, but no introduction was asked of her and she was spared the embarrassment of stating where she was from and what she liked doing. The heavens wept outside, complementing Gwenhwyfar's sense of rising dread. People her age were like hyenas, and in this instance, involving alpha female Viola especially, Gwenhwyfar felt much like a limping gazelle.

The repetitive chime of the bell disrupted her thoughts. Emily stood up, forcing Gwenhwyfar to do the same.

'So where are you from, Gwen?'

'Swansea.' Viola's glare of contempt had just managed to subdue hers. She swept her chocolate-brown hair away from her eyes. 'You know, in Wales?'

'Wales?' Emily frowned at her. 'You're not one of those

rebels, are you?'

'Rebels?'

'You know, *separatists*.'

'No, of course not,' Gwenhwyfar replied, insulted. 'Swansea's pro-union.'

Emily's frown vanished. 'So why did you move?'

'My dad got a new job.'

'Won't you miss your old school? What was it like?'

'All right. Everyone knew each other. There were only two hundred students. It was pretty exclusive,' she added. Maybe Emily was the right hyena to hang around with, the one that would protect her, the gazelle, from the rest of the pack. 'This place is huge compared to it.'

'Really?' Emily seemed bemused. 'Logres isn't even that big. St. George's across town is almost twice the size.' They paused in the corridor, where Emily parted from Hattie and Charlotte with a quick conversation identifying where they would meet for break time.

It was hard to keep up with Emily as she weaved through the massing students, daunting in their hordes. The year sevens looked like mere children, too young to be in secondary school, and from year eight to year ten it appeared that ties became shorter and attire scruffier. The year elevens wore their uniform with an obvious amount of pride, and though Gwenhwyfar failed to conform to their generous tie length, her peers didn't seem to notice. The occasional sixth-former pushed through the crowd in their own clothes, their relaxed dress envied by others. Gwenhwyfar was doing her utmost to avoid pushing into any of them, though such a task became difficult as people began to congeal around doors.

'Any idea what room you're in first?' Emily called to her.

Gwenhwyfar pulled her crumpled timetable out of her pocket. 'Twenty-seven H?' All these room numbers sounded so alien.

'History?'

'Looks like it. Where's that, then?' She dodged a group of young boys loitering by the windowsills.

'That's in the other building.' Emily paused a moment to allow Gwenhwyfar to catch up, her ponytail swishing. 'I can walk you, if you like. It's on the way to my lesson. I've got Chemistry with Mrs Brolstone. *Vile.*'

'Who's Mr Caledonensis?' Gwenhwyfar checked her timetable once more, just to see if she also had a teacher who was 'vile'.

'Mr who?'

'Mr Cal-e-don-en-sis,' she felt her way around the name again. 'Is that how you say it?'

They passed through double doors into the rain. Emily produced a pink umbrella to protect their hair. 'I think so. He's a bit strange. Most people just call him "sir".' The umbrella opened, and Emily raised it above their heads. Gwenhwyfar moved close and followed her across the grounds.

There were so many buildings. At the top of the steps leading to the dismal block they had just left, there was a smaller building past a courtyard with benches to the right, a mobile classroom just forward and to their left, and ahead of them, some way on, a large cafeteria with huge windows and at least fifty tables. As they hurried along the path, Gwenhwyfar noticed that the cafeteria was attached to another food hall, which angled to the left. What looked like a groundskeeper's hut sat left past some concrete, and then beyond that there stood a rather out-of-place looking house that seemed as if it were lived in. Only when they walked past it did Gwenhwyfar realise it was a nursery, flanked by two concrete tennis courts lined with rusting wire. After a sharp left over some speed bumps they seemed to suddenly be in a sea of cars and bikes, all parked outside what had to be the main building, red-brick and huge, stretching the whole length of the car park, nursery, tennis courts, and beyond into a giant school field overlooked by a colossal sports hall.

For some reason they weren't heading for the oldest doors of the building. Emily was guiding her around the back, past a bike shed and into an annex, which revealed, through the gap opposite, even more mobile classrooms, grassy banks and sportsgrounds. Left were the girls' toilets, so they pushed their way right into the old smelly building. As Emily shook off her umbrella Gwenhwyfar took a moment to look around, noting the stone floors curved at the walls, the blue and grey pattern vanishing under cream paint in places, though most of it was left bare, shielded on occasion by rows of lockers which better suited the brown and beige palette of the other building. 'Is this it?' she asked.

'Yep.' Emily followed her inside. 'Wormelow. This is the Maths and Science end of the building. The other end is English, Geography and History. *That's* where you need to be.'

She was going to get lost, she knew it; how could she not, somewhere so huge? Before Gwenhwyfar had time to fully absorb all the picture frames on the wall she was pulled forward by her hand, round a corner, through some doors and then left down a seemingly never-ending corridor. 'The other building is called the Badbury Building. The one next to it is the Art block— the Sixth Form block. Then there's the sports hall, but you'll see that later. *Everyone* has to do P.E. I hate it.' Her upturned nose crinkled. 'It's *vile*.'

'Vile' seemed to be the word of the moment at Logres. Grateful that she hadn't been left to fend for herself, Gwenhwyfar listened intently, taking in every feature worth noting.

'*This* is the medical room and reception,' Emily added, almost bragging, as they passed the doors they had avoided earlier. 'And *that's* the library. Upstairs is I.T. and Science.'

'Won't you be late?'

'No,' was the careless answer, 'and if I am it doesn't matter, I'll just tell them I was showing you around.' She sent her a brilliantly pink smile. 'Oh! And left is the way to the English classrooms. You can use that way to get to the back of the assembly hall. We'll have that after lunch.'

There was so much to take in. Once they passed the English corridor, the building suddenly modernised and they were walking through a white hallway past a huge trophy cabinet. There were students massing in the lobby, complaining about the downpour. As they approached yet another pair of double doors she was shown the main entrance to the assembly hall, empty for the beginning of the day.

'We're nearly there,' was what she had been waiting to hear, though now, faced with the prospect of being abandoned by Emily, she wished they weren't. The next corridor went on for some way, the end opening out onto the grassy banks up to the sports field; but near the exit they angled left. There were stairs at the end of this corridor too, but Emily didn't divulge where they led. Some students were already going into their classrooms. Gwenhwyfar's heart was pounding. She wanted to drag Emily in with her.

'Which one is it?' People were looking at her again. For such a big school they noticed fresh blood quickly.

'That one. Come on!' Emily pulled her into the queue, where Morgan Faye stood waiting on her own in silence.

'Thanks for walking me to my lesson,' said Gwenhwyfar. 'I'd have never found it otherwise.'

The queue had nearly dispersed. 'Don't mention it,' Emily replied, her apple cheeks ripening into a smile. 'I'd better go, but I'll see you at break? We're all meeting in the canteen. The one closest to the Wormelow building, not Badbury.'

'I'll see you there,' Gwenhwyfar confirmed. Invaded by the briefest of hugs, she was left on her own again. Some of the boys in the queue had been looking at Emily, hoping she'd notice their overly boisterous behaviour, but their efforts were in vain, as she proceeded down the corridor in her own little world.

They'd been waiting for nearly ten minutes now, and there was still no sign of their teacher. The carpets in this room were green, and there were books piled to the ceiling near the chalkboard. Dust lingered everywhere.

'You're new, aren't you?'

She expected to hear that sentence a hundred times today. Gwenhwyfar looked up from where she was sitting, on her own at the back of the class, next to an unfilled seat. The boy looking down at her was handsome, his olive skin browned by the sun, and he reminded her of the actor that her old best friend had adored. His confident mouth sat in a long smirk beneath a wide pronounced nose, and a comb of dark, gelled hair unbalanced his square face.

'Yes.' She continued to draw spirals on the small notepad she'd brought in for lessons.

'You're from Wales, right?' was the next question. A glance to the front of the class told her that someone else was interested in the answer: a tall, overly broad-shouldered boy with short mousy hair and a wide, open face.

'That's right,' she responded, daring him to tease her. 'Who told you that?'

'Viola,' he shrugged. He didn't seem to think that she might not know who Viola was. He observed her with narrowed brown eyes. 'I'm Tom. What's your name?'

'Gwen,' Gwenhwyfar replied with suspicion.

'Is that Welsh?'

'I suppose.' She looked behind him again. 'Who's that?'

As Tom glanced over his shoulder, the other boy turned back to his desk. 'Oh, that's just Gavin. He asked me to come over because he thinks you're hot.'

She couldn't help it. The moment the words left his lips her cheeks were on fire. 'Excuse me?'

'Will you go out with him?'

Gwenhwyfar didn't know how he'd dared to continue with the glare he was receiving, and though she wasn't that insulted by the potential interest, she was a bit disappointed that it wasn't from him. 'No. Definitely not.'

To her horror, Tom announced her decision to the rest of the class. 'Gavin!' he hollered, 'she's not interested!'

Several eyes were on her now. Laughing as Gavin told him to "sod off", Tom returned to his seat where he received a wounded push from his friend. Gwenhwyfar wondered if Gavin was the same Gavin Miles that Hattie had mentioned, and thought that he could be the candidate, if he was usually the butt of such jokes.

She dared another look around the class. Morgan was sitting on her own working quietly, but occasionally she sneaked a glance at a boy in front of her, who gazed unaware out of the window, his dark blonde hair highlighted with gold in the pale light. The boy sitting next to him looked familiar, and Gwenhwyfar realised that he was in her tutor group. Her eyes turned to the clock. It was quarter past nine.

The door swung open, and in hurried the teacher who had given her directions upon her arrival. He stumbled to his desk, letting the sliding books in his arms collapse there like a house of cards. One fell onto Gavin and Tom's table. Immediately it was swiped.

'Thank you sir, I needed a new one of these.'

'If I could have that back, Thomas, please,' he asked with some exasperation. Tom opened it up and made a big scene in the process. It was a school planner. The teacher ripped it from his hands.

'Hey!' Tom objected. 'Didn't your mother tell you not to snatch?'

'*This*,' Mr Caledonensis stressed, 'is for our new student, Gwenhwyfar Taliesin. Not for sticky-fingered students such as yourself, Mr Hareton.'

'Gwenhwyfar—?' Tom snorted, 'I thought you said your name was Gwen?'

'Gwen's short for Gwenhwyfar, you idiot,' she snapped, hating that he just grinned.

'Yeah, just like Tom's short for Thomas,' Gavin remarked.

'And Dolf is short for Adolf,' Mr Caledonensis contributed, waving the school planner about. 'I suppose you'll need an exercise book too, Miss Taliesin. Well, here you go. You'll have to buy the textbook. In the meantime you can share Morgan's.'

As the books were dumped on her desk, she was pointed in the direction of Morgan Faye, who seemed irked by the sudden development. Mr Caledonensis returned to the head of the classroom, with no mention as to why he was late, and soon the words "Industrial Revolution" were scrawled out before them. Nervously, Gwenhwyfar gathered her things and hurried to move tables, catching the eye of the boy by the window. As she sat, she found herself lost in the warmth of his chocolate-brown eyes.

He had a strong jaw and a pronounced chin, but both sat well proportioned to an honest face that was defined by a broad, straight nose and generous, cushioned lips. Though he was fair, she could tell that he tanned easily, and his smooth skin was softened by a golden undertone. His eyes, though sunken under thoughtful eyebrows, were bright and quick, and his broad shoulders angled to a frame that was sturdy and solid.

It was obvious that she was blushing; she knew it. Suddenly lost over where to look, Gwenhwyfar threw her eyes to the front of the class where Mr Caledonensis scribbled on the board, seemingly oblivious to the rising noise levels behind him. She could still feel the boy's eyes on her. Curiosity pulled her like a magnet, and she looked at him again. Her heart skipped. This time he looked away first.

The lesson went quickly and any attempts she made to speak to Morgan were deflected with curt, one word answers. Mr Caledonensis took points from the class and added them to the board, listing phrases like: *prosperity and productivity, origins of mass production in Great Britain,* and *eventual increase in pollution and natural resources crisis.* He seemed to cover the government's role in tackling climate change uncomfortably, and swiftly moved on, setting them a series of questions to answer instead. Using the final five minutes of the lesson to check where she was next, Gwenhwyfar memorised the number of her English classroom so that she wouldn't look too lost when navigating the halls. She only just registered the due homework before the bell sounded and everyone jumped to their feet. Still shouting over the ruckus, Mr Caledonensis was forced to give up, and returned muttering to his desk.

'Sir?' Letting Morgan Faye go first, Gwenhwyfar picked her way through the maze of chairs scattered in the aisles. 'This textbook, can I have the name? Where do I get it from?'

He perked up immediately and dropped the papers he had been organising onto his desk. 'Ah, of course! I'd almost forgotten. It's quite simple—it's called *1750–2050, An Anthology*. But if you bring in twenty-five new-pounds I can order it for you through the school. You'd be paying sixty, otherwise.'

'Can I bring it in next lesson?'

'Of course,' he beamed. His sharp grey eyes watched her with interest, but then darted to the two boys that had been sitting in front of her as they followed Morgan on her way out. 'Mr Humphreys!' he called, staying the boy who had gazed at her, the one with the chocolate-brown eyes. 'One moment please, I'd like a word.' Mr Caledonensis turned back to Gwenhwyfar. 'Do you know where you're going next?'

'I think so,' she responded, self-consciously edging away.

'Marvellous. I'll see you next lesson, then. Don't be late.'

Gwenhwyfar nodded, offering a small smile to Mr Humphreys on her way out. Her heart sank at his blank response. Suddenly she was fending for herself out in the corridor. English. Left. Gwenhwyfar retraced the steps of Emily's guided tour, trying not to dwell too much on her latest embarrassment. She was sure she would have to endure many more.

ARTHUR HUMPHREYS

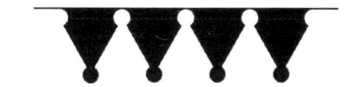

'You must be Gwenhwyfar.'

She was hovering by the open door, eyeing the rows of desks in an effort to decide where she should sit. 'Gwen.'

Her English teacher offered a kind, full smile. She was of average height, but tall to Gwenhwyfar, in her mid-forties and had a strong Roman nose. 'Gwen. You can sit at the back with Hayley. But first let's get you an exercise book.'

Gwenhwyfar followed her to the corner of the classroom and waited awkwardly as the teacher raided the supply cupboard.

'I'm Ms Appelbauer, by the way.'

'Ms Appelbauer?' Gwenhwyfar took the exercise book from her.

'Appelbauer,' she repeated, her hazel eyes lit with a quick spark. 'It usually takes students a while to get it right. Do let me know if you need anything. I know it can be hard, starting at a new school so late. Where are you from?'

'Swansea.'

'Oh? My grandmother was from Swansea, on my father's side.

I hear it's lovely.'

'It is.' She smiled politely. Ms Appelbauer gestured to the back of the class.

'Like I said, let me know if you need anything. Hayley's right there, last row. We're working on Chaucer today.'

Nodding, Gwenhwyfar found her seat. Ms Appelbauer started the lesson, and with everyone working in silence, soon she was struggling to catch up.

The moment the bell sounded Gwenhwyfar followed the masses into the cafeteria, where from the middle of the busy hall she scoured the crowd for Emily. She spotted Viola first, sitting with Tom and Gavin by the fire escape, and as Tom pulled Viola into his lap to give her a prolonged kiss she realised the connection between the two. She felt they suited one another.

'Gwen! Over here!'

She turned to find Emily, Hattie and Charlotte all huddled around the corner of a table. They waved, beckoning her forwards like a dog. 'Come sit!'

She did as she was told. 'How's it going?'

'Good!' Emily said brightly. 'How was History? Did you meet anyone nice?'

'It was all right,' Gwenhwyfar shrugged, unzipping her bag to forage for something to eat. 'I didn't really meet anyone.' Their puzzled silence urged her on. 'Met this completely weird girl though,' she blurted. 'Morgan. I had to share her book in class, which was stupid. She kept it to herself the whole time and practically hissed at me when I asked if I could see it.'

All three faces lit up. 'Really?'

'Really,' Gwenhwyfar confirmed.

'Morgan's just weird though, isn't she? She *never* says hello to us. She's so up herself.' Emily was the first one to spot her. Gwenhwyfar followed her line of sight, and found her sitting amicably with another girl at the other end of the cafeteria. Her gaze swung towards Viola's table again. Gavin still looked uncomfortable as the third wheel. Gwenhwyfar noticed the boy from her tutor group and History class at a closer table, and then found herself searching for his friend.

Emily was eying her. 'What—?'

Quickly she looked away. 'Nothing. I met Viola's boyfriend in History. He was so rude.'

'Tom?' Emily looked over, and Viola glanced back. 'He's not that bad, you know.'

'Yeah. I don't know what he sees in Viola, though. She's so *skinny*.' Hattie sniggered.

The boy twisted in his seat and waved someone his way. It was Humphreys. He was very tall. He passed unnoticed through the crowd, as she wished she could do, and sat down with an easy smile.

'Who's that?' she asked.

'Who?'

'That!' She nodded in his direction, reluctant to point.

'The fat one?' Emily frowned, perplexed.

'No! The tall guy who just sat down; over there by the fire extinguisher.'

'Oh!' Emily suddenly sounded rather smug. 'Why, are you interested?'

'What? No!' Gwenhwyfar pulled a face. 'I was just wondering. He was sat in front of me in History.'

Emily's rather annoying expression told Gwenhwyfar she didn't believe her. 'The good-looking one? That's Arthur.'

'Arthur?'

'Yes: Arthur. Arthur Humphreys.'

Gwenhwyfar's eyes strayed back to where he was sitting, engaged in what looked to be an intriguing conversation. Her teeth began to worry her lip again. For Emily, such behaviour was confirmation enough.

'You do! You *do* like him!' she gasped, laughing at her new-found discovery. Hattie and Charlotte were suddenly on the alert, pouncing in towards the table with anticipation.

'What?'

'Gwen! Gwen fancies Arthur.'

'Arthur?' The two exchanged a glance.

'I do *not*!' she insisted again, wishing that her cheeks, for once, would play on her side.

'Yes you do, it's obvious. Look! You're going all red!'

'It's not like we can blame you, he is quite fit,' Hattie gushed. 'As far as I know, he hasn't got a girlfriend.'

'We should *totally* set you up.' Emily's words made her shrink even further. 'It'll be so cute! Gwen and Arthur, Arthur and Gwen. It so works.'

Gwenhwyfar was beginning to reconsider her choice of hyena. 'But you're completely missing the point. I don't fancy him.'

'How can you not? He's *gorgeous*.' Hattie was gazing his way now. 'Other guys pick on him though. You always see them pushing him in the corridors.'

'Maybe you should go out with him then, if you like him.' Gwenhwyfar found herself glancing over again.

'Look! You can't keep your eyes off him.' Emily's glee expanded. 'We *have* to introduce you. Never know, he might like girls with funny accents.'

'And you're new. That's a definite advantage. Guys like new girls.'

'Hattie's right. You should talk to him. When's your next History lesson?' Emily leant towards Gwenhwyfar as if she was an applicant in an interview.

'Thursday, I think.'

'Thursday. Can you sit next to him?'

'Not really. I could sit behind him though.'

Emily's face lit up. 'If you sit behind him, you can talk to him at least.'

'I suppose…' She glanced over to Arthur. 'Just don't tell anyone, please? I haven't even spoken to him yet.'

'No problem.' Emily sent Gwenhwyfar a wicked grin. 'At least it'll annoy that Morgan girl. She's so in love with him, it's *sad*.'

Charlotte gave a harrumph, her eyes drifting over to where Arthur sat, oblivious to their attention.

Gwenhwyfar was pleased to discover that she was with Charlotte for next period, and as Maths wasn't one of her favourite subjects, this stroke of good luck was all the more welcome. As they made their way up to Wormelow in silence, however, it became apparent that Charlotte was far less interested in her than she had been when Emily was around. Not sure what she had done to offend the hard-faced, orange girl, Gwenhwyfar made one last attempt towards conversation as the bell marked the beginning of lunch. Barely acknowledged and hardly answered, she was relieved to find Emily waiting for them in the corridor.

'Mr Sloane let us out early,' Emily said, saving her with an invasive hug. 'Hattie's got hockey, she'll meet us later.'

Gwenhwyfar's interest was sparked. 'Hattie plays hockey?'

'Yep!' Emily responded, leading them out of the building. 'Why? Do you?'

'I used to play at my old school,' Gwenhwyfar admitted. 'I prefer lacrosse, though.'

'You play *lacrosse*?' Charlotte's words were more a snort than anything else.

'Yep!' Gwenhwyfar said, ducking Charlotte's obvious disdain. 'Do you play anything?'

'No,' Charlotte sniffed, 'why would I want to waste my time playing something stupid like lacrosse?'

'You can play it here then?' Gwenhwyfar remarked.

'The girls don't even get to play football here,' Emily divulged. 'It's either netball or rounders. If you want to do anything remotely interesting you've got to do it after school.'

'I went horse riding a lot, back home,' Gwenhwyfar told them. 'Our school had its own stables.'

'*No*. Really?' As Emily looked to her, Gwenhwyfar nodded. 'You have a horse, then?'

Gwenhwyfar felt her stomach drop. 'I used to. We had to sell him before the move. My dad said he'd be happier where he was, in the country.'

'That must be *horrible*,' Emily enthused. 'He was probably right, though. I'm sure your horse is having a wonderful time where he is. You can always come ride one of mine. We could all have a sleepover.' Charlotte didn't seem too thrilled by the suggestion, but Emily didn't notice. 'It's been ages since we last did that. When are you free?'

Inwardly reluctant, Gwenhwyfar was willing to accept for the sake of forging friendships. 'Would Friday be all right?'

'I'll have to check with my mum,' Emily said. 'If she says no

I'll just ask my dad. He always says yes to everything.'

'You're so lucky,' Charlotte whined. 'My dad never buys me anything.'

'It's just because I'm better at manipulating,' Emily laughed.

'Knowing how to manipulate one's parents is a good skill,' Gwenhwyfar agreed. They passed through the sea of cars and bikes, and headed straight for the cafeteria. 'That's how I got Dillon and Llewellyn.'

'Who?'

'Dillon, my horse; and Llewellyn, my dog. Though he's the family dog now. My dad's more attached to him than I am.' Emily seemed to find this funny, but Charlotte didn't. Gwenhwyfar decided to try again. 'So what does your dad do, Charlotte?'

'He runs his own company.'

'Oh really? What sort?'

'A sales company,' Charlotte shrugged. 'His clients are all super rich. It's complicated. You probably wouldn't understand.'

They were in the cafeteria now, surrounded by noise and the smell of wet coats and umbrellas. Charlotte said something about going to the vending machine, so Gwenhwyfar queued for lunch with Emily, even though she already had one packed.

'What's her problem?'

'What? Whose?'

'Charlotte's!' she stressed. 'She's been acting weird around me all morning.'

Emily's blue eyes cut through the room, seeking their mark. Charlotte was in a queue as well, trying not to look back. 'Maybe she's jealous? You are new, after all. She probably doesn't like not being the centre of attention for once.' They moved along in the queue.

'She doesn't?'

'It's the boys,' uttered Emily. 'She always flirts with them. She's probably annoyed that they're all ignoring her over you.'

She revealed this information with such conviction that Gwenhwyfar didn't think to question it. 'Really? They are?'

'Of course!' her hyena exclaimed. 'Look! *That* guy has been checking you out since you walked in the room, and those boys over there can *so not* take their eyes off you.' Gwenhwyfar followed Emily's line of sight, and she was right, they were all staring. None of them were particularly inspiring, though, and no sixth-formers looked her way. Most of the boys that did sneak a curious glance were similar to her fifteen years of age.

'It's probably just because I'm new,' she dismissed, shifting her eyes away.

'Probably,' Emily agreed. They arrived at the opening of the food hall, where she swiped up a red tray. 'See anyone you like?'

Her nose scrunched. 'Not really, you?'

'*Definitely* not,' was the candid response. 'Though *Charlotte* must like one of them. Maybe that's why she's been acting so weird.'

Gwenhwyfar's attention was snared. Arthur. He was standing at the other end of the food hall, foraging through the chocolate bars. Her chest contracted. A second survey of him confirmed that he was certainly handsome. Unfortunately however, Emily saw him too.

'Look!' she squealed, making the boys in front of them jump. Her voice dropped to a loud whisper. 'It's him!'

Arthur claimed his chocolate bar of choice and waited patiently as his friend dumped mashed potato and peas all over his tray. Gwenhwyfar's look of horror did nothing to dissuade

Emily as she grabbed an apple and crisps and then hurried over to cut the queue. There were loud protests behind them. Arthur was almost a foot taller than Emily, and currently faced with nothing but his back, she was rather adrift as to how to get his attention.

'Emily!' Gwenhwyfar hissed. 'Emily! Please don't!'

'It'll be *fine*! Trust me.' She cleared her throat. It didn't work.

'Em—! Don't you *dare*.'

Emily rammed her elbow into Arthur's back, her tray clattering. It resulted in the hoped-for conclusion. Arthur turned around to see what had hit him and was suddenly faced with two girls, one terrified, one deeply apologetic.

'Oh my God! I am *so* sorry.' He was frowning. Gwenhwyfar thought she detected suspicion in his eyes. 'Really I am. I *completely* wasn't looking where I was going. Are you all right?'

In the commotion Emily's apple had ricocheted past her crisps and across the floor. Arthur's skinny friend interrupted his opinion on national affairs to pick it up.

'I'm fine,' Arthur replied. 'Don't worry about it.' His friend presented the apple to Emily, who took it with a wide, pink smile.

'Thanks. Have you met Gwen?' She gestured to Gwenhwyfar as if displaying a nice framed picture. 'She's new.'

'Sort of.' Arthur sent Gwenhwyfar a quick smile. 'You're in my History class, aren't you? With Marvin.'

'Who—?'

He switched his gaze back to Emily. 'Mr Caledonensis,' he corrected.

'We call him Marv,' his friend contributed, offering Emily a lop-sided grin of his own.

'How funny. What a silly name.'

'I suppose,' added the boy. He was pale and gangly, and had a kind, disproportioned face. His eyes were too small and his teeth were too big, but his cheeks dimpled with a smile that was delightfully wonky, and his brow was creased with the imprint of thought that overshadowed his laughing eyes. 'Aren't you in my English class? I saw you earlier.'

'I think so,' Gwenhwyfar smiled. 'You're…'

'Bedivere,' he said, glancing to Emily again.

'Nice to meet you,' she told him. 'You're in our tutor group too, right?'

He nodded. 'With Miss Ray. She's quite nice, she lets us sit in early before the bell goes.'

'Not all teachers do that,' Emily divulged with a sniff. As they moved along in the queue the boys made a polite effort to converse. Bedivere asked Gwenhwyfar where she was from, and then repeated the questions she had suffered earlier, until Arthur was forced to interrupt him.

'Bed, it's your turn to pay.' He nodded towards the haggard dinner lady who stood old and thin with an impatient frown. A moment passed, and the crowd swallowed them. Emily pulled out a crisp note to pay for her meagre lunch.

'Well, I always knew he was a little strange,' she concluded, batting away the change she was given for her morsel. 'Are you sure you like him? He's a bit… off.'

'I never said I *liked* him.' Gwenhwyfar's face still burned. 'I just think he's good-looking, that's all.'

'*Oh. I see.*'

Something told Gwenhwyfar that she really didn't.

'We probably should have asked to sit with them. Did you see Bedivere? He was practically gawping at me. *Gross.*'

Thinking that was a little bit unfair, Gwenhwyfar nodded in agreement. 'He can't help it—he is a man, after all.'

Emily giggled at this, and took her place at her usual spot in the canteen. The rain had started to drizzle again, and Charlotte was nowhere to be seen. 'So is Arthur, you know. If you want him, Gwen, it won't be hard to get him.'

A gusty breath bellowed through the trees past the window-panes, turning the spittle to hard rain. 'Who says I do?'

'Hello cariad, how was school?'

Overshadowed by the lean figure of her father, Gwenhwyfar glanced up from her favourite lifestyle magazine. Her homework sat abandoned on her desk. 'Fine.'

'Only fine?' He perched next to her. A city of unopened boxes towered around the bed.

'I suppose it wasn't too bad.' Gwenhwyfar turned the page. 'I met a few nice girls. Most were horrible.'

She heard the frown in his voice. 'Horrible?'

'Yep! Or *vile*, as they would say.' A small smile relieved her of further explanation. 'Can't we go home yet?'

'We are home. Besides, Llewellyn's already claimed a spot in the kitchen. We can't move the poor beast now.'

'But where are we going to walk him? You know he prefers the country.'

'There's a few parks we can try. Honestly Gwen, he'll love it. Your mother and I did do our research before we moved. Is your new school really that terrible? I'll bet you that my day was worse.'

'No, not terrible,' she sighed. 'Just… different.' She glanced up to him, and saw the deep creases in his brow. 'It was fine really. I mean it's just like my old school. I have homework and everything.' When he smiled, she did too. 'So how was your day?'

'Terrible!' he expelled, slapping his suited knees with a clap. 'I was late. A police officer stopped me.'

Gwenhwyfar sat up. 'You got stopped by the police? Why?'

'Apparently one of my brake lights was out.'

'Was that it?'

'Yes, but he decided to do a full search anyway. He said that they were doing spot checks on vehicles, something about warning levels being critical, but when are they not?'

'That's stupid,' she scowled.

'It was very unnerving. It was almost like he was looking for something to prosecute me for. The longer he searched the more I began to think about what he might find. Which of course is ridiculous, because all I had in the car were work things. In the end I was a full forty minutes late. Not a good impression to make on your first day.'

'Did your boss understand?'

'Just. Well, he can't fire me for it; I've only just started. I've agreed to work overtime.'

Gwenhwyfar felt her heart lower with disappointment. There was a call from downstairs, a voice straining to be heard in the large townhouse that twisted several floors up.

'Ah yes! Supper's ready. I was supposed to ask you to lay the table. Better hurry.' He stood and stretched, groaning with discomfort as his thin bones crunched in his neck. 'Dere mlân.' *Come on.*

Supper passed with the three of them sitting disjointedly at the over-sized mahogany table. The rain had long since lessened, and now that night was upon them the windows gazed out into darkness.

'Oh, I forgot to mention!' her mother exclaimed, beans suspended halfway between her plate and her mouth. 'Guess who I saw at the hairdresser's today? Gwen? Someone whose child goes to the same school as you! How funny is that?'

Her father stepped in when Gwenhwyfar failed to respond. 'Really? That is quite funny. Who was it, then? Is their child in the same year?'

'Not only the same year, but she's in the same tutor group. I wouldn't have known had I not had to pick up Gwen's timetable this morning. She was called Olivia, and said her daughter was Emily. Emily something? Pass me the sauce please, Garan.'

The sauce was handed to Gwenhwyfar, who handed it to her mother. 'Thank you,' she beamed. 'What do you think, by the way? Of my hair?'

'I think it's lovely, Eve,' Garan smiled. 'Though I do like your natural colour, too.'

Gwenhwyfar twisted the cap of the still water. 'I met an Emily today. She showed me around school. Her surname is Rose. She has horses, apparently. She said I could ride them whenever I want.'

'Well that's kind of her,' Garan remarked, slurping his drink.

'She invited me over this Friday to stay the night. Can I?'

'Of course!' Eve enthused, eager for her daughter to make friends. 'Her mother seemed very agreeable. She gave a tenner to the homeless child that was begging outside.' Eve flicked her newly bleached hair over her shoulder.

'A tenner?' Garan's eyebrows arched. 'She does know that it's probably been given to some man who'll spend it all on drugs?'

'If she's that rich, why would she mind? She even tipped her hairdresser twenty percent. I think she was just showing off.'

Gwenhwyfar frowned at the pointless diversion her parents seemed to be taking. 'A homeless child—? Where were the parents?'

'Their parents are probably the ones gathering the money it collects,' her father explained.

'So the parents are homeless too?'

Garan shook his head. 'Probably not, cariad. The child isn't likely to be homeless, either. It was probably just a scam.'

'He looked fairly homeless to me,' Eve disputed.

'A good scam, then,' Garan maintained.

'His teeth were rotting. I don't know about you, but no parent I know would let their child's teeth rot for a scam. He was too thin and dirty.'

'Well, then he must have been an immigrant. You know how hard it is for them here. Of course he was homeless.'

'He was English.'

'He can't have been. He was probably an illegal.'

'He wasn't foreign,' Eve insisted. 'He wasn't the only one either. The little things try to wash your car if you stop for too long. Honestly, it's like being abroad. Some of them were going through bins.' Her mother's dismissive attitude changed to confusion as Gwenhwyfar's face flooded with distress. 'But darling, it's nothing to worry about. Many people just can't afford homes these days.'

'How come there were never any back home?' Gwenhwyfar looked to her father. The topic seemed to have put him off his food.

'We lived in a rich part of Swansea, Gwen, away from all that,' Eve said. 'It helped we were in the country. They cluster in the cities. Usually if there were too many of them, or if they upset the locals, they got moved.'

'Moved where?'

Garan looked up to Eve, who shrugged.

'To a sheltered community, I think, nearer Cardiff. There are lots there. They help such people get back on their feet.'

'Mobilisation Centres,' Garan divulged. 'Places where the homeless and disabled can work for a living and integrate back into society.' He leant back in his chair, and turned his gaze out of the bare windows.

'It's the recession,' Eve added, 'it makes it hard for people to find work. Besides, some of them don't *want* to find work. They're perfectly happy living off handouts. They're lucky they get that kind of support at all.'

Gwenhwyfar abandoned her food and rubbed the brim of her glass with her thumb.

'Oh, please don't worry about it, darling. People like us don't need to concern ourselves with such things. Your father and I are more than capable of looking after you. It's only the small minority that end up homeless. We'll be fine.'

The table fell to silence. The low whine of Llewellyn, their Catalan Sheepdog, reverberated around the kitchen. His large eyes looked woefully for food.

'I need money for a school book,' Gwenhwyfar blurted out. 'It's for History. The teacher said it would be forty new-pounds.'

'Forty?'

Gwenhwyfar shrugged. 'He said it would be sixty if we don't get it through the school. This way I'll have it for Thursday. I need it to finish my homework.'

Eve looked to Garan. 'I see,' he murmured, reaching into the jacket suspended on the back of his chair. He pulled the correct amount from his leather wallet. 'Here you go.'

Gwenhwyfar thanked him sweetly and clasped the notes in her hand, comforted by the feel of wealth against her palm. After supper she found herself searching the national news for anything about the homeless and disabled, but there was nothing, only reports about the Prime Minister's recent charitable activities and the dispute pertaining to the historical abolition of the monarchy. It was gone ten when she finally abandoned her search, diverted by online shopping websites. She ordered a few coveted items on a whim using her own debit card, subbed on a regular basis by her father, and then switched off her computer to settle into bed. Her mind played over her new possessions, putting herself narcissistically into scenarios that involved the attention of an eager Arthur as she flaunted her new top, mingling at an imagined party.

Logres

The next two days settled Gwenhwyfar into her new routine. She started to learn her way around the school grounds and forged fledgling friendships with teachers and students alike, discovering that Arthur not only shared History with her but all three Sciences, too. As Emily and Hattie became more and more enthused about her pursuit of Arthur, she saw Charlotte less and less, and on Thursday morning all three girls were of the opinion that the recently 'vile' Charlotte had to be off sick.

'I just don't know what's the matter with her,' Emily muttered blackly. 'I thought it was jealousy when she was being horrible to you, Gwen, but now I think it's something else. She's been a right moody cow with me, too.'

They were sitting in their tutor room to escape the cold, and still had some time before registration. Emily was taking the opportunity to perfect her fingertips, scraping pink polish across her nails with a clotted brush.

'Maybe she's having problems at home?' Hattie theorised.

'She would tell us if she was, I'm sure of it.' Emily twisted her wrist to inspect her handiwork. 'Besides, it's no excuse to take it out on us, is it?'

'Maybe she's ill,' Gwenhwyfar suggested, wondering why Charlotte was so determined to dislike her. 'It's not like we've done anything to upset her. If one of us had said something, then it would make more sense, but we haven't.'

'I haven't,' Hattie scoffed.

'Me neither. When would I ever?' Emily pushed the brush back into the bottle and twisted it into place. She let her polished nails harden with splayed fingers. 'I'll send her a text later and see what's wrong. Maybe she's gone and got herself pregnant.'

'What?'

She sent Hattie a knowing smile. 'I saw her in the girls' toilets yesterday morning, and she was *definitely* sick. Kept saying she didn't feel well and everything. She was bent over the toilet for *ages*.'

'Never.'

'It's true!'

Gwenhwyfar frowned. 'But surely... wouldn't she need a boyfriend for that?'

'Not necessarily.' There was a short silence. 'Well, either that or she's bulimic. I don't know. All I know is that it's getting annoying.'

'Chatting about someone, are we?'

The girls looked up. Viola stood next to them with her slender arms crossed. Her hair was down today, long and like dark chocolate, and for a moment Gwenhwyfar wondered if this was why Hattie, Charlotte and Emily bitched about her so; wondered if it was because she was taller than all of them, thinner, and model-like in her stature. 'Go on then,' the slender girl sniped, 'who's bulimic? I'm dying to know.'

'Go away, Viola,' Emily hissed. 'This doesn't concern you.'

'You're right, it doesn't. Shall I go fetch Charlotte instead?'

'Charlotte's not here,' snapped Hattie.

Viola smiled, sarcasm spreading her lips. 'Yes she is. She's hiding in the girls' toilets. *Not* throwing up, by the way.'

Emily huffed. 'What is it you wanted?'

'Nothing. Tom's throwing a party, and you're all invited.' Viola uncrossed her arms. 'Charlotte too, if she's not too busy avoiding you.'

For a moment, all ice seemed to melt.

'A party?' Hattie's excitement mirrored Gwenhwyfar's own. 'When?'

'Tomorrow. Half-seven: at his house,' Viola revealed with reluctance. 'But it's not like you have to come, or anything. I'm sure you all have better things to do with your time. You know, like bitch about Charlotte?'

'Whatever,' Emily remarked. 'Who's going?'

'The usual, but he wanted me to make sure you're coming because one of his friends fancies *her*.' She managed to muster a certain amount of disgust when looking at Gwenhwyfar, who recoiled under the insult.

'Who? Not Gavin again?' The others looked her way with surprise.

'No.' Viola expelled an irritable sigh. 'Tom's other friend, Hector.'

Gwenhwyfar found herself gaining interest. 'Who's Hector?'

'Are you coming, or what?'

The classroom was beginning to fill up. Bedivere was walking to his desk with Morgan, and for a moment Gwenhwyfar's attention was diverted. They were talking amiably, and it annoyed her. The doe-eyed girl had still barely said more than two words to her, despite Gwenhwyfar's continued efforts. Hattie and Emily consulted one another with a quick glance.

'Yeah, definitely,' Hattie enthused.

'Why not?' Emily added. 'Gwen?'

Once again Gwenhwyfar recalled her narcissistic fantasies from a few nights ago, and felt them dance around her head. 'Whatever. I'll go if I have to.'

By the time the bell drove them into the corridors they had forgotten all about Charlotte. English was Gwenhwyfar's first lesson of the day, and she soon caught up with Bedivere. He was not alone. With the lack of hospitality that Morgan had shown her still green in her mind, Gwenhwyfar closed the final few paces between them.

'Hey Morgan.' She flashed the surprised girl a wide smile, positioning herself between her and Bedivere. 'Thanks for letting me share your History book the other day. It was really kind of you.'

Stunned, Morgan failed to respond, then frowned as she realised the other girl had no reason to thank her at all.

'Gwen, right?' Bedivere enquired, pleased by the fresh company. 'Who walked into us on Monday?'

'That's right.' Gwenhwyfar flicked her hair over her shoulder, a move she had seen both her mother and Emily perform numerous times. 'I'm sorry about that. Emily never looks where she's going.' The mention of her friend's name sparked interest in his eyes. 'Bedivere, right?' He nodded. 'It's a cool name. I would've sat next to you on Tuesday, but when I came in you weren't there.'

'Don't worry about it. I'm not usually late. I had to take a detour to the Maths department to hand in some homework. I thought he wouldn't make me do it as I was ill when it was set, but I thought wrong.'

Gwenhwyfar ignored Morgan as she tromped beside her in annoyance. 'How horrible! Was that Mr Slow? He gave me almost a month's worth of homework yesterday, even though I didn't go here last term. He said it was essential I should *catch up*.'

Bedivere laughed. Morgan tried to say something.

'That does sound like him, yes. He's not the most popular of teachers around here. How are you finding Logres so far?'

'Good,' she beamed. 'Everyone's really nice. Everyone I've met so far, at least. I just wish I knew more people in my lessons. I hate sitting on my own.'

'*Bedivere—*!'

Gwenhwyfar looked to her left in annoyance. Morgan seemed bent out of shape.

'I have to go, but I'll see you later, all right?'

Gwenhwyfar walked on, and much to her delight Bedivere did too.

'All right.' He smiled and sent her a brief wave over his shoulder. 'Have fun in Science.'

As Morgan scurried off down the hall, Bedivere was already talking again, and when they came into the stuffy room with verbs and poems scattered about the walls he was happy for her to follow him to his seat. He didn't say much during the lesson, preferring to work with his head down, but Gwenhwyfar didn't mind, as she was often the same. Looking at the cover of his exercise book she discovered that he had a delightfully long name, Greenstone-Jones, which in full made him sound like a gentleman of the past.

When the time came to pack up, she decided to go for it. 'So how long have you known Arthur?'

'Arthur? Since year eight. I only met him when I moved here. How about you and Emily?' Nervously, he filled his rucksack. 'Did you know her before you came here?'

'No. She's been really nice though. Are you friends?'

'Not really.' They slipped out of the classroom and made their way through the busy corridors. 'She hangs around with other girls all the time. What have you got next?'

A current fired through her stomach and made her whole body fill with warmth. She didn't get to sit anywhere near Arthur in Science, but he was still there, sitting in the same class as her, still there for her to gaze at secretively. 'Biology. I don't know anyone there, either.'

'You'll get to know people, don't worry,' he assured her. 'Would you like me to walk you?'

'Please. I've got lost so many times this week, it's ridiculous.'

He laughed his musical laugh as they scaled the stairs together, Gwenhwyfar using the brass railing as a means to haul herself up around the cold stone walls. 'So you didn't always come here, then?'

'No, my parents moved here from East Anglia. They were worried about being so close to the coast and flooding.'

'Did you mind?' She slipped through the door he held open for her. 'Moving, I mean.'

'I hated it at first,' he admitted, 'but I made some friends, met Arthur, then things didn't seem so bad. This place isn't so terrible once you get used to it. It's actually supposed to be the best school in the area.'

Gwenhwyfar's attention turned to the queue outside the laboratory she was due to be sitting in for the next hour and a half. Above the level of everyone else's heads she could see Arthur's, his eyes boring into the lockers opposite him as he stood cross-armed against the wall. Her plan to tell Bedivere this was where he could leave her vanished the moment he spotted him.

'Arthur!' he grinned, bounding towards him. 'I forgot you had this now.'

Drawn out of his reverie Arthur blinked, and then smiled. 'Bedivere, what are you doing here?'

'Chaperoning our newest student to her lesson. She says she doesn't know anyone.'

'Well, we have something in common, then.' Straightening, Arthur stood away from the wall. 'You can sit with me if you like. Or I can sit with you. I was getting tired of being so close to the front, anyway.'

'This is your class?'

'Yep!' Gwenhwyfar did her best to appear confident. 'I think so, at least. I'm pretty sure this is the room I was in last time.'

'It should be, as you've been coming here for the past two days.' Arthur smiled, and Gwenhwyfar found her heart fluttering with the notion that he had noticed. The teacher called them in, and Bedivere peeled himself away.

'I should probably go,' he told them. 'Don't want to be late again. I'm never late. I'll see you at break though, yeah? Bye, Gwen.'

Suddenly they were standing in a disastrous silence with no Bedivere to mediate. Gwenhwyfar offered Arthur an inviting smile, hoping he'd strike up conversation, but he merely smiled back and followed her into the laboratory, looking as awkward as she felt.

'So where are we sitting?' she tried, hiding her reddening cheeks beneath the veil of her hair.

'Where you usually sit, perhaps?'

They reached her empty desk at the back of the classroom. She pulled out a stool and climbed onto it, finding them as ever to be stupidly high, while Arthur glided sideways onto his seat with casual elegance.

'I feel like it's been raining all week,' Gwenhwyfar said, keeping her eyes on the chalkboard.

'It hasn't been raining that much,' Arthur shrugged, missing the point entirely.

'We've had rain pretty much every day since I got here,' Gwenhwyfar disputed. 'Maybe I brought it with me. From Wales.' He was watching her with a frown. 'So I thought you knew those people you were sitting next to,' was her next attempt. 'Don't you know anyone?'

'I know you,' Arthur quipped. Gwenhwyfar smiled, and that seemed to please him.

'But you've only just met me.' She tucked her hair behind her ear. 'I meant other than me.'

'Oh. No, then. I guess I know them, but we're not friends.'

'How come?'

'I don't know, we just don't talk much.'

'You don't? Well, then that's their loss, isn't it? And it means I get to sit next to you, instead.'

As he smiled her heart did a cartwheel. It seemed that neither one of them knew what to say after that, but their teacher soon rescued them. The lights were switched off and the blinds were shut, leaving the room in the blue glow of the ancient television suspended above the door.

Gwenhwyfar leant towards Arthur, half as an excuse to talk to him, half as an excuse to get closer. 'What are we watching?'

'Something about osmosis,' he whispered. 'I don't know, I wasn't really listening.'

'Me neither.'

'Something about plant cells and water.'

'Oh,' she said, 'how interesting.'

'Very,' Arthur stressed. 'It gets better—it'll probably cover facilitated diffusion next. Exciting.'

She let out a laugh which was definitely too loud. Their teacher shushed them. Gwenhwyfar tried to focus on something other than her euphoria, but failed and giggled in silence, and soon Arthur was telling her off too, half-amused, half-perplexed how he could be so witty.

'It wasn't that funny.'

'Sorry,' she gasped, 'I can't help it.'

As soon as his eyes met hers again she smiled, and he did too. 'You're peculiar, you know that?'

'I am? Thanks. That's nice.'

'No, in a good way,' he corrected, forgetting to lower his voice. The three girls sat in front of them glanced back, wondering what the joke was.

'Oh, thanks then, I think.'

'I said *quiet*!' Gwenhwyfar jumped. The teacher's voice cut through the class. 'Do you want to go to the principal's office?'

This was threat enough to silence the two, albeit an amused silence with hidden smiles. Most students preferred to avoid the headmaster, as he was an ominous figure, one who stalked the halls in a blue suit with an expression of thunder. Dr Ravioli was often called the Nutcracker, due to his resemblance to one, though this name stemmed from the more boisterous groups of the school and was largely only used by them.

Gwenhwyfar found Emily, Hattie and Charlotte waiting for her in the canteen at break, huddled around their usual table. She predicted the interrogation before she joined them.

'Was that *Arthur*?' Hattie gushed, knowing full well it was.

Teasing, Gwenhwyfar looked over her shoulder. 'Where?'

'There. You were just talking to him. I saw you walk in together!'

'You did?' Emily sat up to look for him.

'Only because we had Science,' Gwenhwyfar dismissed. 'We were just talking, that's all.'

'And?'

'And that's all!' She gave them both a sly smile. 'Honestly, I only sat next to him in class. *Nothing happened.*'

'*Nothing happened* always means *something happened*. Doesn't it, Em?'

'What did you talk about?' Emily demanded. 'How, even? You said you were stuck at the back of the room, miles from where he sits.'

Suddenly Gwenhwyfar launched into a full account of her lesson with Bedivere, how she'd sent Morgan packing, and how Arthur had 'practically begged' to sit with her.

'Morgan looked so morose when she walked past us on our way down here,' she revealed, remembering the look on Morgan's face when she spotted Arthur with another girl. 'You're right, Em. She clearly fancies him. But he didn't look at her, not once.'

'So he likes you then?' Hattie persisted. Charlotte alienated herself from the group with a large scowl. Gwenhwyfar shrugged. She liked Arthur, and he was pleasant and polite to her, but she had the feeling he was pleasant and polite to everyone.

'I don't know. We get on so well though. We could hardly stop talking. The teacher had to tell us off three times.'

'Is he going to the party tomorrow?' Emily's excitement was palpable. Both her hyenas craned to get closer.

'Oh! You should see if he's going. Is he?'

Gwenhwyfar felt silly for not having thought of it herself. 'I don't know, I didn't ask. Should I?'

'*Definitely*. Where is he?' Emily hunted for Gwenhwyfar's prey, scanning the hall for the correct table. Viola was laughing hysterically at something Tom had done, while someone Gwenhwyfar hadn't seen before spoke quietly with Gavin. She wondered if it was Hector. If it was, his appearance didn't match his heroic name at all; he had a weak chin and a resentful scowl that darkened his already dour demeanour.

'Over there, by the fire escape,' she confirmed, her eyes slipping past the unmemorable Hector and straight to Arthur. 'Stop staring! He's looking at us!'

'He is?' The moment Emily spotted him her eyes dropped to the table.

Gwenhwyfar was going red. 'I'm not going to ask him now, if that's what you're thinking.'

'Why not? It's either now or in History, where everyone will hear. I can come with you if you like.'

'No, it's fine.'

'Do you want him to go to the party or what?' Emily was already on her feet.

'I'll do it *later*!' she hissed, sinking lower. 'It'll look silly if I go now.'

'Gwen's right. I think it will make her look desperate.' Charlotte's words were as stiff as the mouth they left.

'Oh, don't be so ridiculous! Come on Hattie, *we'll* go.'

'No!' Gwenhwyfar leapt up. That was the last thing she wanted, she didn't need Arthur to think he was being ridiculed. 'I'll go. But you're coming with me, as it was your idea.'

They made their way towards Arthur's table. Bedivere had already spotted Emily and was staring at her in awe. The frown in Arthur's brow nearly put Gwenhwyfar off, but Emily wasn't cowed. She joined them both with a wide, pink smile. 'Hey!'

The boys said nothing. Bedivere gazed at Emily open-mouthed, while Arthur eyed her with distrust.

'Sorry to bother you again,' Emily proceeded, 'but Gwen and I were wondering if you were coming to the party tomorrow night.'

Arthur frowned at her. 'What party?'

'Tom's party.'

Their blank response wasn't promising.

'You know, Tom! Tom Hareton. Viola's boyfriend?'

'I know Tom,' Arthur said. 'We're not invited.'

'You are,' Emily insisted. 'Viola asked us to ask you. You *have* to come.'

He shifted and looked to the other end of the hall. 'When is it?'

'Tomorrow night.'

'Can't, I have work. Tell Viola I'm sorry.'

Emily scoffed. '*Work*? Who has to work?'

'What time?' Bedivere interrupted.

'Half-seven.'

He looked to his friend eagerly. 'Don't you finish at half-five on Fridays?' Arthur shrugged. 'I can go,' Bedivere volunteered.

'Great,' Emily uttered, not interested. 'Arthur?'

'I'll have to see,' he evaded.

Gwenhwyfar began to rethink her earlier assessment of his interest in her. 'Well, we'll both be there,' she dared. 'So if you can make it, it'd be nice.'

He seemed unsettled, but mustered an encouraging smile. 'I'll think about it.'

There was little promise in his words. Feeling hope deflate within her, Gwenhwyfar strode back to their table. Hattie and Charlotte had been gossiping; not unusual, but the sudden halt of the intense whispering on their arrival made her uncomfortable.

'Well, is he going?' Charlotte asked, smugly.

Gwenhwyfar sent her a false smile. 'Of course he's coming. Isn't he, Em?'

Emily glanced back to the table where the two boys were seated. Bedivere was harassing Arthur doggedly. 'Definitely.'

Proverbial Daggers

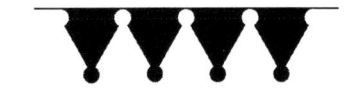

Gwenhwyfar wondered if she'd misheard Emily.
They had organised to meet at the back of the Maths block, but after waiting patiently for ten minutes Emily was nowhere to be seen. Deciding she must have forgotten, Gwenhwyfar investigated their other meets, but to no avail. As she explored the grounds around Badbury, checking the small pockets in the walls of the music rooms, her stomach began to growl. Familiar voices drew her out towards the tennis courts. She stopped the moment she saw Viola, but turned back too late.

'Are you lost?'

Viola approached with her arms crossed, and reluctantly Gwenhwyfar turned to face her. 'No. Have you seen Emily?'

The thin girl observed her with narrowed eyes. 'Why? Has she discarded you already?'

'What does she want?' Tom was surprisingly intimidating for someone so slight. Not quite as intimidating as the giant who stood behind him, though. Gavin Miles towered above all their heads and had a thick, florid face that, though babyish, was threatening due to his muteness. He had wide blue eyes that gazed out from under a high forehead and low, expressive eyebrows. The boy she had seen in the canteen stood beside him, whom Gwenhwyfar had guessed to be Hector. He was staring rather evidently at her chest.

'I'm looking for Emily,' she explained, 'and Hattie.'

'Hattie?' Tom repeated, finding something amusing.

'Hattie,' she confirmed. 'Have you seen her?'

Not one of them offered an answer. Hector was still staring. She didn't like the way he gawped.

'No? How about Emily?'

This time she got a series of unhelpful shrugs, but then Gavin broke his silence.

'Wait, you mean that blonde girl who's obsessed with Lance?' Gwenhwyfar frowned. Blonde matched her description, at least. Gavin pointed up the slope that eventually led to the canteen. 'I saw her by the Art block, with that friend of hers. Not Hattie, the other one.'

'Charlotte?' He shrugged again. 'Thanks.' Quickly she turned to leave.

'I don't know why you hang out with her,' Viola said, separating herself from the others. 'With Emily. You don't seem like the type.'

Gwenhwyfar crossed her arms. 'The type to what?'

'Associate yourself with that lot.' Viola watched her closely, her fists stretching her malformed pockets. 'They're two-faced. Emily has a new best friend practically every week.'

'She does, does she?'

'You've no idea what they've been saying about you behind your back.'

Gwenhwyfar looked beyond Viola to Gavin. He averted his eyes. 'Don't I? All right then, what did they say?'

'Maybe you should ask Emily?' Viola challenged.

'No, I'm asking you.' Gwenhwyfar squared closer. 'Come on, what did she say about me?'

Viola rolled her eyes, as if it were obvious, as if she should already know. 'She called you a sheep-shagger, what else?'

Gwenhwyfar scowled as, suddenly, her cheeks burned beetroot. For a moment words failed her, and she struggled to crawl through the shock. 'A sheep-shagger?' she repeated, appalled. Her eyes slid beyond Viola to her entourage, and she caught a smirk upon Tom's lips. 'You don't know what you're talking about,' she suddenly snarled, 'so why don't you just shut up? If anyone's two-faced around here, it's *you*.'

She spun on her heels and stormed up the hill. She expected to hear laughter in her wake, but none followed. Moments later her vision blurred with tears that she struggled to blink away.

'Gwen!'

Starting, Gwenhwyfar looked up to see Hattie jogging down the hill. The other girl soon fell into step beside her.

'I've been looking for you everywhere,' she said, obviously out of breath. 'Have you seen the others?'

'No,' Gwenhwyfar remarked, avoiding eye contact. 'Someone said they saw Emily by the Art block, though.'

'Was Charlotte with her?' Hattie demanded.

'I think so. Why?'

'I'm just curious.' Hattie glanced to her doubtfully as they climbed the steps to the path running aside the drama studios. 'It's just... I think she's been saying things to Emily about you. Earlier when you went to go talk to Arthur she told me that you said I was fat.'

'Fat?' Gwenhwyfar lapped it up. 'I never said that!'

'You didn't?'

'Of course not! Unlike *some* people, I don't bitch.'

'Charlotte's been telling Emily you've been saying nasty things about us.' Gwenhwyfar's insides were boiling. Hattie continued to pry. 'Have you upset her or something?'

'I haven't said *anything* to that girl,' Gwenhwyfar hissed. 'Not a thing! She's been rude to me since I got here. So no, I *don't* like her.' She stopped and turned to Hattie in distress. 'Has Emily said anything about me to you?'

Stunned, Hattie shook her head.

'Are you sure?'

'Not to me, she hasn't,' Hattie answered. 'Why? Has she said anything to you?'

Gwenhwyfar shook her head. She strode towards one of the back entrances of Badbury, which was nestled next to cordoned off grass.

'So it's just Charlotte, then,' concluded Hattie. Gwenhwyfar nodded stiffly. 'Her uncle's in the army… maybe she just doesn't like the Welsh.'

She wished that Hattie had never found her. The other girl launched into some scandalous story about Charlotte's uncle and how he'd had an affair while posted abroad in Israel. Hattie revealed that Charlotte was convinced he'd fathered a child with his lover, because a few weeks after he had returned they'd received a phone call from an accented woman. Charlotte had told Hattie she could hear a baby crying in the background. After that Gwenhwyfar found her mind closing to the particulars. Her life was mutating into a vortex of "she said, he said".

Gwenhwyfar arrived at History that afternoon to find that Morgan was still ignoring her. She was curled over her textbook with a hard shoulder erecting a barrier between them, and when Gwenhwyfar offered her a pleasant greeting, she received an icy silence for her trouble. The stillness of the car park engaged her for a while as she blurred out the rising noise levels of her class. Their teacher was late again, but more surprisingly, so were Arthur and Bedivere. They arrived right before Mr Caledonensis, who stumbled in organising papers and notes.

'Hey, Arthur,' Gwenhwyfar offered him her widest smile. 'Bedivere. Have you decided if you're coming to the party tomorrow night?'

Arthur and Bedivere both sat sideways in their chairs. 'I'm coming,' Bedivere confirmed. 'Though I don't know if I've managed to convince Arthur yet.'

He laughed at this, so Gwenhwyfar did too. 'Oh, please Arthur, you have to come. It won't be the same if you don't.' The compliment made him blush, and he began to fidget. 'I'll hardly know anyone there. Charlotte and Hattie will be chasing after boys all night. I was hoping that Emily and I could hang around with you guys.'

This hooked Bedivere all the more. 'That should be all right, shouldn't it?' he consulted, eagerly.

'I don't know if I can make it,' Arthur murmured. 'I have other things to do, you know.'

'Can't you postpone them?' Gwenhwyfar suggested. 'Just for a few hours?'

'I don't know…'

'Oh, come on, I know you want to,' Bedivere pressed. 'Just

get someone else to look after her for a bit, she'll be fine.'

Still unconvinced, Arthur shifted and glanced out of the window. Bedivere used his silence as an opportunity to ask Morgan instead.

'Probably not,' Morgan shrugged, as Arthur's eyes settled on her expectantly. 'It sounds pretty lame. If I want to become legless, I'll go swim with sharks. I don't feel like going to one of Tom's parties, anyway.'

The four looked across the room. Tom Lincoln Hareton was currently heckling Mr Caledonensis about his choice of jumper. He was wearing woodland green.

'Still,' Bedivere insisted, 'it'll be good. Even if it's just to make fun of the idiots.'

'And you're definitely coming?' Arthur's brown eyes fixed on Gwenhwyfar. She felt a jolt through her stomach.

'Definitely. I'm the new girl, I have to go.'

This seemed to appease him. His shoulders dropped, and he relaxed back into his chair. 'Well, it seems like I don't have a choice, either.'

Gwenhwyfar spent most of Friday gazing at the clock, hoping in silent desperation that her new top would arrive in time. She'd had a moment to check with Bedivere during tutorial that he and Arthur were still coming, but since then sightings of either boy had been scarce. Science that afternoon was Chemistry, though due to a stricter teacher, swapping seats was impossible. When it was time to pack up and leave, Arthur grabbed his belongings and strode hastily out of the door.

She was eager to get going. The moment her mum parked the car in the driveway she flew towards the house to pick up the bag she'd prepared the night before. Eve followed at a leisurely pace, peeling away her coat in the lobby. Gwenhwyfar came charging back down the stairs.

'Mam? Did any parcels arrive today?'

Eve eyed her with surprise. Her school uniform was gone and she was wearing a large maroon hoodie with worn jeans. 'We're leaving now?'

'I don't want to be late.' Gwenhwyfar strode into the lobby to pull on her trainers. 'Were there any parcels?'

'But we just got in! What was the point of coming home? I could have brought your bag with me, if I'd known.'

'Mam! The parcel?'

'What parcel? I didn't know you were expecting one.'

Gwenhwyfar huffed, muttered something and then proceeded to panic over what she was going to wear.

'Can't you just go in something else?' Eve tried, pulling her driving gloves back on.

'But I wanted to wear that!' Cursing, Gwenhwyfar ran back up the stairs. Eve shouted after her, proclaiming she was going. As she opened the front door a yellow van crackled onto the driveway and blocked her car. Out came a man with a soft parcel.

Shrugging on her coat Eve positioned herself in the doorway. '*Gwen*!' she yelled.

Soon they were back in the car, driving through their affluent neighbourhood to Emily's house. The central navigation system told them they would be there in ten minutes, but her mother was a slow driver, and would probably take longer.

'So how's school going?'

'Good.' Gwenhwyfar kept her eyes fixed out of the passenger window, willing her mother to go faster.

'You'll get used to it. You may even prefer it, after a while.' There was a long silence. 'So who's going to this party? Anyone nice?'

'I only know the girls I'm going with,' Gwenhwyfar shrugged. 'I haven't really met anyone else yet.'

'Well, maybe now will be a good opportunity to get to know people. Where is it?'

'At a boy's house. He's got a girlfriend, before you ask. We probably won't stay long. We're going to watch films, later.'

'You're still going riding tomorrow, though?' Gwenhwyfar nodded. 'You know, your father and I were thinking. Once we're more settled, if the stables here are any good, maybe we can get you a new horse. Would you like that?'

'I don't want a new horse,' she muttered. 'If so, what was the point of selling Dillon?'

'He's old, Gwen. The trip would've been too much for him. He hadn't been in a horse box for over ten years.'

'Well, maybe we shouldn't have moved, then,' she bit, glancing to her mother who gazed ahead with crinkled eyes. She looked young for her age, but it was a youth bought with expensive creams and relentless face yoga. Gwenhwyfar knew she was handsome, however, and that she herself had been given the best of her mother's features: a heart shaped face, a small, rounded chin and full lips; though she was often told she'd got her short legs and petite frame from her paternal great-grandmother. She tanned easily and darkly, like her father, and it was his almond eyes she felt she bore, though sometimes they seemed more like the green, hooded eyes of her mother. Her mother's nose was sterner than her own; and though the similarities didn't end there she had dyed the thick, chocolate locks they both shared bleach-blonde for as long as she could remember.

'We had to move. Your father was going to lose his job. If he hadn't have been headhunted we would've had to sell up, anyway. We wouldn't have ended up in such a good neighbourhood. Do you want to be one of those kids living in the slums?'

'What happened to you and Dad being able to look after us?'

'We can, Gwen, thanks to moving here. Without this job your father has nothing.'

'We must have savings,' she contested.

'If we do, they're none of your business.'

'How come he has to work so late all the time?' she scowled. 'I thought this job meant fewer hours.'

They passed Logres, still open, although the classroom lights were switched off for the night. On the sports field there were afterschool clubs playing cricket and rugby, with some students still in their uniforms lingering to watch the games.

'It does,' Eve insisted. 'But it's only his first week. Once he's settled, I'm sure we'll see more of him.' There was a moment's silence. 'Actually, now that you're back in school I was thinking of getting a job. Nothing big: just something part time. What do you think?'

'Would you still be home for after school?'

'I don't see why not.'

'I think it's great. What were you thinking of?'

Her mother shrugged. 'Your aunt and uncle say they could do with some help at their firm. I may not have worked since I had you, but I still know how to be a secretary. If not, there's always a craft shop in town looking for extra help. Just something to do.'

'Couldn't you work from home? You could start your own business.'

'I wouldn't know what.'

They pulled into Emily's street. Gwenhwyfar peered out of the window in an effort to spot the right house number, which ended up being at the far end of the road.

'Beautiful houses,' her mother observed, as she brought the car to a halt. 'We wanted to buy here, but nothing was on the market. Which one is it?'

'That one, I think.' Gwenhwyfar grabbed her bag. Her mother undid her seatbelt and pulled the keys out of the ignition. 'Mam, I can find it myself.'

'I'd just like to say hello to Olivia. It won't take a moment.' She opened the door and got out onto the empty street. Huffing, Gwenhwyfar followed. The whole community had the feel of a holiday resort, and each colossal building could have been its own hotel. Some of the long driveways were gated and housed expensive cars. As they approached Emily's front door the property greeted them with an air of exclusivity.

They rang the doorbell. Olivia Rose welcomed them both politely and invited them in, directing Gwenhwyfar to Emily's bedroom where Emily, Charlotte and Hattie were already waiting. Later, Eve called up the stairs to announce she was going, and then they were all given pizza, hardly eating a few hurried slices before rushing back upstairs to get dressed.

At first Gwenhwyfar was annoyed that, unlike Charlotte, she hadn't opted for a dress, but once ready she felt satisfied with her choice. The emerald green sparkles of the scale-like fabric clung to her perfectly, and dark jeans coupled with silver heels balanced out the fact it was backless. Her make-up was light, but reminiscent of Viola's dark, smoky eyes. When she returned downstairs to find the others waiting, Charlotte's jealousy was evident.

'Ready?' Emily stood, looking uncomfortable.

'Yep!' she exclaimed. It was obvious they had just been talking about her, but refusing to dwell on the matter, Gwenhwyfar grabbed her coat and strode towards the door.

It wasn't a forgiving night. As they walked together, huddled in their jackets, Gwenhwyfar found her gaze drifting upwards to a night sky inferior to the one back home. They found Tom's house with the door shut and the curtains drawn, the low rumble of sub-bass faint but definite. A sudden wave of heat washed over them as they came inside. Coats were heaped by a coat stand, and loud music boomed from the first room to their left. The air was pungent with deodorant and perfume.

'Made it, then?' Viola offered a smile that could have been considered sarcastic. Surprised, Gwenhwyfar only stared. She looked like an undiscovered supermodel.

Viola had one of those faces that could wear any hat and any hairstyle, with a long swan-neck and a refined celestial nose. Her eyebrows were thick and arched, and her cheekbones angled to a striking profile. For a few moments Gwenhwyfar was overcome with jealousy, though it was mostly for Viola's slender height. She had to be no more than a few inches shorter than Arthur. Her complexion was flawless, smooth and like bone china, and she wore jeans with a dark corset, softened by waving hair.

'Where are the toilets?' Gwenhwyfar removed her coat. Viola took it from her.

'Upstairs. I'll hang this in the closet. It'll get stolen, otherwise.' She gave Gwenhwyfar a knowing smile; one that this time almost seemed kind. Perhaps she felt guilty for being so horrible to her yesterday, Gwenhwyfar mused, or perhaps she was going to throw her coat in the bin. Whichever, Viola was gone without an insult. Gwenhwyfar then realised that the others had abandoned her too. Stealing the opportunity, she hurried upstairs with her clutch to preen herself.

She ran into Arthur and Bedivere when she came back down to join the party. They were standing by the door in the hallway, eying their surroundings. Bedivere had shed his coat onto the pile, and Arthur held his awkwardly, not quite willing to part with it. Eventually he hung it on one of the pegs, half-concealing it beneath the other coats.

Bedivere saw her first. 'Gwen!' he exclaimed. The formalities of school suddenly crumbled as he moved in for a quick hug. 'You been here long?'

She shook her head the moment she was released. 'I only got here five minutes ago. You?'

'We just arrived,' Arthur said, jumping in. He offered half a grin. 'I'm surprised I could remember the way.'

'You've been here before?'

'Not since year seven.'

Bedivere searched beyond them both, keen to dive headfirst into the throng. 'So where's Emily?'

'I think she went to get a drink.'

'Do you mind if I go look for her?'

Their silent shrugs were encouragement enough; and Bedivere was off, hunting for the apple of his eye. Gwenhwyfar sent Arthur an encouraging smile. 'That jumper looks good on you.'

He looked down as if to remind himself what he was wearing. 'Thanks. You look nice too.'

'Want to get a drink?'

'Sure.'

She turned to lead him after Bedivere, her heart thrumming like a humming bird. The air thickened as they passed through the living room, and though she recognised a few people from school most faces were new to her. They found the drinks table in the kitchen, littered with empty cups and half-filled bottles. A few names had already been emptied, cheap rum and another unidentified spirit; and all that was left was known as "solution", a potent home-brew with the appearance of clouded lemonade. She mixed two cups with cranberry juice, gave herself an undersized straw, and then handed one to Arthur.

'So what you been up to?'

'Not much.' He drank, apparently indifferent to the taste. To Gwenhwyfar it tasted like cough syrup, and it burned down her throat. 'Just had to sort a few things out.'

'Well, thanks for coming.' She looked up at him and offered a grateful smile. 'It's nice to have someone here that I know.'

'I don't think I'd have bothered, if you weren't here,' he confessed. 'It wouldn't have been much fun for me following Bedivere while he chases after Emily all night.'

'Well, he definitely likes her. Maybe he found her already?'

'Does she even like him?'

'She was going on about him a lot yesterday.' Gwenhwyfar shrugged, trying not to feel too guilty about the lie. 'Why?'

'I just thought she liked someone else, that's all. One of Tom's friends.'

'Who? Is he here?'

'Probably not. He's been suspended for two weeks. He slashed the tyres of the principal's car.'

'He what? Why?'

'I don't know. He's a complete idiot. He usually does that sort of thing.' Arthur leant against the kitchen counter. Gwenhwyfar joined him, already feeling tipsy. She slid closer so that their sides were touching. 'Did you go to many parties back in Wales?'

'A couple. Usually we could get the alcohol from our parents' liquor cabinets. Most of it was from the black market anyway, so they could hardly ground us for it.' She took another sip of solution, feeling more accustomed to the taste. 'My parents are pretty strict. I'm not allowed alcohol, even though I've had wine before.'

'Wine?' he asked, surprised.

'Yeah, from Bordeaux. My dad got it through work as some kind of favour. I found it in their room.'

'And?'

'And what?'

'How did it taste?'

'Terrible,' she laughed. 'It was disgusting. But then, I was eight when I tried it.'

'You know that's illegal, Gwen,' he teased.

'And? What are you going to do about it?'

'Nothing! You're just lucky. You'll probably never see another bottle like that again.' There was a moment's silence. 'Have you ever had real chocolate?'

Gwenhwyfar frowned at him. 'Real chocolate…? What do you mean?'

'I mean, not that horrible stuff that they *call* chocolate. *Real* chocolate. That's actually made from the cocoa tree. These days they just use artificial replacements. It's not the same.'

'Chocolate comes from a tree?' Gwenhwyfar eyed him sceptically. 'You're joking.'

'I'm not.'

'So why do they make it artificially, then?'

'The cocoa tree's endangered, so it's cheaper to use substitutes. Any real chocolate goes straight to the rich like meat and wine, or like caviar and truffles used to in the early twenty-first century. To the people who run things.'

'Have you?' Gwenhwyfar asked, mixing her drink with her straw. 'Ever had real chocolate?'

'Once. My grandfather gave me a bar for my tenth birthday. It tasted good. Strong, bitter. We still have some somewhere, I think. Not much, but my grandmother says it's worth its weight in gold.'

'It sounds nice. The only other thing I tried was a cigarette, and that was disgusting. It was worse than the wine. I don't know why people smoked them.'

'Nicotine, of course. It's a bit like alcohol—addictive and bad for you.'

'Well, it may be bad for you, but I'm having another one. You?' She refilled his cup before he could object, and then the walls rushed past them in a blurry lurch as she grabbed his hand and tugged him into the living room, lured by the loud music. The unexpected crowd forced her to stop suddenly. Arthur wrapped an arm around her to prevent them both from falling.

'Sorry!' he exclaimed.

Laughing, Gwenhwyfar turned towards him, willing him closer with her eyes. 'At least we're even now. I've bumped into you, and you've bumped into me.'

Someone squeezed through the door and pushed past them. Arthur slid closer. 'You're really pretty, Gwen,' he breathed.

He was going to kiss her, she was sure of it. His expression darkened with lust as she looked up at him, her eyes on his lips, her head tilting as her drink slopped forgotten to the floor. Eagerly he stooped to catch her half-open mouth.

Their lips never met. Arthur's drink tipped all over Gwenhwyfar's jeans. She gasped, the soaked fabric sticking to her skin. Charlotte had barged into them.

'Oh my God!' she said loudly. 'I am so *sorry*.'

Arthur shook his hand and wiped it on his leg. Suddenly Charlotte was trying to brush off his wet trousers, false concern on her otherwise gleeful face.

'Really I am. I *totally* wasn't looking where I was going. I haven't ruined your clothes, have I?'

'No, it's fine,' Arthur responded stiffly, pushing Charlotte's hands away as they batted dangerously close to his crotch. He looked to Gwenhwyfar apologetically. 'Sorry, Gwen.'

'Don't be. It wasn't *your* fault, Arthur.' Gwenhwyfar's eyes narrowed at Charlotte, who responded with a thin smile. 'Where's Emily?'

'Getting cosy with Bedivere.'

Arthur frowned. 'What? Where?'

'Upstairs. Why, want to join them?'

He left them without retaliation, striding off urgently through the house. Gwenhwyfar moved to follow him but Charlotte caught hold of her arm. 'Hattie's looking for you,' she informed her haughtily. As she let go, white finger marks lingered in her paling skin. 'She says she needs your help. She's upset about something. She told me to come and get you.'

Gwenhwyfar resisted, eager to follow Arthur and see if he was all right, but the concern suddenly present in Charlotte's eyes forced her to reconsider. 'Fine, where is she?'

'Downstairs toilet.' She was pushed in the right direction.

Gwenhwyfar strode as Arthur had done, driving angrily through the busy house. When she couldn't locate a single bathroom, she tried to find Charlotte again. She had vanished. There was no sign of Hattie, either.

'Gwen!'

She was pleased to see a familiar face. Bedivere hurried towards her, his hair a mess, his clothes dishevelled. His grin split from ear to ear and when he came to her he crushed her in a surprisingly firm hug.

'Good to see you! Have you seen Arthur? I've got to tell him something!'

'What?'

'Huh?'

'What have you got to tell him?' she shouted.

He shook his head vigorously. 'I can't tell you! It's a secret,' he slurred. 'Have you seen him?'

'No,' she responded, fighting to get her breath back. He smelt heavily of Emily's perfume. 'Not since he went to look for you. You might have just missed him.' She hesitated. 'Have you seen Hattie?'

'Who?'

'Hattie! You know, my friend.' He shook his head. Emily appeared at the far end of the room. 'Never mind!' she called to him, and then he was off again, hunting for Arthur. Emily's greeting was almost as ecstatic as Bedivere's, but weaker in the hug department. Soon she too was shouting at her.

'Gwen! I've been looking for you *all over*!' Her hands latched tightly onto her shoulders. 'Where have you been?'

'Looking for Hattie! Have you seen her?'

Emily shook her head.

'Charlotte just told me to go find her. She said she was upset about something?'

'Upset?' Emily repeated.

'Yeah, and that I could find her in the downstairs loo?'

'Gwen, there isn't a loo downstairs!' Emily revealed, smiling at her as one would a joke. 'Charlotte's tricking you. You *know* she's got a problem with you. Look, I just spoke to Arthur, and he wants to meet you! He says he *really* likes you. He wants to talk to you upstairs where it's not so loud.'

Her interest dispelled her earlier suspicions completely. 'He said that?'

'Yep! Isn't it *amazing*? Arthur and Gwen, just like I said!' She squealed, and Gwenhwyfar squealed too. 'It's so cute! You *have* to go meet him. He wants to see you there at ten. That's in like, three minutes. He'll be in the spare room. Tom's outside, so he won't know. I have to go though—I need to keep Charlotte away. She'll do *anything* to sabotage this.'

She was gone before Gwenhwyfar could register the full implications of what she had said. Arthur liked her. She felt euphoric. Quickly she checked the time on her phone. Three minutes? Why so precise? She was too intoxicated to care, examined her ghostly reflection in her pocket mirror and pinched the colour back into her cheeks. She had to go. She would be a fool not to.

Hector Browne

Gwenhwyfar's head spun as she carefully lowered herself onto the bed.

She wasn't aware of her inability to balance herself, only that the moments between her being downstairs and entering the spare room had been consumed by a void. She put her clutch beside her, steadying her breathing with her head between her legs. Inhaling upside down helped, and when she sat straight again she felt more human. Organising her hair for the umpteenth time, Gwenhwyfar observed the room around her. It was plainly decorated, nothing special. There were a few photoframes dotted here and there, but apart from the picture of Tom, none of them were of anyone she recognised.

The opening and closing of the door drew her back to her senses. Something was wrong. 'Who are you?'

'Someone's had a little too much,' was the candid response. 'You know who I am.'

'No,' she bit, though she knew him from somewhere. She stood, and for a moment her frosty exterior paused him. 'Would you leave? I'm expecting someone.'

'Yeah, I know. Charlotte said.' He slunk closer. Gwenhwyfar moved away from the bed.

'Charlotte?' Quickly she looked to the door. 'Hector, right?'

'So you do know me,' he smirked.

'Yeah, I do. Now get out, I'm waiting for someone.'

He laughed and lurched for her. She twisted her arm away as his fingers grabbed at her wrist. The repulsive mix of beer, solution and sweat caused her to back away as he encircled her small waist with his thick arm.

'Get off me!' She pushed at him, but he barely seemed to feel it, and then his cold lips pressed hard down upon her own. Shrinking backwards she hit the cabinet behind her, knocking the photo of Tom flat. Through the clatter of objects she heard the door open. Immediately Hector backed off. Arthur stood open-mouthed in the doorway.

'Sorry—' he stammered, eyes wide, '—I thought—I mean—'

'Arthur!' She pushed towards him, but her plea was rejected. His face contorted to an expression of pain and he slammed the door. He was gone.

'Idiot!' she expelled, gripped by sudden fury. 'Why did you go and do that?'

Hector's confusion transformed to humiliation as he realised his mistake. 'Do what?'

Gwenhwyfar strode across the room and snatched up her clutch. 'Kiss me! I didn't want you to!'

He scowled at her. 'That's not what I heard.'

'What?'

'I said *that's not what I heard.*'

'Why would I want to kiss *you*? I don't even know you.'

'Do you think you're too good for me? Is that it?' He cut her off from the door.

Gwenhwyfar tugged her wrist away as he grasped for it. 'No, of *course* not.'

'I'll bet you'll go off and laugh to all your skanky friends about this, won't you?'

'What? *No.*'

'Yes you will, you and Charlotte. This was a real funny joke, wasn't it? Real funny.'

He grabbed at her angrily. She slapped his hands away and hit him in the face, kicking at him as he forced her down her onto the bed. The moment he had her pinned he paused, as if he wasn't sure what to do with her. His vacillation cost him. A lamp smashed across the back of his head, shattering the hollow ceramic. Terror paralysed Gwenhwyfar as Hector slumped across her, but then large hands pulled him off and launched him across the room. For a moment she thought it was Arthur and was crippled with hysterical relief, but then a not-so-familiar face appeared, frowning with concern.

'Is she all right?' Viola joined Gavin, who stood beside the bed. She still had the broken lamp in one hand.

'I'm not sure,' the deep voice rumbled. 'Maybe we should help her up.'

As the two faces floating above her distorted even more, Gwenhwyfar realised her face was wet with tears.

'We should call the police,' Viola muttered, concerned.

'We can't do that—not with all that alcohol downstairs. Everyone will get arrested,' Gavin argued.

'If they were interested in arresting teenagers they would have crashed the party already,' Viola disputed, dropping the broken light to the floor. 'Besides, there's that protest on in London tonight. They have bigger things to worry about.'

'You think they'll just overlook the booze if we call them?'

'We'll just have to get rid of it all, then,' Viola snapped, coordinating their movements to prop Gwenhwyfar up. She sat down and offered a supporting arm, into which Gwenhwyfar collapsed gratefully. She began to sob.

'Maybe we should just call her parents?' Gavin frowned.

'Good idea,' Viola agreed. 'Get her phone—it's on the floor. And get rid of Hector. I don't want to look at him.'

Gavin looked down to the crumpled heap and prodded him with his foot. Hector groaned. 'He doesn't look too good. I think you hit him pretty hard, Vi.'

'Well, then call *his* parents. Say he passed out or something. Here—' She took the clutch from him and placed it in her lap. 'I'll deal with her parents. They'll probably freak if a guy calls them up. You sort him out.' She glanced at Hector with an obvious degree of disgust. 'And tell Tom to shut this party down. It's a disaster.'

Gavin hoisted Hector off the floor and dragged him out of the room. Composing herself, Gwenhwyfar pulled away from Viola, her eyes stinging. 'Don't say anything about this to anyone, will you?'

'Gavin said he heard Charlotte tell Hector that you wanted to meet him here,' she said, eying her sympathetically.

'Emily told me that *Arthur* wanted to meet me here,' Gwenhwyfar cried. 'I didn't want to meet Hector. I never wanted to meet Hector.'

'I know.' Handing Gwenhwyfar her phone, Viola removed her arm from her shoulders. 'Arthur will understand, once he knows.

It's not your fault Hector's a drunken lout.'

'You didn't see the look on his face when he opened the door. He didn't even let me explain... practically locked me in with that... that...' A strangled burst of tears ended her words. Viola fished some tissues out of Gwenhwyfar's clutch, and she took them, shaking.

'It's all right. Hector's gone. You could get him into a lot of trouble for this.' She offered a strained smile. 'He's been asking for it for ages.'

'Why do you hang around with him anyway?' Gwenhwyfar accused.

'I don't. He's obsessed with being part of Tom's entourage, and Tom's too eager for one to tell him to get lost.'

Slowly, Gwenhwyfar felt herself calm down.

'You can't go home like this. How about we get you cleaned up? Then we can call your parents, go downstairs and show those bitches that their plan failed.'

Gwenhwyfar nodded, and Viola offered a serene smile. 'Come on. The bathroom's this way. We'll worry about Arthur later.'

When Gwenhwyfar descended to the dwindling party, Emily, Hattie and Charlotte had already gone, even though she was supposed to be spending the night at the Rose household. Slowly, all evidence of the party was removed, until at long last the only indicator of the alcohol consumed lingered in the final few houseguests. Leaning against the kitchen counter, Gwenhwyfar stared down at her mobile, wondering what excuse she would use when she called her parents. It was past twelve and her father would be getting ready for bed.

'You can still stay at mine,' Viola offered again. 'We can stop off at the garage to get you a toothbrush.'

'No, it's all right.' Gwenhwyfar attempted a smile. 'I think I'd rather just go home.'

There was sudden shouting. A breathless boy ran hollering through the house, his skin sweat-glazed, eyes wide.

'Police!' he yelled. '*Police*!'

The news brought an onslaught of wordless cries. Gwenhwyfar stood dumbstruck; watching as Tom rapidly waved the dwindled few out through the back door.

'Go, go! Hurry up!' He pushed the next one across the threshold as Viola blitzed the kitchen. A strong air freshener was fired around the premises while windows were flung open. Sirens could be heard in the distance. Cheeks were pinched and ice-cold water was rubbed into flushed faces. Someone stuffed the last of the illicit substance into a bin liner and ran with it out into the garden and beyond the back fence, the bag dripping as they went.

'You should go, Gwen, before they get here,' Viola advised. She pushed two small spray-bottles into her hands. 'Here. Use the pink one for your mouth, the yellow one for your eyes. You don't want your parents to know that you were drinking.'

'Thanks.' The music was switched off, the litter cleared away. It was almost like magic, seeing the evidence of the whole evening vanish before her eyes.

'I'm going to head off too. I'll walk you,' Gavin declared. Suddenly he didn't seem so intimidating. He was more like a large guard dog than anything else: her guard dog. Abruptly she realised that there was an unmistakable gentleness to his eyes. 'We shouldn't wait here.'

'All right.' She collected up her belongings. Her hands still trembled when Viola handed her coat to her. 'Thanks, for what you did.'

Viola merely nodded. 'See you Monday, Gwen. Don't let any of this get to you.'

Soon Gwenhwyfar and Gavin were out in the cold, pulling on their coats as they hurried down the garden, through the fence and along an alleyway that led out onto the street. The sirens grew ever louder until, eventually, they stopped. As they paced Gwenhwyfar searched for the new house phone on her mobile. Gavin stood patiently to one side while she recounted some tale of not feeling well, the excuse a migraine. Angrily she stabbed the disconnect button with her thumb.

'I have to meet him at Emily's. How am I supposed to do that?'

'He won't pick you up here?'

'No, he can't. He thinks I'm at her house. And they still have my bag. That's if they haven't burnt it already.'

'Where does she live?'

'High Ashbourne?'

Gavin frowned. 'I know it. That's through patrol. When will he be there?'

'Fifteen minutes.' She drew in a sharp breath of cool night air. It expanded softly in her head. 'How bad is it?'

'They'll stop us if they see us,' Gavin said. 'It's after twelve. I know how we can avoid it, though. It shouldn't be too difficult here. It's a rich neighbourhood.'

'You'll come with me?' she asked hopefully.

'Of course I will.'

'Thanks.' They set off at a brisk pace. Gwenhwyfar kept her phone clutched in her fist, just in case her father called. 'And thank you, for saving me earlier.'

'Viola was the one who smacked him round the head with a

lamp,' he confessed.

'Still, if you hadn't been looking out for me...' Once again her eyes threatened to overflow.

'Not everyone calls them Charlotte and Emily, you know. We call them the Furies. Emily's the Avenger and Charlotte's the Jealous. You know, Trisiphone and Megara.'

Gwenhwyfar's frown told him that she didn't.

'From the legend?' Gavin tried. 'They torment sinners in Greek mythology. Except everyone's done wrong, in Megara's eyes.'

She eyed him curiously, and smiled. 'Who came up with that one?'

'Arthur. It was brilliant, because they had no idea what we were talking about. They still don't.'

'Arthur?' Gwenhwyfar asked, surprised. 'Are you friends with him then?'

'I used to be.' Gavin shrugged. 'He's all right, but he keeps his distance and I keep mine. Lance hates Arthur and usually reminds everyone else to as well.'

'Lance...?'

'Yeah, he's suspended.'

'You mean the idiot that slashed the principal's tyres?'

Gavin snorted. 'He didn't do anything. Lyndon framed him. He knew Lance would get blamed for it.' They turned onto a new street. 'Lance and Arthur used to be best friends, until the Furies started a rumour about Lance and a girl Arthur liked. It got pretty nasty. Arthur ended up spending all his lunches in Mr Caledonensis' room. Until Bedivere arrived, at least.'

'What was the rumour?'

'That he'd kissed her, or slept with her, or something crazy like that. It's complete bollocks. Lance and Ellie denied it, but Hattie insisted she'd seen them together. That was when Hattie became Alecto, the un-resting. The third of the Furies.'

They fell into a long silence.

'If you still liked Arthur,' Gwenhwyfar began, 'why didn't you stay friends with him? Why side with Lance?'

'Same reason you wouldn't speak to Viola when you were friends with Emily,' he quipped. 'To fit in.'

Gwenhwyfar scowled.

'Besides,' Gavin muttered, 'Arthur doesn't associate himself with thugs.'

'You're not a thug.'

'Tell him that.'

Suddenly, he stopped her. They were at the corner of one of the wider streets, hidden by the shrubbery skirting someone's front garden. 'What?' asked Gwenhwyfar. Gavin shushed her.

'Watchmen.' He pointed to the end of the adjoining road. Gwenhwyfar saw two men dressed in the grey uniform they shared with their Welsh counterparts. 'They'll check to see if we've been drinking. They're always looking to give out penalties round here.'

He waited with his arm barring her for a minute, but the moment the Watchmen had turned the other way he hurried quietly across the street. Mindful of her heels, Gwenhwyfar tip-toed after him as quickly as she could.

'Come on!' he whispered, waving her over. 'Seriously, faster would be good.'

'I've never had a penalty before,' she admitted as she joined him.

'You're lucky,' he murmured. 'I've heard stories.'

'What stories?'

'They like to do something they call a forfeit, if they don't feel like logging a penalty. It's a complete abuse of power. It can be pretty nasty. Especially if you're a girl.'

Gwenhwyfar felt her stomach turn. 'Isn't that just a rumour?'

'Rumour has to come from somewhere,' Gavin argued.

They rounded another bend and were suddenly on the approach to Emily's house. More sirens keened in the distance. Gwenhwyfar faltered.

'Oh God, maybe I should just leave it?'

'Why? They'll freak if you show up after what they've done. It'll be worth the photo.'

'But I don't even want to look at them.'

'You just have to pretend like you don't care, that it doesn't bother you. That's the thing that annoys them most, trust me.'

He was right. She could do this, she knew she could; but that didn't make the prospect any less terrifying. Her sudden lack of courage only upset her further. She drew a deep breath and quickly walked up to the house. A glance down the drive told her that Gavin was still there, eyeing the street apprehensively. She rang the doorbell. Emily's mother answered.

'Gwen?'

'I'm here to pick up my stuff,' she blurted, 'I have a headache.'

Confused, Mrs Rose stepped aside. 'Of course! I'm sorry, Emily told me you'd gone home already.'

'I forgot my bag,' she excused, her heart pounding.

'Oh. Well, the girls are upstairs.'

She didn't bother to knock when she came to Emily's bedroom. The surprise on their faces would have been amusing had she been there for revenge, and she envisioned how much more dismayed their expressions would be if she had brought a police officer with her. Unfortunately the fantasy didn't last long.

'Where's my stuff?' she snapped. Emily opened her mouth. Silence. It was funny how scared they all looked. Gwenhwyfar's dark eyes cut through the room. Her bag had been opened, and many of her belongings were strewn across the floor.

'You went through my bag?' she hissed in disbelief. Stomping around the room she whipped everything up. She noticed her hoodie was missing and then saw it in the bin by Emily's desk. Pulling it out from under the soiled make-up wipes, she eyed it furiously. It was ripped. 'Which one of you hippos did this?'

The girls all looked to one another for help. High on adrenaline and fear, Gwenhwyfar grabbed her sports bag and stuffed everything into it, swinging it onto her shoulder. Charlotte's dress was hanging on the door to the wardrobe. She couldn't resist.

'No!' screeched Charlotte, as Gwenhwyfar tore the skirt from the bodice. Satisfied, she rushed out of the room and flew down the stairs. Emily squealed for her mother. Gavin was waiting for her in the drive. When he saw her running, he fled too.

'What did you do?' he demanded as they charged down the street then stopped for breath round the corner. 'You trying to get us clipped?'

'You should have seen their faces—horrified, all of them. It was like I was some sort of ghost.'

Gavin looked over his shoulder, as if he half expected to see the three Furies flying after them. 'Did you vanquish them?' he panted.

'No. I vanquished Charlotte's meringue, instead.'

Gwenhwyfar waved to Gavin as the car turned and then set

off down the road. She knew that her father was plucking up the courage to discover what she had been doing out on the street with a strange boy, but kept her eyes fixed ahead in the hope that he might not ask. After a few minutes of silent driving, however, Garan tried his luck.

'He seemed nice.' Gazing out of the car window, he indicated to go left.

Gwenhwyfar held her forehead in her hand, feigning her headache. 'I suppose.'

'Is he a friend from school?'

'He's in one of my classes.' The movement of the car made her feel queasy. 'He walked us home from the party.'

'That was good of him. Did you have any trouble with patrol?'

Gwenhwyfar shook her head. 'We didn't see them.'

For a few moments nothing was said. Her father looked for relevant road signs, as always choosing not to use the navigation system installed in the car's dashboard. Gwenhwyfar ignored his concerned glances, glad she had remembered to use Viola's sprays.

'How are you feeling?'

'Not too great,' she admitted. Her stomach lurched when her father slowed the family car to a halt. Police tape cut across the road ahead, and blue lights flashed off of the dancing ribbon. He wound down the window as a bright-vested man approached.

'Road's closed due to an incident,' the man barked. 'Power's out—you'll have to follow the diversion.' Gwenhwyfar met the policeman's eyes. He sniffed in consideration. 'Been anywhere nice, this evening?'

'I just picked my daughter up from a friend's house,' said Garan. 'She wasn't feeling well.'

The policeman shone his torch into the car. Gwenhwyfar felt her pupils contract in protest. 'I see. Party, was it?'

'Sleepover,' Garan corrected. Another car pulled up behind theirs, hooting. The policeman was distracted.

'Just follow the signs.' He waved them on.

A long while passed. For some reason the diversion took them through the outer wall to London, where they were stopped and asked to show identification. Such checkpoints could be troublesome at the best of times, but it was late, and the sentry seemed unconcerned enough to let them pass without too much fuss. When they didn't come back through the wall in the opposite direction Garan grew concerned. The scenery soon changed to the densely populated area of South London, litter as well as decay becoming frequent. They were lost.

'Bloody diversion,' Garan muttered, peering about. Gwenhwyfar sat forwards and turned on the car's navigation with a huff. It recalculated their route home, and Garan turned the car around in a side street. They drove back. Traffic was sparse.

'Awfully quiet, isn't it, Gwen?'

A brick collided with the bonnet and bounced up the window, spider-webbing the glass. Garan swerved, but then veered to get back on the road. The car behind them blasted its horn and careered into a lamppost.

'Dad!' Gwenhwyfar yipped. The bonnet of the other car bellowed with smoke. No one got out. Garan thrust his phone into her lap. She grasped at it, shaking.

'Call the police,' he advised.

'Dad, stop! Why aren't we stopping?'

'Call them!'

'We need to stop!'

'Just call them, Gwen!'

Fumbling, she punched in the digits. A figure ran across the road, followed by another and then another, and then scores of people were streaming through the street, slipping between buildings and jumping fences. Windows were smashed; buildings were torched. A toothless man bounced into the side of their car and then dozens of hands were grasping at the body. They were surrounded. Garan slowed but kept the car moving. In his rear view mirror a man was pulled from the crash site.

'Can't we help him?' she cried.

'The police will help him,' her dad responded, his jaw rigid. 'Have you called them?'

'I'm being transferred!'

He revved the engine. Eggs splattered onto the windshield. Small gangs of children swamped the vehicle and, laughing, pressed their grubby faces against the glass. Gwenhwyfar turned to see riot vans descending. Officers armed with bludgeons pulled the man free from the mob. The windshield wipers came on, the washers squirting, the broken eggs smearing across the glass.

'Galla i ddim weld blydi unrhyw beth!' *I can't see a bloody thing!* Garan swore, slipping into Welsh. A woman leapt up onto the bonnet. There was an opening in the crowd. Garan's foot hit the floor and Gwenhwyfar was thrown back in her seat. The woman vanished over the windshield, tumbling over the roof. Several houses were on fire. Gwenhwyfar snapped the phone shut and abandoned it on the dashboard. They accelerated away.

'Are you all right?' her father asked, his voice urgent. 'Gwen?'

'I'm fine.'

'Good. I'll get us home.'

He didn't stop the vehicle to scrape the mess off the windshield, but pressed on, hunched over the steering wheel to peer through a thin sliver of clear glass. It was nearly three by the time they heard the crackle of gravel sound their approach to the house. They pulled up by the front door, and then the engine fell silent.

Garan sat still, his eyes lingering on the destroyed, sticky windshield looming before them. He expelled a long sigh. 'Your mother's going to go crazy. She was going to the spa in this tomorrow.'

'Why did they pull that man from his car?' Gwenhwyfar asked.

'I'm not sure, cariad,' Garan admitted. He withdrew his keys from the ignition. 'Maybe they wanted to steal it.'

'But it crashed,' she scowled.

'Or take things from it,' he tried.

'It was on fire!'

He paused. 'A lot of people can't afford cars, Gwen. And they resent people who can.'

'Why?'

He shook his head. 'They just do. They were probably from the protest in London. They must have started looting once the power went out.'

She gazed through the mottled glass. 'What were they protesting?'

For a moment Garan's features were suspended with the look of someone with an opinion dangling on their tongue, but then his eyes softened, and his words were swallowed.

'Nothing, cariad. Don't you worry about it.'

'I had another one of those dreams the other day, Marv.'

Mr Caledonensis looked up from his desk, his lanky frame bent over an open drawer. 'Oh yes?' he invited, rummaging for a pen. The playful screams of year sevens could be heard through the closed windows, but Arthur kept his eyes on his desk. 'Was it the same as your other one?'

'Similar,' he admitted. His mind was still on Friday night. History that morning had been difficult, but by ignoring Gwenhwyfar and Bedivere completely he had made it through. 'It was different, though. This time there was a lion.'

'A lion?' Marvin sat down. 'And in what context did you see this *lion*?'

Frowning, Arthur looked out beyond the window. He was perched on one of the tables with his feet in a chair. 'It's not important, really.'

'I will be the judge of whether or not it is important, Arthur,' Marvin encouraged. 'Come on, your dream. Tell me what happened.'

'Well, I was in a forest, lost. I came across that alligator, you know, the one I've dreamt of before? It was sitting on a rock. It hissed at me and snapped, and I knew it was going to eat me.'

'And then what?'

'Then a lion leapt out of the forest, just as the alligator was about to spring, and tore the head off and dropped it at my feet. There was a flash of light—something like a comet, or a fireball, exploded in front of me, and suddenly the lion's mane turned to fire—white-hot flames burned all around it.'

There was a silence. 'Is that how it ends?'

'No.' Arthur went on. 'It burns so big that all the trees catch fire and it traps me with it. The lion's skin burns too. It turns from gold to black, like charcoal, and leaps towards me. I try to run but the claws—they're hot—like coals—tear me down… and that's… that's when I wake up.'

He glanced across to his teacher, who gazed at him with glinting eyes. 'Interesting,' Marvin murmured. 'And the lion you say is new, but the alligator isn't?'

'That's right,' Arthur nodded. 'I've dreamt of that before.'

'How curious.'

'I've tried looking the meaning up. My grandmother has this old encyclopaedia on dreams, but what I read hardly makes sense,' Arthur said, twisting his thumbs.

'And what did you read?'

'Something about hardships, and great strength, but it all seemed to unravel after that. It's strange… my dreams keep getting more and more destructive. I keep dreaming of death.'

Marvin expelled a releasing sigh. 'I'm sure it's nothing to worry about, Arthur. It's probably just part of growing up, like nosebleeds and spots.' He smiled at him kindly. 'I remember having bad dreams when I was your age. Not of flaming lions and evil alligators, but they were quite interesting.'

'But do dreams actually mean anything? Are they important? My grandmother says they're just your brain organising memories or recent experiences—like it's filing them away in a big archive,' he recited.

'Anything's important, Arthur, if a person believes it is. Were you at the protest, on Friday? The people there believe change is important, even though most do not.'

'No. I heard it got quite violent after the power cuts. Several people were injured. I saw it on the news.'

'Typical! Don't tell me, the news focused on the riot and hardly mentioned the peaceful protest at all?' Marvin shook his head. 'Yes, there *were* a few people taking advantage of the situation, but that wasn't part of the protest. Though it *is* a sign that people aren't happy with their lot. Not that the government will see it that way, though. I assume you've heard about what they plan to do?' When Arthur gazed at him blankly, Marvin ploughed on. 'The New Nationals were just waiting for something like this to happen.'

'Waiting for what to happen?'

'This riot! A riot, any riot: any illegal, dangerous activity to justify the nation-wide increase to the area where protesting without the police's consent is illegal. Do you know what that means? Censored speech for all. If they don't like what you decide to protest against, then your freedom of speech, your *right* becomes illegal by default.'

'I thought protests near parliament were only banned on May Day,' Arthur ventured, disturbed by his teacher's fanaticism.

'No,' snapped Marvin. 'Every day: all three-hundred-and-sixty-five of them. All throughout London: right down to Epsom. Soon the rest of the country will be silenced too.'

Arthur frowned. 'But surely if people don't want to promote extremist ideas, there won't be a problem.'

'But what's extremist? Who decides? Do you decide, Arthur, does the individual decide? What seems perfectly reasonable to one may seem like madness to another,' Marvin imposed, angered. 'It'll be Milton and the New Nationals who decide right from wrong, and one day you may wake up to find that the beliefs they've taken a disliking to just happen to be yours.'

There was a tense silence. For a while both reflected, Arthur feeling wounded by the harsh reprimand. Eventually he found himself enforced to break the quiet, but only once he was sure

Marvin had calmed down.

'I thought you said they were protesting the poor excuse for democracy that parliament is exercising?'

'Well, they were! A few people that I know, at least.'

'But the news said—'

'That they were all yobs? Disillusioned youths? I'm sure it did. I don't rely on the news, Arthur. They make half of it up; either that or they don't report it,' Marvin said scornfully. 'Milton is quite chummy with the head of UK Broadcasting, so I'm sure that everyone in the country was informed that they were marching against all that's good in this world. You can't believe everything you hear, you know.' The clock was bringing the lunch hour to an end. Soon everyone would be swarming back in to sit through another assembly. 'Have you fallen out with Bedivere?' he suddenly asked.

'What? No.'

Marvin studied him closely. 'Are you sure? This morning you both looked put out. You didn't say a word to him or Gwenhwyfar.'

'I was working,' he countered with a dismissive shrug.

'In silence? You would be the only one in the whole class, save for Morgan. Is something wrong?'

'Nothing's wrong,' Arthur insisted, rising to leave. 'I should probably go and find him now, actually. I said I'd meet him for assembly.' He knew his teacher didn't believe him, but that didn't matter. Slinging his rucksack onto his shoulder as the bell rang, Arthur hurried towards the door. 'I'll see you later, Marv.'

He felt his teacher's eyes on him as he slipped out into the empty corridor, and they burned into his back until he turned out of sight.

New National

Arthur kept his head bent towards the table. The classroom began to fill with students still buzzing from their lunch hour. Frowning, he concentrated on the open Politics textbook that he'd taken from the teacher's desk. The empty chair beside him loomed for a while, but was then disturbed as an apologetic Bedivere slunk down to fill his usual seat.

'Arthur?' There was a prolonged silence. 'So you're just going to ignore me, then.'

Arthur glanced at Bedivere, and flicked to a new page.

'I didn't know, you know.'

He clenched his jaw and kept reading.

'I had no idea what was going on. I was only told that Gwen wanted to talk to you, nothing else.'

'By Emily,' Arthur pointed out, his voice rigid. 'Why didn't you tell me it was coming from her?'

'Because! You wouldn't have listened to me, otherwise.'

'I wonder why?' he hissed.

Bedivere opened his mouth to retaliate, but Mr Graham

silenced them all with a great huff as he rose to stand by the chalkboard. Struggling to conduct the lesson on two feet, their Politics teacher leant heavily on the edge of his own desk, which groaned under the pressure. The next hour and a half was spent in a working silence. With the eventual sounding of the bell, Arthur packed to leave.

'I'm not lying, you know,' Bedivere murmured to him, struggling to match his haste. 'I swear I didn't know what she was up to.'

'Yeah, right.' Arthur stood up.

'If I had said anything about Emily, you never would've gone to meet Gwen.'

'And then the prank wouldn't have worked, would it?' He grabbed his blazer.

'Prank or not, Gwen *wanted* to meet you.'

'Emily said so, did she?'

Bedivere huffed. 'I didn't *know* it was a trick, Emily just told me to pass on a message. I *thought* I was doing you a favour.'

Arthur kicked his chair under the table and forced his way behind Bedivere. The other boy scrambled up.

'It's not what you think,' he continued.

'How do you know what I think? You don't even know what I saw.'

'I know exactly what you saw. Gwen told me.'

'Oh, so you've been talking to her about this, have you? I bet you're all laughing about it behind my back: you, her, and the Furies.' He cut through the room and sped for the door. Bedivere followed.

'Gwen had nothing to do with it.'

'Really?' Arthur snorted. 'Then why doesn't she tell me that herself?'

'Because you practically locked her in there with him, you idiot!' Bedivere pushed him in the back, and Arthur caught himself on a desk. There was a loud exclamation of protest from Mr Graham. 'I had nothing to do with it!'

'You know what Emily's like, so why did you even listen to her? Oh, wait, I know: because she let you stick your tongue down her throat.'

'Boys!' the teacher hollered again. He launched himself upwards but Bedivere didn't linger, hid the tears welling in his eyes as he rushed out of the room. For a moment Mr Graham twitched to go after him, but with a face like thunder beckoned Arthur over instead. 'And what, may I ask, was that about?'

'Nothing,' Arthur said, surprised by how upset he felt.

'Nothing?' Mr Graham echoed.

Arthur shrugged. 'Just a disagreement.'

'A "disagreement"?' Purpling, Mr Graham shook his head. 'How dare you disrupt my class? The two of you were behaving like animals. Animals!' Angrily, he flicked through the papers on his desk. 'I should call the principal. You're lucky I haven't. As it is, I have something I want to discuss with you. It's about your latest paper.' He drew a breath, and suddenly his demeanour was suspiciously sweet. 'You seem to have misunderstood the question. I asked you to outline George Milton's party policy and how he became Prime Minister.' He waved Arthur's work at him. It was covered in red graffiti.

'But that's what I did,' Arthur objected.

'No, you can't have done. There's not one reference to the article I asked you to read from your textbook. Where are your approved sources? The content is wrong. And where on *earth* did you find all these references?'

'Archives,' frowned Arthur. 'Independent journals... Why? What's wrong with them?'

'Nothing's *wrong* with them as such, they're just... not *correct*. You didn't find any of them in the library here, surely?'

Arthur shook his head. Scowling, Mr Graham examined the essay. 'Claims such as this... you say that George Milton has exclusive access, along with his favoured followers, to rare luxuries such as red meat, wine and chocolate, but that argument cannot be true. Everyone knows that George Milton is a simple man, with a simple diet. And here, for example, you say, *"the authenticity of Milton's success in previous elections has been widely debated since it became apparent that Milton's party, New National, is suspected to have enlisted votes from those imprisoned, and several voters unfortunately deceased."* Is that what it says in your textbook? That the Prime Minister is a fraud?'

'No,' Arthur replied stiffly.

'Here, even! Ah yes, my favourite part. You go on to say that in relation to previous governments, Milton's *regime* is dangerously close to mirroring a dictatorship, even comparing it to *Ingsoc* from Orwell's *1984*... *"a party that has long since used threats of national security to exterminate the liberties of its people in return for their perceived safety."* If I didn't know any better, Arthur, I'd say you were in severe danger of sounding like a separatist. Not to mention the issue of where you found a copy of *1984* and why on earth you've read it.'

Arthur felt a moment of inward panic. 'My grandfather read it to me before it was banned,' he lied, fervently hoping Mr Graham wouldn't ask to see what was in his bag.

'And what about the rest of this nonsense?' he asked,

suddenly livid. 'Where on earth did it all come from?' Again the paper was flapped around, its stapled pages cackling.

'I thought it would be beneficial to do some external research.'

'Beneficial?' snorted Mr Graham, his jowls flapping. 'The school could get into trouble for this, don't you realise? If this had been an exam? All our funding, gone!'

'But other teachers encourage us to read outside the textbooks,' Arthur reasoned, 'to find alternative truths.'

'I don't care about the truth, I just care what's in the syllabus!' Mr Graham snapped, standing with a jolt. The desk creaked under his podgy hands. 'And so should the other teachers! Who's been telling you otherwise?'

The sudden change in tone caused Arthur to bolt up. He stared back into Mr Graham's receding eyes, his own distant.

'No? Not going to share? Fine!' A crisp rip sounded as his chubby fingers tore apart the paper, pieces falling to the desk as he shredded it again and again. 'You are to rewrite this paper in the *correct* fashion for tomorrow afternoon. If you do not, I will be sending you to the principal's office to be punished for your knowledge, use, and reference of a banned book and for your questionable research into sources supportive of such ludicrous ideas. Do you understand?'

Arthur nodded, quelling his rising anger.

'Oh, and *some* thought to my job security would be appreciated before you pull another stunt like this. I shouldn't have to expect it from you, Arthur.'

Arthur nodded, and when that failed to satisfy his purple-faced teacher he cleared his throat. 'Yes sir.'

'Go on; get out of my sight. I don't want to see you again until you've redone it, you hear me?'

Arthur hurried out of the classroom into an empty corridor. The voice of Mr Graham followed him down the hall.

'And don't forget! Rewrite it for tomorrow!'

The streets felt empty, sparsely populated with residents sitting purposelessly on front doorsteps and lingering on street corners. Lower Logres was the lesser-funded part of town; littered, tired, and rarely ventured into by people who did not live there. Its separation from the bustle of the ever-constant centre was absolute, which existed as a tidy labyrinth of chain stores and big businesses. Arthur turned his head against the wind as a cloud of grit rolled along the un-swept street. Water was short, and cleaning was only possible after heavy bouts of rain.

The residents were grey, with grime worked into their browned clothes and dirt rubbed deep into their skin. The dust got everywhere, and Arthur washed it off every night with gratitude that he could. When their water had been cut off he had collected rainwater when it came, filling up bottles from the water fountains at school. This had meant he could wash at least, but less often; and every day he had arrived at Logres with the self-consciousness of someone aware of their own odour.

The kiosk was one of the few smaller establishments left open. Whenever he had the time Arthur took advantage of the cut-price meals left over from the previous day, and purchased two pre-packaged lunches, not yet stale. Sometimes he brought food that he had prepared at home, but it seemed wrong to deplete the supplies that had to last him and his grandmother the week. He missed days, of course, and the guilt for skipping a drop was usually heavy in his mind. This was his cost, his responsibility, and now that he had started he didn't think he could stop.

He selected something large, cold rice with lumps of meat that promised to be chicken, and a hefty sandwich. Protein was good. He always chose the meals with the highest calorie count. Arthur went to the checkout with a feeling of guilt, snatching a chocolate bar as he waited in line. The till beeped, the cash machine pinged. He handed over two hours' wages and got just over half back. Wrapping the bag into a tight bundle, he tucked it under his arm and ducked outside.

The sky seemed heavy. Posters were layered like cards along the peeling walls of the houses running parallel to the road, some messages long-concealed, some reappearing under newer sentences that had been half torn down. A few were community notices, a couple were slogans, but most were New National speak, the words of which jumped out at him in angry letters as he hurried by.

Smile and the world smiles with you, read one. *A happy worker is a happy person*, read another. *You have the things in life you deserve*, proclaimed the next. And, *Would you know if your neighbour is housing illegals?*

The occasional police officer frequented the main road that led to the clock tower, but running into one at this hour was rare, and Arthur was fairly confident he would not get stopped. He fished for the chocolate bar he had bought himself and ate it absently, stuffing the empty wrapper back into the bag when he was done.

There was a quiet park two streets away. Opposite it ran a small road with second-hand charity shops and bookies. At the end of this road by a disused bus stop was a bin, open-topped and skirted with iron grating. The movement was so rehearsed that he needn't think to do it. As he passed the bin he dropped in the whole carrier bag with the food, and then nipped across the road to cut through the park.

Giving aid to the homeless was an offence, he knew: particularly as many of them were illegals. He didn't know if the older woman who scavenged through the bins in this area was an immigrant, only that so far she had avoided arrest, evading the ever-constant risk of being moved out of the area.

He couldn't help himself. Quickly he stole a glance over his shoulder as he threatened to turn out of sight. The particularly grimy woman half-vanished into the bin to fish out what he had dropped, and then hurried off into a side street, trusting that she had been given something good.

The next morning arrived with a sky the colour of dull lead. September was slipping by with cold winds and the promise of heavy rain, forcing students to don thick, navy jumpers beneath their summer blazers. Arthur, escaping the sudden drop in temperature, was sitting in Marvin's classroom. With Bedivere now avoiding him completely, he was using his newfound unpopularity as an opportunity to churn out Mr Graham's mindless essay. The traditional glowing praise of Britain's prosperity as a conclusion allowed his mind to tend to other thoughts: his destroyed relationships, his unwelcome solitude and worries over the price of heating his grandmother's house.

At about twenty to nine, when most students were still arriving, Marvin appeared with a mug of coffee that slopped onto the already stained carpet. 'Ah! Good morning Arthur,' he chirped, putting his papers down on his desk. 'In early, I see?'

'I had a paper to finish. It's for Politics.'

'Politics?'

'Could you read it?'

'I don't see why not. Did Mr Graham set you some surprise homework?' He collapsed into his chair. The foam padding protruded through the rips in the cover.

'I had to rewrite it,' Arthur explained. He dropped his essay onto Marvin's table. It slid across the slick surface and met his teacher's curious hands.

'Why?'

'Just read it.'

Marvin's eyebrows contracted to a thick line as his pupils scanned the page. After a while he held it out, and Arthur retrieved it expectantly.

'Well...' Marvin began, chewing his words. 'It's... well-written.'

'Well-written?' echoed Arthur. 'I wouldn't call it that. I know it's rubbish—that's the whole point.'

'Not *rubbish*, as such... but yes... I can't say I agree with this perception of George Milton. Which references did you use? Not those propaganda books?'

'We always have to use those. Either that, or anything else on the reading list.'

'And why did you have to rewrite it?'

'Because I took your advice,' Arthur shrugged. Marvin stared at him blankly. 'Remember, to use different sources when writing a paper?'

'Oh, I see. Mr Graham didn't like seeing things from another perspective, then?' A smile played at the corner of his lips.

'No, not really.'

'Well, aren't you lucky you didn't decide to experiment for an exam? I knew you had access to other sources, Arthur, but I thought you were just reading up on them, not utilising them for school papers.'

'I got bored of always writing the same nonsense. The amount I've discovered just from looking at other sources is incredible. None of it is covered in any of my classes. It makes me wonder what else is being kept from us, and why. Even History—what you teach is better than most, but it's not complete, is it? You miss things out, don't you?'

Marvin leant back in his old chair, and sighed. 'Not because I want to, heaven knows! I encourage students like you to read around because I can't teach you everything. I'd be out of a job if I didn't respond to the syllabus. I sometimes think I should just go back to lecturing. The universities used to be more lenient.'

'Wouldn't it be overlooked, if we all just said what we have to in the exams?'

'I can't control what people write if I start putting alien ideas in their heads,' countered Marvin. 'Besides, Ravioli's a stickler for doing things by the rules. He'd crack heads if he discovered any freedom of information in his classrooms. His brother's a New National.'

The shrill school bell ended their conversation as it had done so hundreds of times. Marvin glanced to the clock on the wall, though he knew the time to the exact minute. 'By all means read around, Arthur; but for goodness' sake, don't put anything you learn from any external research into your schoolwork. And watch who you talk to about such things, too,' he advised. 'Times aren't what they used to be, and you never really know what people are thinking, or who else might be listening.'

The hallways were riddled with massing students. Arthur, well practiced in the art of weaving through crowds, picked his way through with swift expertise. He was halfway up the stairs to the laboratories when someone called out to him.

'Hey! Arthur!'

A sharp pain seared through the back of his skull as a half-filled water bottle hit him squarely on the head. He turned to see who had thrown it. Tom Hareton was laughing, but he wasn't the culprit.

'Where you off to in such a hurry?' Hector barked. A few over-stretched strides, and he was standing on the step above him.

'Science.' Arthur ascended the stairs. Eagerly, Hector cut him off.

'Why so fast? You've still got time.'

Arthur tried to find a way around, but quickly he was blocked.

'You know, Art, you shouldn't be so rude. I'm only trying to talk to you. I wanted to see how you were doing.'

'Don't you have a lesson to get to?'

'I'm serious. I really did want to talk to you, Art.'

Arthur stopped, resisting the urge to push him.

'I wanted to apologise,' Hector continued. 'I just wanted to say that I'm sorry Gwen picked me over you.' A snigger from Tom echoed through the stairwell. 'But we have to respect the girl's wishes, don't we?'

'Of course.' He moved a step up, but Hector persisted.

'I mean, it can't have been nice for you to walk in on us like that, but that sort of thing happens, right?'

'All the time.'

'I'd like to think we were still friends, and friends talk about everything, don't they?'

Arthur darted around him and stomped up the stairs. Hector shadowed his steps, snapping at his heels.

'Am I right? Like Gwen and me. I'd like to think we can talk about her without the hard feelings.' More muffled laughter. 'Like how many times we did it and how she moaned for more.' Tom was in hysterics and Hector was finding it hard to keep a straight face. 'I just thought I should let you know that we're thinking of making it official, now. Like friends with benefits?'

Arthur slammed his hand into the double doors at the top of the stairs. Hector's shorter paces soon relented, and the two teenagers fell behind, whooping like wild dogs. Arthur's Science room was fast approaching and immediately he spotted Gwenhwyfar in the queue. She approached him, worrying her bottom lip between her teeth.

'Arthur? Please, about Friday—I wanted to explain—'

'Leave me alone, would you?' he exploded. 'I don't care! I don't care what you and Hector got up to, I don't care how funny you think this is; so just get lost, and stop pretending you're any different from *them.*'

She fell back, stunned. Ignoring the leaden silence that had fallen over his queuing classmates, Arthur hurried into the laboratory and sat at his old table, the eyes and whisperings of the gossipers pressing hard down upon him.

Science crawled by in isolation. Sitting alone at the back of the class, Gwenhwyfar tried to brush away the sting of Arthur's words before they rubbed too deep. The memory of Tom's party had faded into a sickly and indecipherable blur, interrupted by the ugly rearing of Hector and his cold, unwelcome lips. Like yesterday, Arthur left abruptly at the sounding of the bell. Crestfallen, Gwenhwyfar began the slow walk to the cafeteria. Her mind was lingering on the grinning faces of the grubby, squealing children when she heard her name echo in the hall.

'Did you hear? After Arthur left they just kept on kissing. How *cruel* is that?'

Charlotte. Or Megara, as Gavin would say. Trisiphone was with her, as was Hattie, also known as Alecto. It took Gwenhwyfar a moment to realise that they were with Viola's old acquaintances: Rhea Morte and Rebecca Woods. The five girls swarmed down the corridor like a section of a hive.

'I heard they did more than that,' Rebecca contributed, flicking her thick black hair over her shoulder. 'I heard they had *sex*.'

'*No.*' Rhea gasped. 'Really?'

'Really.'

'But he's so *ugly*,' Rhea snorted, her upturned nose wrinkling. 'I thought it was just supposed to be a prank?'

'It was,' Charlotte told them. 'It was all Gwen's idea.' Gwenhwyfar noticed that she now walked central to their small group. Emily had been demoted.

'Poor Arthur,' Rebecca sympathised, her arms linked with Hattie and Rhea's. 'He must be *devastated*.'

'I spoke to Rupert yesterday,' Charlotte announced. 'Apparently Arthur thinks Gwen is absolutely *vile*. He can't stand her. He never wants to speak to her again.'

'*No.*' Emily's mouth hung open.

'So he doesn't like Gwen, then?' Hattie asked.

'Even if he did like her, it's too late,' scoffed Charlotte. 'It's not like he'll forgive her for what she did, and besides, she'll have whatever Hector has now, and I hear he has a lot. He's slept with practically every girl in the school.'

Hattie made a sound of disgust. 'I'm never going to sit near either of them again. *Gross.*'

Their voices faded as Gwenhwyfar slipped down the nearest staircase, her fingers tingling with rage. How dare they blame this on her? It took her longer than usual to make it to the canteen, and all the while she found herself replaying Charlotte's words. Would Arthur really believe such a thing of her? Did he really hate her?

It took her a moment to realise she was being called. Striding purposefully through the crowded hall, she joined Gavin and cast off her bag next to Viola's. 'Where's Tom?'

'Band practice.' Viola removed her feet from a chair so Gwenhwyfar could sit. 'Where've you been?'

'I just saw the Furies,' Gwenhwyfar started. She picked at her half-painted nails. 'They're saying that their stupid prank was *my* idea.'

'No one's going to believe that,' Viola told her.

'No? I think Arthur does. He said so. He told me I was just like *them*.'

'You spoke to him?'

'If you can call it that,' Gwenhwyfar muttered. 'I tried to apologise, I tried to explain, but he just shouted at me and told me to leave him alone. He *hates* me.'

'Really, he's the one who should be apologising to you,' Gavin remarked. There was a low rumble from above.

'But he doesn't know what happened,' Gwenhwyfar reminded him. 'It's not his fault. I'd be angry at me, if I had only seen what he saw.'

'I can talk to him. He might listen to me.' Another rumble

caused Viola to turn her eyes to the window. 'It's getting dark, out.'

'Thunderstorm, probably,' Gavin observed. He leant forward into their table. 'Did you hear? They've made fifty arrests in relation to that protest on Friday. Ridiculous.'

'How is that ridiculous?' Gwenhwyfar prickled. 'I was there, remember? They practically set fire to half of London.'

'It's ridiculous because they didn't say *who* they arrested. According to some independent news websites they're detaining the organisers of the peaceful protest beforehand. The riots were the perfect excuse.'

There was a moment of silence between them, and then a ripple of excitement through the hall as the thunder clapped louder.

'Oh Gwen! I was just telling Gavin. I have news.'

'News?' Gwenhwyfar leant a little closer.

'You can't tell a soul, though. I don't want Emily and that lot knowing.'

'As if I'll ever speak to them again,' she assured Viola, glancing across to where Emily usually sat, where she used to sit. 'What is it?'

Viola looked to Gavin, and smiled. 'I've been scouted. By a top London modelling agency, can you believe it?'

'What? When?'

'I was in London on Saturday, and a booker stopped me in the street. They asked me to go to their agency. I just heard that I have a test shoot this Saturday.'

Gwenhwyfar felt a twinge of jealousy. 'A test shoot? What's that?'

'They take some pictures, and if they're any good, they sign me. I might have to start going to castings. They say girls can make a lot of money modelling. A lot of them have bought their own house and one for their parents by the time they're twenty.'

'What's the agency called again?' Gavin questioned. 'I want to look it up on my phone.'

'*Quantum Models*. It's supposed to be the best,' she boasted. 'All their girls get contracts with the big names abroad. Like *Supra Models* and *Fashion First*.'

'But what about school?' Gwenhwyfar asked.

'I can work weekends and half terms,' Viola explained. 'Besides, it's not far to London. I can always go to the occasional appointment if it's important.'

'True.' Grinning, Gavin held out his mobile. The screen displayed the agency's online books. 'Looks professional.'

'That's because it is,' Viola smirked. A flash of lightning illuminated the hall. Outside, heavy rain streaked past the windowpanes. Gavin and Viola flicked through the portfolios of the other models. Gwenhwyfar pictured herself at a photo shoot, then in a glossy magazine, and she contemplated the benefits. Why didn't Viola want Emily to know? She'd be green with envy—they all would. Another flash flooded the hall, and a few excitable girls screeched. Something pulled at her attention. From the other side of the cafeteria Gwenhwyfar saw Hector's eyes illuminate. He was watching her.

The Nutcracker

Mr Graham was spread out at his desk.

He wasn't a particularly tall man, but he was intimidating, and he had a large stomach that started above his heart and rounded off far below his middle. As Arthur approached him with his newly written paper, Mr Graham ordered him to wait with a fat extended finger. He didn't hurry himself to finish the page that he was reading, and by the time he closed his crisp copy of *Politics in New National England* others were beginning to wander into class.

'Well?' Mr Graham's eyebrows rose expectantly.

'I rewrote it, as you asked.'

Mr Graham snatched the paper off him, a thick scowl shadowing his features. 'This is hand-written. You know I can hardly read handwriting,' he grunted. 'You're supposed to type up all your work.'

'I couldn't at such short notice, sir.'

'What, no computer? Don't tell me you didn't have time to print this, Arthur. What about that library you're always working at? Why not do it there?'

'I can't do schoolwork during work hours,' he excused. 'And my computer's not working.'

Mr Graham considered this for a moment, squinted, and then abandoned the essay on his desk. 'Very well,' he relented, 'but next time make sure it's printed. Handwriting is only for exercise books. It works the muscles.'

'Don't you want to read it?'

'Later. Now hurry up and sit down. You've already wasted enough of my time this week.' He pulled himself up out of his chair. Arthur retreated, though his destination was no haven. Bedivere ignored him and when he tried to reach his seat the other boy made it as difficult as possible. 'Hurry up and sit, all of you!' Mr Graham barked. 'I don't have time for your dilly-dallying. Sit!' He turned to the chalkboard and scrawled something nearly incomprehensible across it.

The lesson was long and tedious. Not once did Bedivere's brown eyes shift from the surface of their desk, and a hand-drawn spiral on the front cover of his exercise book expanded and intensified. With yesterday's behaviour clearly at the forefront of his mind, Mr Graham kept a close eye on them, squinting after them both suspiciously as they exited the classroom at the eventual sounding of the bell.

With nothing else to do at lunchtime, Arthur went to sit in Marvin's musty classroom with a mushrooming headache. Idly, he traced the proclamations of infatuation and foul language engraved into his desk. Marvin was marking papers.

'What kind of imbecile thinks that the Industrial Revolution originated in the United States?' he harrumphed, exasperation creasing his features. 'Have I not been making my lessons clear enough? The United States, as we know it, didn't exist until 1776.'

Arthur peered over his school bag. 'Who came up with that gem, then?' he asked, pleased that he at least knew the origins of England's most done-to-death historical event, second only to the World Wars.

'Now now, Arthur. What sort of teacher would I be if I told you that?' His eyes smiled. 'Let's just say their name begins with a T. That leaves three options, no?'

'Three?' asked Arthur.

'Oh no, that's in one of my other classes,' Marvin corrected. 'Never mind. I suppose it's rather obviously Mr Hareton, anyway.'

Arthur rolled his eyes. 'That's hardly surprising.'

'No?'

'I don't know why you don't just smack him around the head with a textbook.'

Marvin seemed amused. 'Is that what you would do?'

'It might give the rest of us a chance to learn something. He never shuts up. Why don't you just throw him out?'

'Oh, believe me, the thought has crossed my mind on several occasions.' Slowly Marvin shook his head. 'But I learned long ago that the best form of punishment for Mr Hareton is the lesson itself. Why throw him out into the corridors when he clearly hates learning so much?'

Arthur grinned. He loved his lessons with Marvin, loved spending his extra hours in this room. Yes, it smelt as if it hadn't been cleaned in fifty years, and yes, the pile of books next to the teacher's chair was so precariously stacked that all the students had bets on when it would finally collapse, but Marvin was at his level, thought in the same manner as he and Bedivere did, as opposed to all the other students at Logres, who looked at him as if he were mad if he ever tried to hold an intelligent discussion with them.

'Ah!' was the next exclamation. 'This genius seems to think that steam engines ran on oil. What a Hawking!'

Arthur laughed. 'Not Tom again, I hope.'

Marvin scribbled red ink across the page. 'No, not this time,' he sighed. 'Do you know what the worst thing about marking students' papers is, Arthur? It's the fact that I can't simply write, *wrong*. No, one must never write *wrong* on a student's paper. Nor may I write *incorrect*. It all has to be *good try*, or, *wonderful attempt*. Or my personal favourite, *not quite right*.'

Arthur flicked back through his exercise book and frowned. 'I've got a couple of *not quite rights* in here, Marv.'

'Well of course! No one can always be *quite right*.'

'Next time just write *wrong*, please. I won't sue you for it.'

'You might not, but the committee of teachers and parents would have my head.' Abandoning his marking, Marvin stretched. 'So, how did that *not quite right* paper go down with Mr Graham?'

'I have no idea. He didn't even read it. I don't think he's going to.'

'He probably just wanted to make a point.' Marvin rubbed his deep-set eyes. 'I wouldn't worry about it. I don't. I feel confident enough in your abilities to be sure that having to write such drivel won't brainwash you, like it has nearly every other student at this school.'

'I'd say that the teachers are more brainwashed than the students,' Arthur duelled. 'Has it always been this way?'

Marvin's quick eyes locked onto him, his hands linked behind the back of his head. His brown jumper had ridden up his shirt, and he had bruises of ink ingrained into his fingers.

'I mean has the educational system always been so… so limited?'

'Limited?' For a moment Marvin considered his words. 'Well, any system of education is limited. Do you think they cover the Nanjing Massacre in Japanese schools? Do we cover Britain's involvement in the development of biological warfare?'

Arthur watched him closely and chewed the inside of his cheek.

'No, we don't,' Marvin ploughed on. 'So I suppose the answer to your question is yes, the educational system has always been limited. As time goes by however, we see variations on that limitation. I would say that today, it is particularly limited.'

Arthur's headache threatened to bloom into something more substantial. 'But why?'

'Aha! Thank you Arthur, thank you.' Marvin waved his hands about, brimming with excitement. 'You have just brought us to another vital point.'

'I have?'

'Yes, you have. There is a lot that our government would rather we didn't know, but even their best efforts can't censor out everything. Something, *somewhere* will always get through. The intellectual is the single most dangerous thing to a government, and do you know how? I'll tell you. It's because they never stop asking *why*.'

There was a moment of silence.

'I always knew you were a smart one, Arthur. From the moment I saw you on your first day, I knew you were different.

You always asked questions, always wanted to know, always were the first to pick apart inconsistencies. You were always, always asking *why*.'

Arthur bit at the dry skin on the inside of his lip. He gazed at Marvin as his teacher stopped gesticulating and his hands dropped to the table. He swallowed.

'*Why* is the most important question in the universe. *Why* can change the world. Remember it, Arthur. Never stop asking *why*.'

French was long, and once again Gwenhwyfar found she learnt little due to her disruptive class. Afterwards they spent lunch in the packed canteen, with the wet weather raging beyond the windows. Geography was her last subject of the day, a lesson shared with Viola, and it commenced without much fuss. It was later, when students were supposed to be working quietly, that she heard Emily and another girl whispering doggedly.

'Who?'

'Who what?' Emily murmured.

A quiet cough from Miss Barnes caused their voices to hush even more. Viola sent Gwenhwyfar a sidelong glance.

'Who's asking who out?' the other girl hissed. Gwenhwyfar couldn't recall her name.

'Arthur!' Emily responded, giggling. She glanced deliberately over her shoulder. 'Charlotte's *devastated*. Then again, she's totally deluded if she thinks he will ever go out with her. She's too short.'

'Who's he asking?' The girl almost sounded hopeful.

'Morgan. That sad, skinny girl that always looks at him with lovesick eyes. I don't know why, though. She's so *dull*.'

'But tall enough, at least,' the other girl remarked.

Gwenhwyfar felt her heart perform something rather incredible. It both expanded and imploded at the same time. She didn't care if it was obvious she was staring now. She did it anyway.

'Where did you hear that?'

Emily's voice lowered to a wicked murmur. 'Hattie says she saw them talking at the end of break, by the girls' toilets.'

'And he's asking her out?'

'Apparently. Poor Charlotte. Then again, I can think of someone else who'll be just as *devastated*.'

Viola's sharp kick to the back of Emily's chair pulled Gwenhwyfar out of the trance she'd fallen into. She refused to make eye contact with the girls in front, even though they both glared at her. 'What?' Emily hissed.

'Sorry.' Viola pulled a fake smile onto her lips. 'My foot slipped.'

Disgruntled, the two turned back to bend their heads together.

'Just ignore them,' Viola whispered.

Gwenhwyfar couldn't. Morgan had vanished from the cafeteria towards the end of break, and had been absent during lunch too. The whispering resumed, but she tuned out to the particulars. Morgan liked Arthur, she knew she did. What if Arthur liked Morgan too?

'Gwen?' Class work halted, and all eyes turned to the front. The deputy head stood waiting with his hands clasped behind his back. Miss Barnes looked at her sternly. 'Mr Hall here requests that you accompany him to the principal's office.'

A susurrus of speculation followed her words.

'Now?'

'Yes please. Take your belongings with you.'

Gwenhwyfar packed her bag, picked up her blazer and

bundled everything under one arm. 'I'll see you tomorrow,' she said to Viola, as she self-consciously edged towards the door. The sniggering started before Gwenhwyfar was led out of the room. She heard Viola kick Emily's chair again. '*Ouch*!' the first of the Furies screeched.

She was in trouble; she knew it. As Mr Hall escorted her through the corridors she picked through everything she might have done wrong. Was it the money she had taken from her father? Or the nasty comments she'd made when friends with Emily? It didn't take long for a more frightening prospect to prise its way into her mind: perhaps what Charlotte said had spread, and she was about to be blamed for what had happened on Friday.

Mr Hall ushered her into a polished, large office. Immediately Gwenhwyfar felt claustrophobic. Waiting for them both was Dr Ravioli.

'Miss Taliesin, I presume?' He offered a welcoming smile, but it was stiff and cold. 'I've met your parents, but I don't think we've spoken. That will have to change. I generally feel it's best to hold a meeting with new students to see how they're getting along. Sit down, won't you?'

She took her place in the chair indicated. On the wall behind Dr Ravioli's desk was a framed New National poster. The crimson flag, circling the un-lidded eyeball inset with a black triangle and crimson iris, watched her intently; the circles of which not only representing the all-seeing nature of the party, but the unity of all.

'Have I done something wrong?' she asked. Mr Hall stood at the closed door behind her, blocking any chance of escape.

'Why don't you tell me?'

She contemplated her options. 'I can't think of anything.'

'No—?'

'Should I be able to?'

Ravioli straightened his name plaque carefully. 'I've received a tip-off from another student. A very serious accusation has been made. I've summoned you here because I would like to ask you some questions.'

'Who? What accusation?'

'I understand that you attended a private party on Friday night, hosted by one of our students?'

Reluctantly, Gwenhwyfar nodded.

'I just wanted to clarify one or two things with you. Firstly, were there any illegal substances at this party?'

She shook her head instinctively. 'No.'

'No? No solution, no beer? No narcotics?'

'Not that I know of.' Gwenhwyfar shrugged. 'I suppose people could have brought stuff along themselves, if they wanted. I didn't see any. It wasn't supplied or anything.'

'I see.' He made a note about something. Gwenhwyfar craned her neck to try and see what, but he moved the paper away. 'Secondly, my source tells me that you were attacked by one of our students on Friday night. Is this true?'

Her heart thumped. Suddenly she was stuck, and the reality of Hector's unwelcome advances rose in her stomach like hot bile. She looked away.

'Well? Were you?' He folded his front over his desk.

'Define attacked,' she responded icily.

'Did one of our students assault you?'

Crossing her arms and legs Gwenhwyfar glared fixedly at the

carpet, and nodded.

'It would be helpful, Miss Taliesin, if you could tell me what happened.'

'Someone forced a kiss on me,' she said, hating the triviality of the words. She drew a breath. 'Then he... he pinned me down.'

'Did he sexually assault you?'

She couldn't speak.

'Did he rape you, Miss Taliesin?'

'No.'

'Did he intend to?'

'I... I don't know.' She fidgeted in the small chair. Dr Ravioli scribbled something else down.

'Could you tell me what you were wearing on the night of the assault?'

'Does it matter?' The principal gazed at her mutely. 'Jeans,' she relented, 'and a strappy top.' She felt sick.

'And your attacker's name?'

'Hector.'

'Hector who?'

'I don't know what his surname is. He's friends with Tom Hareton.'

Dr Ravioli clenched his jaw into a hard square. 'I see. Is there any possibility that you may have encouraged Hector to believe that you wanted to be intimate with him?'

'No,' she spat.

'Don't lie, Miss Taliesin. This is a boy's life we're talking about.'

'I didn't do anything.' Gwenhwyfar shifted uneasily, and looked to Mr Hall, static by the door. 'Does he need to be here for this?'

He didn't even answer. Gwenhwyfar felt hot tears slide down her cheeks. The principal went on.

'Now tell me. I've heard that others were involved in this *incident*. Is this correct?'

'Yes.' She recited the full names of all three Furies. Dr Ravioli added yet another note to his investigation.

'Did Miss Rose, Miss Mulberry and Miss Stone tell Hector to kiss you?'

'I don't know.'

'Did Mr Humphreys know what was going on when he found you?'

'I don't want to talk about it! I... *no*, he didn't know.'

'I was wondering, Miss Taliesin, why you haven't reported this to the police. The school hasn't been notified of any investigations.'

Gwenhwyfar wiped her cheeks with the back of her sleeve. 'I... I didn't know if I should. I didn't think it was worth it.'

He looked down to his notes. 'Tell me. What happened after Hector "pinned you down"?'

'Someone hit him on the head and pulled him off.'

'Who?'

She glanced to the New National poster looming behind him. 'I don't know their name. I can't remember.'

'You are aware that Hector had to go to casualty?'

She nodded. Dr Ravioli beckoned Mr Hall, who hurried to his side. Quiet words were exchanged and then his cold eyes settled upon her.

'I think it's best to inform you that I will be talking to all parties involved. Rose, Stone, Mulberry. Hector Browne, as well. I took the liberty of informing your parents.'

'You called my *parents*?' she repeated, appalled. 'Don't you think I should've had the chance to tell them?'

'You've had all weekend to tell them, Miss Taliesin. You do understand that if you pursue this, it will be your word against Hector's. If I discover that either you or my source has been lying, then your punishment will be severe. Understood?'

She nodded, utterly dismantled.

'That will be all.'

Numbly, Gwenhwyfar rose to her feet. She was escorted out of the office and then shut out in the corridor, where she stood for a while, alone. She didn't want to go back to class, but her Geography lesson was far from over. It was easy to decide to leave early. After a long, meandering walk she arrived at home. As she passed the threshold another wave of tears gripped her. She couldn't stop them.

'Gwen?' Eve rushed to her. Llew followed, too old and stiff to make it first. 'Are you all right? What's wrong? I had a call from the principal. Is what he said true?'

She couldn't go through it again. Dropping her bag on the floor she ran past mother and dog and catapulted herself up the stairs.

'Gwen!' Eve shouted, hurrying after her. 'Gwenhwyfar!'

She slammed herself into her bedroom and vaulted onto the bed. She wished she'd never come to England. For the first time since moving she cried in earnest; cried for home, her friends and for her old school. She cried for her old life, and for Dillon, her horse. She sobbed away the day's events and then, heaving, she wept for Arthur.

Merlin

Garan paced back and forth, wearing down the plush living room carpet. His hand swept across his thinning hair. Eve stood to one side, arms crossed.

'This is ridiculous!' he barked. Gwenhwyfar cringed again, crunched up on the sofa, wrapped in her bathrobe with her wet hair hanging in cords. 'So that's why you wanted to come home early on Friday night? Because you were part of some practical joke?'

Llew was by the armchair, watching the scene with brown, anxious eyes. He gave a quiet whine. Eve perched on the sofa arm. 'Shouting about it isn't helping anyone, Garan. Don't you think she's been through enough as it is?'

'I should have never let you go to that party! You're only fifteen, for God's sake, and look what happened!' Gwenhwyfar opened her mouth to speak, but was immediately cut off. 'Were you drunk? And don't lie to me, Gwenhwyfar, because I could smell the solution on you when you got into the car.'

'I wasn't drunk,' she insisted. 'I tried a little solution, but only a tiny bit. I couldn't drink it! It made me feel sick. Hector was drunk, but I definitely *wasn't*.'

'Do you know what sort of trouble you could get into if the police find out you were at a party with solution?'

'I didn't *know* there'd be solution,' Gwenhwyfar countered.

'Yet you still drank it!'

'As if you've never done the same! You and Mam have had wine before.'

'That's different, Gwen,' he scolded. 'You're way below the legal age limit. The laws are getting stricter. How are we going to notify the police if illegal substances were involved?'

'I don't *want* to tell the police,' she maintained, 'it'll just be my word against Hector's. If the principal doesn't take me seriously, then why would they?'

'We'll be talking to him about that, Gwen, don't you worry,' her mother assured her. 'It's appalling how he handled it. I've called the school and we have a meeting scheduled. They will have questioned the other students by then. He should be more on side.'

'It's disgraceful,' her father growled. 'Who does he think he is? Interrogating you like that… and without parental supervision! I don't care what he says—you're still a child. We should have been with you. He made *no* indication that he'd pull you out of class like that when he called your mother.'

Llew barked nervously. Garan snarled at him. 'Will someone please shut him up?'

'Llew! Be quiet!' Gwenhwyfar tried, as the sheepdog continued to yip. Another aggravated whine and he silenced himself, grumbling to the floor.

Garan finally stopped pacing. 'What did you say those girls' names were? Emily, Hattie and who?'

'Emily, Hattie and Charlotte,' Gwenhwyfar repeated. 'The ones I thought were my friends.'

In the silence that followed, Garan seemed to calm down. Sighing, he looked to Eve. She returned his gaze questioningly. 'I just wish... I just wish that we didn't have to hear this from your principal. When were you going to tell us?'

'Soon!' she insisted. 'I just—didn't know how to bring it up. I was going to mention it to you at some point.'

'Some point.' He strode the room again, and his anger returned. 'This *Hector* character... I'd like to break his neck, that's for sure.'

Eve nodded. 'I'd rather he was castrated, myself.'

'We could always set Llew on him,' Gwenhwyfar suggested. Upon hearing his name Llew lifted his head, gazing at Gwenhwyfar expectantly.

'I think he wants his supper,' Garan remarked.

'He can have Hector for supper,' Gwenhwyfar added, cheering up a little. She smiled and turned to her beloved old dog, who slowly began to wag his tail. 'Would you like that Llew? Hector for supper?'

Encouraged, Llew hauled himself off the floor and padded over to poke at Gwenhwyfar's crossed arms. He dislodged them both, and was rewarded for his efforts with a scratch behind the ears.

'I think we could all do with something to eat,' Eve concluded. 'It is late. How about we get a takeaway? Will Chinese do?'

'Sounds fine with me,' Garan approved, deciding enough was enough for one evening. 'Gwen?'

Gwenhwyfar nodded eagerly. 'Yes please. I'm starving.'

'Right. I'll see what they have,' Eve said, pleased to be doing something. 'I picked up a menu in town today. They've just opened. They come highly recommended.'

Garan moved into the kitchen and Llew followed him, also in search of food. Idly Gwenhwyfar spent a few moments in reflection before succumbing to the lure of the remote. Switching the media station on, she gazed at the images that flashed before her, mindlessly absorbing the day's news.

'I've been thinking.'

Arthur's attention returned to Marvin. The older man was standing behind him and to his left, observing the windows, hoping to discover what it was that Arthur found to be so captivating.

'About what you mentioned yesterday; about not being able to learn certain truths. Well, what if there was an after-school club? Where such alternative views—be they truths, or not—were taught?'

Arthur's interest was sparked. 'Would that be possible?'

'Perhaps.' Marvin walked across to his desk, and sat down. 'Obviously it would be secret, and we'd have to be careful about who attended, but it could work. It might be dangerous job-wise to have it off school property, but then again, it might be safer. I'd have to think of a cover story, otherwise.' Marvin fell silent for a few moments, and sucked his teeth. 'There's a lot of hoops to jump through to get an after-school club here. It has to be fully approved by several people, and the principal likes to have staff drop in on them from time to time.'

'Couldn't we just meet somewhere neutral? In a library,

perhaps?'

'No, not a library, libraries are much too quiet. Everyone would hear what we were discussing. It can't be in public. I could host it at my house, if people were careful. If I get any grief for it I could claim I'm offering extra hours' tutoring.'

'Wouldn't you get into trouble for that?'

'Less trouble than I'd get into for teaching you all "radical" ideas,' Marvin chuckled. 'But remember, no chatting about this to just anyone. If we're doing this, we must be discreet.'

'We will be,' Arthur assured. He was burning to learn more, know more. 'So does that mean that I'm the first member?'

'Of course!' Marvin grinned. 'I was thinking of asking Bedivere too. An hour a week should be enough. I know that might be difficult for you, but if we work around your shifts I'm sure we can agree to some sort of schedule.' Arthur didn't really feel like sharing the experience with Bedivere, but kept quiet. 'How about we invite Morgan? I've been keeping an eye on her, and she's smart. She'd do well with something like this. What do you think?'

'About Morgan?'

Marvin nodded. 'Is she trustworthy?'

He thought for a moment. 'I think so.'

'Good. Morgan, then.' Glancing to the clock, Marvin lifted his bag onto his desk and unzipped it quickly. 'Before I forget: I found this when I was clearing out my attic. I thought you might like it.' He pulled out a small, thin book with a tattered and broken spine. 'It was banned quite some time ago. Worth reading if you're interested in current affairs. It's surprising how the author manages to highlight issues so potent today in a time when such changes had only just begun.'

Arthur carefully removed the book from Marvin's hands. It read: *The Human Condition*, by Marcel E. Whittler. The cover was simple, a black and grey divide merging into the illusion of a human eye. Beyond the front cover, scrawled in messy ink, was Marvin's full name, Marvin Ambrosius Caledonensis. 'Ambrosius?' Arthur questioned, a smile playing his lips.

'I know. You would have thought Marvin was a bad enough name to give a child.'

Arthur grinned, and reread the signature. It was in pen, and difficult to read, but his grandmother had schooled him well in the art of deciphering old handwriting. He frowned, thinking he'd mistaken a few letters. No, he was sure.

'Marvin? Why does this say *Merlin*?'

Marvin peered at the open, browning book. 'Oh! I'd almost forgotten.' He slipped his bag under his desk. 'It was a nickname I had in school. I already had a ridiculous name, but for some reason "Merlin" just sounded cooler.'

'Merlin…' Arthur mused. He grinned. 'Can I call you Merlin?'

Marvin expelled a loud laugh. 'If you like. Not in front of the other students, though.' The bell went. 'Ah, time for registration! Go on, sit.' Arthur returned to his desk, *The Human Condition* clutched tightly in his hand. 'The book!' Marvin hissed. 'Put it somewhere safe. Don't let anyone find it!'

'Sorry, Merlin.' Resisting the urge to start reading, Arthur stowed it away in his rucksack. The classroom began to fill.

Gwenhwyfar was eager for the day to end. The milder weather allowed for lunchtime to be spent in the cold sun, so she and Viola claimed an old picnic bench nestled between Badbury and Wormelow. After talking extensively about her upcoming test shoot that weekend, Viola broached the topic weighing heaviest on Gwenhwyfar's mind.

'So what did the principal want yesterday?'

Reluctant to linger on the details, Gwenhwyfar skirted over the experience and focused instead on the principal's behaviour, exaggerating how he had looked her up and down when he'd asked how she had managed to get away. 'It was gross, really,' she remarked. 'It's almost like he was just looking for an excuse to check me out.'

'Well, he does hang around the girls' changing rooms a lot,' Viola said, a half-eaten apple suspended in her hand.

'But seriously,' Gwenhwyfar prompted, 'I didn't mention you or anything. I didn't want to get you into trouble.'

'Thanks.' Viola smiled. 'I don't really feel like a trip to the Nutcracker's office. Though I'm sure my name will come up at some point, even if it's just mentioned by a vengeful Emily.'

They laughed again.

'They'll get bored with you eventually, you know,' Viola told her. 'Then they'll move on to their next target.'

'Poor soul.' Gwenhwyfar twisted in her seat as Viola's gaze slipped up the hill. She frowned. 'Is that *Gavin*?'

He could move fast, for someone so tall. As he cantered past students leapt aside as if run at with an out-of-control car. Soon he was towering above them.

Viola swallowed. 'What on earth's the matter?'

'You'll never guess what I just saw,' their messenger panted. 'All three Furies coming out of the principal's office.' He climbed over the bench and sat next to Gwenhwyfar. 'They were absolutely ashen, all of them. I overheard a member of staff saying they'd be called back in with parents for a severe talking to.

Didn't you say Gwen was called in during Geography yesterday?'

'That's right,' Viola admitted. 'It turns out Ravioli wanted to question her about what happened on Friday.'

'I just didn't realise it would be so soon,' Gwenhwyfar fretted.

'It means that they'll be punished, at least.'

'If my word is better than theirs.'

'Well, we have witnesses,' Gavin reminded her. 'Tom and I both heard Charlotte tell Hector you wanted to meet him. Bedivere was a part of it too, not to mention Arthur and Vi. We outnumber them.'

'I don't think we can count on Arthur's support.' Viola threw her apple towards the nearest bin. It went in with a clang. 'I tried to speak to him about it before Maths, but he wouldn't listen. He thinks Gwen and Bedivere helped mastermind it.'

'Ridiculous,' Gavin muttered.

'I know.'

'I still don't get how Ravioli found out,' he added. 'I mean, did you tell him?'

Gwenhwyfar shook her head. 'No. Did you say anything?'

'Not a word.' Gavin shot his gaze to Viola.

'I haven't either,' she said. 'What about Arthur?'

'Definitely not. He hasn't a clue,' Gwenhwyfar insisted.

'He might have told on you, if he thinks you set him up,' Gavin pointed out.

'But he doesn't know about Hector,' Gwenhwyfar reminded him. 'That's what Ravioli was asking me about.'

'Have you told anyone else?' Viola asked.

'Bedivere knows, but I don't think he's the sort to go and do something like that.'

The three shared a moment of silence.

'I've got another meeting with him tonight.' Gwenhwyfar confessed. 'My dad's not pleased with the way Rav handled things.'

'Do you think he'll involve the police?' Viola asked, suddenly anxious.

'I think it's up to Gwen if the police are involved or not,' Gavin observed.

'I don't want to make a big deal out of this. I just don't want to talk to Hector, Emily, Charlotte or Hattie ever again.'

Viola shrugged. 'I know. But if they get expelled, you won't have to.'

When Gwenhwyfar met her parents in the foyer after school, the principal was running late with a prior engagement. They were forced to wait outside his office on low, uncomfortable chairs as the building emptied, leaving only a few teachers to wander the halls. Mr Caledonensis offered Gwenhwyfar a smile as he passed them in the corridor, carrying an empty, tea-stained mug. No sooner than she had smiled back he was gone, his footsteps echoing around the corner. Abruptly the door opened.

'Good afternoon, Mr and Mrs Taliesin. Miss Taliesin. Please, come in.'

Her mother went in first. Last in, Garan shut the door behind them.

'Take a seat, won't you? I apologise for the delay. I was stuck in a call.' He smiled at them as he positioned himself at his polished desk, but it was the same cold smile as before. Garan pulled out two chairs from the side of the room and sat down with Eve, the angles of his blue suit crinkling.

'How can I help you?'

'We were wondering what the developments are on the

situation involving our daughter,' Garan started, his legs too long for the plastic chair. 'Yesterday on the phone you mentioned meetings with the other pupils involved.'

'So I did.' Dr Ravioli propped his elbows on his desk. 'I can assure you that progress has been made. I have spoken to all three girls involved in the incident.'

'And?'

'And their accounts were somewhat different from your daughter's, Mr Taliesin.'

'Are you calling my daughter a liar?' Eve snapped. Her hair was scraped back into a formidable bun that pulled her cheeks taught.

'No, Mrs Taliesin, of course not. I am merely saying that there is more than one version to compare. I am afraid that it is rather a case of four against one.'

'If it's numbers you're worried about, there are others who can vouch for me,' Gwenhwyfar interjected. 'Like who heard Charlotte get Hector involved, or the person who pulled him off.'

'I thought you couldn't remember who that was, Miss Taliesin?'

Her father was losing patience. 'Could you tell us how the versions differ, at least?'

For a moment the principal looked uncomfortable. 'According to the girls, Gwen asked to meet Mr Browne *and* Mr Humphreys upstairs. They say that they had no idea what Gwen's intentions were.'

'That's not true!' she burst out.

'That has to be made up,' Garan argued, astounded.

'Hector's version is consistent,' Dr Ravioli added. 'He claims that Gwen was consenting until someone hit him on the back of the head. Whoever that was, by the way, will be in serious trouble when we find them. Mr Browne had to go to casualty.'

'Despite any uncertainties you may have regarding the incident, what is it you propose to do next?' Garan demanded, his face set like stone.

'I intend to investigate further. Despite these inconsistencies, rest assured, I will get to the truth. Once I have established who is responsible and understand what took place, I will deal out swift and harsh punishment.'

'Be that as it may, I find the way you've handled this situation to be absolutely appalling,' Garan snapped. 'Gwenhwyfar was devastated when she came home on Monday. Your insensitive questions were intrusive and unnecessary, and she tells me there was even another teacher present. Who was this?'

'Mr Hall,' Ravioli responded calmly. 'He's the deputy head. He escorted Gwen from her lesson.'

'Escorted? What is she, a criminal? Or was she being escorted to ensure that Hector didn't attack her again?'

'Gwenhwyfar tells me this *Hector* has a history of harassing girls at this school,' Eve interrupted. 'Is this true?'

Dr Ravioli shifted. 'There have been a few incidents, yes.'

'Then why on earth hasn't he been dealt with before? All of this might have been avoided!' Garan exploded.

The principal didn't seem to have an answer.

'I should string you up,' he growled. 'You knew he was a risk, and did nothing! If anything, this is *your* fault. Why don't I go and find the parents of the other girls who have had a run-in with this boy? We could have you done for negligence.'

'Are you threatening me?' Ravioli asked, his voice steady.

'No,' Garan growled, 'I'm merely stating the facts.'

'Facts aside, I need to be sure I have all the information to avoid making any rash decisions,' he insisted.

'You have all the information,' Garan disputed.

'And I will use it, Mr Taliesin, I assure you.'

Eve gave a stiff smile. 'Well then, I am sure that your knowledge of Hector's record will play in Gwen's favour. I think for now, however, we can ask for a little more sensitivity. Gwen is the victim here.'

'Exactly,' Garan added. 'We've already had to make one formal complaint. If we feel that this isn't being dealt with in the appropriate manner, we will be going straight to the governors.'

Garan and Eve rose to their feet. Gwenhwyfar and Dr Ravioli did the same.

'Of course, my only concern is that the matter is dealt with thoroughly.' The principal stiffly extended his hand, and reluctantly, Garan shook it.

'It's probably best to inform you that we're also considering going to the police,' he said, his shoulders rigid.

'I understand completely. Assault is assault, regardless of school procedures. Logres is always invested in what is best for our students.'

'Good. We look forward to hearing from you.'

Ravioli grimaced and remained standing as they exited his office and slipped into the corridor.

'New National nut,' Garan muttered, as they clustered into their family unit on their way out. 'Did you see that poster? That's hardly appropriate. He's headmaster, for God's sake.'

'It's just a poster, Garan,' Eve huffed as they came out into the cold. 'It's normal. I'll bet all schools have them.'

'Maybe so, but what do you think every child sees when

they're in there? That poster, that's what. It's not right.'

'*Garan*,' hissed Eve. 'Can you not, just this once? It's not helping.'

They bundled into the car. Gwenhwyfar slammed her door.

'And you're all right with that, are you? Our daughter's new school churning out New National cant?'

'I don't know why you're so worked up. It was there last time.'

Garan started the engine. 'Not as I remember.'

'Well, you remember wrong.'

'Stop it, will you?' Gwenhwyfar snapped, leaning forward to remind them both that she was still there. 'The last thing I need is you two bickering. Who cares about a sodding poster?'

'Gwenhwyfar!'

She sat back with a huff. 'I don't even *want* to go to the police. I thought we were going to let the school deal with it?'

'We are.' Garan turned the car out of the car park, and rejoined the traffic to the main road. 'But it doesn't hurt to consider it. The principal needs to know what we're thinking. That way he knows we're serious.'

Eve gazed out of the passenger window. 'You're not going to make a fuss about this, are you?'

Garan looked to Eve. 'What do you mean?'

'The poster. If we go to the governors, it should be about Gwen, not about what you find ethical or not.'

'I won't mention anything!' Garan exclaimed, defensively. 'Now who's going on about it?'

Eve muttered something that Gwenhwyfar couldn't hear, and then they all descended into a thick, unhappy silence.

Morgan Faye

Gwenhwyfar stuffed her hands further into the gloves lining her pockets. Her cold lips blew into the folds of her knitted scarf, puffing out a cloud of moisture that plumed in the frigid air. Ahead of her Llew padded slowly, while her father kept an eye on the dog's dangling lead.

It was just the three of them. Gwenhwyfar's mother didn't really do walking, least of all walking with the dog. With hardly any sleep, Gwenhwyfar had risen reluctantly on Thursday, wishing once again that it were the weekend. She huddled further into her coat. Garan coughed.

'Dad?'

'Yes?'

Gwenhwyfar thought for a moment. She watched the leaf-scattered path pass beneath her feet. 'This thing with Ravioli… do you think it'll be all right?'

'I don't see why not. I think the meeting with him went relatively well, don't you?'

Unsure, she nodded.

'And your mother really had him with that point about Hector's previous record. The principal can't side with him now that he's aware we know about that.'

'True…'

'It'll be fine, trust me.' He tucked her into his side, and they linked arms. Gwenhwyfar looked up. Llew had plodded ahead and was sniffing at a tree, his lead tangling in the dead leaves. Her father was right; this was a nice park. It seemed to be a favourite spot for early morning dog walkers. There was one at the top of the hill.

'I'm sorry.'

'Sorry for what?' he asked, a frown present in his voice.

'For not telling you about what happened. I was going to, I just… didn't know how.'

Garan looked ahead. 'You should always tell us if something like that happens, Gwen,' he urged. 'No matter how silly it may seem to you, or how embarrassed you are. If you tell us, we can do something about it. Even if we only help prevent it from happening to someone else.'

'I know.'

'What upsets me most is that you felt you couldn't talk to us. We're your parents.'

'I know, and I'm sorry, but—'

'I want you to promise me that you won't hide things from us from now on. Doesn't matter what it is, I want you to know that your mam and I are always there for you. If anything is worrying you, or if anything like this happens again… I want you to tell us. Can you promise me that?'

She gazed at him for a moment, but then diverted her eyes to the path. 'I promise,' she murmured, and her words caused him to impress a squeeze upon her arm.

'Good.'

'Do you think I should have told the police?' Llew scouted up ahead, tackling the steady hill at a stiff pace.

'You weren't worried about getting those girls into trouble, were you? Just because there was alcohol at that party?'

'No. I couldn't care less if they got into trouble. It was my new friends that I was worried about... it was their party.' He looked at her. 'It wasn't their solution, though,' she added quickly. 'I actually think Hector supplied that.'

'Why doesn't that surprise me?' Garan muttered. 'We still have time to go to the police, Gwen. If you decide it's best.'

'Do you think I should?'

'It depends. I can't see them making too much of a fuss about the alcohol, if it was out of your control.' There was a moment's silence. 'Perhaps we should see what the principal comes up with? You may feel it's adequate.' A tan dog, thickly built with a distinctive stripe down its spine shot into view and halted by Llew. Alarmed, Llew cowered but then some civil sniffing ensued. Garan frowned. 'Is that a Rhodesian Ridgeback? You don't see many of those, these days.'

The handsome dog shot off again.

'I'm glad you've found some new friends,' he added. 'I was a bit concerned that you might not have anyone to talk to.'

'No, I have friends,' she assured him. 'They're actually really nice. Nicer than those girls, at least.' Suddenly Gwenhwyfar recognised the lone dog walker. The Ridgeback had returned to him, and he clipped it back onto the lead. It was Gavin.

They met as they crossed on the path.

'Gwen!' he exclaimed, his face lighting up with surprise. 'I didn't know you had a dog. Is he yours?' He gestured to Llew who looked back with concern.

'Yes, that's Llew.' Beaming, she looked down to the handsome animal at his side.

'This is Cass. Family dog, but of course I'm the one who ends up walking her.'

'Sounds familiar,' Garan remarked. Gwenhwyfar noticed that Gavin stood a few inches taller than her father.

'Sorry. This is Gavin. Gavin, this is my dad.'

'I think we've met, actually,' Garan recalled, shaking his hand. 'When I picked Gwen up after that party.'

'That's right,' Gavin nodded politely.

'You walked her home. Thank you.' Their hands separated. Gwenhwyfar watched the transaction with interest. 'So what do you do, Gavin? Do you play any sports?'

'Rugby mostly,' he said, relaxing. 'I'm on the school team. Do you play?'

'No, the extent of my involvement is shouting from the sidelines,' Garan admitted. Gwenhwyfar's eyes wandered. 'So Gavin, do you work?'

'Dad!' she interjected, feeling the interrogation was wholly unfair.

'Gavin doesn't mind; do you, Gavin? I'm just getting to know my daughter's friends.' He paused. 'You can hardly blame me, after what the last lot did to her.'

'Yes, but you don't need to worry about Gavin,' she stressed, deeply embarrassed. 'He walked me home, remember?'

'No, it's fine, really,' Gavin assured, offering a toothy smile. 'I do work. Only part-time though, two nights a week. At Bellini's, the Italian in town. Do you know it?'

'I do actually,' Garan said brightly. 'What do you do there?'

'I just wait tables, but you know, it keeps me in pocket.'

A phone rang. Garan jumped and immediately fished it out of his coat. 'Sorry,' he excused, 'I've got to take this. See you again, Gavin.'

He sidestepped away from the path. Gwenhwyfar bit her lip as he hunched under a tree and proceeded to mutter into the receiver. She looked up to Gavin with rosy cheeks.

'Sorry about that.'

'Don't worry about it,' Gavin said, his voice deep and warm. 'Actually, I'm surprised I didn't get any of that when he picked you up on Friday. So how are you?'

'I'm good. Still recovering from Rav's grilling session.'

'Of course, that was yesterday, wasn't it? How did it go?'

'I'm not sure. My dad thinks it went all right, but it was pretty horrible. He practically called me a liar.'

'What a knob.'

'I know, right?'

Gavin looked down to Cass, who considered her surroundings with a curious sniff. Gwenhwyfar hunted for Llew. She couldn't see him.

'Listen, I'd better go, yeah? Got to get this one back to the house and get ready for school. But I'll see you at break?'

'Yeah, see you at break,' she repeated, still smiling. Awkwardly Gavin wandered off, his tall frame towering over the attentive Cass. Gwenhwyfar watched him amble down the hill.

'Sorry, cariad,' her father said as he rejoined her. 'Apparently we have another client to worry about. We should probably get back home. I've got a few things to sort out before work.' He turned on the spot. 'Llew!'

'Llew!' Gwenhwyfar called. The old sheepdog's head popped out from behind a tree. She called him again and he began a slow, reluctant plod back to the path. They turned to leave.

'Who's the new client?' Gwenhwyfar asked, her breath clouding.

'No one important,' her father dismissed. 'Just another cog in the corporate machine.'

'Everything's all right, isn't it?'

'Of course it is,' he exclaimed, a little too brightly. 'Why do you ask?'

Gwenhwyfar turned her eyes to the gate far off at the other end of the park. The cold morning sun peered over the buildings in the east. 'No reason.'

Gwenhwyfar was finding it hard to concentrate. All three Furies had been absent during registration that morning, probably summoned to Dr Ravioli's office so that he could trawl over more particulars. Huffing, she flicked through her textbook in an effort to find two compatible poems. Bedivere sat next to her in silence, hunting through his own copy of *Poetry: Level Four*. Keeping a sharp watch over the class, Ms Appelbauer marked essays at her desk. Bedivere shifted next Gwenhwyfar, bored. As he stretched his bones gave off a loud crack.

'I've never really been one for poetry,' he admitted, removing his glasses to rub his eyes. 'I don't quite get it.'

'I don't think you have to get it,' mused Gwenhwyfar. 'You just read.'

'Unfortunately, *just reading* isn't enough for exams. It's not long until our mock Level Fours, you know. I'm dreading the English Language paper. I hear it's a killer.'

'I'll worry about that one after Christmas,' Gwenhwyfar whispered. Ms Appelbauer looked up, prompting them to a short silence. The moment her eyes returned to her marking, Bedivere abandoned his pen and leant back into his red plastic chair.

'So how are those meetings with Ravioli going?'

'Horrible. He's convinced that I'm making it all up.' With her chosen verse neatly copied, she flicked back through her textbook.

'Really?' Bedivere propped his chin in his palm. 'When I spoke to him he seemed to take it all very seriously.'

Gwenhwyfar stopped reading. 'When did you speak to him?'

'The other day, when he called me in for a meeting.'

'You never said.' Ravioli hadn't, either.

'It wasn't a long one or anything. He just wanted to know my involvement.'

'But he hasn't even bothered to question Arthur yet,' she pointed out. 'So why would he need to question you?'

There was a silence. Bedivere seemed to consider his options, but Gwenhwyfar's darkening expression soon forced him to panic. Both expelled a huge sigh as suddenly, Bedivere confessed.

'I'm sorry Gwen, I didn't mean to, really I didn't. I just thought it would be best to tell someone!'

'Don't you think I would have told someone if I had wanted to?' she snapped, turning her head to the front. 'You have no idea how horrible all of this has been! I meant it when I said he doesn't believe me; he really doesn't.'

'Gwen, I'm sorry—!' he whispered, eyes pleading.

'Why even tell Ravioli in the first place? You know what he's like—you've been going here for nearly three years!' Ms Appelbauer glanced up, searching for the disturbance. Gwenhwyfar lowered her voice. 'I can't believe you'd betray me like this, Bed.'

'I only wanted to help, I swear. I thought if something was done about it, Arthur might realise what really happened.'

'Haven't you heard? Arthur doesn't care,' Gwenhwyfar replied bitterly. 'He still thinks we were in on it. I mean, how could he *actually* believe that?' She returned to her work and angrily flapped through several more pages. It took her a while to calm down.

'Gwen?'

She was silent for as long as she could manage. 'What?'

'I'll make it up to you. I'll talk to Ravioli. I'll even try to explain things to Arthur again, if you want.'

She contemplated his offer, then sighed, her frustration dissolving. Hector had taken enough from her already. 'No, it's fine. Well, it's not *fine*, but I suppose you were only trying to help. Just ask in future, please?'

Bedivere nodded extensively. 'I will,' he promised.

'Bedivere?'

Ms Appelbauer was sitting straight, with her marking pen pointed towards him. Bedivere looked up.

'The others are managing to keep things to an acceptable level. Would it trouble you to do the same? You too, Gwen.'

'No, miss.' Bedivere donned his glasses and resumed his work.

'Sorry, miss,' Gwenhwyfar added, wondering how much had been heard. Embarrassed, she returned to her search, flicking through Tennyson, Thomas, and then halting on Auden, trying to make an interesting choice that wouldn't prove too hard to examine.

It had to be bad luck that Science was the most frequent lesson in Arthur's timetable. There was a moment of panic when their teacher split them into pairs, but thankfully Gwenhwyfar was allocated to work with someone else instead. Deciding to spend his break time alone in the library, Arthur found a corner that wasn't too visible to the main desk and pulled out Marvin's book. Now gloved in a different book jacket, *The Human Condition* was disguised as *An Unfortunate Encounter with Alfred*: an easy and vaguely intellectual crime-thriller. He flicked through the thin leaves, halted by a chapter entitled: 'The Rise of CCTV.' Cautiously, Arthur observed his surroundings. The librarian at the main desk was busy. He returned to the book. It read,

> *It is a little known fact that closed circuit television was first developed by the Nazis during World War II. Mostly used to observe V2 launchings in 1942, it was also utilised in video recording technology, and introduced the idea of surveillance in areas labelled 'unsafe' for humans.*

He skipped down the page, scanning for key words. The clock behind him ticked quietly. A muffled cough sounded at the other end of the room.

> *Widely used, closed circuit television has swiftly become a means of keeping an eye on the masses. Integrated into businesses, coffee shops, public transport and open spaces, it uses the pretext of protecting those on film to gather information and monitor behavioural anomalies. From employee and customer surveillance to crime prevention, closed circuit television has become a controversial addition to daily life, many cameras becoming so discreet that it has become hard to know when one is being watched, by whom, and for what purpose.*

For perhaps the first time in his life, Arthur looked up and observed the small glass sphere nestled in the ceiling. He stared at it, and it stared back. His eyes crept along the premises, and he noticed another, and then a third, all placed in strategic positions. Nervously he shrank into his chair, bringing *The Human Condition* closer to his chest.

> *... with new technologies such as emails, mobile phones and the Internet, it is sobering to explore how this rise of surveillance has developed. It is well known that governments take liberties with the privacy of most Internet users, tapping into email accounts and online correspondence...*

A chorus of pages flapped and wobbled as half a shelf avalanched to the floor. Two aisles down Morgan hurried to tidy up. Arthur jumped to his feet, stuffing *The Human Condition* into his bag. Morgan looked up as he joined her, her eyes wide with surprise. He helped her gather the laminated books off the floor.

'You're not a true library-goer until you've annoyed Mrs Paisley,' he said, glancing to the main desk where the librarian sat scowling, her glasses illuminated by an old-fashioned computer screen. 'Are you all right?'

'I'm fine,' she murmured, lowering her gaze. 'My bag just caught.'

Arthur stood and put the books back into their rightful place. 'Were you looking for something?'

'I've got a study to do for class on the Fauvists. You?'

'I was just reading.'

'Anything good?'

He was tempted to tell her, but the urge quickly faded. 'Not really, just something I picked up from home.'

She bent down and retrieved the last two books. Arthur took one and pushed it back where it belonged.

'Thanks,' she smiled, standing again. 'For the damage control.'

'You're welcome.'

A thought suspended her as she turned to leave. 'Is it true? Bedivere tells me you're not talking to him. He says he's not talking to you, either.'

'He's not.'

She leant against the end of the shelf unit and observed him with concern. 'What happened?'

'It's a long story,' Arthur muttered. 'He can stuff it, as far as I'm concerned. He's been teaming up with Emily.'

'So that's why you haven't been in the canteen all week.'

'I'm spending lunch with Marvin. It's better, really,' he shrugged. 'I can't stand the canteen, anyway. It's too busy.'

'You can always come and sit with me if you like.' He thought she went a little pinker as she spoke, and she soon shrugged to look elsewhere. 'I mean, if Bedivere's not talking to you and Marvin's busy, or something.'

'Thanks.' He wondered how, after all this time, he and Morgan had hardly spoken. 'I can't today though, Marvin's expecting me.'

'That's all right, I'm working in the art rooms anyway.' Morgan stood straight. 'I should probably go and find this book. Want to help me? You know, so I don't destroy half the library.'

He offered her a lop-sided smile. 'I'm sure you'll manage. I've got some reading to catch up on. But I'll see you in History?'

Disappointment shadowed her face, but then the sun came out with a wide smile. 'Sure, I'll see you then.'

She turned and headed for the Fine Art section of the library. Arthur watched her for a moment but then returned to his seat, and opened up *The Human Condition* once again.

He was pleased to find Marvin in his classroom at lunch. He'd found time to read through a little more of his book during English, and as he discovered the chapter covering hierarchies and the monarchy had realised that the author lived in a time before the abolition. Marvin was halfway through eating a sandwich when Arthur joined him. He nodded to him, still chewing.

'And—? How are you finding the book? Interesting?'

'Very.' Sitting, Arthur pulled his lunch out from his rucksack. 'I've just finished the chapter on CCTV. I've been wandering around the school with my eyes open to cameras—I had no idea there were so many of them.'

His teacher nodded to the back of the room. Arthur twisted round and, sure enough, there loomed another tiny black sphere.

'You know they have microphones on them, these days,' Marvin mused. 'The smarter ones have facial recognition, but these models are old. They were designed to pick up key words in suspicious conversations. I mean, what's a suspicious conversation? Who decides?' He took another chunk out of his sandwich, ripping the crust from the bread. 'Oh, don't worry,' he added, swallowing thickly, 'that one's been broken for years. My friend Mr Pick, the technician, overlooks it so long as I read through his children's papers.'

'Is there one in every classroom?' Arthur broke into his lunchbox. Marvin nodded. 'Why?'

'To keep an eye on things, I suppose. Just in case students bring something dangerous into school. I don't see the point of the microphones, though. Maybe that's to keep an eye on the content of our lessons. Speaking of which, have you thought of any names for our afterschool club?'

'Not yet,' Arthur admitted. 'When are we having it?'

'Friday. What time do you finish work?'

'Half five.' He started to eat. 'I'd like to be home for seven, though.'

'How about we do quarter to six to quarter to seven? I would have liked to do an hour and a half, but I think an hour is stretching it enough. It's probably safest if you invite Bedivere and Morgan.' He hesitated. 'Do you think that Gwenhwyfar would be interested in something like this?'

'Probably not.' Arthur shrugged. 'She doesn't seem like the type.'

'No?' Marvin crumpled his sandwich bag in his hands, and then dropped it into the open-mouthed bin next to his desk. 'I thought she might have potential. She seemed like an intelligent girl to me.'

'Maybe we should wait with the name until we're all there,' Arthur suggested, eager to change the subject. 'Then we can vote on the best one.'

'Aha! Spoken like a true democrat. Let me know what Bedivere says. You can ask him in History, no?' Marvin popped open a packet of crisps, and began to crunch. Arthur still didn't know how to tell him that they were no longer friends.

'Good afternoon, class! If we can settle down, that would be good.'

Marvin was peering over the room of noisy students, hands elevated, in an effort to gain their attention. Gradually the pupils began to fill their allocated seats. Arthur did his best to ignore Gwenhwyfar, who sat waiting with her chin propped in her hand. His eyes wandered across the room. Tom was harassing Marvin doggedly.

'Mr Hareton, if you would *please* stop using that mouth of yours for one minute, the rest of the class might get the chance to learn something,' Marvin stressed. He picked up some heavy books and began to do the rounds, dropping one on each desk. 'We'll be looking at military history today!' he exclaimed. 'One between two, please. You won't be needing your textbooks.'

'Why didn't you tell us that last lesson?' complained Tom. 'I've done my back in, carrying that brick around all day.'

'That's what your *lockers* are for, Thomas.' Marvin clapped his hands together twice. 'Come on! Page forty-seven. Chop chop! We don't have all day.' He turned to the board, seemingly deaf to the buzz behind him. Arthur was wondering how to tell Bedivere about the club without him mistaking it for forgiveness.

'Marvin wanted me to speak to you,' he ventured, already on page forty-seven. He examined the old photographs, garish in their colouring. In one picture, servicemen stood before an iron fence twisted by an exploded missile. Other photographs were of long dead politicians, practising gestures of diplomacy. 'He's setting up an after-school club on Fridays, at quarter to six. He wants to know if you want to come.'

'What sort of club?' Bedivere responded, surprised he was no longer being ignored.

'History. We'll be looking at alternate truths, stuff he can't teach us in school. The darker side to England and all that. You interested?'

'I don't know.' Bedivere gazed at Marvin's back as he scraped chalk letters across the dusty board.

Arthur twisted round in his seat. 'Morgan? Marvin's setting up an afterschool club about world affairs,' he murmured. 'You're invited too, if you want to come.' He caught Gwenhwyfar's eye, felt his chest contract, and quickly looked away.

'When is it?'

'Friday, next week at quarter to six,' Arthur said. Bedivere was still listening. 'What do you think? We need to come up with a name for it, so if you have any ideas…'

'I'll let you know,' Morgan smiled, playing with a lock of her hair.

'It's a secret, though. You can't tell a soul.'

'I won't,' Morgan promised, glancing to Gwenhwyfar.

'Can I join?' Gwenhwyfar interrupted.

Arthur shook his head. 'No, sorry.'

She scowled. 'Why not?'

'It's by invitation only. If you want to join, you'll have to ask Marvin.'

'Why can't you ask him?'

'Because you should ask, if you want to join,' Arthur insisted.

'Can't we just ask him now?' Bedivere tried.

'And let the whole class know?'

'Gwen just heard it. I thought it was a secret?' he argued.

'Gwen's not going to tell anyone,' Arthur disputed. 'Are you, Gwen?' She didn't seem to know how to react. 'If she really wants to join she'll have to ask Marvin herself. It's not that hard.'

Obviously hurt, Gwenhwyfar pulled her eyes away and across the room. Arthur looked to Morgan and offered a smile. 'So did you find something on the Fauvists? Without destroying anything, I mean.'

'I managed,' she said, glancing to Gwenhwyfar anxiously.

'I'm sure Mrs Paisley was pleased.' There was an awkward silence. Bedivere gave him a sidelong glance. 'So I was thinking… are you up to anything tomorrow lunchtime?'

She fiddled with her pen. 'I don't think so. Why?'

Arthur shrugged. 'I was just wondering if I could take you up on your offer. That is, if you're not busy.'

'Well, I was going to throw more shelf units on the floor, but I think I could give it a miss.' She offered a quick smile, and lowered her voice to a diplomatic murmur. 'Aren't you doing something with Marvin?'

'Not tomorrow. Besides, he's probably getting sick of me by now.' He glanced to Gwenhwyfar. She seemed to be staring at the other side of the room. 'Shall we meet by the Art block?'

'Sounds fine to me,' Morgan enthused.

Marvin, finally prepared for the lesson, turned to them all with another great clap and began his monologue on the First and Second World Wars.

BUNSEN BURNERS

Viola leant across the basin, eying her hair in the stained mirror. She'd worn it up that morning, but during the walk to school the wind had teased things out of place. Adjusting a few strands, she shouted to Gwenhwyfar. 'So what did Arthur say to her, exactly?'

The toilet flushed, a lock sounded, and Gwenhwyfar joined Viola at the basins. 'He asked her if she wanted to spend lunch together. *Right* in front of me, too. He's going to ask her out, I'm sure of it. You remember what Emily said,' she huffed. 'I thought he didn't even like Morgan? I thought he liked me.'

'He *does* like you, Gwen. Why do you think he's been so upset over this whole Hector thing? It wouldn't have bothered him at all, if he didn't care.'

'*Care*—?' she snorted.

'Oh, you know what I mean. Why do you think he asked Morgan to lunch in History? Because you were there, because he wanted to make you jealous.'

'You think?' Gwenhwyfar went to dry her hands. The dryer

didn't work, so she vanished into one of the cubicles to get some toilet paper instead.

Viola leant against the sink. 'And Emily was obviously making it up. Why would Arthur want to ask Morgan out? It's obvious he likes you. He's just upset about the prank.'

'He didn't even let me explain it to him,' she despaired. They left the bathroom. 'And now he's sniffing around *Morgan*.'

'We don't know that.'

'Well, Morgan likes him. It's obvious. Surely he must know that, at least.'

They came to their classroom. Morgan was sitting in her usual seat, drawing in her sketchbook. As they sat down, Bedivere ambushed them.

'Can I join you?' he asked hopefully. Gwenhwyfar gestured to a chair. He moved it closer. 'Thanks. I just couldn't bear it. Morgan keeps pushing me to talk to Arthur, as if *I'm* the one ignoring him.' He looked over his shoulder, and then turned back to them with a scowl. 'You know, I used to think she was interested in me? But of course not, everyone only ever wants Arthur.'

'I didn't know you liked Morgan,' Gwenhwyfar probed.

'Me neither,' Viola admitted. 'What happened to Emily? Gwen told me that not so long ago you were dazzled by her.'

'Let's just say I'm now aware of her true colours.'

'What, pink?' Viola remarked.

'Besides, I never said I liked Morgan. I just thought she liked me. And I was pretty certain Arthur liked Gwen.'

The lights cut out. There was a wave of excitement. Their tutor, Miss Ray, appeared in the doorway. Carrying her coffee she flicked the light switch on and off, and huffed.

'Settle down!' she demanded, coming into the room and

shutting the door. 'It's just a power cut. Another one,' she added under her breath.

'Does that mean we can go home, miss?' someone called from the back of the class.

'Miss, I think we should leave early,' another girl shouted from her small group of friends.

'Hattie's afraid of the dark, miss,' Charlotte teased, giggling.

'It's light outside,' Miss Ray declared curtly, her honey-dyed hair up in a small bun. She put her mug down and began to search through the papers on her desk. 'Look, you know we have a generator. It'll be on in a few minutes. A bit of natural light never hurt anyone.'

'I'm so sick of this,' Viola complained. 'I swear it's happening more often.'

'It is,' Bedivere murmured. 'The New Nationals aren't making enough to power the country. The rural areas go first, then houses in the slums. Then it's towns and residential neighbourhoods. Hospitals go last.'

'I don't think they've ever had to cut power to a hospital,' Viola observed. 'Not yet.'

'But we have a generator?' Gwenhwyfar asked.

Bedivere nodded. 'Courtesy of all the rich parents.'

'We have blackouts all the time in Wales. You're right about the rural areas.' She sighed. 'How long do they last here?'

'A couple of hours. Longest one I had was four days. I went completely insane. No Internet, no telly, no oven. Nightmare.'

'I hope the power's still on at my house,' she fretted.

'That depends on where you live.'

The lights came back on. There was a murmur of disappointment. Miss Ray looked up with a wave of her arms. 'See? What did I tell you? Two minutes.' She settled in her chair and proceeded to take the register.

'Where were you at break today?'

Marvin watched Arthur expectantly as he came into the room, shutting the door behind him.

'Outside. I bumped into a friend,' he said, sitting on one of the tables.

'Oh?' Marvin sounded pleasantly surprised. 'Someone I know?'

'Just Morgan.' He unzipped his bag and rummaged inside for his lunchbox. 'She's actually really nice. We're spending lunch together. I hope you don't mind.'

'Of course not.' Marvin hooked both hands behind his head, and stretched back into his chair. 'How did she take to our offer? About joining the club?'

'She's in. She came up with loads of suggestions for names.'

'And Bedivere?'

Arthur frowned. He'd never really confirmed either way. 'He didn't say.'

Marvin sighed. 'I know you two have had a bit of a falling out. It's hard not to notice, with the way you've been behaving.'

Arthur turned his gaze out of the window. 'We're not friends anymore.'

'Why ever not?'

'It's complicated.'

'I see.' Marvin rested his chin on the bridge of his hands. 'This wouldn't have anything to do with that party on Friday night, would it?'

'How do you know about that?'

'I overheard Mr Hall talking to Agnes Brolstone in the corridor this morning. Apparently Gwen was involved in some sort of incident.'

'You could say that,' Arthur muttered.

'What do you know about it?'

'Just that I was the subject of a rather nasty practical joke. And that Gwenhwyfar and Hector are now an item.'

'Are they?' Marvin's eyebrows furrowed. 'That's not what I heard.'

'What did you hear?'

'I heard that Gwen was assaulted.'

Arthur paled. 'What? When—?'

'On Friday at that party. Someone came forward on Tuesday and told the principal. The school wouldn't have known about it otherwise. She wasn't hurt, thank goodness. One of our students clouted Hector. If there was a practical joke involved, Gwen was the victim, not the perpetrator.'

Suddenly, Arthur felt queasy. 'So you're telling me—what—that Gwen was set up, and that Hector…?'

He couldn't finish. Marvin nodded. 'I'm afraid that's rather what it sounds like.'

Arthur retreated behind his own hands. How could he have been so blind? Of course Gwenhwyfar had nothing to do with it! Of course this was the work of the Furies! Even Bedivere had been innocent. He, just like Gwenhwyfar, had been manipulated, and they had all been made fools of in the process.

'Arthur?'

He expelled a loud groan. He couldn't make amends now; he didn't know how. 'Why hasn't Hector been expelled? Or arrested?' He buckled over and snarled at his own stupidity. 'I'm a fool, Merlin, a fool!'

'No Arthur, you are not a fool,' his History teacher countered, solemn. 'How are any of us to know such things? The important thing is, you know now. It's not too late to fix this.'

'It's too late for me. How is what I accused Gwen of forgivable?' His head snapped up, turmoil in his eyes. 'I thought she was a part of it.' He shook his head violently. 'What are they doing about it?'

'The principal's been holding meetings with parents this week, that much I do know. I should imagine that he's reluctant to go to the police because of bad press concerning the school.'

'And Hector? What about him?'

'Hector? His surname's Browne, as is the principal's cousin's. Now that may not mean much, but I'm fairly certain the two are connected. It may explain why this hasn't been officially announced in the staff room yet. It'll be suspension, at the very most, for Hector. Gwenhwyfar's parents will demand that, at least.'

'Sounds like Ravioli has quite a dilemma on his hands,' sneered Arthur.

'I don't understand why Mr Hall isn't being more discreet. Granted, Agnes is Hector's tutor, but I'd have thought this sort of thing should be kept highly confidential, at least until a resolution and plan of action is found. Particularly given how much Agnes likes to talk.'

The two fell silent.

'I'm sorry if this has upset you, Arthur, but I thought you'd want to know. It won't be long until the entire school is discussing it.'

'I know.' He looked to the clock, and sighed. 'I should go.'

'Where to?' asked Marvin, concerned.

'Morgan. I was supposed to meet her five minutes ago.' He stood, and slowly hoisted his bag. How was he going to rectify this? Gwenhwyfar wouldn't forgive him easily, and why should she? Bedivere and Viola both deserved an apology, too.

'Then you'd better hurry!' exclaimed Marvin, trying to lighten the mood. 'Maybe it'll take your mind off things? Being outside for a while.' He picked up the day's paper, flicked it out, and began to read. 'Tell her to keep thinking of names for our club.'

Arthur nodded, wished Marvin a good weekend, and then vanished through the door.

Lunchtime passed with a strong gale that bowed trees and flattened grass. Inside, the rustling branches could be heard through the closed windows, which whistled in the darkening corridors. Gwenhwyfar stared up at the bruised clouds through the window opposite her Science room. Just one more lesson, she thought, and then she would be granted respite. The laboratory door opened and she found her seat in silence. Their teacher, Mrs Watson, announced that they would be working in pairs and then shouted them out to the unsettled class.

'Jo, Max; Rupert, Jack; Sue, Lucy; Arthur, Gwen…'

Her head shot up. Scowling, she turned her eyes to Arthur, who hesitantly rose to his feet and wandered over, reclaiming his temporary seat for the first time in days. As the list of pairs continued, Gwenhwyfar kept her eyes fixed on the chalkboard at the other end of room.

'How's Morgan?' she bristled.

He gazed at her, wide-eyed. 'She's fine.'

'Did you enjoy your lunch date?' About them, the rest of the class played an ad-hoc game of musical chairs.

'It wasn't a date,' he told her.

'No?' She shot him a sharp look. 'So what was it?'

'We just had lunch together, that's all.'

Mrs Watson called for their attention.

'Test tubes are in the back cupboards, Bunsen burners by the sink. Remember, we'll be looking at the reactions of carbon with metal oxides when heated. The carbon is here at the front with the magnesium, copper and iron oxides. *Don't* forget the heat resistant mats or your goggles, *please*.'

Gwenhwyfar jumped to her feet. As she began to gather the apparatus Arthur hurried to follow.

'I wanted to apologise,' he said, cramping her. 'I've made a terrible mistake.'

She moved to the supply cupboard, snatched up the test tubes and then crushed them into his hands.

'We need a magnet. And the chemicals.'

'Gwen, please. I'm trying to talk to you.'

'Well, now you know how it feels, don't you?' She left to get the last few necessities, and soon she was back at their desk.

Arthur tried again. 'I know, I'm sorry; I shouldn't have ignored you, especially not when you tried to explain things to me.'

She began to set it all up. 'No, you shouldn't.'

'I shouldn't have shouted at you either,' he added. She slapped the heatproof mat onto the table, and then slammed the Bunsen burner on top. 'I'm sorry.'

'Where does this go?' The rubber tube from the apparatus was choked in her hand. Arthur took it off her.

'Even if you had kissed Hector, that would have been up to

you, and I had no right to treat you the way I did.' Gwenhwyfar remained still, listening, but not looking. 'I was just under the wrong impression.'

'I was under the same impression as you,' Gwenhwyfar responded. 'And I didn't kiss Hector. I would have told you, if you had let me. He kissed me.'

She sat down and tried to light the Bunsen burner. Arthur turned it on.

'I know, I'm sorry. I was just... upset. I was stupid, really stupid. I didn't mean to hurt you, Gwen.'

Gwenhwyfar heard the sincerity in his words. As she glanced across to him, she saw it in his eyes, too.

'And... and I'm really sorry about... when I shut the door, I had no idea. Had I known what was going on, I would've... would've...'

How did he know about that? Scowling, she blinked back tears and stared at the dancing flame. 'You weren't to know.'

'I should have known that Emily and Charlotte would do something like this. I just didn't know they were that evil. I hope they get expelled.'

'They won't. Their parents give too much to the school. I don't know about Hector, though. He might go.' Gwenhwyfar finally felt sturdy enough to look his way. He still seemed troubled, but sent her a tentative smile. She turned back to their work, donning the oversized goggles that were much too big for her head. Arthur did the same.

'I like you, you know,' he ventured. She jerked her dark eyes to his. 'I do.'

'And what about Morgan? She fancies you, you must know that.'

'Don't be silly.'

'She does,' she insisted. 'It's obvious. Even Bedivere knows. She wouldn't stop blithering on about your little lunch date.'

'It wasn't a date!'

She sent him a narrowed stare. 'Does she know that?'

'Look, I've just spent the past half hour talking to her about how I should apologise to you. She even knows I like you. I *told* her.'

She stopped what she was doing. 'You told Morgan about this?'

'It won't be long until the whole school knows, Gwen. Marvin overheard Mr Hall talking to Mrs Brolstone in the corridors about it. He suspects that he's been discussing it more carelessly than he should.'

The temperature of her face seemed to skyrocket and suddenly she was rendered speechless. It was as if a noose had tightened around her throat. 'He does?'

'I'm sorry.'

She felt a sickening twist of rage and mortification. 'Bydd fy'n nhad yn wallgo,' *my father will be furious*, she hissed.

Arthur gazed at her anxiously. 'Gwen, I really am sorry.'

'I know, I know you are.' She adjusted the flame to make it hotter, and then recorded the reaction of carbon with iron oxide in her exercise book. 'I'm just angry. I can be angry, can't I?'

'Of course you can.' He watched her for a while as she worked in silence, and then began to write some of their findings down.

'You should talk to Bedivere, you know,' she said after a while. 'Emily took advantage of him to get to you. He had no idea what was going on.'

'I'm going to talk to him about it this weekend.' There was a moment's silence. 'What are your plans?'

'Viola's got a photo shoot. I might be going with her to that,' she lied.

'A photo shoot?'

'Yes. You can't tell anyone, though. She doesn't want people knowing. She might become a model.'

'A model?' He shrugged. 'Good for her. You'll have to tell me how it goes. I can't say I agree with the whole thing, though.'

'No?'

'My grandmother's always going on about it. Every time she sees an advert or a fashion spread, she says: *They should have used me! It would have been more of a challenge for them to make me look vapid.*'

'She sounds interesting, your grandmother,' Gwenhwyfar observed, amused by his impression.

'She is. I think she'd like you. Maybe you should come and meet her, sometime.'

Gwenhwyfar offered him a growing smile. 'I'd like that.'

He grinned at her, and for a moment she forgot they'd ever fallen out at all.

Free Countries

'Gwen? Is that you?'

Her mother spied her from the kitchen, and resumed the preparations for supper. The smell of home cooking filled the house, and as Gwenhwyfar closed the door she realised that she was standing on the day's post. She stooped to gather it up as Llew whined her a welcome, padding up to her side. After an affectionate hello to her old friend, Gwenhwyfar sorted through the letters. Nothing much of interest or import was posted anymore, yet despite this they still received a New National leaflet detailing what had been done for their local community each week.

'What are you making?' she called to her mother, as she kicked off her shoes and dumped her bag.

'Apple crumble!' Eve exclaimed. Gwenhwyfar paused at a flyer that had been wedged between two envelopes. It was ripped. 'How was school?'

'Fine,' she replied, scanning the flyer. It read: *Do you dream of a free Britain?* She wandered through to the kitchen, where her mother's hands were buried in a bowl of flour. 'I think I'll go and get changed.'

Eve seemed distracted. 'We'll be eating a bit later tonight. We have to go and pick the car up from the garage. You don't mind keeping an eye on the supper, do you?'

'Just let me know when.' Gwenhwyfar vanished up the stairs.

Once she'd changed into something more comfortable, she settled down on her bed. Her room was beginning to feel a little more homely now that some of the boxes were gone and all her furniture was in place. It wasn't as big as her old bedroom, but it was definitely cosier, and she had a nice view of their small garden and the large townhouses beyond.

She examined the flyer again.

Do you dream of a free Britain?

Many like you have decided to fight for a life free of repression, observation and poverty.

Many like you are tired of living under a government that we did not vote for.

Many like you want freedom, prosperity and independence.

If you think a free Britain is for you, join the revolutionary cause. If you think freedom is for you, join **Free Countries**.

Rising against the regime.

Thoughtfully, Gwenhwyfar booted up her computer. The small device activated just as her phone beeped at her, presenting a message from Viola.

Feel like going to the cinema on Sunday night?

She tapped her thumb quickly over the touch-screen and messaged back, *sure, what time?*, then sat down. The torn flyer lay before her. She accessed the Internet, typing in a few key words to examine the results. The first page rendered little. The second, too, had nothing of interest, and so she tried again but with different words. *Free Countries* brought up scarcely anything, and *Revolutionary Cause* produced too much. Eventually, she tried typing each word with *Rebels*. This time she had some success.

The fourth website down on the second page seemed like a promising source. Curiosity caused her to click. When she did, the entire text from the flyer flashed up on screen. It was a simple site, with black font on a white background. Gwenhwyfar scrolled down until she no longer recognised it.

> *What do we believe?*
>
> *We at* Free Countries *believe in the right to choose our leaders, the right to freedom of speech, and in the importance of protecting human rights.*
>
> *We at* Free Countries *believe in independence from a no-longer-united Kingdom.*
>
> *We at* Free Countries *believe that the New Nationals are abusing their governmental powers, and that George Milton has no intention of ever holding his long-overdue elections.*
>
> *We believe in a free Britain.*
>
> *How do I join* **Free Countries***?*
>
> *If you complete the security check,* Free Countries *will contact you anonymously with further details.*
>
> *This website is a smart site and only appears to non-governmental, safe networks.*

Please don't forget to click the 'erase' button at the bottom of this page to wipe your browser history and evidence of your visit to Free Countries.

Thank you for your interest in our cause.

Alarmed, Gwenhwyfar pressed the button immediately. The page vanished. She checked her browser history; it wasn't there. Neither was any indication that her computer had been connected to the address at all. Curiously, and with *Free Countries'* promise in mind, she checked her email, but there was nothing new. By the time her parents left for the garage she was shopping online, and had to force herself to complete some homework. The rest of the evening passed by quickly, her mind preoccupied with the words of the website. Before bed she realised that she'd left the flyer out on her desk, so she ripped it up into small pieces, and then flushed it down the toilet.

'Garan! Gwenhwyfar! Good to see you.'

It was Saturday afternoon. Gwenhwyfar's uncle came into the room, his arms stretched wide. Garan caught him in a firm handshake.

'Hello George,' he said, his claim that their relatives were causing him a great inconvenience by visiting forgotten. 'Glad you could make it.'

They released one another, and then Gwenhwyfar was engulfed in a padded, affectionate hug. The moment she was free her aunt had taken hold of her.

'Aunt Melissa,' she said, with due enthusiasm. 'It's so good to see you. What do you think of the house?'

'It is lovely, isn't it?' Melissa replied, admiring the furnishings and then the high ceiling. 'It's a great space. Lots of light.'

'I love the front,' George told them, hovering in the middle of the kitchen. 'The brickwork is very handsome. What's the neighbourhood like?'

'Good. So far the neighbours seem friendly enough. Most people keep themselves to themselves,' Eve told him, moving in for a kiss on the cheek.

'It was like that when we first moved in too,' Melissa told them. 'People will warm to you, once they realise you're here to stay.'

'So are you all settled in?' asked George.

'Basically. There's still a few boxes of old stuff in the attic that I need to go through, but everything else is unpacked.' Eve sat down. 'Would either of you like a drink?'

'Tea would be lovely.' Melissa joined her sister at the kitchen table. 'George?'

'Coffee for me, thank you.'

Garan, still at the counter, went to boil the kettle.

'So where's Grace?' Eve asked. 'At home?'

'No, she's here.' Melissa turned in her seat, and frowned at the door. 'Grace?'

'She said she was getting something from the boot,' George explained.

'She was supposed to be going out with her friends this afternoon. I said she could postpone it, this once.' Melissa sighed. 'Grace!'

'I'm *coming*!'

The front door slammed, and soon Gwenhwyfar's cousin was in the room, observing them all resentfully.

Gwenhwyfar hadn't seen her since Grace was about eight. Her

last memory of her younger cousin was the impressive waterworks she had displayed whilst out on a hack in the Welsh countryside, after being told that she couldn't ride Eve's horse. Worn down by the screaming, Eve had allowed her to sit up front with her on her eighteen-hander with the pony tethered close; only for Grace to kick the poor beast in the shoulders, spooking the Shire and sending her spurned ride galloping off across the hillside. It was later found wandering alongside a motorway after a long hunt to track it down.

Grace was thirteen now, and could still be mistaken for Gwenhwyfar's sister. Her hair was auburn and her chin was squarer, but it was the freckles she had inherited from George that really marked the two cousins apart—her face was peppered with them.

'Hello Grace,' Garan said, much too sweetly. 'Would you like a drink?'

'No.' Adding a quick 'thank you' as an afterthought, Grace went to sit at the end of the kitchen table, away from her parents. Gwenhwyfar sat at the breakfast bar and observed as Grace produced her phone and scrolled through it.

'We meant to come by sooner, but things have been so busy at the firm,' Melissa said, taking the hot tea off Garan. 'We're working on a new case. Tell them about Roehill, George.'

'We're trying to claim compensation and a better settle price for houses that are no longer habitable due to repeated flooding along the Thames,' George explained as Garan handed him his coffee. 'The argument is that the government hasn't done enough to prevent flooding in the area. The clients and property owners are hoping to claim under negligence.'

'And would that be the New Nationals you're suing, then?'

Garan asked with interest. Eve shot him a look.

'No, it's the Department for Environment and the Ministry of Defence,' George explained. 'It's a big case. We're only involved with the property side. They have others working on it too. They're going all out.'

'None of this would be happening if the area wasn't largely owned by property developers. Many of the houses are rentals, but at least this way the independent homeowners might see some compensation.' Melissa sipped at her tea. 'There's a chance the court may just grant an injunction, which wouldn't be a bad thing either.'

'What's an injunction?' Gwenhwyfar asked.

'An injunction means they'd have to intervene to prevent the problem from happening in the future,' she explained.

'I thought the New Nationals were supposed to have a good hold on climate change?' Eve frowned.

'You can't control the weather,' George disputed, 'but you can cause over-saturation through poor land management. And it's a historical case. Yes, the New Nationals are supposedly getting a handle on climate change now, but previous governments didn't do enough.'

'I'm surprised this isn't a problem elsewhere in the country,' Gwenhwyfar remarked.

'Oh, it is. Cities have taken the right precautions, but in many cases that means dams upstream which flood rural areas. It's the coastal towns that are the problem. Many are now below sea level and are relying on dykes. I rather feel they should just relocate further inland, if possible. Or look at some of these land-reclaiming projects they have going, you know, like they used to do in Singapore.'

'Except then you leave massive holes in the earth elsewhere,' Melissa pointed out, looking to George. 'Really, I don't know why anyone would buy on anything other than a very high hill these days. Can you imagine what would happen if the dams and dykes in London failed?'

There was a moment's silence. Gwenhwyfar could tell that her father was holding his tongue.

'I'm making tortillas tonight,' Eve announced. She turned to her sister. 'Would you like to stay for dinner?'

'That would be nice, wouldn't it?' Melissa beamed. 'Grace? What do you think?'

Grace pouted. 'But I said I'd meet Josey at six.'

'You can always see her tomorrow,' George suggested.

'I already had to change my plans once today,' Grace huffed. She turned to her mother. 'Can't Dad just drive me home? You can have dinner here, if you want.'

'Grace, I don't think that's entirely practical,' Melissa started, her voice low.

'You don't have to stay. Some other time, maybe?' interjected Garan.

'No, we'd love to stay for dinner,' George said firmly. He looked to Grace. 'Wouldn't we?' Grace said nothing. 'Grace?'

'*Fine*,' she muttered.

'Shall we do a tour?' Gwenhwyfar stood up, and the tension in the room dissolved. George and Melissa were keen, so she led the Swan family upstairs to explore the rest of the house, showing them everything but Garan's office.

Grace didn't stay for dinner. George drove her home and then came back just in time for supper. Afterwards, he and Melissa left early to pick Grace up from her friend's house. Gwenhwyfar marvelled that her cousin's brattish tactics had won the day, but her parents seemed happy to let it pass without comment.

On Sunday evening Gwenhwyfar went with Viola to the cinema, where she received a full account of the test shoot the day before. Viola went into detail about everything, from what she'd worn right down to her specific poses and facial expressions. When Gwenhwyfar tried to mimic them, the interplay became so absurd that they both fell apart laughing. Afterwards she made Viola promise to take her to any modelling parties, insisting that she should get first refusal if Viola was ever given any extra free clothes.

Monday morning was soon upon her again. They were gathered in their tutor room early, and Bedivere was explaining to them both how Arthur had apologised over the weekend.

'Turns out he's found out all about it, at last,' he commented, enjoying his new place at their table. 'Marvin told him. Annoying, given he wouldn't listen to us.'

'I wonder if he'll apologise to me?' Viola mused, her chin propped in her upturned hand. 'He had a real go at me when I tried to explain everything to him.'

'He did say that he would,' Bedivere assured her. He turned to Gwenhwyfar. 'I also asked him about Morgan. What was it you heard, again?'

'That he's going to ask her out,' Gwenhwyfar said. 'Though admittedly, it's Emily who said it.' She exchanged a glance with Viola. 'So what did he say?'

Bedivere shrugged. 'Nothing much really, but I definitely got the feeling that as far as he's concerned, they're just friends.'

A few other students were beginning to find their way into the classroom, Morgan included. She glanced over to their table as she passed, and seemed to reflect over something, but then she adopted her usual seat and produced her sketchbook in silence.

'God, when are they going to call?'

'Who?' Bedivere asked.

'Her agency,' Gwenhwyfar explained. 'She had a test shoot on Saturday.'

'For a modelling agency,' Viola interjected. 'I'm waiting to see the pictures. They'll only put me on their books if they like them. They looked all right when they took them, but you can never tell with that sort of thing.'

'Still, you said that the photographer seemed really positive,' Gwenhwyfar reminded her. She turned to Bedivere. 'She's just paranoid.'

Miss Ray strode into the room, keys and papers in one hand, her coffee and I.D. badge in the other. 'Gwen?' she called, setting her things down at her desk. 'I've just spoken with the principal. I'm afraid that he wants to see you in his office, before first period.'

She twisted around in her chair. 'What for?'

'He didn't say. It's all right, you won't miss the register—I'll mark you in as present.'

She didn't really feel like facing another meeting on her own. It must have shown, because Viola and Bedivere both looked to her with concern.

'Do you want one of us to go with you?' Viola offered.

She doubted that such a prospect was an option. 'It's all right. I'll see you both at break.'

'And History,' Bedivere reminded her. They waved at her as she slipped into the corridor, and she wondered how well they would get along in her absence.

'Miss Taliesin. I'm glad you could join me.'

Reluctant to go into his office, Gwenhwyfar hovered by the door, her hand squeezing the strap of her rucksack. Eventually she plucked up the courage to enter, and sat down stiffly. 'You wanted to see me?'

'Yes,' Dr Ravioli began. 'First of all, I have spoken to your father. I would like to assure you that I am looking into the breach in confidentiality that has occurred at this school. As it is, Mr Caledonensis had already informed me of the situation. I can assure you that Mr Hall won't be present for any of our future meetings.'

Gwenhwyfar nodded, knowing that the damage had already been done. The principal glanced down to his desk for a moment, fingering the fountain pen that lay across his papers.

'I've also come to a decision regarding the incident. Now, I want you to understand that these are just precautions that the school is taking. If you feel the need to involve the police, you're free to do so, but I think we both understand that's not necessarily the best way to proceed.'

Gwenhwyfar knew he was right, in this case, as far as the particulars involving the solution went. She also knew that she did not like being told what to do. 'Yes, well, I think I'll be the judge of that.'

'Of course,' he agreed.

'So what's the verdict? Are they going to be expelled?'

'Not quite. I've decided that three days' suspension is best.'

'Suspension?'

'Unfortunately, *expelling* a student isn't so straightforward.

There has to be a good reason, prior concerns, and all four students have merits that make them worthy of a second chance.'

'Like what? Rich parents?' Gwenhwyfar snapped. 'Hector's done this sort of thing before. Why should he get another chance?'

'You're lucky that I've decided to rule in your favour. Had I simply taken their word over yours, it would be you and Mr Greenstone-Jones who would be facing suspension.' He leant forward, and offered her another one of his crocodile smiles. 'I can assure you that I've taken none of this lightly.'

'No?' she retorted.

His countenance suddenly darkened. 'No. This will go on their permanent records. *Which*, might I add, will be very detrimental to this school's reputation.'

He looked pointedly at her, as if this was her fault. Brimming with rage, Gwenhwyfar said nothing.

'I thought I should inform you of this now so that you know where Browne, Stone, Mulberry and Rose are, and why they will be absent from school this week. I have also insisted that they apologise. Is that acceptable to you, Miss Taliesin?'

Gwenhwyfar never wanted to speak to any of them again. Eventually she nodded. She felt she could do little else.

'Very well. Now, it might be a good idea if you get to class.'

The bell rang on cue. Eager to separate herself from his company, Gwenhwyfar hurried to join the stream of students ambling through the corridors.

She was a little late by the time she made it to Mr Caledonensis' room. Bedivere and Arthur were both talking as she found her seat, and though Morgan seemed to be working in her exercise book, she was clearly listening. Only when Gwenhwyfar sat down did she realise that the other girl was sketching something in the book margins: a woman in a medieval gown.

Bedivere turned to her immediately. 'What did Ravioli say?'

'They've all been suspended.'

'For how long?'

She shrugged, and busied herself with preparing her exercise book. 'Three days.'

'You spoke to the principal?' Arthur interrupted. 'When?'

'Just now,' Gwenhwyfar told him. She sent Bedivere a wry smile. 'He said we were lucky that he hadn't chosen to suspend us, instead.'

'Why hasn't he expelled any of them?' Arthur asked angrily. 'Did he tell you that, at least?'

'Apparently they all have merits that make them deserving of a second chance,' Gwenhwyfar repeated, bitterly. 'Money.'

'I suppose he can't really expel a student for a practical joke,' Bedivere murmured. 'Even though it got out of hand, are the Furies really responsible for what Hector did?'

'Of course they are—they know what he's like,' Gwenhwyfar muttered. 'And Hector—'

'I know,' he added. 'He should have been kicked out. Actually, I'm surprised he wasn't.'

Arthur turned to Gwenhwyfar. 'There must be a way around this. Can't you appeal?'

'To who? Ravioli—? I'm not sure if I want to. It's over, and I'm glad.'

For a while they said nothing. Amongst the racket of the class Morgan's pen scribbled noisily across the page. Gwenhwyfar looked to the door to see if there was any sign of Marvin. Tom was taking full advantage of his absence by shouting mindlessly and flinging things across the room.

'So how was the photo shoot on Saturday?' asked Arthur.

'Oh! It went really well, actually,' Gwenhwyfar beamed. 'We should be getting the pictures soon.'

Bedivere sat sideways with his arm draped over the back of his chair. 'When?'

'By the end of the week, at least,' Gwenhwyfar guessed. 'What did you get up to?'

'Visited family,' Bedivere shrugged. 'My grandparents have just bought a new shed. It's more like a log cabin, to be honest.' There was an awkward silence. Morgan was still bent low over her exercise book, scratching long black hair onto her delicate figurine. 'How was your weekend, Morgan?'

She looked up, surprised to be asked. 'It was good.' She coloured, and looked across to Arthur. 'We went to an exhibition on the Pre-Raphaelites in London.'

'We?'

'Me and Arthur,' she added.

Arthur shifted, and offered Bedivere an uncomfortable smile. 'Yes. It was good, actually. I was impressed.'

'I didn't know you liked art, Art,' Bedivere teased.

'You went to London?' Gwenhwyfar echoed.

Morgan nodded, and looked at her with her big, brown eyes. 'We went to see a movie, too. That wasn't as good though.' Suddenly she laughed. 'Arthur went into the wrong toilets in the cinema. He got chased out by a five year old.'

Arthur fidgeted as Morgan fuelled the fire of her own amusement. For perhaps the first time in her life, Gwenhwyfar experienced real jealousy, the kind that burns and nauseates, that causes the heart to twist into a painful knot; like the wringing out of a wet rag, whose worth is wrung out with its waters.

She had never been so thrilled to see Mr Caledonensis. The moment he loped into the room she gave him her full attention. Time seemed sluggish with two hours to one, but after a long monologue and a lesson filled with chatter, the clock ticked its final minute.

'Don't forget to answer questions four to seven with two paragraphs each by next lesson!' Marvin shouted, as the class erupted to its feet. Packing away as if the room were on fire, Gwenhwyfar hurried to leave, eager to catch up with Gavin and Tom as Bedivere struggled to match her haste.

'I'll see you later!' she called brightly to Arthur and Morgan, with a brisk wave over her shoulder. Arthur nodded back with a smile that belied his confusion, while Morgan ignored her completely, offering Arthur another happy grin.

'Why didn't he tell me?'

They strode down the corridor, their fellow students parting for Gavin who stalked through the crowd as if it were the Red Sea. Gwenhwyfar looked to Bedivere apprehensively. 'Why didn't he say he was seeing Morgan on Saturday?'

'I don't know,' Bedivere murmured, as they both struggled to keep up with Gavin's giant strides. 'Maybe he didn't think it was important?'

'It was obviously important enough to keep it secret,' she argued. 'I mean, did he mention anything to you?'

Bedivere shook his head. 'He only mentioned Morgan when I brought her up. There was nothing about them going to London together.'

'I thought he came to see you on Saturday?' she accused.

he corrected.

'...y wasn't going to say anything if she hadn't,' she remarked. 'I mean, what; now he's seeing her at the weekends? If they're just friends, why not mention it? Why lie?'

Bedivere shrugged.

'You don't think he fancies her, do you?'

'How should I know?'

'I thought you were his best friend?'

'He's with Marvin all the time,' Bedivere retorted. 'I've barely spoken to him since the party.'

'I *told* him she fancies him,' Gwenhwyfar declared, angered. 'Who hangs out with someone who likes them, if they don't like them back?' She wheeled on Gavin. 'That's weird, right?'

'Who's this?' Gavin asked with a frown.

'Arthur,' Bedivere said, ruefully.

'It is weird, isn't it?' she said again.

Tom was walking on the other side of Gavin, his wide jaw and small chin set with concern. 'Has anyone seen Hector?'

'No,' Gavin replied stiffly.

'He was supposed to meet me this morning.'

'He's been suspended,' Gwenhwyfar snapped, still too angry with Arthur to really be enraged about Hector.

His face contorted. 'Why? What the hell for?'

'For trying to *rape* me?' She couldn't believe he couldn't connect the two. Looking across to the brown-haired teenager, Gwenhwyfar wondered what on earth Viola saw in him. He turned a light shade of red.

'Oh, come on, you can't have honestly thought he didn't try it. How do you think he got those scratches on his face? I don't know why you still hang out with the bastard,' scowled Gavin.

'Sorry,' Tom eventually mumbled, 'Hector told me he'd been scratched by his cat.'

Gwenhwyfar huffed. They came out into the large foyer of new Wormelow.

'Well, he wasn't. Gwen scratched him, and now he's been suspended for assault.'

'Charlotte, Emily and Hattie, too,' Gwenhwyfar told them.

'Not going to the police, then?' Gavin enquired.

'How can I? If I did everyone would be in trouble, especially *you*, Tom.'

There was a loud crash and a series of bangs that sounded as if something had collided with lockers. As they turned into the English corridor, a dishevelled boy limped past them with wild hair and a bloodied lip. Alarmed, Gwenhwyfar stared.

'Great,' Bedivere muttered, clearly disturbed.

'Looks like Lance is back,' Gavin remarked with a frown.

Tom was grinning like an idiot. 'Yep, and he's doing the rounds.'

There was shouting in the other corridor, but then it passed, and faded to an excited murmur. Gwenhwyfar gazed up at them both, appalled that they could be so cavalier. Was this Lance character responsible for what she had just witnessed? Arthur's description of him suddenly seemed fitting. Gavin may have protested at Arthur's appellation of *thug*, but judging by what she had just seen, it was now all she expected.

Lancelot Lawson Lake

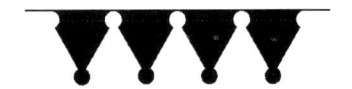

The back corridors of old Wormelow were nearly emptied. Class was over, and as Bedivere had been detained to discuss his homework with Ms Appelbauer, Gwenhwyfar was walking to their designated meeting spot alone. She was halfway down the corridor to the assembly hall when she saw him, a boy in her year, inappropriately dressed in a scruffy, oversized interpretation of their school uniform. He punched the locker in front of him with a sharp jab of his fist, and the door clattered as he struggled to un-stick the lock.

He had dark, wild hair that curled; his loose chocolate locks messed by a recent scuffle, and though he was not quite as tall as Arthur he held himself with a sure-footed assertiveness gained through obvious athleticism. His nose was proud, adding to an unusual sullen profile defined by high, sharp cheekbones and wide surly lips.

She wasn't sure why, but she stopped. Something about him irritated her.

'What?'

She quickly pulled her eyes away with the realisation she had been staring. 'Nothing.'

He hit the locker door again. This time it swung open with a bang. The bruises on his knuckles were plum and blueberry, a dark smudge across his blushed ivory skin. 'You need to be here, or something?'

She shook her head. 'Why'd you punch it?'

'Lock sticks,' he muttered, stuffing the contents of his bag haphazardly into his locker. He slammed it shut. 'It works.'

'Can't you get someone to fix it?'

He studied her with earthy eyes crowned by dark lashes. 'Who did you say you were?'

'Gwen. I'm new here,' she added.

'Oh,' he remarked flatly, as he tugged the key from the lock. 'So *you're* the new girl.'

She was expecting him to introduce himself—to perhaps make a comment about her 'odd' accent as so many others had done—but instead he turned, and left.

For a moment she lingered, trying to figure out why she felt so discomfited. Reluctant to retrace her steps simply to avoid him, she followed at a distance, catching up with him at the double doors. He eyed her suspiciously.

'You're not following me, are you?'

'Don't flatter yourself,' she glowered.

He didn't hold the door for her. Gwenhwyfar had to catch the heavy wood before it struck her in the face.

'You are following me,' he said irritably, as they turned the same way.

'No, I'm really not,' she insisted. They came to another door. This time Gwenhwyfar pushed through it as he did.

'Go to the principal's office if you're lost,' he suggested curtly.

'I'm not lost!' she claimed, trying to overtake him.

'Don't you have some friends you can annoy?'

'Yes, that's where I'm going.'

His face contorted to something ugly. 'And that happens to be in the same direction that I'm going? Yeah, right.'

Gwenhwyfar huffed. 'You really think I'd *want* to follow you? You must have a high opinion of yourself. Either that, or you're crazy.' She eyeballed him. 'I'm heading for the *exit*, you idiot.'

His jaw clenched. 'Why are you even here, anyway?'

She rolled her eyes, hoping they'd part ways the moment they came outside, but they both stomped in the same direction. 'My dad got a job here, so I had to move schools.'

'No, I mean *why* are you *here*?'

'Believe me, I'd rather *not* be here, if I had the choice,' she said, her cheeks crimson. 'What did you say your name was?'

'I didn't,' he grunted. They passed the Wormelow wing of the canteen. He wasn't going there, either.

'What, afraid I'll start stalking you?' she sneered, desperately searching for her friends.

'Aren't you already?' he jibed.

As they turned the corner she saw Viola and Gavin sitting on a bench, talking. It took them a while to notice her, and when they did, they stared.

'Where do you think you're going?' the boy warned, as suddenly, they started to head for the same bench.

Gwenhwyfar stared at him, dreading what she knew to be true. 'To sit with my friends.'

'No, you're not.'

'What, disappointed I'm not stalking you after all?'

They both came to the table. Gwenhwyfar dumped her bag and sat down resolutely. She smiled at Viola and Gavin.

'What's this?' the boy demanded.

'This is Gwen,' Viola begun, 'Gwen, this is Lance. Gwen sits with us now—we're friends,' she explained, offering a smile.

'So you're Lance?' Gwenhwyfar mocked. 'I've heard so much about you. Do you beat people up as a hobby, then?'

He shot Gavin a questioning look. Viola launched straight into their break-time conversation.

'I just heard from the agency. They loved the photos. They're going to email them to me, but I can pick up the prints later in the week.'

'Does that mean…?'

Viola nodded. 'I'm officially on their books!'

There was a moment of shared excitement.

'I'm sorry, what?' Lance was still standing by the bench, his brow knotted into a black scowl.

'Oh!' Viola continued, 'and I have a casting, too. They're going to see if they can place me with other agencies abroad. They've already had a lot of interest.'

'Hang on. You're both friends with her?' Lance looked to Gwenhwyfar with a sour expression. 'Where's Tom?'

'Music rooms,' Gavin grinned, pleased to have his friend back. 'How was your little holiday? Did you get to do much?'

He stuffed his free hand into his pocket. 'No. I was grounded. Don't you think I'd have come to Tom's party, otherwise?'

Viola rolled her eyes. 'Oh, sit down, Lancelot. Stop being so stroppy. Wait until you hear what you've missed.'

'Yeah, Vi's a model now,' Gavin added with enthusiasm. 'Like those thin ones you see in magazines.'

'*And* Bedivere's sitting with us,' Gwenhwyfar added. She wouldn't have guessed that Lance was short for Lancelot.

'He is?' Gavin asked.

'Yep!' Gwenhwyfar enjoyed seeing Lancelot's expression blacken. 'He asked if he could join us in English. Apparently Arthur's spending lunch with Marvin. Then again, it could be Morgan. I just found out that they went to London together on Saturday.'

'They did?' Viola asked. 'As friends, or what?'

'Beats me.'

Resigning himself to the situation, Lancelot sat down. 'What's this about that idiot Arthur?'

'He's not an idiot,' Gwenhwyfar snapped.

'Gwen likes him,' Viola explained.

Lancelot snorted. 'That loser? Why?'

'He's *not* a loser. Not everything is because you say it is.'

He laughed at her. 'But he's such a moron!'

'He's nicer than *some* people I've met,' Gwenhwyfar remarked.

'No way are we letting Bedivere sit with us.'

'Come on, Lance. Bed's all right. Besides, it's not like it's *Arthur*,' Viola teased.

'It's too late now anyway, he's here.' Gwenhwyfar waved to him as he headed their way. Soon he was amongst them, squeezing onto their bench.

'I just saw Morgan, *not* with Arthur,' Bedivere announced. 'At least he's definitely with Marvin. I don't think you have to worry about them being more than just friends, Gwen.'

Suddenly the whole table descended into a discussion of the triangle that was Arthur, Morgan and Gwenhwyfar. Lancelot observed the scene with a black scowl.

'Where's Hector?' he blurted out, bored.

'Hector's been suspended,' Gavin explained. Gwenhwyfar surveyed Lancelot's profile, trying to comprehend why he was so antagonistic.

'Suspended?' he snorted. 'Why?'

'He attacked Gwen,' Viola explained.

Lancelot's eyes shot to Gwenhwyfar. 'Attacked how?'

'You know, *attacked*. Tried to… y'know…' Gavin's words trailed off with an uncomfortable shrug.

'Hector? Really?' He looked to Gwenhwyfar again, disbelieving. 'Says who?'

'Me,' Viola snapped.

'And me.'

'No one asked you anything, Beddy,' Lancelot flared.

'Don't talk to him like that,' Gwenhwyfar cautioned. 'No one asked for your opinion, either.'

'And no one asked for yours,' he sneered.

'What is your problem?'

'Nothing. I'm just not accustomed to having two berks sit at my table.'

'Lance!' Viola's eyes flashed. 'Either shut up, or bugger off, all right?'

His gaze was uncompromising. Gwenhwyfar glared at him while Bedivere tried to make himself less conspicuous. Eventually Lancelot expelled something akin to a hiss, got up, and took his bag with him.

The four watched him lope away. After a few moments of mutual irritation, Gavin sighed. 'I'd better go and see what's bothering him.' He pushed himself to his feet grudgingly. 'I'll see you at lunch. Just ignore what he said. He's always moody after a suspension.'

Gwenhwyfar didn't think she'd ever met someone so argumentative. As conversation resumed, she propped her chin in her hand and gazed after Gavin as he hurried to catch up with Lancelot.

'Did you hear about Hector?'

Julie Appelbauer stood with her tea in one hand and her satchel over her right shoulder, fat and full with papers. As Mr Slow shook his donkey-like head, Agnes Brolstone went on.

'The principal is trying to keep it under wraps. Rumour has it he's been suspended for attacking a female student.'

Mr Slow frowned. 'What? When—?'

'Two weeks ago, off school grounds,' Agnes whispered, not quietly. Mr Slow cast his sullen gaze across the room as if he wasn't entirely sure he should be party to such information. 'I heard it from Jason. The principal made the decision last week. What I want to know is this: why weren't we informed?'

Julie shifted the strap of her bag as it dug uncomfortably into her shoulder. 'I'm sure the principal has his reasons,' she theorised. 'Student safety?'

'Exactly,' Mr Slow agreed, loudly. 'He probably just felt it inappropriate to circulate the details.'

'Oh, come John; we all know why he's keeping this schtum,' Agnes murmured. Julie eyed the clock. Third period on a Tuesday was always a challenge, as it was the bottom set: Year Nines who couldn't care less about Chaucer or Shakespeare. 'It's outrageous, really. What if one of us had left the boy unsupervised with a female student? It would've been our fault, not his.'

'If you're dissatisfied with things, Mrs Brolstone, I suggest you take your complaint to the principal.'

They turned, surprised to find Marvin Caledonensis had joined them. Mr Slow immediately ducked out of their company. Agnes drew herself up, her old willowy frame strengthening. She looked at Marvin with contemptuous eyes.

'You do, do you? I had not taken you to be a supporter of the principal's methods, Marvin.'

'You misunderstand me, Agnes.' He cast his eyes calmly across the room to where Andrew Graham was sitting, his large stomach barely contained by the arms of the chair that bore him, and to Mr Eaves who sat opposite, projecting the illusion of working when in fact he too was listening. 'I am merely suggesting you speak to the principal about your concerns, before *someone else does*,' he murmured. 'You remember what happened to Martell.'

Paling, Agnes nodded curtly and made a brisk exit as the first bell marked the start of their shift.

'Julie,' Marvin said warmly. 'I had thought you wiser than to be involved with Agnes' gossip.'

'I thought so too,' she admitted. 'But she got me on my way out with her granddaughter again. You know what she's like.'

'Agnes and her grandchildren,' he remarked. 'Really, I'm not sure who we hear about more, Daisy or Dr James Ravioli.' Smiling, he reached for her satchel. She relinquished it gratefully. 'How are you finding our new student?'

'She's doing well.' She followed him into the hall. 'She seems to have found a friend in Bedivere.'

'In my lessons, too,' he said, pleased, 'and in Arthur.'

'How is Arthur?'

'He's coping. Gwen's arrival has been good for him, I think.

You heard what happened?'

'You told me, yes. And as you know, Agnes has been giving her opinion on the matter.'

'I don't know why he didn't just announce it last week. He was probably acting on behalf of James. The principal seems a reasonable man when I speak to him, yet his management of this school speaks otherwise.'

Students were starting to fill the corridors, bustling about in an apathetic effort to make it to their lessons on time. Old Wormelow always felt much cosier to Julie than the newer wing of the building, and she was glad that she got to spend most of her time in it.

'I fear I have neglected you of late, Julie.' Marvin smiled, and looked at her in that rare way he managed, that made a person feel worth something. 'I know I'm never in the staff room when I should be.'

'I'm aware of it. I had to cover for you twice last week.'

'I've been encouraging Arthur to spend more time with people his own age,' he admitted.

'Such a thing can't be bad.' Julie pushed open the door to the English wing of the building. 'The sooner the better.'

'Speaking of teenage troubles, how are your boys?'

'Good. Daniel's studying Economics next year. He's hoping to get into London; he doesn't like the idea of being too far from home. And he'll be able to see his father more often there.'

'And Erec?'

'Still sleepwalking,' she said, briefly. 'I think it's his meds. They're helping with the hallucinations, but God, Marvin: it freaks me out when I see him walking about at night. His eyes are wide open, but it's like he can't see anything. He was standing over my bed at four a.m. on Sunday. I nearly screamed.'

They came to her English room. Noticing that she was with Marvin, a few of her Year Nines made crude remarks, which they both ignored.

'Will I see you in the staff room at lunch?'

'That depends on Arthur,' he told her, 'but I expect so.'

'Good. I miss you when you're not there.' Now that her class was completely gathered the shouting had started. She unlocked the classroom door. 'Andrew keeps trying to school me on the joys of supporting the New Nationals.'

'And you haven't given in?' he asked. 'Most teachers here support the New Nationals, according to Andrew. Everyone just tells him they do to get him off their back.'

'And the principal, too. Did you know it's all but official? They're only accepting new teaching applicants who actively identify with the New Nationals. I heard it from Diane. She's seen the notes on the applications.'

'A paper trail is official enough,' Marvin remarked.

'What do you tell Andrew?'

'Oh, he knows I disagree with him completely. I think it gives him great pleasure to debate party policies with me. It keeps me clued up when it comes to discussing the school's leanings.'

'A brave endeavour,' she teased.

'Watch out for Davidson,' he added, eying a blonde boy who ambled past and went to sit at his desk. 'I hear he's developed the habit of throwing his pencil case at teachers when their backs are turned.'

'Wonderful.'

She traced him for a moment as he left, his tall lanky frame cutting straight down the corridor, and then followed the last of her students into her classroom, shooting down any vulgar questions they had about her and Mr Caledonensis.

'*Suspended?*'

Garan stared at Eve, still standing by the lobby. He set his briefcase down at the back of the sofa and shrugged out of his raincoat. 'What do you mean, suspended? For how long?'

Gwenhwyfar was leaning against the armchair. Llew fussed at her father's side. 'Three days,' she said, trying to mask her disappointment. 'It's better than nothing.'

'It may as well be nothing,' Eve muttered, clearly upset. 'What's going to happen after the suspension's up? I'm assuming that *boy* will be allowed to continue as normal. Did the principal mention if he would be putting any safeguarding steps in place?'

'I told you; he didn't say anything, only that he would make sure they apologise.'

'And have him in the same room as you? I think not,' Garan said stridently. 'I can understand the girls being suspended, but what justification do they have for keeping him in school?'

'We've logged a formal complaint,' Eve pointed out. 'Perhaps we can appeal?'

'I don't want to appeal,' Gwenhwyfar insisted. 'The suspension will go on his record. Hopefully he'll learn his lesson.'

'And why don't you want to appeal?' Garan took his suit jacket off and threw it on the sofa.

'I just—I don't want to go through it *again*,' Gwenhwyfar said, distressed. 'Once was bad enough.'

'We'd be with you the whole way this time, darling,' Eve assured her. 'There'll be no way for the principal to make you feel anything less than taken seriously.'

Gwenhwyfar doubted that was possible. 'But it's over now, it's done with. It's not like anything actually happened.'

'He assaulted you,' Garan pointed out. 'That's hardly *nothing*, cariad.'

She didn't want to talk about it. Once again she felt as if she was the one who was being interrogated when she had done nothing wrong.

'We should at least talk to the police,' her mother said.

'But I don't *want* to talk to the police.' Gwenhwyfar stood away from the chair. Giving up on her father, Llew padded over to nudge at her instead. 'What good will it do?'

'Good? It'll do plenty of good. It'll get you compensation and a restraining order on Hector, if we're lucky. Why are you so opposed to it? It's your right.'

'Hector will just say I was drunk.' She drew in a deep breath, but it wavered. 'He's not going to *admit* to attacking me, he still says I was up for it.'

'The police are equipped to deal with such things,' Eve said, softly. 'They'll see through it.'

Gwenhwyfar rubbed at her cheeks, smearing away her sudden tears. Neither of her parents moved to comfort her. 'Isn't it too late? If I were reporting it, surely I should have done it when it happened.'

'Crimes get reported historically all the time,' Garan said, his voice short. 'I hardly feel a week is going to make much difference.'

'But what about Viola? The only reason *she* hasn't been suspended is because no one's told the principal she hit Hector!'

'We can worry about that later,' Eve interrupted. 'Right now the most important thing is to make sure that this *Hector* is dealt with properly. How would you feel if after his suspension he goes and does this, or worse, to another girl?'

That wouldn't be my fault, Gwenhwyfar thought bitterly.

'I know you're concerned for your friends, love, but I really don't think the police will care. I mean, after all, she *saved* you. They can hardly charge her for that.'

Gwenhwyfar petted Llew absently, feeling isolated in the corner she had been backed into.

'Daddy won't mind calling for you. You'll only have to give a statement.'

Llew left her again, bored by the half-there attention he was receiving, and plodded lazily into the kitchen. As Gwenhwyfar stared into the carpet, the woven pattern blurred and distorted into something barely recognisable.

'Gwen?'

She didn't look at her mother. Instead she sniffed and wiped her nose on the sleeve of her hoodie.

'I'll call them now,' Garan declared. 'You're obviously devastated by this, cariad. Really I don't blame you. This is awful, just awful.'

Her eyes began to dry as her yearning for comfort evaporated. Eve turned to her and offered a sympathetic smile. 'I think it's best, darling, don't you?'

Gwenhwyfar nodded, feeling as if she had little choice. Their minds were made up. She supposed it made sense, but sometimes she wished that they would just listen.

Her parents were silent. It was dark now. Gwenhwyfar gazed out of the passenger window, her mind closed off. She didn't know what she was thinking within the small box she had constructed for herself. Nothing, really; just staring: a dull frequency that birthed no words and offered slim comfort. Her father set his eyes upon the road, his hands stiff at the steering wheel. It was Tuesday evening, and they had just left the local police station. It had been everything Gwenhwyfar had expected.

'It's madness,' Eve volunteered, her sigh producing no enquiry to her thoughts. 'I mean it was *assault*. How can they just brush it off like this?'

'You heard what they said,' Garan remarked. 'Unless we can prove that it wasn't just a misunderstanding...'

'Of course it wasn't a misunderstanding. He *assaulted* her. How could they have heard anything different?'

'They heard some lecherous boy kissed a girl he liked without thinking, that's what they heard.'

'And pinned her down,' Eve spat out, almost choking on the words. She fell silent for a moment, and then shook her head. 'Perhaps we shouldn't have mentioned we were considering going to the police.'

'You think that man has the time to interfere with something like this? He's a school principal.'

'I saw that officer's face change when Gwen gave him Hector's name,' Eve disputed. 'I'd have thought they would be a little more understanding.'

'We can still press charges. They have Gwen's statement. All we have to do is make a call.'

Eve ran an unsteady hand through her hair. 'What should we do?'

Garan sighed. 'What are we pressing for here...? Believe me, I want to see this *basdun* get his comeuppance as much as you do, but you heard what they said. A misunderstood kiss. A house party. *Alcohol.* If the police had been more inclined to overlook certain particulars, then I would have said it would be worth it. But now I think it will only cause Gwen further upset.'

Gwenhwyfar jerked her eyes to her father, and watched his half-lit profile illuminate as the car passed under the streetlights lining the road.

'She's been through enough already. We don't want to give the police an excuse to put a magnifying glass over our lives—because that's what they'll do. Hector's lawyers will make sure of it.' For a short while they drove in silence. 'Though of course it's up to Gwenhwyfar.' Looking in the rear-view mirror, Garan offered her a stern frown. 'What do you think, cariad?'

She was conflicted. Despite her reluctance to talk to the police, once there she had been hopeful for their support. The more she had explained herself, however, the more their scorn had fledged into full-blown discouragement. She had thought the female officer might be the more understanding of the two, but ultimately her position had been the most unsympathetic, and had felt like a betrayal to their sex.

'You don't have to decide yet,' Eve prompted. 'We still have time.'

'Would we have to go to court?'

'Probably, yes.'

It wasn't hard to envisage how that would unfold. She suspected it would be much like Ravioli's questioning, but worse.

'I'm not sure. I mean, it was definitely worth trying, but like Dad says, it sounds like it wouldn't go anywhere.'

'We can't know that,' Eve objected.

'Yeah, he shouldn't have done it. Yes, it was horrible. I just—I really don't feel like having to convince a bunch of strangers that

I wasn't asking for it. Especially not when it's probably not going to result in anything, right?'

She looked to her parents. Eve's mouth hung open as she tried to find the right words. Garan's face was set like stone, his eyes far off at the end of the road.

'We don't know if it will result in anything,' her mother said, finally. 'But if you can face it, it's worth a try.'

'But that's just it. I don't know if I can *face it*. I mean, quite frankly, I have more important things to worry myself with. Like school, and not being told I'm a liar.'

Eve looked to Garan for protest, but found no support.

'I don't think it's worth it,' added Gwenhwyfar.

'*Garan.*'

'I'm sorry, but I think in this instance, Gwenhwyfar's right. Considering everything—and I don't say this lightly—it's just not worth pursuing.'

Gwenhwyfar could tell that her mother didn't agree, for she sat back violently and cast her gaze out of the window. For a moment Gwenhwyfar thought she was going to press her opinion further, but she said nothing.

'I think you've made the right choice, cariad.' Garan offered her a half-relieved smile. The car turned another corner and then the next left, and soon they were driving through the suburbs of Upper Well Street, closing in on their still-new home.

It was Wednesday evening when Gwenhwyfar was reminded of *Free Countries*.

She was sitting on her knees at her desk, huddled by her computer, when a small window popped up to fill the screen. Irritated, she clicked it away, but it followed her from page to page. Only when she looked properly did she realise that it wasn't just any pop up window. It was trying to say hello.

There was a small box in which she could key in words, like an old-fashioned messenger portal. When she failed to cross it away, the pop up box grew impatient.

Is anyone there?

She didn't know what to do. Her instincts told her to ignore it for fear it was a virus, but curiosity soon prevailed.

Who's this?

Nothing. She waited two minutes in apprehension, watching the clock tick by. Finally,

Free Countries. *Are you there?*

She faltered, considering.

Yes, I'm here.

We said we'd get in touch. Hope you don't mind.

How did you find me?

When you visited our page we made a note of your IP address. We noticed you were online. Not to worry, we severed the connection so your interaction with Free Countries cannot be traced.

Who is this?

I told you, Free Countries.

She considered turning the power off. As her finger crept closer to the restart button, text flashed up again.

If you're not interested in our cause, we'll leave you alone.

If you are, we'd like to meet.

Are you interested in working with Free Countries?

Panic flooded through her. Suddenly she felt as if she'd done something dangerous, that this was too suspicious. She pressed the power button before she could stop herself. Relief washed through her as her computer rebooted with a clear screen. Nervously Gwenhwyfar waited for a few moments and then opened up the Internet, just to be sure.

That wasn't very polite.

Her heart froze.

My computer crashed. Who are you?

I told you, Free Countries.

No, I mean, what's your name?

She waited while the pop up window digested her question. It seemed to chew it over for a while.

If you'd like to work with Free Countries, we can meet and I can give you more information.

Gwenhwyfar frowned.

I'm not meeting anyone unless you tell me your name.

More deliberation. She picked the last scraps of nail polish away from her thumb.

What is your name?

Isolde, the pop up box relented.

Really?

Yes, it's Celtic.

You're a girl?

Yes. I'm Irish.

Gwenhwyfar suddenly felt less threatened.

Are you interested in Free Countries?

She thought for a moment.

Yes. Where can we meet?

Is the park by Woodlands Road good for you?

She was unnerved that they knew her location in detail. Drawing another deep breath, she calmed herself. Public, she should meet her somewhere public.

Is there a coffee shop near by?

Yes. How about Saturday at one?

Sounds good.

What's your name?

Gwen.

Look out for me at one in Mocca Coffee. I've got light blonde hair and will be wearing a green coat. I look forward to seeing you, Gwen.

The conversation ended itself. Suddenly there was no sign of it ever happening at all.

For a while Gwenhwyfar continued to browse the Internet, making sure that there wasn't anything else. Was she crazy, doing something like this? She didn't even know if she agreed with *Free Countries*, but it sounded appealing to be part of a forbidden cause. Just to be safe she deleted her browser history, switching off her computer. It was just gone ten o' clock, not quite late enough for bed, and so taking a few moments to stretch, Gwenhwyfar made her way downstairs.

Her parents were watching the media station. She moved to sit in the armchair, stepping carefully over Llew, who gazed at her with rheumy eyes. There was a man on screen reporting world events with an emotionless expression. She glanced to her mother and father. They were both transfixed.

'What's going on?'

'You just missed the announcement,' her father said. 'George Milton is holding a general election next May.'

Gwenhwyfar tried to read his expression. 'Is that good?'

'It is. He was supposed to hold one last year. Parliament has to have one once every five years, or more often, depending on the Prime Minister's discretion,' he explained.

'So why didn't he hold one then?'

'The five year time limit of a parliament can be varied by something called an Act of Parliament. Milton extended his term by six months at first, but then increased it by another six. He claimed it was due to the financial crisis. We couldn't *afford* an election. Not that the New Nationals minded, of course, but there were plenty who did.'

Eve propped her head in her hand. 'Weren't there all those protests about it?'

'There was almost a civil war,' Garan corrected. 'He made a joke out of democracy.'

'That's right, I remember it being on the news.'

Gwenhwyfar frowned. 'When was it on the news?'

'Last summer. They clamped down on the protesters quite hard. It got nasty when someone died.'

'Who?'

Eve shrugged. 'I don't know, just some woman. A policeman hit her and she fell. I don't think it was his fault. She was just in the wrong place at the wrong time.'

'They were trying to kettle the crowd into too small a space,' Garan added, angered. 'It was completely their fault. What do they think is going to happen if they trap ten thousand people in Parliament Square? They'll panic, that's what. No wonder they turned violent.'

'They were only doing their job,' Eve huffed. 'You know that those boys they arrested had petrol bombs. They *intended* to hurt someone, police or not.'

'So they said,' Garan remarked. 'They also said that the woman was part of the group allegedly caught with the petrol bombs. They only backtracked when her family threatened to sue for libel.'

'*Fine*,' Eve snapped. 'You're right: it was the Met's fault. I mean, I don't know, do I? You're so *strident*.'

Quickly, Eve's gaze flicked back to the media station. The images changed again, and suddenly the newsreader was talking about the ongoing effects of the historical privatisation of the NHS. Gwenhwyfar bit the dry skin off her lower lip. It bled.

As the news turned to local headlines, she wished her parents goodnight and pulled herself up the stairs to get ready for bed. She'd never really followed world affairs before; her old life at Ysgol Annwfn had consisted of little more than worries over what to wear to each social event. Now that she found her eyes opening, however, she wondered if the world had always been so frightful. Sleep welcomed her slowly that night, bringing her unsettled visions that abated when she woke.

Quantum Models

The lights flickered, threatening them with another blackout. It was Thursday, so the Furies were back, and the next-door table was monopolised once again, a circus routine of all three girls applying make-up, ruffling their hair, checking their reflections, then repeating all the former; until at long last they concluded their beauty routine with the toxic spraying of deodorant under their shirts and the dousing of their wrists, legs and necks in perfume. Forty-four B was again filled with the smog of strong-smelling substances in the mornings. Gwenhwyfar hated it.

'This is giving me a headache,' Bedivere complained, sinking low to keep his head beneath the hanging cloud. 'I can barely breathe with that stuff in the air. It *stinks*.'

Gwenhwyfar looked across to the Furies. Word had spread about what had really happened the night of Tom's party, and as a result she now endured renewed whispering and rumour in times of recess. Charlotte gave Gwenhwyfar a sidelong glance that suggested she had heard Bedivere's complaint. 'How is it even allowed?' she whispered.

'It's not,' he murmured back. 'Miss Ray banned it ages ago, but she's stopped dealing out the detentions. They don't work, so she pretends not to notice.'

'How can anyone not notice this?'

'They'd all shrivel up without their smellies,' Viola declared loudly. 'I think she knows she'd be liable.' Smirking, she folded her arms and leant back in her chair. 'So have you spoken with Arthur?'

'Not since Tuesday.'

'And?'

'I didn't want to bring it up. He says they're just friends.' Gwenhwyfar looked over her shoulder, but Morgan wasn't at her desk yet. 'I don't know if I can say anything without seeming weird.'

'He *did* hide it from you,' Viola reminded her. 'Why didn't he mention it, if it was so innocent?'

'It was just an outing. It's not that weird, is it?'

'You seemed to think so on Monday,' Bedivere remarked.

'I've had time to think about it since then. Besides, she *knows* he likes me.'

'And he knows she likes him.' Viola's brown eyes settled on Gwenhwyfar. 'I don't care what he says, that's *weird*.'

Suddenly her resolve unravelled. 'It *is* weird, isn't it?' she fretted. 'I mean, who hangs out with someone that fancies them if they don't like them back?'

'I don't know why they're suddenly such great friends,' Bedivere muttered. 'Before you got here, Morgan followed me everywhere, yet when I was with Arthur she barely said more than two words to him.'

She scowled. 'So what am I supposed to do?'

Viola shrugged. 'Nothing. What can you do? Arthur says they're friends, so you'll just have to trust him. If he *does* like you, he'll soon forget about Morgan. When's your next lesson together?'

'Second period.' She now knew her timetable by heart. 'Science. Then History this afternoon.'

'Make sure you get to sit with him in Science, then,' Viola advised, her voice low. 'And make sure it's clear to Morgan how close you and Arthur are. She'll soon back off.'

'I think I can manage that,' Gwenhwyfar murmured. She turned her eyes to the door. Morgan came into the classroom with her tatty sketchbook pressed close to her chest. Gwenhwyfar felt no sympathy for the doe-eyed girl as she sat alone. Morgan clearly had a strong dislike for her. It was a mutual feeling, and once again Gwenhwyfar found herself wondering what on earth Arthur saw in Morgan other than a pretty face.

As she joined the queue outside her Science room, Arthur greeted her with a lavish smile.

'Gwen,' he expelled, uncrossing his arms. 'Is it still all right if we sit together?'

'Of course! If Mrs Paxton will let us get away with it. You know what she's like.'

He grinned boyishly. 'She won't mind. I think she likes me.'

The door was opened to grant them access to their lesson. 'So what are your plans for this weekend?' she teased. 'Any more secret trips with your stalker?'

'She's hardly a stalker, Gwen,' Arthur said as he followed her to her seat. 'Actually, she's quite nice. I think you'd like her, if you got to know her.'

'Well, that's not going to happen.' Gwenhwyfar slipped her bag off her shoulders and pulled out her exercise book. 'She hasn't said a word to me since I started here. Or haven't you noticed?'

'I don't think that's true,' he frowned. 'She's probably just shy.'

'Being shy is no excuse for being rude,' she said, unzipping her pencil case. She offered a good-natured smile. 'I'd be perfectly happy to talk to Morgan. I'm not the one ignoring her.'

Arthur watched her surreptitiously. Gwenhwyfar waved her arm and expelled half a laugh.

'All right, you just wait until History, and you'll see. When has she *ever* done anything but hiss at me?'

'I just don't understand it,' Arthur said. 'She's perfectly nice to me.'

'Of course she's nice to you,' Gwenhwyfar replied, writing out the date. 'You're a boy. She's clearly one of *those girls*.'

'Which girls?'

'You know, the ones that are nice as pie to anything male, and that turn into a harpy the moment they're on their own with something with any form of *ovaries*.'

'I don't know about that.' He dropped his bag on the floor. 'But no, I'm *not* going on some secret outing with her. I only didn't tell you about last weekend because I thought it wasn't important.'

'I know.' She shrugged. 'It's not. Really, I don't care who you hang out with. I just thought that when you said you weren't going out with her, you weren't going out with her. In whatever context.'

His jovial demeanour collapsed. 'And that was my fault, I know. I should have mentioned it. Sorry.' Gwenhwyfar felt a flare of inward irritation, and she hated herself for bringing it up.

'Look, I don't particularly want to talk about Morgan all lesson, do you? If you say you're just friends, you're just friends. I trust you.' She sent him a winning smile. 'So what *are* you doing this weekend?'

'I have a Saturday shift at the library. Then I'm spending Sunday with my grandmother. You?'

Her mind jumped to *Free Countries* and immediately her pulse quickened. 'Just meeting a friend,' she lied. 'We're going shopping.'

Mrs Paxton silenced the class with the clap of a wooden ruler against her desk. Her grey eyes honed in on Arthur and immediately she asked him to move. Gwenhwyfar sent him an apologetic smile as he ambled back to the front of the classroom, quietly and without protest.

He waited for her once the bell rang, and together they came out into the corridor.

'So where are you off to now?' she asked, moving closer as they streamed with the crowd, at a pace that annoyed others.

'Marvin's.' His palm brushed the small of her back as he guided her through the masses. 'You?'

'Cafeteria,' she called up to him. 'To sit with Vi. Want to join us?'

He shook his head. 'I can't.' He seemed to sense her disappointment. 'I'll walk you there though, if you like?'

'Sure.'

Though the sun shone outside, the cold wind sapped all warmth from the pale rays and left her fellow pupils shivering in inadequate coats. They made their way down from Wormelow in silence, and stopped together just outside the canteen on the cut grass, which lay a good distance from the congested doors.

'So I'll see you in History?'

'Of course.' He stood a little closer. 'Maybe… if we're not so busy next weekend… we could hang out, or something?'

'Or something…?'

'You know, go out together… go and do something.'

She smiled up at him. 'Are you asking me out?'

Immediately he coloured. Saving him from the embarrassment of trying to formulate a response, she stepped towards him and clasped his hands gently.

'I'd love to. We'll work something out?'

A pleased grin split across his lips. 'Sounds good.'

'Want my number?'

They fumbled for their phones. 'Thanks,' he murmured, once he had it. Gwenhwyfar looked up at him, reluctant to go.

'I'll see you later?' He nodded. Standing on her tiptoes, she cupped his neck and planted a feather-light kiss upon his cheek. A group of boys saw it and ambled by, whooping. As Gwenhwyfar blushed Arthur did too.

'I'll see you later,' he promised, half-stunned by the gesture. Eventually they parted, and his eyes shadowed her until she found her way through the throng and into the cafeteria.

Her friends were all sitting at their usual table. Lancelot was there too, and looked just as moody as he had been the day before. Since first meeting him on Monday, he had thawed very little towards her.

Gwenhwyfar scoured the crowd as she joined them. Hector was nowhere to be seen, despite the fact his suspension ended today. 'Everyone all right?' There were varying positive noises, and a grunt from Lancelot.

'Viola was just showing us her pictures from Saturday,' Tom announced. Before the couple sat a smart-looking folder.

'I was going to show you this morning,' Viola added. 'I went into the agency after school to pick them up. I'll be on the website soon.'

'Can I see?' Gwenhwyfar reached for the portfolio. It was heavy with a soft, matte cover. The letters QMS were embossed in the middle. She opened it. 'Oh Viola, these are gorgeous!' she exclaimed. Her friend took the compliment in silence, while everyone around her craned their necks for a second look. 'Your hair looks amazing… I'm so jealous!'

'Me too,' Gavin said, and everyone laughed.

She turned the page and studied the second and third picture with just as much awe. The portfolio was empty after that, but Gwenhwyfar could tell that Viola, along with everyone at the table, was made proud by the content.

'You'll go far, I think,' she encouraged, closing it carefully and handing it back to her. 'I wish I could be a model.'

'I think you could be, if they didn't have this silly height restriction. One of the girls at the agency told me that her friend was dropped for being too short. She was fourteen when she started, so her agency thought she'd grow. When she didn't, they stopped promoting her effectively. That was after they told her to quit school to model full time.'

Tom's face contorted. 'That's a bit unfair.'

Viola shrugged. 'That's the industry.'

'Did your agency do that?' Gwenhwyfar asked, thinking that perhaps modelling wasn't for her after all.

'No,' Viola said, clutching her book to her chest. 'That was *Fashion First*. She couldn't find work with other agencies after that. She was too short, and too old.'

'How old was she?' Gavin enquired.

'Nineteen.'

'I thought you were going to say thirty, or so,' he confessed.

'Not that thirty's exactly retirement age,' Lancelot snorted. They all looked to him. It was the first contribution he'd made in days.

'I suppose they prefer working with girls when they're younger and thinner,' Gwenhwyfar theorised.

'Only because most of them haven't finished puberty yet.' Viola stowed her portfolio away. Gwenhwyfar was beginning to play over her arrangement on Saturday. She was experiencing second thoughts.

'Do any of you know anything about a group called *Free Countries*? I got a flyer about it in the post the other day.'

'I think I've had one of those before,' Bedivere confessed. 'I usually just throw them away.'

'Apparently they have a website.'

'They do?'

'Yep! That's what I've heard, at least.'

'I heard they were some extremist organisation,' Tom remarked. 'Apparently they were involved in the rioting the night of my party. Did you hear about that?'

'Yeah, I was there,' Gwenhwyfar reminded him.

'I don't think they were involved in the riots,' Gavin said. 'All I know about them is that they're some kind of collective that's completely anti-Milton.' He frowned. 'I don't think I've ever heard of them *doing* anything.'

'We probably shouldn't be talking about them really,' Bedivere said, half-jokingly. 'What if we're overheard by a spy?'

'A spy?' Gwenhwyfar asked.

'Yeah, you know how the government likes people to inform for them. I hear they like the young.'

'Usually it's the farter who first smells the fart,' Tom mused. 'Like the spy who suggests there's a spy.'

Bedivere laughed. 'Me? Funny, Tom.'

'Why do you want to know about *Free Countries*, anyway?' Lancelot was quite handsome when he wasn't scowling. Finding that suddenly they were locked in each other's stare, Gwenhwyfar shrugged uncomfortably.

'I was just curious. We *did* get a flyer through the door. I don't want the police thinking our house is radical.'

'They shouldn't,' Bedivere shrugged, 'I mean, everyone has the right to free speech, don't they?'

The blare of the cafeteria seemed to amplify. 'Hypothetically,' Lancelot muttered.

Curiously Gwenhwyfar observed him, wondering what he meant.

'Gwen! Supper!'

The call was sharp and impatient. Frowning, Gwenhwyfar abandoned her half-finished Maths homework and hurried down the stairs. Her parents were already at the dining table as she joined them, her father still on his feet, helping her mother to dish up.

'You should've called me,' he was saying, as he took the plates off the side and dumped them on the large kitchen table. 'You shouldn't have let them in.'

'What was I supposed to do?' Eve snapped, her cheeks burnished. 'They had a *warrant*, Garan. I couldn't very well send them away.'

'Any Tom, Dick or Harry can print a false document like that and pretend it's legitimate,' he said, slamming the salt and pepper down as Eve carefully put out Gwenhwyfar's supper. 'How did you know they weren't going to take something? They could've hurt you. Did you not think of that?'

'What's this?' Gwenhwyfar asked, sitting down.

'Your foolish mother didn't think twice about letting two policemen into the house, that's what,' he snapped. Eve's lips pursed shut in anger. 'And with that attack on that woman that happened last week, too! Did you not *think*?'

'I *told* you, I called the local police station before I let either of them past the threshold,' she retorted, her eyes blazing. 'I'm not an idiot, Garan! I checked their registration numbers—they were *happy* for me to. They even *encouraged* it.'

'The police were here?' Adrenaline bolted through Gwenhwyfar. 'Why?'

Her question only seemed to incense her father further. 'To search the property, that's why. I can't even *begin* to get my head around that one. What were they looking for? What did they take?'

'They didn't *take* anything.'

'Did you let them into my office?'

'Of course I did!' she exclaimed. 'They had a warrant. How many times do I have to say it?'

'You'd think they'd have more important things to do,' Garan hissed, livid. 'Like arresting sexual predators.'

Gwenhwyfar looked to her mother. 'Why did they have a

warrant?'

'That's what I want to know.' Garan cut into his supper, forked a mountain of it into his mouth, and chewed noisily. 'What in God's name could they be looking for? We've just moved in, for Christ's sake!'

Eve snatched up her glass of water. 'It's nothing *we've* done,' she insisted. 'Milton's introduced spot checks on residents new to an area. It's the government's way of tackling housing of illegals and the homeless. It seemed perfectly standard.'

'Standard?' Garan repeated, appalled. 'Standard my arse! They probably singled us out because we're Welsh,' he bit, his face distorting to an angry sneer. 'That house opposite us has just been sold. I'll bet whoever's bought it won't be receiving a "spot check" when they move in.'

Eve's cutlery clattered as she dropped it onto her plate. 'I'm not Welsh,' she argued, 'as your mother always liked to remind me. Nationality has nothing to do with it. I think it's good that the police are checking up on who is moving into the area. For all we know there could be six terrorists next door plotting to blow something up.'

'Such people know how to avoid getting caught,' Garan countered. 'At the end of the day it only impacts the average citizen. *Me. You.*' Suddenly he leant forward, urgency in his eyes. 'You didn't let them out of your sight, did you? Tell me you didn't do that.'

'Why?' Eve's eyebrows arched. 'Have you got something to hide?'

'Of course I haven't,' he grumbled. His back snapped straight. 'It's *outrageous*, can't you see it? It's a massive invasion of privacy! They have time to search our house but they can't be bothered to look out for our daughter? For all we know they've bugged us.'

'I told you—I didn't let them out of my sight! They barely touched anything. They had a sweeping look around each room, and were mostly interested in the attic and the cellar. They were just checking for illegals.'

'What were they going to do with them if they found them, exactly?'

'I don't know! Send them off to Hastings? Isn't that where they all go? With the asylum seekers before they get shipped back home?'

Gwenhwyfar swallowed the mouthful she had been chewing, and looked to her mother. 'They didn't touch anything in my room, did they?'

'No, they just had a look. They left after ten minutes, even warned me of burglars operating in the area. It was legitimate, one hundred percent.' She fired a glance at Garan. 'So I'd appreciate it if you didn't treat me like I'm some kind of idiot.'

'I'm not treating you like an idiot,' he insisted. 'I'm just alarmed. I had no idea this was happening. I mean, when did that start?'

'Last year, apparently.'

'I suppose we wouldn't have known, would we?' He offered them both an apologetic smile. 'I'm sorry. I just wish I had been here. I feel like my home has been violated.'

In the quiet that followed the argument dissolved, and suddenly it was as if he hadn't lost his temper at all. He asked Gwenhwyfar how her day had been, to which she answered the usual 'fine', with a bit of information about teachers and her homework. Soon they were eating in silence again, interrupted by a low grumble from Llew.

Eve put her fork down. 'I'm not sure if it's anything to worry about, but I went to the market earlier. Usually on my way I run into that little boy—do you remember? The one with the rotting teeth—but today he wasn't there.'

'I can't imagine that he's there every day, is he?' said Garan.

'But that's the thing, I've taken to buying him soup. I always see him without fail at the exact same time each weekday. Last time he brought his sister.' Eve caught the disapproval in Garan's eyes, and scowled. 'It's only soup, Garan.'

'If you get caught—'

'He's a *child*. I know you're not supposed to give them anything, but it's not like it's money. Olivia Rose is always giving them money.'

'Maybe he's moved to a different area?' Gwenhwyfar suggested, battling with the urge to check her computer, just to be sure that the police definitely hadn't interfered with it.

'I'm sure he'll turn up,' Garan remarked through a quick smile. 'Really Eve, you're too kind for your own good. You shouldn't feed them. What if we go on holiday? He'll become reliant on you.'

'He's not a wild animal,' Eve reminded him sharply. 'What was I supposed to do, ignore it? Let him starve?'

'You'll be wanting to bring him home, next. He has parents.'

'How do you know?'

'Like I said—'

'It's a scam, right. I see him every day. I was considering calling social services, for him and his sister.'

'If you think it will help.' There was a long silence. Eve stiffly rose to clear the plates. Gwenhwyfar stood to lend a hand.

'I'm sure he'll turn up, Mam. Maybe social services have

picked him up already?'

'I would have liked to have known about it,' Eve said. Smiling, she shook her head, and turned the taps on full blast. 'Never mind. I just thought it was odd, that's all. He's probably just found someone who buys him sweets instead.'

Gwenhwyfar put the condiments back in the cupboard. The legs of Garan's chair scraped across the floor. Garan kneed his way past Llew, who was hovering for scraps. 'I'm going to check my office,' he declared, stalking out of the room. Gwenhwyfar looked to her mother, who offered a sympathetic shrug.

'He's just stressed,' she excused. 'Work's a bit hectic for him at the moment. He'll be back to his old self in no time, I'm sure.'

Gwenhwyfar hoped so. There wasn't an evening since they moved here that hadn't involved some sort of spat between her parents. Most of it was passive-aggressive, but it was draining, and she didn't know how to rectify it or why it was suddenly a continuing problem.

French had traditionally been a lonely affair until Lancelot returned to school, and unfortunately for Gwenhwyfar the empty table she had chosen to sit at just so happened to be his. It was Friday, and encouraged by the last few break times she had decided to try and get to know him a little better. Finding a topic he didn't immediately explode over was difficult, and whenever she did his responses were either venomous quips or amounted to Neolithic grunts.

They were sharing a textbook, attempting to translate sentences such as *J'ai un stylo rouge* and *Où est la piscine, s'il vous plaît?* when Lancelot finally asked her something without being prompted. Taken aback, Gwenhwyfar had to ask him to repeat it.

He huffed at her. 'I said, how did you become friends with Gavin and Vi?'

She wasn't certain if this was curiosity, or a jibe. 'I don't know really,' she admitted. 'It just sort of happened.'

'Was it after that party?' Lancelot enquired, staring intently at his exercise book.

Nodding, Gwenhwyfar abandoned her pen. 'They helped me fend off Hector.' Maybe he just took longer than the average person to adjust, she mused. She studied his profile, suddenly noticing the rich chestnut spun throughout his curling hair. Her prolonged gazes were becoming an unconscious habit. 'I'm sorry if you think I've hijacked all your friends while you were gone or something, but it really wasn't like that. They're just nice people.' She had been expecting a snarl, but instead he shrugged. 'So how long have you known them?'

'I've known Gavin since primary school. He wants me to join the Royal Marines with him when we graduate.'

'Really?' She was surprised to think Gavin would be interested in such a path, and the idea of Lancelot obeying any rules seemed far-fetched. 'Don't you want to go to university?'

'Not everyone can afford to go,' he snapped, his shoulders hunching. 'Though I suppose you can. You look like you've got rich parents.'

He'd fired it out like it was an insult. 'What do you mean?'

'I mean you look like you've got rich parents,' he repeated, his dark eyebrows knotting.

'They're not *that* rich,' she objected, suddenly feeling as if she had to apologise.

He snorted again. 'You have to be rich to have ended up hanging out with Emily and Charlotte. They're like metal detectors.'

'Don't be such a snob.' She picked up her pen to resume the translating activity.

'I'm not a snob,' he disagreed. 'Only rich people can be snobs.'

'Is that why you're so grouchy all the time? Because you're not a snob and you don't have rich parents?'

The space around him seemed to darken, and lightning sparked through his eyes. Sensing she'd gone too far, Gwenhwyfar found she couldn't correct herself because she didn't know how. She waited for the onslaught, but none came. For a while she enjoyed Lancelot's silence, but eventually the tension buzzing within him was just too taut to ignore.

'Sorry,' was her eventual attempt, 'I didn't mean to upset you.'

'I'm not upset.'

'Even so, I'm still sorry,' she pursued.

'So what?' Lancelot scribbled in each rectangle in the margin of his exercise book. His hiss was enough to convince her to leave it, so she resumed her schoolwork. She moved on to something more challenging, French poems they weren't supposed to be examining until next year. The final word of one sentence eluded her. As Lancelot sat brooding beside her, she repeated it in her head methodically.

L'ombre se transforme en nuit, et de la nuit à la poussière.

The Round Table

Arthur had never seen anything like it.

It was a small town house, pocketed away at the end of a long road, tall in stature and deceptively thin. It wasn't the exterior that had him wondering, however, it was Marvin's apparent obsession with unusual things. The walls were cluttered from floor to ceiling with them.

Arthur guessed that at some point in his life, Marvin had travelled extensively. Exotic pots, carvings, wind chimes, musical instruments and obsolete weapons covered the walls, interrupted by the odd oil painting. The unpolished floor groaned beneath their feet as they moved deeper into the house. Overlooking the staircase was the head of a great stag, grey with age.

'That's Rudolph,' Marvin explained as he took Arthur's coat. 'My great-great-grandfather shot him sometime in the 1930s. I should dust him, really, but I like that he looks his age.'

Marvin left Arthur to hang his coat out of sight. Noticing an old photograph by one of the closed doors, Arthur bent down to inspect it, realising that it was of Marvin in his early twenties.

Next to him was another man similar in age and stature.

'The others should be here soon, no doubt.' Marvin reappeared from the closet, and clapped his hands together. 'Let me show you around. I was thinking of using the study. What do you think? Will it do?'

It wasn't the biggest room of the house, but Arthur suspected it might have been, had the walls not been lined from floor to ceiling with books. Most of them were coated in thick dust, but a few had recently been read.

'I think this is where we'll sit,' Marvin said, circling the room excitably. 'I have to say that I'm rather nervous. I just hope the others will find it as interesting as you do, Arthur. Would you like a drink?'

He nodded dumbly, and was surprised when Marvin unlatched a compartment in the bookcase. Inside was an old bottle with several glasses.

'What's that?'

'This? Oh, this is where I keep my consumables,' Marvin grinned. He took out a corkscrew, and placed the bottle on the round, polished table. 'Have you ever had wine before, Arthur?'

'Once,' he admitted. He picked the bottle up with interest, wiping the grain-like sawdust away to clear the label. 'Where did you get it?'

'The black market.' Marvin closed the hatch in the bookcase and commandeered the wine. 'This particular label is my favourite. It's too expensive to drink on a regular basis, so I save it for special occasions. It used to be abundant on the market but the drought and dry winds of 'forty-eight damaged Europe's wine supplies. Now most of it goes to parliament, and what little is left to be sold on the sly has more than tripled in price.' The cork popped as it came struggling out of the bottleneck. Once the glasses were dusted, Marvin poured Arthur a small taster. 'I know you're not legally allowed to drink until you're twenty-five, but I thought this would be a good way to start our sessions. To demonstrate to you what else is being forgotten.'

The doorbell rang. Marvin shoved the bottle into Arthur's hands. 'Ah! Squirrel this away if that's not our other two members, would you?' He hurried to answer the door. Curiously, Arthur read the date on the label. *France, 2021*. His nose hovered over the neck, and he inhaled. The smell was overpowering, but that was to be expected for something that was thirty-one years old.

'Come in, come in. I was just telling Arthur about enjoying things long forgotten. Would you both like some?' He hurried to the glasses, and reclaimed the bottle.

'You mean that's *actual* wine?' Bedivere seemed more eager than Morgan, who hung back, afraid of doing something wrong.

'Yes, it's *actual* wine, one of the many things being withheld by Milton. I suppose you've never heard of his particular weakness for French red?'

The burgundy liquid glugged into each glass, and Morgan and Bedivere received them tentatively.

'No, no I haven't,' Arthur grinned. He smelt it again, and found it was less potent than before.

'We should have a toast.' They all looked to Marvin and mirrored the raising of his glass. 'To truth, and knowledge.'

They murmured the words uncomfortably, waiting for their cue to drink. Bedivere coughed, and Arthur winced. Morgan screwed up her face then raised her glass again to discreetly spit it back out.

'It does take some getting used to, freedom. I believe it is an acquired taste, one that develops the more you're subjected to it.' Marvin sat, his pale eyes scanning across the nearly empty table. 'Before we begin, we should decide on a name. Are there any suggestions?'

No one wanted to go first. Morgan stared at the books opposite, and Bedivere swirled his glass.

'Arthur! You're usually the first to come up with such things,' Marvin tried. 'Have you thought of any possibilities?'

Arthur racked his brain, concentrating on his little-used creativity to try and think of something witty. '*History Club?*' he eventually shrugged. Morgan looked at him, and smirked.

'We can do better than that. Anyone else?'

Encouraged, Bedivere cleared his throat. 'How about *Marvin's Maniacs?*'

'Clever, very clever… though I don't think that's quite appropriate, do you, Bedivere?'

Morgan's eyes rose up to meet Arthur's. 'How about… how about *Round Table?*'

'Round Table Club?' Bedivere questioned, not getting it.

'No: *The* Round Table. We'd say; we have another meeting with *The Round Table.*'

Marvin seemed pleased.

'Well, the table is round,' Morgan pointed out.

'How about *Tabula Rotunda*, to make it less obvious?' Steeling himself, Arthur took another sip of his wine.

'*Tabula Rotunda* could work. A bit of Latin never hurts.'

Morgan looked to Marvin. 'But it's too hard to pronounce. Why not just stick with *The Round Table*? No one will know what we're talking about, anyway.'

'We should have a vote,' Arthur insisted.

'A vote! Ah yes, our first attempt at democracy. All in favour of *The Round Table*?'

Bedivere and Morgan both raised their hands.

'All in favour of *Tabula Rotunda*?'

Marvin and Arthur raised their hands. The others looked displeased.

'Well, that's no good.' Bedivere dipped his finger in the warm wine, tasting it on his lips. 'So much for democracy.'

'This won't do,' murmured Marvin, scraping his scalp with blunt, bitten nails. 'Won't someone relent?'

Silence ensued. All eyes looked to one another, Morgan adamant, Bedivere shy. Eventually Arthur gave in. 'I suppose *The Round Table* will do,' he muttered, irked. Marvin beamed.

'That's settled then. Now, I thought we'd begin with the darker side of human cloning—there are longstanding rumours that Asia and the States have been using clone technology to test biological weapons. Or we could look at the politics of Milton's party, and those preceding it. Arthur's been reading a rather interesting book on surveillance. *1984* is a good one too—you must have heard of that.'

Arthur was the only one who didn't look at him blankly.

'Well, I have a copy of it upstairs somewhere. If you give me a moment I'll go and fetch it. That can be your homework for this week: reading.'

As Marvin vacated the room, Arthur took another sip from his glass, savouring the taste. The burning of the alcohol no longer seemed so intense. Bedivere surveyed the towering books, his eyes wide with wonder.

'Where did he get all of this stuff?' he whispered. 'Do you

know?'

Arthur shook his head, and sucked the wine off his bottom lip. 'I didn't get the chance to ask. He must have got most of it abroad.'

'He can't have gone to each country to get each thing he has,' Bedivere contested, frowning. He strained to get a peek of the littered hallway.

'It would be impressive if he had,' Arthur said. 'I'm pretty sure that a stuffed duck-billed platypus isn't allowed to leave Australia.'

'Where was that?' Bedivere asked quietly.

'By the stairs.'

He leant back in his chair. 'He must have bought it somewhere,' he concluded.

'Maybe they're all antiques? The stag belonged to his great-great-grandfather, but I don't know about the bison skull. It's not like the US will just let anyone in, and if you get a travel visa they make sure you only leave with what you came in with.'

'I didn't see that either,' complained Bedivere.

'It was by Rudolph,' Arthur remarked, his eyes trailing the wall of books behind his friend. 'It was on a plaque with an American flag, so I'm assuming it was a bison.'

'What is a bison, anyway?'

'You know, a buffalo.'

Morgan was being quiet. Arthur had listened in on her interaction with Gwenhwyfar in History yesterday afternoon, and though he had heard Gwenhwyfar make countless attempts to strike up conversation, the effort had indeed been wholly one-sided, a point he'd had to yield to today during Science. 'Are you all right?'

She nodded, her long fingers tightly wound around the stem of her wineglass.

'You should drink that, you know. Marvin says it's expensive.'

'But I don't like it,' she murmured, her cheeks pink. She looked to the door apprehensively. 'Can't one of you just down it? I don't want to seem rude.'

'Drink it then,' Bedivere said. 'I saw you spit back out into it.'

'Excuse me if I'm not comfortable with my History teacher getting me drunk.' He rolled his eyes. Morgan retaliated by pulling a face. Her gaze then settled on Arthur. 'Do you want it?' she whispered.

'Not particularly,' he frowned.

'Please?'

Arthur looked to Bedivere. 'You really can't just drink it?' She shook her head. Roughly, and a little irritated, he sighed. 'Fine. Give it here, then. If I must.'

Bedivere made a face as Arthur gulped it down, coughing and spluttering as some of it went the wrong way. 'Backwash,' Bedivere said with a sound of disgust.

'It's not like I've *got* anything,' Morgan hissed at him. Arthur slid the glass back across the table. As she took it off him, their fingers touched. He withdrew his hand sharply. 'Besides, I can't stay long,' she added. 'I have an exam tonight.'

'You do? For what?'

'Singing,' she replied, looking to Bedivere with her arms firmly crossed. 'So *wine* is the last thing I need right now. I should be practising.'

Faint thuds and footsteps could be heard from the rooms upstairs. It was already dark outside, and Marvin had long since closed the heavy, Victorian-style curtains that were decorated with the antique designs of William Morris.

'Go then, if you're so worried. Arthur and I will finish the wine, won't we, Arthur?'

He felt he'd already had too much as it was, and said so, only the words seemed to tumble out of his mouth like drunken acrobats. His next sip went down more easily. Bedivere looked up at the ceiling at another mighty thud.

'What's taking him so long?'

'Maybe we should go and check?' Arthur suggested, though he made no effort to rise. Shortly footsteps sounded back down the stairs, and Marvin was with them again, looking flushed.

'Sorry about that,' he apologised. 'I found one copy but the other wasn't where I left it.' He gave one each to Bedivere and Morgan. 'Ah! Finished already, I see?' He picked up Morgan's glass. 'Would you like some more?'

'Actually, I think Morgan's had enough,' Arthur announced, when he realised she wasn't going to object. 'She's got an exam, later.'

'An exam?' Marvin looked to her with interest. 'Is this for your singing?'

Morgan nodded. 'I have to leave early, I'm afraid. I can't be late.'

'A shame! Let's not waste any more time, then.' He frowned at Arthur's empty hands. 'What am I going to give you? *Animal Farm*, perhaps?'

'I've already read it,' Arthur confessed. 'I felt particularly sorry for Boxer.'

'As did I,' Marvin remarked. 'But I trust you're still on the other read I lent you?' Arthur nodded. 'Well, perhaps you can keep going with that. Or refresh yourself with *1984* instead. We'll be discussing it next week.'

'You mean we have to finish this in a *week*?' Bedivere asked, flicking through the discoloured pages.

'It's only a book,' Morgan told him. 'I could read it in an evening.'

'Now!' Marvin interjected. 'You must all be wondering why I invited you here. Well, you know why you're here, Arthur; and I assume you've explained a little about the club to our members—'

'We're looking at alternative truths, right?' Bedivere asked. 'The darker side to Britain, and all that.'

'Yes, yes, Bedivere, we shall cover that. We shall look at Europe, why we left and why ultimately the EU was disbanded; we shall look at the tragic situation in the United States, and we shall look at the abandonment of the Commonwealth states and the blight of Indonesia. But as well as that we shall also be looking closer to home, at our own histories, and I use the plural intentionally; at the rising rebels in the old Celtic countries, at the redefinition of New National Britain's borders, and at our absolute ruler himself, George Milton, who thus far has used all his electoral power to claw hold of democratic immunity, whose Party has long since been a change-hand, change-face game of musical chairs with the same policies and people from one party to the next. This brings me to my former point of why I invited you here: because I believe that you three are the smartest, the most open, the most questioning, and that you will benefit most from hearing things from an alternative viewpoint—not always my own, and not always comfortable—that the three of you may one day take what you have learned here and remember it when the world darkens, and this country truly forgets that which it once was.'

There was a deep silence. Even Arthur, who was used to Marvin's tangential speeches, was momentarily confounded, and in the quiet that followed he observed Bedivere to see what he thought of this side to their teacher. His eyes then slipped to Morgan, and he was surprised to find that she was transfixed.

'But I must stress to all of you, it is my job at risk in doing this, my life at stake. So when you speak of this, speak only amongst yourselves, and tell no one what it is we discuss here. Understood?'

There was a series of dumbstruck nods of consent. Bedivere cleared his throat with a small cough.

'And here I thought this was just going to be an extracurricular History club,' he joked.

Morgan's phone beeped. She jumped to her feet and looked to Marvin apologetically. 'Sorry, I have to go. Are we still doing this next week?'

Marvin nodded. 'If you're willing to come.'

'I'll be here.'

He grinned at her, and followed her out of the room to fetch her coat. Bedivere left soon after, and then it was just Arthur, watching the clock apprehensively and mindful of his need to get home.

'I don't think Morgan took to the wine, do you?' Marvin remarked, as he rejoined Arthur at the depleted table. There were twelve seats, ten of which now sat empty, though most of the chairs were squashed together in a space which was definitely too small. 'I suppose it could be quite distressing to be encouraged to break the law, but I didn't really think of it at the time. Do you think she minds?'

'I think she was just concerned about holding a sober slur for her music exam,' Arthur grinned, rubbing the brim of his empty glass with his thumb. 'I don't think she took to the taste, either.'

'I did say that it takes some getting used to.' Leaning back into the soft leather of his chair, Marvin cradled his wine in his palm. 'I think we wasted most of our time coming up with *The Round Table*. So how are you finding *The Human Condition*?'

'Good. I'm not reading it in the right order, though. I'm on the chapter exploring the need for social hierarchies at the moment.'

'Ah yes, that's a good one,' Marvin reminisced. Suddenly he leant towards Arthur and set his drink aside. 'Now, before you go, I was hoping to gauge your interest in something. Do you remember that conversation we had before the summer holidays? When you asked about going into politics?'

Arthur nodded.

'There's an emerging political party that's looking for people to join: young applicants in particular. They're too small for the current government to worry about.' He got to his feet and went to the desk in the corner of the room, which was surrounded by stacks of boxes and files. 'Their policies are relatively safe. It'll be a good thing to have on your record, especially if you're still thinking of applying for a scholarship.' He scribbled something down and passed it to him. 'All you have to do is hand out leaflets and get to know the people higher up. You'll have to complete voluntary service for the New Nationals, to counter your unfriendly interest, but if you're keen you can then apply to be a prospective parliamentary candidate.'

Arthur took the paper from him and read Marvin's messy handwriting as best he could. It read, *The Eco Party*.

'The hours are flexible—you could even do a couple at the weekend. I'll help you if you get stuck, but I think it's worth you looking into.'

'Thanks, Marv.'

'Please. Merlin.'

'Merlin,' he corrected, crumpling the note into his pocket. He looked at the clock once again, and this time Marvin did too.

'We've run over our hour!' he exclaimed, immediately clearing away the glasses. Rising to help, Arthur followed Marvin into the kitchen. 'Give your regards to your grandmother for me, would you? Will you be coming next week?'

'Of course.' Arthur smiled. Marvin led him into the hall and then vanished to retrieve his coat. 'This stuff, Merlin… where did you get it all from?'

'These? Abroad, mostly. I travelled in my younger years, but most of it belonged to my father and grandfather. They were much bigger explorers at heart than me.' His face stretched into another crooked smile as he helped Arthur into his sleeves. 'This is a greatcoat, unless I'm mistaken.'

'It was my grandfather's,' Arthur responded with some pride. 'He left it to me when he died. It's been in the family for years.'

'It must be ancient,' Marvin admired, enthused.

'It was never really worn before he got it. Between us we've had it repaired dozens of times.' He looked down at the old, woollen green. Marvin unlatched the door.

'Thank you for coming tonight, Arthur. Do you think our first session went well, all things considered?'

'I think it was very interesting,' he said, even though he had learnt little. 'I'm sure we'll get down to things next Friday.'

The two exchanged their farewells. Marvin stood waiting at

his doorstep until Arthur had disappeared from sight, his oversized greatcoat billowing behind him in the gloom.

The house greeted him in the cold, its windows gazing out into the dark with open lids. The lights were on, and as he closed the front door he heard sounds in the kitchen.

'Arthur! Is that you?'

His grandmother appeared in the doorframe, her lilac jumper rolled up to her elbows and her slim jeans muddied at the knees. Her clothes were never age-appropriate for a seventy-two year old; they were worn for practicality's sake, for digging in the garden, for working on her jewellery and for the Alexander Technique, which she no longer taught. Her hair was dyed red with home-dye kits, and her nose was proud and not like his at all. She came towards him with her arms extended and kissed him on the cheek.

'How was it? You must tell me how it was. How is Bedivere? Did he like the club?'

He took off his coat and hung it on the stand. 'He did, and he's fine. The club was good. We talked about books,' he added, thinking it was mostly true. 'I invited Morgan, too. Do you remember Morgan?'

'Of course I remember Morgan!' She led him into the kitchen. 'She's the blonde girl, isn't she? The one you had a crush on last summer?'

'No, that was Catherine. Morgan's got brown hair. She's interested in books, too.'

She frowned at him. 'What's her surname?'

'Faye.'

'I'm sure she was blonde.'

He could smell smoke. 'You've left the hob on.' Arthur hurried over to the stove and snatched up the smouldering wooden spoon. 'What did you have the hob on for?'

'I had to cook, didn't I?' his grandmother snapped. He ran the cold tap to cool the wood. 'Have you eaten? I made lasagne earlier, just for you.'

'You shouldn't have made anything,' he said, turning off the tap and drying the spoon. 'There's food in the fridge so you don't have to cook.'

'I like cooking,' she objected. She went to busy herself at the kitchen counter. 'I'll make you some tea.' Hissing, she retracted her hand from the stove. 'Why is that thing on?'

'What did you do?' Arthur said, rushing over to her.

'It's nothing.' She waved her hand away. 'It's fine.'

'It's not fine—you've burnt yourself. Are you all right?'

'I'm fine! Really.' She yanked her hand away from him when he tried to inspect it. 'Don't fuss.'

'Run it under the cold tap,' insisted Arthur, turning it on again.

'I know what to do.' She stuck her hand under the water willingly, and kept it there.

'I'll heat up that lasagne. Would you like some?'

'I already had some. Honestly, I don't know why you're making such a fuss. It only took five minutes.' She turned the tap off, dried her hands, and went to peer out the back window. 'Damn cat scared off the woodpecker this morning,' she muttered. 'It's such a beast. It's left three heads on the kitchen floor this week. I'd kick it out, if your grandfather hadn't loved it so much.'

'He needs a bell,' Arthur said for the hundredth time. 'I can buy him one, if you like.'

'And have him tinkling about the house all day? It'd drive me mad.'

'Are you sure you're not hungry?' he asked again. 'I can warm you some up anyway, just in case.'

'All right then,' she relented.

Relieved, Arthur hunted in the fridge for what she had made, finding that though she had cooked a lasagne, she hadn't eaten any of it at all. He pushed it into the oven, grateful that they had power. 'So where is Lionel?'

'Outside. I haven't seen him all day.' She frowned at him, waiting for the kettle to boil. 'How was the library? You don't have to work, you know. I can give you money if you need it. Where's my wallet?' Searching her surroundings, she found it on the kitchen table and pulled out an old, crumpled note. 'Here, you must take it. No Arthur, I insist. Go on.'

Reluctantly, but with a grateful smile, Arthur folded the ten new-pounds and stuffed it into his pocket. 'Thanks Gran. I know I don't have to work. I work because I enjoy it.'

'I know what you're like. I don't want you paying my bills for me. I mean it. Your grandfather left me with enough when he died. I can manage it.'

'I know.' Arthur checked the clock. The last time he had failed to pay a bill on time their water had been cut off. 'I spend my earnings on junk I don't need, don't worry. I even bought these shoes last week.'

He showed her his school shoes, which looked fairly new, and she was appeased. Soon they were sitting at the small kitchen table with cups of tea in their hands, waiting for their supper to be ready.

'I was thinking… maybe after my shift tomorrow we could go to the supermarket and get something nice for lunch on Sunday,' he said after a silence. 'What do you think?'

'I think you should be spending your weekends with your friends, that's what I think,' his grandmother told him. 'What about that girl from Wales? What happened to her?'

'Nothing happened to her. We've been hanging out at school, when she's not with her friends. She's nice.'

'I'm glad to hear it. I thought you'd forgotten about her.'

'I haven't forgotten. I just hang around with Bedivere as well,' he lied, not wanting to get into the particulars about Marvin. 'But I'm seeing Gwen after school, too.'

'What about Lance?'

'What about him?'

'How's he doing?'

'He just got back from another suspension. For slashing the principal's tyres, remember?'

'Lance? Little Lance?' She looked at him disbelievingly. 'But he was always such a lovely boy. Why would he do such a thing?'

'I don't know.' Arthur pushed himself to his feet and checked on their supper. Deciding it was suitably heated, he served two large portions, knowing that he would finish whatever his grandmother didn't. She always ate sparingly, and yet was constantly insisting that she was full, and had just had breakfast, lunch or dinner.

This wasn't the first time she had almost set fire to the house, and such incidents were becoming more frequent. Coming home from school was often a gamble in itself—sometimes she would be out, and then he would spend the evening worrying whether she would return, and if she didn't, who might find her lost and confused across town—whether it would be a neighbour, or the police, whom he often had to call.

Later, when his grandmother had settled down to watch her favourite show, Arthur snuck upstairs to her bedroom and found the wooden box in which she kept her frugal savings. Into it he placed the ten new-pound note she had given him, shuffling it into the bottom of the fives so that she wouldn't get too suspicious.

Gwenhwyfar waited nervously in *Mocca Coffee*, a hot chocolate clasped firmly in her hands.

She was early, and kept her eyes on the swinging door. It was busy in the small café, as it was Saturday, and many walkers were taking refuge from the flash storm outside. She didn't know how she was going to recognise Isolde. Several blonde girls had already entered and left the building, some with dark coats and a few with green.

She checked the clock. It was just gone one. Suddenly it dawned on her that she should have told her parents where she was going and when she would be back. What if Isolde wasn't who she said she was? Another candidate wandered into the heat of the coffee house, with near-white hair and a pink flush to her cheeks. She was clutching an expensive looking phone and a large statement bag. As she approached, Gwenhwyfar put her drink down and sat forwards.

'Are you Gwen...?'

She was tall and reminded Gwenhwyfar a little of Viola, though she was not as waif-like. Her deep-set eyes were bright blue and she had thin, carefully plucked eyebrows that defined the arch of her strong, bumped nose. 'Yes.' She jumped to her feet. 'Are you Isolde?'

The pale girl nodded and they both shook hands.

'It's nice to meet you,' Gwenhwyfar added. 'Would you like a drink?'

'I'll go and order one, thanks.' She offered a quick smile. 'I won't be a moment.'

On her own once again, Gwenhwyfar powered through half of her hot chocolate, keeping her eyes on the bar. She wasn't sure what she was looking for, a suspicious character perhaps, or something that would tell her that what she was doing was a bad idea. Isolde soon returned with a latte, and settled into the armchair opposite.

'Thanks for taking the time to meet me,' she started. She couldn't be older than twenty, and Gwenhwyfar found herself wondering why someone seemingly so pampered was recruiting members for a rebellious cause. 'It's much easier to talk in person.'

'I can imagine,' she agreed. 'Thanks for meeting me here. It's not really park weather.' Rain sheeted down the windows, and a man was hurried past the café with an inside-out umbrella.

Isolde rummaged through her giant bag, her forearms vanishing. 'Let's get started, shall we?' She produced a large notebook and a pen. 'So why are you interested in *Free Countries*?'

Gwenhwyfar hadn't been expecting questions. 'I'm not sure, really. I just saw the flyer and was curious.' Isolde fiddled with a small trinket hanging around her neck. Gwenhwyfar was distracted. 'Is that gold?'

'You can see it if you like.' Unfastening it, Isolde held it out for Gwenhwyfar to handle. She took it delicately, turning it to see it shine.

'Where did you get it?'

'It was my grandmother's,' Isolde explained. 'My grandfather gave it to her when they first started dating. She left it to my mum when she died, and then my mum gave it to me.'

'It's lovely.'

'Thank you,' she beamed. She fastened it back around her neck.

'So how long have you been living in England?' Gwenhwyfar asked, feeling more at ease.

'Seven years.' Isolde leant into the soft cushion of the armchair and put her notebook to one side.

'Where in Ireland are you from?'

'Fermanagh, in the Lakelands.'

'Do you miss it?'

'Sometimes,' she shrugged. There was a short silence. 'You're Welsh, right?'

'Yep,' Gwenhwyfar nodded, pleased to talk about her heritage. 'I just moved here. My dad got a job in the city. My mam's English though. She's wanted to move back for some time.'

'I don't see why,' Isolde remarked.

'Closer to my aunt. So how come you moved here?' She took another sip of her lukewarm hot chocolate. 'If you miss Ireland so much?'

'My dad got transferred to run Heathrow. It's not all bad. We get free flights, so we go away a lot.'

Gwenhwyfar nodded. Isolde had to come from a wealthy family if she wore gold. Her father had once told her that there were hardly any reserves left and that everything had to be recycled at a high cost.

Isolde picked up her notebook again, positioning it on her knees. 'Have you ever been part of a political group before?'

'Not really.'

'So you won't know what's involved then, or what we do.'

'I read what was on your website, but that's as far as I got.'

'Well, we're quite different from other causes. I'll start with the basics. Ultimately we'd like the reinstatement of Northern Ireland, Scotland and Wales as sovereign states.'

Gwenhwyfar frowned. 'So you support the *Celtic Rebels*, then?' She wasn't sure about that. They had been responsible for a strain of violence in the Highlands, as well as in what the New Nationals were now calling Southern Ireland, a small area in the south of Ireland which had changed coats and was now considered to be part of a newly-defined United Kingdom. There had been trouble, too, at the Welsh borders, with random attacks on any Welsh citizen deemed not "Welsh" enough. Isolde shook her head.

'No,' she insisted, 'we believe in independence gained through non-violent means. The *New Celtic Rebels* have nothing to do with *Free Countries*. In fact, we believe they're only hindering any positive developments.'

Gwenhwyfar drew her eyes away from an older man sitting in the corner of the café. She imagined he was watching them, but her suspicion subsided when his wife joined him. 'What else do you believe?'

'We think we should disarm all nuclear weapons and remove supplies of viruses in laboratories which can be used for biological warfare. We also want to work towards free and unbiased education, gender and race equality, the redistribution of wealth and the eradication of poverty. Oh, and we're very keen on helping the environment, and on the importance of free and uncensored speech,' she added as an afterthought.

'So you're against nuclear weapons, then?' The rest of the list sounded logical to Gwenhwyfar, and the Welsh nationalist inside her was easily seduced by the notion of being free from English "tyranny". 'How many members are there in *Free Countries*?'

Isolde put her mug down on the small coffee table between them. 'That's the thing... because we're so anti-Milton, we prefer to operate what we call a chain-group. There's a few people in charge of flyers and the website. When they get a hit, they have a contact, who contacts their contact, telling them the server address of the person interested. That person, in this case me, messages the person interested and gets them to meet. If the person interested, you, decides they want to join *Free Countries*, their only point of contact would be me. It means that if one of us is ever questioned, we won't be able to reveal other *Free Countries* members because we won't know them.'

'So basically, apart from the person who recruited you, you've no idea who you're working for?'

'Nope.' Isolde seemed happy about it, careless even. 'There are code names, obviously, but if I passed them in the street I'd be none the wiser. I think it's cool, in a way. It means my identity is safe.'

'But what about protests? How do you organise things like that?'

'We don't. We can attend any protest individually, but we'd have no idea if anyone else from *Free Countries* was there or not. We don't believe in protests as a method; it brings too much attention and just gets you on the heightened surveillance list. At the moment we're recruiting.'

'And then what?'

'And then we do what the Alpha tells us to do. They're in charge. When the time comes we'll get a message through the grapevine, and then we'll act.'

'Act how?'

'I don't know. We don't believe in the current government though,' she murmured quietly. 'We think the call of elections in May is going to be a televised sham.'

There was another silence. Gwenhwyfar wondered how Isolde could be so dedicated to something she knew so little about. 'So what's your code name?'

Quickly she scribbled something down, tore out the page from her notebook and handed it to her. It read *Omega Iota Zeta.*

'Each code name indicates a member number, or rank,' Isolde explained. 'That's why the Alpha is the first. The second is Alpha Beta. The six hundred and twenty fifth would be Alpha Beta Alpha. I figured it out, even though we're not supposed to know. I'm five thousand, one hundred and nineteenth. You'd be five thousand, one hundred and twentieth.'

Gwenhwyfar tried to catch the threads of her calculation. How on earth had she arrived at that number? 'What would my code name be?'

Isolde wrote it down on another piece of paper. It read *Omega Iota Eta.* Gwenhwyfar wasn't sure how she was supposed to pronounce it.

'So there are over five thousand members of *Free Countries*?' Her stomach felt the pumping of her heart. She hadn't expected to get involved in something so huge.

'And counting,' Isolde said, proudly. 'If you join you'll recruit our next member, and then they'll recruit someone else. We only ever have to recruit one person each, but as the Alpha recruited many, somehow the cause seems to expand. I think there may be different branches of code names, which means my estimate of numbers could be much too low.'

She frowned. 'Can you leave once you've joined?'

'Yes. It's quite easy, as no one knows who you are. We get contacted every now and then to check we're still active and alive—it's usually something coded that we have to respond to—and if you don't reply in the timeframe, the whole pyramid shifts up a level. Everyone gets promoted to the number above. Technically, if you want to leave you can just not answer to the check-ups. I was Omega Iota Sigma not too long ago.'

Gwenhwyfar was beginning to feel seduced by the secrecy. She could join for a little while, couldn't she? Isolde had just told her that it wouldn't be permanent, that she could always drop out. 'What happens now?'

'Now you wait to hear from us. If you're in, I'll phone my recruiter and tell him. Then he'll pass it on and get it to the top. They keep any information they have on us completely safe. In the meantime you'll be sent a key for coded messages. You have to memorise it and destroy it afterwards. It's easy once you get the hang of it, almost like learning a second language.'

'What information do they have on us, then?' Gwenhwyfar asked.

Isolde shrugged lightly. 'Just your phone number, and it's not like that means anything to anyone. So, are you in?'

'I'm in,' Gwenhwyfar gushed before she could stop herself.

'Great. I'll let Omega Iota Epsilon know. Don't tell anyone we're on a first name basis, by the way. We're not supposed to be.'

'Couldn't they see us talking online?' Gwenhwyfar stood with Isolde, who gathered up her coat, bag, phone and notebook.

'Not as far as I know. It's encrypted.'

That relaxed her slightly. At the end of the day she would just be connected to Isolde and whoever came beneath her. It wasn't as if the Alpha would ever come knocking on her door, demanding that she rebel.

It didn't take long for the two to part ways, and Gwenhwyfar remained in the coffee shop a little longer to allow Isolde a head start. She wondered where the other girl went to college, concluding that it had to be somewhere local. Eventually she donned her coat for the rain, pulling up the waxy hood. When the weather showed no signs of relenting, she braved the storm and began the long trek back home.

Lower Logres

She half expected to hear something from Isolde or *Free Countries* on Sunday, but after checking her inbox and Internet browser several times, resigned herself to a much longer wait. Monday morning arrived with a sky cleared by the weekend storm, and once again the weather was brilliant and blue, as if they had been given a second summer. She debated with herself whether or not to tell Viola and Bedivere about what she had signed up for on Saturday, but as they talked over the most recent celebrity scandal, she decided against it.

It was after registration when Mr Hall came into their tutor room with Emily, Hattie, Charlotte and Hector in tow. It took a few moments for the class to fall silent, but when it did, the atmosphere was thick and uncomfortable. The Furies stood sheepishly beside the deputy head with red faces, while Hector hovered nearer to the door, his arms firmly crossed.

Mr Hall eyed them all sharply. 'Well?'

Charlotte elbowed Emily in the side.

'Sorry,' Emily blurted out, not meeting Gwenhwyfar's eye.

'Sorry for playing that prank on you.'

Miss Ray seemed surprised that this was happening now, in front of everyone. Gwenhwyfar felt her face heat up with embarrassment. Was she to be denied her dignity, on top of everything else?

'Sorry Gwen,' Charlotte added, her face red like beetroot. 'Sorry I ripped your hoodie.'

'Sorry I tried on your clothes,' Hattie mumbled.

Emily's blue eyes slunk to Bedivere, who observed the scene with a scowl. 'Sorry Bedivere, for tricking you,' she added. 'It was wrong of me.'

Blushing, Bedivere looked away.

'Hector?'

The boy looked to Gwenhwyfar blackly. His cheek had almost healed, though there was still a faint imprint where Gwenhwyfar's nails had been. She hadn't seen him at all last week, and wondered if he had been in school.

'Hector!' Mr Hall barked.

'Sorry,' he obliged, and despite the sneer the deputy head was satisfied. Gwenhwyfar averted her eyes, insulted. Where was her apology from Mr Hall? Then again, what good would it do? Sorry didn't solve anything. The group hovered while the deputy gazed at her expectantly.

'Gwen?'

Her countenance blackened. She wouldn't say they were forgiven, because they weren't. 'All right,' she mustered. 'I appreciate the fact you realise you were wrong.'

Mr Hall looked to Miss Ray, his mouth open to scold, but her tutor stepped forwards quickly and waved an end to the scene.

'Thank you girls, you can sit down now.' She nodded to the

deputy. 'Mr Hall, I suspect you'll be wanting to get Hector to his lesson?'

With a final displeased glance at Gwenhwyfar, Mr Hall stiffly escorted Hector out of the room. The rest of the class returned to their normal buzz, whispers rippling across each table.

'Well that's that, then,' Viola said to Gwenhwyfar, who was exuding false indifference to what had just transpired. 'Hector didn't look happy, though.'

'I'm not surprised,' Bedivere remarked, glancing awkwardly towards Emily's table with ruddy cheeks. 'Think we'll be seeing much more of him?'

'I won't,' Viola declared. 'Tom's ditched him, too. I made sure of that.'

'And Lance?'

'As far as Lance is concerned, his and Hector's friendship never existed.'

Gwenhwyfar nodded. It was comforting to know that her friends stood beside her. She also knew, however, that all she had gained Hector had lost, and doubted that he would soon forget it.

'Arthur!'

He was waiting for them outside their History room with the rest of their class, standing on his own, half-in and half-out the doorway to their empty classroom. He brightened when he saw them. Bedivere hurried over.

'You'll never guess what,' he told him. 'The Furies just apologised. Hector too. Mr Hall brought them all into our tutor room before registration and made them do it.'

Concerned, Arthur looked to Gwenhwyfar. 'He did?'

She nodded, reluctant to trawl over the particulars. 'He

would've got me to apologise too, if he could, but I didn't. I mean, what have I got to be sorry for?'

'Nothing, that's what,' Bedivere declared stridently.

'Are you all right?'

She met Arthur's worried gaze. 'I'm fine.'

'You sure?'

'Yeah, really.' She forced a smile. 'I'm just glad it's over. I hope that's it.'

They let themselves in when the second bell rang. Marvin Caledonensis wasn't as late as expected, and by the time Gavin and Tom arrived he was already writing on the board.

'You're a little early aren't you, sir?' Tom remarked, obviously thrown, as he and Gavin found their desk.

'Early to you, late to others,' Marvin muttered, his back to them as he scribbled out his clean, chalk letters. 'Yes Tom, I am indeed *early*. But I thought I'd put a bit of effort in, as your mock exams are fast approaching. I hope you're all ready to use those brilliant minds of yours.'

There was a murmur of discontent at the mention of exams, but with the threat of failure the class soon settled to work from their textbooks. With the low hum of chatter still present, and with Marvin occupied at his desk, Gwenhwyfar prodded Bedivere firmly in the back.

'How did it go on Friday?' she whispered, craning over her desk. 'You know, the after-school club?' Morgan looked up, and Arthur turned around.

'It was pretty weird,' Bedivere said, eager to share. 'Good, but weird. He gave us wine and everything.'

'Wine?'

'Red. Vintage, too.' He looked to Arthur. 'Where did you say it was from?'

'Bordeaux, in France. It was over thirty years old.'

Bedivere's eyebrows arched. 'No wonder it was expensive.'

'I didn't like it,' Morgan volunteered. 'It was too bitter.'

'You still should have drunk it,' Arthur said. 'I'm not finishing it for you next time.'

'You had to finish hers?' Gwenhwyfar asked.

'I didn't want it going to waste,' he remarked, his eyes shifting to Marvin, who was spread out across his desk with his latest read in his hands. Gwenhwyfar caught Bedivere's gaze. He made a face, and she felt she was missing something.

'So have you spoken to Marvin yet?' he asked her when Morgan looked up and the grotesque was gone.

'No. I'm not sure if I should if it's by invitation only.'

'He won't mind.' Bedivere turned to Arthur. 'Will he?'

'He shouldn't do.' Arthur shifted. 'Maybe I should ask him for you?'

'I thought you said it was better if I did it myself?' Gwenhwyfar glanced to Morgan, and felt the bitterness resurface with the reminder of her exclusion. 'When's the next one?'

'Friday.'

'I'll do it. It might not be this week, though. My aunt and uncle are coming for dinner, and I don't think I'll be able to get out of it.' She was still half-expecting a summons from *Free Countries* or Isolde. She sent them a masking smile. 'I'll let you know.'

The rest of the lesson passed quietly, with a low murmur that Marvin rarely achieved from his pupils. Even Tom was subdued. After a brief speech covering their homework, the bell rang and Morgan scurried off in an effort to walk alone.

'It's because I'm here,' Gwenhwyfar said as Arthur frowned

after her. 'I'm sure if I weren't, you and Bedivere would have the pleasure of her company.'

'She's probably just got somewhere to go before class,' he excused. 'So what have you two got next?'

'English,' Gwenhwyfar replied, gathering her coat. 'You can walk with us, if you like?'

'Sure.' He hoisted his rucksack onto his shoulders and followed them both out into the corridor. They were caught in the current.

'What are you doing for break?' Bedivere asked brightly. 'Don't tell me you're sitting with Marvin again?'

'I was going to read in the library, actually. Refresh myself on our homework for the week.'

'Homework?'

'Marvin asked us to read *1984*,' Bedivere divulged.

'Well, if you need a break from it you can always come and sit with us,' Gwenhwyfar suggested. 'Bedivere hangs out with me and Vi now, anyway.'

'You do?'

'I'm only doing it to irritate Lance,' he grinned.

'Lance? You sit with him?'

'Technically he sits with me.'

Arthur looked to Gwenhwyfar. 'You too, Gwen?'

She hadn't anticipated that Lancelot would be a problem. 'Yeah, but only because he's friends with Tom,' she explained. 'It's not like I *like* him.'

'Can't we all just sit somewhere else?' Arthur appealed. 'Just the three of us?'

'We can't do that, it's not fair on Vi,' Gwenhwyfar objected. 'Besides, Lance will be on his best behaviour. If not, he'll get kicked off the table. It happened a lot last week.'

Arthur's scowl thickened.

'It'd mean we could all spend some time together at least,' Gwenhwyfar pursued. 'You never know, you might like them. They're actually really nice. They don't hang around with Hector, anymore.'

'And they can't stand the Furies,' Bedivere encouraged. They strolled three abreast down the busy corridor.

'I'll think about it,' he relented. 'Not for break, though. Maybe lunch? Where will you be?'

'The canteen,' Gwenhwyfar told him, as they paused outside their English room. 'You'll see us. You'd better come.'

'I will if I can. See you later?' Smiling, he shrugged out of their company. Put out by his reluctance to make plans, Gwenhwyfar watched him stride down the corridor.

'He'll sit with us,' Bedivere assured her. 'Don't worry. He's probably just reluctant to be seen with the *cool crowd*.'

He grinned at her, and then Ms Appelbauer opened the door and called them promptly into class.

'Where is he?'

Gwenhwyfar dumped her mobile phone on the wooden table. They were still waiting for Arthur to join them, but with much of their lunchtime gone his sudden arrival was looking all the more unlikely. They were sitting outside in the warm sunshine on a bench opposite the Wormelow wing of the canteen. Viola was boasting about her latest test shoot, while Tom held a protective arm around her, gazing at her proudly.

'Maybe he got held up with Marvin?' Bedivere murmured, looking over his shoulder for the fifth time. 'It's not like he can't find us.'

'He'd see us, if he was looking for us.' Gwenhwyfar rubbed her thumbnail, and pushed away the varnish. 'I'll text him. I wanted to see if he'd like to walk home together, anyway,' she whispered. 'What's his last lesson?'

'Politics, same as me.' Bedivere pressed his chin into his fist. 'Though he won't be going home, he'll be going to work.'

'I can walk him to work.' She punched out a quick message to Arthur and then fell back into watching the others idly, paying particular attention to Lancelot, who sat with his jaw cupped in his bruised hand, his dark eyes tracking every slight movement. The conversation had migrated to the Furies' apology.

'So they came in with Mr Hall, then?' Gavin was asking, with a folded frown. 'What did Hector say?'

'He barely apologised at all, did he, Gwen?' Viola asked. Gwenhwyfar sat forwards with Bedivere, and shook her head.

'Hardly. Mr Hall made him. He definitely wanted me to say sorry, too. Though I don't know what for.'

'For what you were wearing, obviously,' Lancelot remarked, with a slow roll of his eyes. 'Or maybe for what you were drinking. I don't know, it's usually one or the other.'

'That's not Gwen's fault,' Bedivere objected, rising quickly to the remark.

'Still—' Tom started.

'Still nothing, Hareton—' Gavin snapped, '—he's being *sarcastic*. Obviously.'

Tom reddened, as did Bedivere.

'You know, given what Ravioli said to me, I was hoping that Mr Hall would apologise too.'

'Yeah right,' Gavin remarked. 'He wouldn't do that, and

definitely not in front of your whole tutor group. If he does, it'll be in a private meeting with you and your parents, with the principal's hand up his arse, puppeteering his mouth.'

Lancelot smirked at this, and Tom sniggered.

'The Furies didn't look too happy, either,' Viola went on. 'None of them actually apologised for what they got Hector to do.'

'No, but Emily *did* apologise for the prank at least,' Gwenhwyfar reminded her. 'Sort of.'

Gavin looked to Bedivere. 'Didn't you make out with her?'

Bedivere's face lit up with immediate embarrassment. 'We kissed, if that's what you mean.'

'Didn't she apologise for that too…?' Viola started, looking to Gwenhwyfar. 'She did, didn't she? Completely unprompted.'

'Christ, Bed, how bad was she?' Tom laughed.

'It was a *prank*, remember?' Gwenhwyfar pointed out. 'That's why she was apologising, because she used Bedivere to get to Arthur and me.'

'Oh, really? And here I was thinking that she snogged you because she has the hots for you,' Viola teased, rolling her eyes.

'Emily has the hots for Bedivere?' Tom asked. His face crinkled up drastically at such a notion. 'What happened to her fancying Lance?'

'I almost feel hurt,' Lancelot quipped.

'At least you came out of it unmolested.' Gavin nudged Bedivere in the side. 'I can't say the same for you, Bed.'

'Jealous?' Bedivere scowled.

'Completely,' Gavin gesticulated. The table laughed.

'Well, you're welcome to her if you like,' Bedivere retorted. 'She's a crap kisser.'

Viola gasped, and the boys all voiced non-verbal opinions of his daring.

'Ooh, that one's going to go around like wildfire,' Gavin observed.

'Well, she is!'

'Emily won't like that,' Tom mocked.

'I couldn't care less,' Bedivere muttered, his cheeks blooming with crimson. Angrily he twisted his hair.

'We're only teasing, Bed,' Viola tried. 'We know it was a prank. It was cruel of her.'

'At least you didn't have to knock her out with a lamp,' Gavin added.

'Yeah, and if you can't laugh about it, what can you do?' said Tom.

'Nothing,' huffed Bedivere, irked.

There was an uncomfortable silence. 'Someone got out of the wrong side of bed this morning,' Lancelot muttered. To Bedivere's obvious relief, he then changed the subject; and as Gwenhwyfar watched Lancelot talk and joke with Gavin, her thoughts soon returned to Arthur.

She met him when the final bell of the day went, and together they walked under the long shadows that cut across the school grounds, out of the gates and onto the main road.

'So how was Politics?'

'Good,' he said. 'I mean, it was all right. It's all a load of nonsense, really. I feel we never learn anything.'

'I have that in General Studies,' she smiled. 'Sometimes I think there's no point in attending. It's all just general knowledge that's not really general and not really knowledge at all.'

'At least you don't have to write propaganda papers,' he reasoned. 'In Politics it's all I ever do. I feel like I'm being brainwashed.'

She laughed. 'Science is a reprieve, at least. We're looking at man-made cells tomorrow, right?'

'Oh, don't get me started on those.' They crossed the road, and then meandered up a gentle hill lined with small, suburban houses. 'The Second Genesis. Well, the third technically, as they discovered a cell completely separate to the one we're all descended from at least fifty years ago. But they can't use that to produce natural resources. Or incurable diseases.'

'How about cures for diseases?' asked Gwenhwyfar. 'Can they use it to do that?'

He looked to her and smiled. 'Good point.'

'So what happened to you at lunch? We waited for you.'

'I was going to come,' he offered, 'I just lost track of time. Sorry.'

'That's all right. Tomorrow, maybe?' She smiled up at him, but he kept his gaze fixed steadily ahead. 'How long have you got to work for tonight? It must be hard having a job and studying at the same time.'

'Two hours. It's not too bad. If it's quiet they let me do my homework.'

'Which library is it?'

'Lower Logres. It's connected to the school—that's how I got the job.'

They fell victim to a prolonged silence. As they walked together Gwenhwyfar almost thought she could feel his body heat transcend the gap between them. The sensation was swiftly interrupted.

'Is there a reason you hang around with Lance?'

She frowned. 'What do you mean?'

'I mean, why are you friends with him?'

'I'm not friends with him,' she disagreed. 'I actually can't stand him.'

'No?' He looked at her quizzically. 'Then why do you hang around with him all the time?'

'I don't hang around with him all the time. He just has the same friends as me. We don't even talk.'

'You don't?'

'No. Would it make a difference if we did?'

He shrugged. Gwenhwyfar turned her eyes back to the road. They were quite far from the school now, and she realised that she should have been paying attention to the route they were taking. She lived in completely the opposite direction.

'I was just wondering. Last I heard Lance and Hector were pretty much best friends; Tom, too.'

'Well, all that's changed now,' Gwenhwyfar assured him. 'None of them even speak to Hector anymore.'

They turned the corner at the end of the tree-lined road. Across the street, by a small playground skirted with balding grass, sat a dismal building with a damaged sign indicating it was *ower ogres bra*.

'Is this it?'

'It needs new funding really,' Arthur told her. 'At the moment we're running on donations. It's the last one in the area.'

She looked up at the grey concrete block that was her local library. At least she knew where it was now, and since Arthur worked most nights she could do her homework here to be near him. 'It doesn't look too bad.'

'It's nicer on the inside. Want to see it?' His eyes always seemed wider when he looked at her, as if he was trying to see her whole.

'I'm all right, thanks. I'd better get home. Though I might have to come and find you if I get lost. Which way is it?'

He sidled closer, his front lightly brushing her back, and pointed. 'That way: down George Street, then left at Victoria Lane. You should come to Potters Park. Do you know your way home from there?'

'I should do.'

'If not you can always come back and find me,' he said.

'I hope you're not sending me the wrong way on purpose, Arthur.'

They gazed at one another. He was much more amiable when he wasn't talking about Lancelot, Gwenhwyfar thought.

'I'll see you tomorrow,' he breathed.

'You will,' she promised. As she turned to retrace their steps, Arthur retreated through the library doors and waved at her with one last lopsided smile.

'Did you hear about Scotland?'

Gavin clenched his abdominals into his twenty-second sit up. Beside him Lancelot rose and reclined in a long line of Cadets, all exercising on the order of their SSI, the Staff Sergeant Instructor.

'No.' Lancelot sat up again, his breathing controlled, his words effortless. 'What about it?'

'The *New Celtic Rebels* have occupied Fort William. Killed fifty people.'

'I didn't hear that,' Lancelot murmured, his cheeks hollowed with concentration.

'I found an eyewitness account on the Internet,' Gavin remarked, lowering himself onto the cold grass, wet against his back. 'They're talking to the Irish and the Welsh. They think they should have full independence, and that this is the only way to get it.'

'Let me guess, any Scot or person of "Celt-origin" not on their side is an English bastard? I know they want what they feel the New Nationals have taken from them; I know that they don't want to suffer under this government any more than the rest of us—but blowing up buildings and shooting civilians—? That's not going to get it.'

'Ever since we left Europe there's been unrest,' Gavin puffed, now on fifty-two. 'The upper one percent has nothing foreign to blame anymore.'

'They'll find someone, they always find someone. The disabled, for example, or the poor—it's *their* fault that we're circling the plughole. Don't you know it?'

'I know it,' Gavin remarked. 'If the New Nationals place the blame, the average citizen will be happy to point the finger, too.'

'As long as it's not at themselves,' Lancelot said with a sidelong glance.

The SSI wandered their way, scrutinising every rise. It was cold, and the frigid air burned Gavin's dry throat. He waited until their superior passed them, nearly at the benchmark. 'You changed your mind yet?'

Their gaze crossed again as Lancelot sat back up. 'About what?'

'Joining up when we finish school. If you studied, got through your exams, I reckon you could sign on as an officer.'

'Don't you need a degree for that?'

'Not these days.'

Lancelot frowned, his heavy brow darkening. 'Where are you getting this stuff from, anyway?' He paused to rest a moment, and Gavin sat up to join him. 'You've been banging on about rebels, rights and the poor for weeks.'

'I told you, the Internet.'

'Not on one of those crackpot conspiracy sites?'

Panting, he shook his head. They had just done track. 'Nah. Some encrypted blog that posts up eyewitness accounts. Whistle-blowers use it. It's one of the ones that helped blow the lid on the Poppy Scandal.'

His thick eyebrows twisted. 'What, the one about that girl?'

Gavin nodded. 'It was a mass cover up. People being too poor to afford healthcare: more specifically the new generation of antibiotics. People dying of throat infections, cuts and scrapes.'

'I remember,' he said solemnly. 'What did they do about it?'

'After the fuss? Nothing. People are still dying. Christ, it's bad enough paying my own health insurance, let alone contributing to my brothers', but my parents think it's fair. Those who work, chip in. Until I sign up, of course.'

They both leant back and resumed the exercise.

'You're not still taping over your webcam, are you?' Lancelot asked with a huff.

'Webcam, phone camera, any camera on any device I own.'

'You know it's illegal now.'

'I know. I also know they're not going to find out. I don't want the New Nationals watching me shit, shower and shave. You can't tell when they're using them.'

'I'm beginning to think you're wasted on the army,' Lancelot said.

'It'll be a waste if I don't join. You too, Lake.'

'Don't think there'll be a regime change. What we're stuck with now, we'll be stuck with then. If you sign up you'll be taking your orders from him.'

'Is that what put you off? Milton?'

'I don't want to be anyone's attack dog,' Lancelot scowled.

'You know what they say. If you're not police or army, you're little people.'

'I thought you were all for the little people,' Lancelot duelled.

'I am,' Gavin frowned, 'but I can hardly watch out for them if I'm one too.'

There was a moment's silence between them. Gavin had hit their target about ten sit-ups ago, but there was no order from the SSI, so he kept going.

'Maybe,' Gavin said after a while, 'maybe things can be changed from the inside.'

'You'd need to be top dog, for that.'

'I could manage it,' he grinned.

The SSI stalked back towards their end of the line. Gavin had a shift at Bellini's after this: an evening of dealing with the punters, customers who were inflated with a false sense of their own autonomy; because they had money, because they had comforts, even though they were nothing but small pebbles at the bottom of a vast and unchanging pyramid.

Lancelot sat up to join him, panting with his arms draped over his knees. 'You're wasted on the army, Miles,' he said again. His smile was short and quick, and as they were all told to stand to attention, he sprang obediently to his feet.

BEETHOVEN

It was Tuesday morning, and the sky was still dim in the east. Gwenhwyfar huddled in her coat, her mouth and nose expelling vapour as she hurried down the slight incline to Badbury. The moment she entered the building, warmth enveloped her, and she was grateful that the heating was functioning at a useful hour. She unbuttoned her coat with numb, tingling fingers, pausing by the practice rooms to unwind her scarf. Usually at this time in the morning she could hear the odd wavering note sung by a girl, but today her ear was drawn by the muffled sound of a piano.

She knew the piece, but from where? It was perfect, flawless even. Taunted by the familiar melody, she approached the last door on the right and peered through the small window. Immediately she stepped away. It was Lancelot.

Vaguely she remembered hearing him speak with Tom about music. She looked again. He looked different hunched over the keys. His bruised hands danced. There was sheet music before him though he didn't seem to need it. She squinted to read the title, but quickly her eyes drew back to him. The room around him blurred, and soon he was all she saw, and for a moment it was as if she were carried with the music.

'Spying on people, are we?'

She spun around, her heart pounding. The adrenaline rush left her when she realised it was just the Furies. Quickly she moved away from the door. 'What do you want?'

Emily folded her arms and glanced towards the practice room. 'Is your boyfriend in there, or something?'

'Maybe it's *Arthur*,' teased Hattie.

'Maybe it's *Hector*,' spat Charlotte.

'Maybe it's none of your business?' Gwenhwyfar commented, rolling her eyes. 'If you stalk me like this, people are going to talk.'

'Eww! Why would we want to stalk you?' Emily's face distorted.

'I think she fancies us,' Charlotte muttered, eyes narrowed.

'Oh, get over yourselves,' Gwenhwyfar snapped. There was a trip in the flawless music.

'Better keep away, or she'll infect us with all sorts,' pursued Emily. 'She did catch a lot when she had sex with Hector.'

'You're still harping on about that? *Please*. We all know that if anyone's got something, it's Charlotte.'

'What's that supposed to mean?'

'You mean you don't remember calling her a whore?'

Charlotte's eyes widened. Her lips were thin. 'She didn't.'

'She did.'

'That is such a lie!' Emily screeched. The music faltered again. There was a loud bang of the keys. 'She's lying, Charlotte. *Gwen's* the one who said that. I told her to stop being so mean.'

'Oh, and while we're on the subject of boys... Bedivere was talking about you yesterday, about how crap a kisser you are.' Emily's face crashed. 'He said he never wants to go through anything like it again. What was it he compared you to...? That's right, it was a fish. A wet, sloppy, slimy fish.'

The music halted again. Emily didn't have the chance to retaliate. As Hattie and Charlotte revelled in their friend's misfortune, the blue door was ripped open.

'Will you lot shut up?' Lancelot snarled, livid. 'I'm trying to play the *sodding* piano here, in case you hadn't noticed, so how about you all go and have your bitch fest in the bus lane?'

He slammed the door. Emily spun around, striding towards the other staircase. Hattie followed her. Charlotte lingered for a moment, then scurried off. Angrily the piano started up again. Gwenhwyfar listened to the frantic notes for a minute before she made her way up to registration, satisfied that for once, she had given the Furies a taste of their own medicine.

The power was out again, and there was a problem with the generator. The last time there had been a blackout Gwenhwyfar's neighbourhood hadn't been affected, even though many houses had gone without electricity for two full days. The class was restless, unsettled by the lack of lighting. She came to her Science table to find Arthur waiting for her, and felt her heart lift when he returned her smile with equal warmth.

'Hasn't Mrs Paxton moved you yet?' she teased as she climbed onto her stool.

'You know how she likes to shout at me in front of the entire class,' Arthur grinned. 'Besides, I told her I can't see the board properly from the front. I can sit here, as long as I behave.'

'And? Are you going to behave?'

They grinned at one another. Gwenhwyfar put her bag on the table, unzipped it, and pulled out her belongings.

'Ready for some synthetic cells?' Arthur asked, opening his exercise book.

'Oh, definitely.' She plucked a pen from her pencil case. 'You?'

'I hope so. Ignore me if I start ranting, though. This sort of thing has the tendency to irritate me.'

'You were telling me yesterday,' she recalled. 'You don't think such advancements are good?'

'No. Why, do you?'

'If they're for advancing the field of medicine. Synthetic cells and other cellular types of research can only make the world better. Don't you agree?'

He frowned. 'I just don't think that meddling with the foundations of nature can ever truly be good.'

'But we already meddle with the foundations,' Gwenhwyfar countered. 'We meddle when we cure diseases.'

'And where has that got us?' Arthur retorted. 'The world is overpopulated, resources have run out and other species have become extinct. That's what I mean when I say that it can't ever be "good".'

'But you're here today because of the advances we've made,' Gwenhwyfar told him. 'You can guarantee that somewhere in the history of your family, someone will have been saved by such necessary *evils*. Call it "natural selection" if you like: the smartest being is the most successful and therefore out-competes other species.'

'I know. But when you start to wipe out what you rely on

yourself, your environment and said species in order to maintain and further such advances, you only fuel your own demise. I don't mean it in an individual sense, just in a wider context of ecological exhaustion.' He looked to her ruefully. 'I told you that it irritated me.'

'Don't worry about it,' Gwenhwyfar replied, favouring him with an affectionate smile. 'I'm sure we can agree to disagree.'

Mrs Paxton silenced the class in her usual brisk manner and outlined their subject for the day. A while later, when power had finally been restored to their classroom, a twenty minute educational film was inserted into the ancient television device. Still wondering how she could navigate his apparent issue with Lancelot, Gwenhwyfar whispered in Arthur's ear.

'Do you want to sit together at lunch?'

He looked at her. 'Alone?'

She hesitated for a moment. 'Of course.'

Her heart pounded as he looked away. A moment passed, and he leant towards her again. 'Can you meet me in our History room? I have to see Marvin about something, first.'

She tried not to scowl. It was something, at least. 'What time?'

'Quarter past?'

'Perfect,' she agreed. 'I'll be there.'

The room went dark and was illuminated by the short documentary about RNA. Gwenhwyfar started a silent correspondence in the back of her school planner, and spent the rest of the film passing it to and fro with Arthur, with the occasional hushed snigger.

'So how come you work so much?' she asked once the lights were back on and the film had ended. She copied a complex diagram of RNA into her exercise book. 'Most people I know have never had a job.'

'Maybe in this area they haven't,' Arthur remarked.

'I haven't,' Gwenhwyfar admitted, as she filled in the blanks. 'My mam doesn't work, either.'

'Does your dad?' Gwenhwyfar nodded. 'What does he do?'

'Private security for computer networks... he's pretty high up. He works in the city. You live with your grandmother, right?' She hesitated for a moment. 'What happened to your parents?'

He was caught off guard. Suddenly he seemed unable to meet her gaze. 'There's not much to tell. My mother left shortly after I was born. I grew up with my grandparents. My dad died when I was five.'

'I'm sorry to hear that,' she said softly.

'Don't be,' he responded, attempting a smile. 'I'm lucky to have had them both. My grandfather passed away about a year ago, so now it's just my grandmother and me. Oh, and Lionel, our cat.'

'You have a cat?' She was glad for the chance to change the subject. 'What sort? I have a dog. He's called Llew.'

'A British Shorthair. Llew's lion in Welsh, right?'

She was pleased that he knew what it meant. 'Right.'

'When we first got Lionel, he pulled one of my grandfather's books off the shelf and tore out a page. My grandfather couldn't get it off him, because Lionel thought it was a game. He destroyed all of it, apart from one strip. It was a list of the Knights of the Round Table, and the only one spared was Sir Lionel. He's been known as that ever since.'

'I'd like to meet Sir Lionel, sometime.' Gwenhwyfar smiled.

'I'm sure he'd like to meet you too. You could always come over this weekend, if you want.'

She felt her heart leap. 'I'd love to. But don't you need to check with your grandmother first?'

'She won't mind. She's always asking when I'm going to bring a girl home to meet her, anyway,' he joked.

'We could go to the cinema, there's a film on I want to see. It's called *An Inspector Calls*. It looks good.'

'How about Saturday?' Arthur suggested.

'Saturday's perfect,' Gwenhwyfar told him, wondering if this counted as a date. As he gazed at her his eyes lit up, and she was subjected to the full force of another of his charming smiles.

Break time came and went with a cloudy sky that threatened rain, but failed to deliver it. The canteen emptied at the sounding of the bell, and Bedivere, Gavin, Tom and Viola all set off to their lessons. As always, Lancelot took his time to get organised and Gwenhwyfar found herself waiting impatiently for him. Refusing to make a comment that would set him off, she remained silent, even when he joined her at an indolent pace.

'I heard you this morning, you know,' he drawled, much to her surprise. 'Telling Emily what Bed said. Does he know?'

She rolled her eyes. 'You know, Lance, it's none of your business.'

'It becomes everyone's business when people like you go shouting it out in the corridors,' he countered. His dark hair twisted in the wind as they walked, and as her own hair danced about her she reeled it in with persistent fingers.

'I didn't shout it out. And no, Bedivere doesn't know. So I'd appreciate it if you didn't tell him. Judging by the look on Emily's face, she's not going to repeat it to anyone, anyway.'

'I wouldn't count on it,' he said. Gwenhwyfar was beginning

to notice how other boys went to great lengths to avoid him, while girls drew closer, tittering their schoolgirl giggles. 'Charlotte's probably told the whole school.'

'Why are you so concerned?' she sniped, dearly wishing that she could swap her lessons and spend French with Arthur instead. 'I thought you didn't like Bedivere. Anyway, after all those three did to you, I'm surprised you didn't tell her yourself.'

He bristled. 'What's that supposed to mean?'

'Aren't you just a little bit annoyed that they managed to destroy your and Arthur's friendship?'

She'd struck a nerve—that much was plain—but why she suddenly wanted Arthur and Lancelot to become friends again, she couldn't fathom.

'How do you know about that?'

'Gavin,' she admitted. 'I asked why everyone calls them the Furies. That was before I knew you.'

'I miss those days.'

Gwenhwyfar shoved him. His eyes widened.

'So now you're beating me up, too? What happened to Little Miss Pacifist?'

She sent him a sarcastic expression and he retaliated in kind. They came to the entrance to Badbury, next to the Sixth Form block. This time he held the door for her.

'So that music you were playing earlier, what was it?'

'You mean that music I was trying to play but couldn't, thanks to you?'

She doubted she would ever have a civil conversation with him. 'Yes,' she retorted flatly. 'It was pretty good. I didn't know you could do sophisticated stuff like that.'

'Sophisticated stuff?'

'Yeah, anything other than beating the living daylights out of people.'

His dark brows knotted. 'Is that how you see me?'

'You mean as a thug?' This time he pushed her. Scowling, Gwenhwyfar tried to compose herself. She punched him hard on the arm, though doubted his muscles felt it. 'You're not *supposed* to hit women.'

'I didn't hit you,' he mocked. 'Besides, women aren't supposed to hit men.'

They both stomped up the stairs, wearing down the old carpet even more.

'You didn't answer my question,' said Gwenhwyfar, rubbing her arm. 'You know, about the music you were trying to play? What was it?'

'What's-his-name. Beethoven. Don't tell me a rich snob like you hasn't heard it.'

'Of course I've heard it, I just couldn't remember.' Her cheeks felt a little rosier than usual. They were in the computer room this week, attempting to learn French by clicking buttons and playing games. 'What piece was it?'

'Moonlight something,' Lancelot shrugged.

'Sonata?' Gwenhwyfar asked, remembering.

'Could be,' he grunted.

'So where did you learn it?' she pursued, as they queued by their room.

'Learn what?'

He had to be doing it to annoy her. 'The piano!'

'My mum taught me, all right? It's not like I do it for fun, or anything. I do it for the band.'

She gazed at him blankly. 'The band?'

'You know, my band? Our band? Tom's band?'

'You're in that?'

'What?' Lancelot said, indignant.

'Nothing.' She led him into their French room.

'No, what?'

'Nothing! I just find it hard to picture you in a band, that's all.'

'Why is it so hard to believe?' he grunted. Violently he pulled out a chair and let his bag thump onto the floor.

'What do you play?'

'What?'

'In your band, what do you play?'

'Guitar.' He was beginning to sound Neolithic again.

'Not the piano?'

'No, not the piano.'

'I thought you played it for the band?' He grumbled. Gwenhwyfar smirked. 'So who sings?'

'I do,' was his black response. He turned on the old computer, waiting for the ancient system to fire up. Gwenhwyfar couldn't contain her amusement. 'Oh, *what?*'

'Nothing! It's nothing.' His aggravated expressions were priceless. 'So what's this *band* of yours called?'

He eyed her suspiciously through his long dark lashes. '*The Oxymorons.*'

'So that would be shortened to *The Morons*, then?'

The scowl on his face was so exaggerated that she had to turn away and snigger.

'Oh, make fun of it if you want to, *Gwenhwyfar.*'

She gasped. 'Where did you learn my name?'

'Gavin told me,' he said with some satisfaction. 'I actually quite like it. I think I'll call you it more often. Gwenhwyfar.'

'If you do that, I'll call you *Lancelot*, and see how you like it,' she threatened.

'You'd better not,' he warned.

Her eyes narrowed to small slits. 'Oh, I will.'

'Fine, *Gwenhwyfar*,' he hissed.

'All right then, *Lancelot*,' she jeered.

The two made a point of turning their heads away; both determined to ignore the other.

Bedivere came to find them all at lunchtime, his face like thunder. 'You know what I just heard?' he demanded, looming over their table.

'What?' Gavin ventured.

'That someone told Emily I said she was a crap kisser!' His pupils danced across the table, accusing each person they fell upon.

'But you did say that Emily was a crap kisser,' Lancelot pointed out.

'It was you, wasn't it? Oh yes, it sounds like something you'd do, just to be funny. Well, it isn't funny, Lance. The whole school's talking about it.' Lancelot opened his mouth to object, but was cut short. 'Not to mention the new rumour that's going around because of you.'

'What rumour?' Viola interrupted.

His cheeks reddened. 'It doesn't matter *exactly*—'

'Yeah it does.' Lancelot sent a pointed expression to Gwenhwyfar. 'What rumour? We're probably going to hear it, anyway.'

'I'm not repeating it!' Bedivere snapped, distressed. 'For her to even know such a thing we'd have to have done more than just kiss, which we definitely did *not* do.'

Gradually the group began to form their own ideas. Their amusement just made Bedivere grow hotter. 'This isn't funny! One of you told her, so tell me who, all right?'

'It wasn't me,' snorted Lancelot. Viola shrugged, and Gavin shook his head.

'Not me,' Tom murmured.

'I don't know anything about it either,' Gwenhwyfar lied.

Lancelot offered him a shrug. 'Looks like it wasn't anyone.'

'Sorry Bed,' Viola started, 'maybe someone overheard?'

'You do get eavesdroppers here,' Gavin tried. Their newest addition was not satisfied. His poised stance suggested he was thinking of leaving, but ultimately he pulled out a chair. As he sat his head fell into his hands and he groaned.

'People will be talking about this for *weeks*.'

'Nah,' Gavin tried, 'I mean, just get Lance to hit someone. Then they'll all be talking about that, instead.'

'I wish he'd hit whoever did this,' he muttered. Lancelot leant back in his chair and propped his foot on his knee.

'That can be arranged. For a small fee, of course.'

'Is eternal gratitude small enough?' he begged.

'Works for me.' Lancelot looked at Gwenhwyfar, and her gaze was pulled to his as if their eyes were opposite ends of two magnets. 'You'll have to tell me who did it first though,' he added. Suddenly uncomfortable, Gwenhwyfar stood abruptly and plucked her things off the table.

'Sorry, I said I'd meet someone for lunch.'

'Who?' Viola enquired, her interest peaked.

She glanced briefly at Lancelot. 'Who do you think?'

'Arthur?'

Gwenhwyfar nodded. 'I'll see you in Geography. Bye, everyone.' She hurried away, weaving expertly through the crowd.

'Tell me about it then!' Viola shouted after her. She turned and offered them one last wave, trying not to feel too guilty about telling on Bedivere.

Gwenhwyfar hurried to Mr Caledonensis' classroom, expecting Arthur to be waiting outside. When she arrived, however, he was nowhere to be seen, and it wasn't until she heard voices that she thought to check the room itself. Feeling as if she were intruding, she knocked softly, pushing on the door the moment she was beckoned in.

'Ah, Gwenhwyfar!' Marvin beamed. 'Arthur told me we were expecting you. Going on a lunch date, are we? Sounds very nice, though I can't say the weather's good for it.'

It was as if she'd just interrupted an important conversation. There was an atmosphere lingering, a sense that she'd come too early, and that they both still had things they were burning to say.

'It is a bit miserable out,' she agreed, venturing a little further into the room. 'Am I interrupting? I can come back later if you like.'

'No, no, not at all! Arthur was just returning a book I lent him,' Marvin explained, still holding *The Human Condition* in his hand. Gwenhwyfar spotted it before he could hide it, the grey and black cover glaring at her with its large, human eye.

'Is that it? What is it?'

'Oh, it's just something for Politics. It's not very interesting, is it, Arthur?' He stowed it away. 'I already have another student lined up to read it.'

'Is it good?'

'Good? I'm not sure about *good*.' Marvin busied himself at his desk. '*Useful,* if you're interested in that sort of thing. You're welcome to borrow it, of course, but it's quite dull. Very stuffy prose, if you know what I mean.'

'Boring,' Arthur corrected, offering a smile.

'I think I'll pass,' Gwenhwyfar said, sensing the hollow gesture in Marvin's words. He clapped his hands together.

'So! Are you two off?'

'I think so.' She turned to Arthur. 'Shall we go?'

'Of course.' He followed her to the door, and soon they were out in the empty corridor.

'So… what's *The Human Condition* really about?' Gwenhwyfar asked, once Marvin's room was some way behind them.

'You saw the cover?'

'It was hard not to, with him waving it around,' she teased. Arthur remained silent. 'Was I not supposed to?'

'Not really, no,' he murmured, 'and I wouldn't go telling anyone you did. He could get into a lot of trouble, Gwen, and so could I. He shouldn't be lending me stuff like that, and I shouldn't be reading it.'

'Stuff like what?'

'You know, banned books.'

'Marvin gives you banned books? Isn't that a bit dangerous?'

'Yes. That's why I'd appreciate it if you didn't tell anyone. And I mean anyone. Not even Viola, because she'll tell Tom, and Tom can't keep anything to himself.'

'She won't tell Tom if I ask her not to,' she started.

'Yes she will. They're going out. They'll tell each other everything,' he remarked matter-of-factly. 'Marvin's the best teacher in this school, and I don't want him getting into trouble because of me.'

Gwenhwyfar felt like he was scolding her for something she hadn't done. 'Right, I get it. I won't tell anyone.'

Her words seemed to appease him. 'Thank you.'

They walked in silence for a while, until they braved the cold and found a bench on which they could perch. Huddling in her coat to keep herself warm, Gwenhwyfar brushed some flyaway hair from her eyes. 'So what is it about then? You know, that *book*.'

'It's a study on what led to the restriction of human liberties.'

'Is that the kind of stuff that he gives you to read at that club?' Arthur nodded. 'So then why can't I read it?' she challenged.

'Because you're not technically a member yet.' He smiled at her fondly. 'Are you cold?'

'A little.'

Immediately he removed his coat and draped it around her shoulders. His arm lingered there, and he pulled her closer. 'Better?'

'Yes, thank you,' she nodded, extremely pleased with her current position. 'What about you, though?'

'I'm fine,' he said, as the icy wind blew. 'I'm fairly warm-blooded.'

'I wish I was. I'm like a lizard, I need the sun to warm up.' She shivered, pressing closer to his side. 'Are we still on for Saturday?'

'Of course,' he responded with amusement. 'Why wouldn't we be?'

'Just checking. I'm looking forward to it.'

'Me too.'

She thought for a moment, and wondered why he spent so much time alone. 'So how was work?'

'It was OK.' Gwenhwyfar could feel each breath he took, each word reverberate in his chest. 'Someone came in looking for a book no one could find. That was the highlight.'

'So it's just you and your grandmother living together, right?'

'And Lionel,' Arthur reminded her.

'So… is your grandmother quite rich, then?'

'Not that I know of, why?'

'Oh, it's just—I mean… what about bills and stuff?'

He seemed offended. Gwenhwyfar stared at him, sensing she'd said something wrong. They both frowned.

'Why do you think I work at the library every evening? I pay the bills, or contribute to them at least—it's not like my grandmother's non-existent pension could cover it. That ran out years ago.'

She scowled. 'You mean you pay for everything?'

His arm slipped from her shoulders. 'Who else?'

'Everything?' Gwenhwyfar repeated.

'No, not everything,' Arthur relented, 'most things. She still has a bit of money left over from when my grandfather was alive. I'm just glad the house is hers, otherwise it'd be impossible. How could you think it was all just provided for?'

'I'm sorry if I offended you. It's just—usually an uncle or a relative would pay for something like that.'

'Well, I don't have an uncle,' Arthur remarked. 'Or any other relatives.'

'I'm sorry.'

'Don't be, it's fine.'

This time the silence was short-lived. 'You know, I think it's pretty great that you support your grandmother. Most people wouldn't know where to start with something like that.'

'Thanks.' He folded his arms into his chest in an effort to keep warm. 'I think she appreciates it. Sometimes.'

She hitched closer to him again, and offered his coat to half-cover them both. Gratefully he put his arm around her and rubbed her side. Pleased that they were still friends, Gwenhwyfar held him close, and they sat huddled together until the bell rang.

Arthur walked with Gwenhwyfar to Geography, where they talked together until their lessons started. As Gwenhwyfar left to queue with Viola, Arthur rejoined his own class, feeling the sullen gaze of Lancelot press hard upon him. They were called into their classroom. The moment he approached Lancelot blocked his way with a palm to the chest.

'What?' asked Arthur, in the bored tone he always used: a tone that never failed to annoy Lancelot.

'So you and Gwen are dating now?'

'Maybe.' Arthur twisted past him.

'Lance! Sit *down*,' Miss Church commanded. He did, but without indicating that he'd heard her, and as Arthur took his usual seat behind him, Lancelot twisted around.

'So you are dating? Just for the record, if anyone does tell you I've slept with her, please ignore them, because I wouldn't even want to.'

The best policy with Lancelot was usually to ignore him. His jaw squaring, Arthur occupied himself with collecting the necessary objects from his schoolbag.

'Not that I'm saying you shouldn't, because she seemed up for it, going by what Hector said…'

He opened his books, pulled out a pen, and calmly wrote down the date.

'…and she had to have had *something* along those lines in mind when she invited you both up to that room…'

'*Me.* She invited *me* to that room.' He shouldn't have corrected him. Immediately Lancelot's eyes sparked.

'Yeah, whatever, Arty,' he smirked. 'Next time just make sure you're not getting anyone's seconds.'

His fist tightened around his pen. He hated being called *Arty* and he hated the way Lancelot always threw such disgusting concepts around. What was worse, Arthur seemed to find it nearly impossible to resist the urge to provoke him. 'Don't worry about me, Lotty. Gwen's made it quite clear who she's interested in.'

His assailant scowled. 'Oh, has she?'

'Yes,' Arthur stated, jaw tight. 'So as much as I'm touched by your concern, you needn't worry. I'm not getting anyone's seconds, unlike some people.'

His pointed look was enough to show Lancelot what he meant. Suddenly Lancelot rocketed to his feet, and Arthur's table was flying towards his face as his angry, bruised hands smacked the edge up. Snapping the desk back down, Arthur rose to the challenge. Miss Church yelled.

'What, don't like thinking about her?' Arthur sniped, pleased that for once, it was he who was getting a rise. 'It's just as well— she told me she couldn't stand you, anyway.'

'Arthur!' Miss Church cried. She stormed towards the duelling boys as Lancelot pushed him.

'I never touched her,' Lancelot growled, his heavy brow twisted with rage.

'Lance!' she shouted. 'Sit down!'

'Funny how she left, isn't it? I told her she was welcome to you, but apparently she would rather move schools.' Arthur stood firm as he was shoved again. Their teacher caught Lancelot by the arm and dragged him away from the desk.

'He started it!' he hollered as he was pushed towards the door.

'Out, Lance! I gave you a warning—I want you to go straight to the principal's office, *now*. You're not to come back until you've told him why I sent you there.'

Arthur smiled with satisfaction as Miss Church slammed and locked the door. For a while Lancelot hammered on the wood, but then the knocking ceased and his curses echoed down the hall.

'Arthur!' Miss Church barked, 'If you don't sit down, I'll send you there with him! Sit!'

Her voice rose to silence the class. Arthur snapped down and spent the next few moments trying to restore his disturbed desk. For a while the girl who sat next to Lancelot glared at him through narrowed eyes, but her silent accusation was wasted. Arthur wondered why so many girls seemed to be enamoured with the aggressive teenager. When the class quietened, Miss Church finally had a moment to write her intentions on the board. The lesson would be on the science of predicting volcanic eruptions. Arthur smiled.

Corrected

'Lance has been disrupting Mrs Church's lessons again.'

The final bell of the day had sounded, expelling the students of Logres from the school grounds in an excited hubbub. Though the days were getting shorter, there was still some sunshine left to enjoy, and Julie felt the usual sting of being one of the last stuck in the stuffy, dusty building.

'I heard,' Marvin remarked mildly, stirring the two cups of tea he had just made. 'Apparently she's rather upset. I'd have thought she'd be used to it by now.'

'You don't have him in any of your classes, do you?'

'Not since Year Nine, no.' Carefully, Marvin carried the two full mugs across to where Julie was leant against the small refrigerator that stood at counter height. 'Personally I find Tom Hareton harder work. At least whatever Lancelot has to say is vaguely intelligent. Tom just runs off that mouth of his as if he's got verbal diarrhoea.'

'You shouldn't be so cruel,' she scolded, taking her tea from him and blowing the steam over the brim. 'I know what you mean, though. Since I gave Lance something to work on from a higher set he's settled right down. Where is Jo now?'

'In the deputy's office, giving Mr Hall more black marks for Lance's record.' His brow rumpled, and he sighed. 'Sometimes I think the principal is doing that boy more harm than good.'

'Didn't his mother teach music here?'

Marvin nodded, and swallowed. 'Yes! Emma. She was lovely. One of those rare people that just light up the room. I met her at university. I didn't know Ben that well, but he seemed a decent man. Lance could have used him in his life.'

'Funny how things just happen, isn't it?' Julie remarked. 'One day your life is set—you wake up, have toast, go to work, see friends, come home and have your family—and then the next everything changes. Sometimes I wonder how I got where I am.'

'You seem to be doing well by those boys.' He looked at her, encouragement in his eyes. 'Erec will get better once he settles. He always finds it difficult when they swap him over to something new.'

She sighed. 'I know. So how's Arthur?'

'He's been spending more time with Gwen. It's good for both of them, I think.'

Julie nodded in agreement. 'You should try to limit the amount of time he spends with you. Jason's concerned. He doesn't think it's... proper.'

'Proper?' Marvin questioned. 'Of course it's not *proper*. How many students would rather hang out with their tutor over their own ilk? What have you heard?'

'Just that the principal thinks it's cause for concern, and that's without him knowing the full extent of how much time Arthur spends with you.'

'They won't know that, unless Mr Pick tells them, and he and I have an agreement.' He grinned at her toothily.

'You're so anti-establishment,' she teased. 'It's going to get you into trouble, one of these days.'

'When it does, I'll be sure not to mention your hand. Covering for me in staff meetings? Keeping me up to date with the gossip? You and I make a jolly team, Julie.'

She smiled at him fondly.

'Those biscuits,' he said, eying the coffee table in the middle of the room. 'Do they belong to anyone?'

'They're Mr Hall's. He brought them in yesterday.'

He looked at her with a mischievous glint in his eyes, crept forwards and set his mug on the table.

'Marvin, don't.'

He opened the tin with a pop.

'You shouldn't!' she exclaimed. 'He'll know, I swear he counts them.'

'A couple won't hurt.' He pushed the lid back in place, and scurried over to her. 'Chocolate digestive?'

She took one and Marvin bit into the other, showering crumbs down his front.

'I assume you've read the latest poll results,' Julie remarked. 'The New Nationals still have the majority. I can't imagine who votes in such things.'

'Whoever answers their phone,' Marvin told her. 'Those they call are hardly going to voice support for an opposing party.' Swallowing, he dunked the rest of his biscuit into his tea. 'I have wondered how many of our choices are smoke and mirrors. It's a popular conspiracy theory that the three main parties are essentially one and the same, run and funded by the same oligarchy.'

'Andrew Graham's convinced that life has never been better. Things are *good* under Milton, for men like him.' She glanced to the New National poster hanging on an otherwise empty wall, opposite the notice boards. 'I can't remember when Logres suddenly became so politicised.'

'I think it was about the time when Ravioli became headmaster, shortly after they came to power.'

'It's very tiring.' She offered him a strained smile. 'I'm sure it's what keeps Andrew and other Milton supporters here spouting their praise.'

'Every regime thrives on its celebrating simpletons.' He leant next to her. 'And you? What do you think?'

'Do you even need to ask? If the New Nationals had their way, Erec would be packed off to a mental institution. I know my son—he wouldn't hurt a fly. I even heard from my doctor that he could go into one of those Mobilisation Centres.'

'I would keep him away from those, if you can,' Marvin advised. 'I've heard rumours about those places, and none of them are good.'

She frowned at him. The late afternoon sun cast new shapes through the windows onto the rough blue carpets. 'What have you heard?'

'Julie?'

They both looked up. Mr Eaves poked his head through the doorway, his steely eyebrows knotted. Marvin stepped away from her, and only then did Julie realise how close he had been, close enough to smell, to feel the warm steam off the top of his tea.

'Charles,' she smiled, aware that he liked to listen in on conversations that didn't concern him, and had long-since gained the nickname Mr Eavesdropper. 'Don't tell me, Mr Hall wishes to see me?'

'It'll be the biscuits,' Marvin murmured in an undertone.

'Not Mr Hall, I'm afraid.' Mr Eaves half stepped into the room, reluctant to be pulled too far from his busy schedule. 'Dr Ravioli wants to discuss your latest set of reports with you.' He eyed her sympathetically. 'Did you forget to follow protocol?'

'Oh, probably.' Huffing, Julie strode across to the sink and emptied what was left in her mug. 'Has he spoken to you at all?'

'Not yet; I'm hoping that I've been spared this term,' Charles said without a smile. He ducked out of the staff room and sped off down the corridor.

'Perhaps we can continue this some other time?' Julie said, turning to Marvin. 'I always feel we're rushed, talking in the staff room like this.'

'Why, Ms Appelbauer, are you asking me on a date?'

'Of course,' she teased. 'And what better way to spend it than talking about Milton and his simpletons?'

'Just let me know when you're free, and we'll work something out.'

'I'll check my schedule,' she promised.

'Until then, staff room tomorrow?'

'Staff room,' she agreed.

They parted, and set off to opposite ends of the building.

'So what are you reading at the moment?'

They were sitting at a table for two, nestled at the back of the small room, as close to the corner as they could get in an already full restaurant. It was Thursday evening, and Gwenhwyfar was working her way through her pizza, which was crispy, thin, and bigger than the plate it was served on.

'Something called *Capitalism, the One True Religion*. It basically argues that capitalism and environmentalism can't co-exist. In order for capitalism to be "successful", the environment has to be destroyed.'

'Is it good?'

Arthur shrugged. 'It's all right. It's a bit Americanised. The last book I read was better.'

'You mean *The Human Condition*?' He nodded. Gwenhwyfar bit off a mouthful of crust and took a moment to swallow. 'I'm just going on a hunch here, and ignoring what Marvin said about it. I'll bet it's worth reading.'

'It is worth reading,' Arthur agreed. 'I can ask Marvin if you can borrow it. He won't mind as long as you're careful.'

Gwenhwyfar glanced down to his plate. He had nearly finished. 'Won't someone else be reading it?'

'I doubt it. Shall I ask him?'

'Why don't you give me the highlights?' Gwenhwyfar suggested. She took a sip of lemonade. 'I wouldn't want you getting in trouble with Marvin or anything.'

'You just can't be bothered to read it, can you?' Arthur teased.

'Well, I *am* in the middle of something else right now,' Gwenhwyfar admitted, buoyantly. 'It's about a struggle to claim a kingdom's throne, but the *true* heir is a bastard-born pauper living in the slums. She's only just discovered her true heritage after earning her freedom as a slave and sailing across to new lands.' She grinned. 'I'm on book four. My aunt gets me them for Christmas.'

'What's it called?' Arthur asked.

'*Empire's Call*. Well, that's the name of the series. The first book is *Untold*. Want to read it?'

'Of course! I'm wondering why I've been wasting my time with politics books now. Compared to that they sound boring.'

'You can have my copy, if you like.'

'Thanks.' He folded his cutlery and let his arm rest across the table. Gwenhwyfar still had a quarter of her pizza to go. She was flagging.

'So what's *The Human Condition* about? You never really said. Give me all the details, come on.'

'Well,' Arthur leant across the table, and Gwenhwyfar did the same. 'Mostly it's looking at the social state of the country at the time of publication. Investigating things like the need and use of CCTV, the purpose and effect of hierarchal systems such as the monarchy—'

'It was written before the abolition?'

Arthur nodded. 'In 2001. The most interesting bit is about big businesses and their involvement in politics. It explores how corporations control governments through lobbying and donations. Given that the party with the most money usually wins the election, once in power you could argue that they're indebted to those who gave them funding. If company A gives party B a million new-pounds for their election campaign, and party B wins and comes into power, party B are hardly then going to pass any laws that negatively affect company A, otherwise they won't donate next time.'

'I've heard about this,' Gwenhwyfar said, remembering what her father had told her. 'It happens all the time. With the highest-funded party winning every election, you'd think they'd just cut out the whole voting process and declare the party with the biggest campaign budget the winner.'

'I suppose it would save everyone the trouble of getting to the ballots,' Arthur remarked with an appreciative smile.

'Did the New Nationals have the highest budget?'

'I don't know,' Arthur admitted. 'But as they're currently in power, I should imagine so.'

'I've heard you can't trust the news, either,' Gwenhwyfar added, glancing to her left as a waitress hurried past. 'Often they have interests in particular industries, historically oil and fracking, but currently coal, right? So they peddle the particular viewpoint that benefits them. Such as claiming that climate change doesn't exist—you know, like they used to—and maintaining that it's under control now, that a little more coal burning won't hurt. To guide public opinion and justify continued investment in non-renewable energies.'

'Well, it works to an extent,' Arthur agreed, his voice lowered to a suitable murmur. 'Public opinion on the matter is definitely confused. We have the resources to curb climate change—we're just not investing ourselves in it. I suppose the required steps have always been considered too radical.'

'Or not profitable enough,' Gwenhwyfar remarked.

'I just don't get why it is so hard to look at things differently,' Arthur frowned. 'Everything is a short-term fix. People just keep going. They change some habits, but not quickly or thoroughly enough, and look where it's getting us.'

'People only change when it becomes too dangerous to stay the way they are,' Gwenhwyfar mused. 'Didn't Rollo May say that?'

'Whoever said it was right. Then again, I'd argue that things got too dangerous some time ago, and still we've seen little change.'

'I think I will borrow that book, if Marvin's all right with it,'

Gwenhwyfar declared. 'The one you're reading at the moment, as well. I'd like to know more about capitalism.'

'I'll ask him.'

There was a moment's silence as they considered all that had been said. Eventually Gwenhwyfar looked down to her pizza, and then to Arthur. 'Would you like the rest?'

Eagerly he swapped their plates so he could finish her food.

'We should do this again sometime,' she suggested, pleased that they had chosen a restaurant instead of the cinema. They had been talking non-stop for nearly two hours.

'We will,' he promised. 'How about we go for pancakes after school next week? I think I have one afternoon off.'

'Sounds great,' she beamed. The waiter came by to ask how they were doing, and Gwenhwyfar ordered another drink.

'So how are you finding Logres?' Arthur asked when the waiter had gone. 'Is it very different from Swansea?'

'Yeah, completely,' Gwenhwyfar said. 'There's a different vibe here. Everything's really busy. The Welsh countryside is wilder, but it's green here, which is nice. I don't think I'd have coped if it was like London.'

'London's not so bad,' Arthur reasoned, polishing off the last of her pizza. 'It has some nice parks.'

'The smog is horrible, though. It makes it nearly impossible to breathe. They need to plant more trees.'

'We need more trees everywhere,' he agreed. 'I know they say that this government is the greenest ever, but where's the proof?'

Gwenhwyfar didn't know. She looked up with a shrug, her hand resting on the table, and when Arthur clasped it her heart skipped. She still couldn't believe how handsome he was.

'Pudding?' he suggested, offering her a lop-sided smile.

Gwenhwyfar nodded, rubbing her thumb across the back of his palm. 'Pudding.'

'Arthur! Good to see you.'

Marvin moved aside to let him into the musty hallway, and took his coat. 'Can I offer you a drink—? Tea? Coffee? I'm not sure if I should crack open another bottle of wine just yet. We can't be drinking it like it's water. I can do orange juice?'

'Orange juice is perfect, thank you,' he said. After a moment spent reabsorbing all the artefacts he remembered from his last visit, Arthur followed Marvin into the kitchen. It was cosy, and nearly as cluttered as the hall, with several pots and cooking utensils hanging on the walls. 'Aren't the others here yet?'

'Not yet, you're the first.' Grinning, he handed him a cold glass of orange juice. 'Did you refresh yourself on Orwell?'

'I did.' Arthur took a large gulp. The sugary drink made his mouth water. 'I'd forgotten how grim it is. Even now, I was rooting for Winston. I always choose the wrong characters to back.'

Marvin rubbed his hands together as he leant against the stove. 'It'll be interesting to see what the others think,' he remarked. 'Though I don't want to dwell too long on it. At the moment I'm more interested in what's been happening in these Mobilisation Centres.'

'Those are the institutions that take in the homeless, right?'

'The homeless, the poor and the less able: those reliant either upon the state or in breach of quality of life laws. Such places are supposed to be platforms of reinvention, but… let's just say that I suspect such a definition may be far too generous.'

Frowning, Arthur downed the last of his juice, the glass chilling his fingers. It was cold outside too, though not as cold as it was going to be. Last winter had been a bitter frost from November until March, with six feet of snow decimating transport and cutting off supplies.

'I suppose we'll soon see what comes of it.' Marvin busied himself with clearing away the washed pots. 'I'll be keeping an eye on events, that's for sure.'

Arthur put his empty glass down on the side. 'Merlin? I was wondering... you remember that you originally wanted to invite Gwen? Well, I was wrong. I think she would be interested in this, very interested. Could I ask her to join us?'

Marvin's bushy eyebrows bristled to meet over his hooked nose. 'I think it's best if you don't, for now.' He sucked his teeth. 'Morgan and Bedivere will want to invite someone if you do, and that would double our group. I would like to get a handle on the members we already have, first.'

'But what if you were to invite her yourself?' Arthur tried. 'Could that not work?'

'That doesn't seem fair on the others,' he fretted, but upon seeing Arthur's disappointment, he offered a more lenient smile. 'Maybe next week... this is only our second session, after all. Have you looked into the Eco Party yet? You'll want to sign up quickly, before everything shuts down for Christmas.'

Thankfully, Arthur didn't have to think of a suitable excuse to mask his laziness. The doorbell rang, announcing the arrival of the rest of The Round Table. Marvin gave a loud exclamation and hurried to let them in.

They discussed *1984*, though Bedivere seemed to find their interpretation less engaging than Morgan. Marvin highlighted parallels that Arthur himself had drawn for his shredded Politics paper, but the topic soon shifted. Sitting exactly where he had been last week, opposite the window, Bedivere looked to Marvin curiously.

'The New Nationals… how is it that they got elected?'

Marvin eyed him sharply. 'Well, it's called *voting*, Bedivere.'

'Yes, I know *that*.' He blushed as Arthur and Morgan grinned. 'I mean, *how*. How did a party like this get into power? Who voted for them, and why?'

'Lots of people voted for them,' Marvin said, still standing from his speech on Orwell. 'Despite what people say, I don't think it's true that the New Nationals rigged the elections. What people forget is how frightened everyone was back then. Milton came along with a hard stance on all things pressing, pledging this and promising that.' Stiffly, he lowered himself into his chair. 'Make no mistake, he is charming. He seduced people. Everything about the New Nationals seemed exciting: their uniforms, their policies. People called them crazy at first, and other parties ridiculed them. Perhaps they were crazy in the beginning, but soon the jester dropped his façade and revealed a monster.'

'I don't even know if the façade has completely fallen,' Arthur added, looking to Marvin. 'Many people will vote for them in May.'

'I'm sure people will vote… but willingly?' Marvin gestured at them all. 'Morgan,' he barked. 'Morgan could vote for the New Nationals in May, but why would she? Did you know, Morgan, that if you and Arthur were to have the same job, at the same firm, with the same experience, Arthur would be paid roughly twenty to thirty percent more than you? How does that make you feel, Morgan, working for that percentage of the year for free? Would you vote for the New Nationals? No? What if they called you to ensure that you did? What if they dropped by your house?

Isn't it right, after all, that women are paid less? It's not *feminine* to want to earn as much as men. Women are *less able*. The New Nationals have backpedalled on gender equality quickly and effectively, and now the majority agrees with them, too.'

'But that's not fair,' Bedivere exclaimed.

'Fair? No, it's not fair,' Marvin snapped, wheeling on Bedivere, who sat bolt upright and retreated into the back of his chair. 'But what are *you* going to do about it? Gender equality is your issue, too. Why is it such a horrific thing for you to be seen as feminine? What is so desirable about what we consider to be masculine? It's women that continue to show true strength despite their marks of repression. If anything the phrase "grow some balls" is entirely misdirected. It should be "grow some ovaries".'

'No,' Morgan said suddenly. 'It should be neither. Determining between men and women in the sense that one is superior to the other is the root of the problem in the first place.'

'True,' Marvin conceded. 'My point is, there are all kinds of reasons why people shouldn't vote for the New Nationals, but people will; either because they are ignorant and therefore happy, or because they will be too frightened to vote for anyone else.'

'Cowards,' Arthur muttered.

'Cowards, or sensible?' Marvin countered. 'It's survivalist. If they themselves are unaffected by New National rule to a liveable extent, then why would they risk stepping over the line?'

The table fell to silence. Arthur, Morgan and Bedivere all exchanged a glance as Marvin huffed deeply and then leant into the round table.

'Our time is nearly up,' he told them. 'I think we'll do something different this week. You all have your copies of *1984*? Yes? I'll take those, please. Instead of reading, your task is to find one event in the news—just one, any you like—and research it on the Internet. Probe for the truth; compare accounts. See if you notice anything odd. I think you'll be surprised.'

He smiled at them all and collected up their books. After they had taken their empty glasses into the kitchen, he bade them farewell on the threshold. Arthur left with the others, hurrying out into the night.

Gavin undid his tie the moment he came into his bedroom, throwing it onto the bed.

'I hate Mondays,' he muttered, as Lancelot walked in behind him. 'English. *Maths*. Cadets, work. Not to mention feeding Gareth and Gideon.' He unbuttoned his shirt, whipped it off, and then pulled an old t-shirt over his head. 'I mean, how old is Gideon? Thirteen? When I was his age I was cooking spaghetti for the both of them.'

'Parents not back?' As always, Lancelot investigated anything new or out of place in Gavin's room. He paused by the bookshelf and extracted the thickest novel he could find, knocking over a photo frame in the process. 'You could always teach him. I don't know why they have to eat before six, anyway.'

'Mum's on a late.' Gavin kicked off his school trousers and stepped into some jeans. He bundled up his discarded clothes and threw them on his chest of drawers. 'Anyway, she won't let him use the stove, not since he set fire to it. I suppose I should count myself lucky that I get to go out at all.'

'The joys of being the eldest child,' Lancelot remarked. He righted the picture and returned the book, and stalked along the perimeter of the room. 'Though you wouldn't catch Bobby cooking for Luke. He's too busy smoking his brain away to do much of any real use.'

'Your uncle allows that?' Gavin scowled, sitting in his desk chair. Lancelot came to a standstill at the middle of the room. 'He hardly even lets you use painkillers.'

'Not unless we're dying,' Lancelot remarked. 'Of course he doesn't allow it, he doesn't know. He smells it, though. He thinks it's me. It's insulting. It's my room he searches, not theirs.'

'He'll search their rooms too,' Gavin told him. 'They just won't know. My mum looks in my room all the time—it's infuriating. I don't know if she does it on purpose, but I'll find she's moved something, on the top shelf, or under the bed. Is it that she can't remember where she found it? Or is it her way of telling me she's snooping?'

'Snooping for what?'

He shrugged, unwilling to speculate. 'Beats me.'

There was a scuffle at the door. Gavin sat forwards with a huff.

'That better not be you, Gid,' he called. 'What did I say about listening in on people?'

The door swung open, and Gareth appeared in the frame, looking sheepish.

'How do you turn the oven on?' His fat bottom lip wobbled, and he looked shyly across to Lancelot. His hair was dark and too long, and he had a plump, soft face matched by his podgy, short frame. 'Gideon wants to do a pizza.'

'You're not having pizza,' Gavin told him firmly. 'I've already made dinner. Tell Gideon that if he puts that pizza in the oven, I'll lock him in the cupboard. All right?'

Nodding, Gareth's blue eyes flittered nervously to Lancelot again, and then he slunk out of the room, anxious with the message he had to bear.

'We should eat,' Gavin declared. Lancelot jumped up and eagerly chased him down the stairs.

They stopped the pizza just in time, though Gideon had removed the wrappings. Gavin stuffed it all back into the box and pushed it into the freezer. Cass begged silently for scraps, and as they huddled around the small kitchen table it was all arms and elbows: Lancelot next to Gavin, Gideon next to Lancelot, and Gareth sandwiched between Gavin and his younger brother.

'Gideon's in charge when I'm gone. Dad will be home soon, so I want all this cleared up—*don't* tease the dog—everything washed up and tidied, you hear me?'

His brothers did little to acknowledge his request, and for the rest of the meal Gavin tried to keep their disorderly behaviour in check. As always, Lancelot took their antics well, only snapping when Gideon tried to squirt chilli sauce on his school uniform. For the rest of the meal Gideon sat in a shocked silence, as if he were surprised to find that a razor was sharp.

'Gavin,' Gareth asked, drawing out his name in the babyish manner that their parents adored. 'When are you going to Cadets?'

'Half five.' He snapped a sharp knife out of Gareth's hand as he prodded his opposite palm with the point.

'Gavin,' Gareth said again, 'when can I come to Cadets?'

'When you're old enough,' Lancelot answered patiently, spooning the last of his seconds into his mouth.

'Gavin, when will I be old enough?'

The two boys exchanged a glance. 'Not for a while yet,' Gavin conceded. 'You're only eight.'

'Anyway, you might not feel like it when you're older.'

Gareth eyed Lancelot curiously. 'Why not?'

'It's hard work.'

'Why?'

'Because you have to do army stuff, stupid,' Gideon interrupted. Gavin scolded him and told him not to call his brother stupid. '*I'm* old enough to join, but I don't want to. They teach you how to fight and kill, but I don't think it's fair to fight or kill anything.' He looked to Gareth disapprovingly. 'And you shouldn't want to kill, either. Do you want to kill something?'

'No,' Gareth insisted, distressed by the question.

'Gavin will, won't you? When you join the army. Soldiers kill people all the time.' Gideon leant forwards, narrowed his eyes, and directed his stare straight at him. 'But *Gavin* wants to kill people, because *Gavin* wants to join the army.'

'Gideon—' Gavin warned.

'It's true. Gavin wants to kill people.'

His youngest brother shrank away from him at the words.

'I don't want to kill anyone, Gid,' he scowled. 'I want to help people. People that need helping, and can't help themselves.'

'If you want to help people, then maybe you should be a doctor,' Gideon remarked matter-of-factly.

'But then he wouldn't get to shoot things,' Gareth pointed out.

'Exactly,' Gideon argued.

Lancelot was losing patience. 'Your brother doesn't want to kill anyone, and you know it.'

'What about you? Are you going to kill someone?'

'Not if I can help it.'

'But aren't you joining the army, too?'

'Going to Cadets doesn't mean that you have to join the

army,' Lancelot reasoned. With all forks and knives neatly crossed, he stood to clear the plates. 'I've considered it, but with the current government what it is, I'd only be fighting for what I don't believe in.'

'What's government got to do with it?' asked Gideon.

'Everything,' Lancelot said. 'Ultimately, the government tells the army what to do. If a government wants its army to go and bomb a country for no reason, the army obliges.'

'Lance,' Gavin cautioned. 'He's thirteen.'

'So Gavin *is* going to kill people then,' Gideon concluded triumphantly. 'I thought so.'

'We should go,' Gavin declared, looking to the clock. Quickly he ran a drink from the tap, gulped it down, and then snatched up his sports bag. He paused in the living room as Gareth followed them to the front door. 'Remember what I said. Gideon's in charge. Wash up the plates, and then do your homework. OK?'

Gareth nodded silently. Shouting to Gideon in the other room to remind him he was going, Gavin followed Lancelot over the threshold and slammed the door.

THE DISAPPEARED

The first week of October arrived with mild weather more suited to the early days of June. Gwenhwyfar spent most of Tuesday and Wednesday away from her friends, keeping company with Arthur as much as she could when she had established that he didn't have a pressing reason to be with Marvin. It was Thursday afternoon when she came home to find her mother whispering with her aunt in the kitchen, and sensing that something was wrong, she paused to listen at the half-closed door.

'Something's the matter with him, Mel, I *know* it,' Eve was saying, her voice fragile and worn thin with tears.

They hadn't heard her come in, or perhaps they thought they had, for suddenly there was a tense silence. When Llew failed to alert them to her presence, however, the murmuring resumed.

'He's probably just stressed. You know how hard this new job's been for him,' Melissa said, softly. 'He's in a new role, with more responsibilities than he's ever had before. You said it yourself: he's probably still adjusting.'

'Then why won't he talk to me about it?' she sniffed. 'If I ask him what's wrong, he just shuts down. I'm... I'm going insane here, Mel. I've nothing to do, all day, and I just keep thinking—' there was a moment's silence, '—I keep thinking that he's... he's hiding something from me. It's—it's a feeling. I can't quite place it.'

'What are you thinking?'

The silence that followed was so thick that Gwenhwyfar could almost hear her own heartbeat.

'I don't know,' Eve murmured. 'He's been in London all week, he even stayed in the city one night, with no notice, and when he is home he hides in his study. He won't let me go in, not even when he's at work. He locks it.'

'Does he, now?'

'I think... I think he might be...'

Her mother started to sob again. Gwenhwyfar felt her stomach turn to lead. *Another woman*, she thought suddenly, and though she felt sickened by the notion it was if she had known all along. It made sense of why her dad was never at home, why he was always working and attending business meetings at strange hours, and the anger that suddenly swept over her was suffocating. *How dare he, how dare he* do this to them? How dare he hurt her mother like this? The coward, the traitor.

What was she supposed to do? She couldn't act normally with them after hearing their secret, and it was their secret now. No one had told her, and from the sounds of it, no one was going to.

'I'm sure it's nothing.' Melissa hushed Eve calmly. 'It's easy to get worked up about things when we have too much time on our hands, to blow them out of proportion. Maybe you should come and work for the firm, after all? I think it would be good for you.' There was a silence, filled with more tears. 'Have you spoken to him?'

'No,' Eve replied miserably. 'I know if I do, he'll just deny it. I'm not *stupid*, Mel, I know something's going on. I mean why would he need to hide that bank account from me? He's clearly using it to buy gifts for *her*. When did he last buy me something? When?'

Gwenhwyfar couldn't listen to a word more. No one heard her open and close the front door again, and the moment she was out on the porch she drew in a deep, shaking breath. She had to get away from the house, had to walk, had to separate herself from the anger anchored inside her. As she came to Potters Park, she decided that she would go and see Arthur and tell him what she had heard. When she got to the library, however, she couldn't bring herself to do it, and so lied to him instead and told him that everything was fine.

The table seemed empty with just four of them filling it. It was Friday; their third session at The Round Table, and this week Marvin had supplied them with crisps and other nibbles. There were party sausages and cheese with pineapple on toothpicks, of which Morgan only ate half, leaving Bedivere to snaffle the rejected lumps of cheddar; and bowls of nuts and dried fruit, which remained largely untouched.

'Your turn, Arthur,' Marvin said, his mouth full with a mini sausage roll, which consisted of cheap grey processed meat. 'Morgan and Bedivere have shown us what they learned—' He eyed Bedivere, who had mistaken the brief, and Morgan who had gone for something that yielded few results. '—What have you got for us?'

Awkwardly, Arthur stood up as the others had done, and

looked to the sheets of paper he had before him.

'Vanishings,' he muttered. 'Mentions of homeless people going missing off the streets.'

Flopping into his chair, Marvin crossed his hands over his stomach. 'And?'

'And that's just it. I used a website which publishes amended versions of every newspaper article in the country. Every time an article is corrected, the new version is uploaded against the old. You can see the changes and omissions that the New Nationals make. Here.'

He slid the printouts across the table, the original publication, and the amended version. Bedivere frowned.

'You're telling me that the news changes?'

Arthur nodded. 'It's rewritten without any acknowledgement that it has been. Why do you think it's so hard to get a printed paper?'

'I don't know,' Bedivere shrugged. 'Progress?'

Marvin shook his head. 'Only particular institutions and New National offices get printed papers, these days. Local tabloids may be easier to find, perhaps, but are probably amended the most. Anything that's been published can be recalled, redacted and re-issued. That's why I tell you to always question what you read or hear in the news. It changes with Milton's policies.'

'But that's illegal, surely?' Morgan asked, an upset scowl darkening her features. 'They can't do that. They can change anything?'

'And unless you happen to have access to the original, you can never be sure what. As Arthur says, there is a website on the Dark Net highlighting most changes, but the New Nationals constantly shut it down. It must have been removed and re-launched at least seventy times now.'

'What about live broadcasts?' Bedivere interjected. 'Everyone sees them, knows what was said. Surely they can't amend those?'

'No, but who remembers? You *could* record such broadcasts illegally, but who would ever think to? It's physically impossible, unless you use a device severed from the network. The news is trusted by most, and people take it at face value. Would you have thought to question it, before hearing of this?' He smiled stiffly. 'I told you you'd be surprised.' He gestured. 'Go on, Arthur.'

Arthur cleared his throat. 'If you read the original article, it mentions homeless children going missing in our area, from the seventeenth of September this year. This is a local paper. Now, if you look at the second sheet... *this* amendment replaced the old article on the twenty-seventh of September. I chose it, because it's a drastic change. It's no longer about missing children, but about a series of thefts and missing animals, in particular pets, which are believed to have been stolen for "sustenance" by these same, no-longer missing children.'

He could tell that his discovery was not going down well, least of all with Morgan, who stared at both copies as if they were a cruel trick.

'*This* is what I wanted you to realise. Arthur, I think, already knew it, but you should know it, too. Your government owns the press. Anything and everything they want you to read and believe, you will. Nothing is left untouched. Everything has been tailored for your maximum complicity in a society which is structured and strung together like some nasty, elaborate *lie*.'

Bedivere and Morgan stared at Marvin in silence. A chill rolled up Arthur's spine. Yes, he knew it too, but hearing it again pushed him towards the same uncomfortable feeling he had felt when he first stumbled across it.

'They own technology as well,' Marvin continued. 'When I was young there were promises of great things to come, from in-home 3-D printing to teleportation and Mars colonisation. Science and technology have been sidelined due to the near eradication of funding. No one is *creating* anymore. How can they, when they are watched as they are? Surveillance strangles innovative thinking. Technically we have been in the same place with little-to-no progress for twenty years now. Things are repackaged and old technology is rebranded, but there are no *breakthroughs*. Medically it is much the same.'

Bedivere shifted. 'Gavin knows a lot about this sort of stuff,' he volunteered. 'He's always talking about encrypting. I don't know if he uses the Dark Net or not, but he's probably heard of it.'

'If he does use it he wouldn't admit to it,' Arthur told him. 'Use of the Dark Net was made illegal about fifteen years ago. Thankfully they can't go after everyone who accesses it, so they focus on the hosts, instead.'

'Ah! That reminds me. Arthur asked if he could invite someone new to join us last week, but I don't think it fair that only he gets to choose. I've thought carefully, and I think we can cope with three more. What do you think?'

'We can invite people?' Morgan asked, brightening. 'Who?'

'Whoever you like,' Marvin beamed.

'George Milton?' Bedivere joked.

'Within reason, obviously,' said Marvin. 'It must be someone you trust completely, someone who will really benefit from being here. If they mess up, then you're all out. Understood?' They nodded, weighed down by the responsibility he had suddenly dropped upon them. 'Well?'

'Like I said, Gavin knows a lot about this sort of stuff,' Bedivere mused. 'But Gwen…'

'I'm inviting Gwen,' Arthur said. 'If that's all right.'

'Gwen,' Marvin repeated with a nod. 'Bedivere?'

'It has to be Gavin then,' he said, thinking. 'Yeah, Gavin. I don't think Vi would have time for this. He's more likely to say yes.'

'Morgan?'

'Lancelot,' Morgan said after a moment.

'You can't ask Lance,' Arthur protested.

She glared at him. 'Why not? You're inviting Gwen.'

'Yes, but Gwen's not an idiot.'

'Neither is Lance.'

'Lance will just tell everyone, you know he will,' contested Bedivere.

'Says who? I happen to think that he'd be perfect for this. And if Gavin is coming he'll want to be here. I can ask, at least.'

'But this is Lance we're talking about—! Come on!' Arthur appealed to Marvin, but his teacher averted his eyes.

'I *trust* him,' Morgan insisted. 'Marvin said we could invite who we want.'

'As long as you're happy being responsible for us getting kicked out when he goes and tells everyone,' Arthur muttered.

'He *won't* tell.'

'We'll see what he says,' Marvin cut in, 'we don't have to give all the details out immediately. If they're interested, we can reveal a little more.' He rubbed his dry hands together. 'We'll invite them to our next session. How does that sound?'

The room fell into silence, but eventually the three of them nodded. Arthur gazed at Morgan resentfully, his good mood ruined by the prospect of enduring an encroachment by Lancelot into one of his last remaining sanctuaries.

Viola handed her portfolio to Gwenhwyfar, who opened it up immediately and flicked through the glossy pages to find her latest shots. It was Monday morning of the second week of October, and they were both sitting outside, surprised to find that despite the hour, it was reasonably warm.

'So what was this for?' Gwenhwyfar asked, after she had made suitable noises of admiration.

'Just another test,' Viola shrugged, leaning over the picnic bench to get another look. 'I didn't get paid for it. So far I've earned nothing. It's really expensive going up to London all the time.' She pointed at the photo on the left. 'I got that one in the first shot,' she added proudly.

'It looks great.' Gwenhwyfar flicked back and forth between the pages, comparing each picture. 'This one's definitely my favourite. I love the make-up.'

They were sitting in the large square of grass by the Design Technology rooms. In the wing behind Viola, opposite the drama studios, was their tutor room, which overlooked both the benches and the narrow strip of grounds between Badbury and the perimeter fence.

'Think Bedivere will find us here?' Viola asked, stowing her portfolio away in her schoolbag.

'He should do. We'll go inside in a bit, anyway.' Gwenhwyfar let her gaze drift across the grounds. The bin by the steps down to the Badbury changing rooms was overflowing, picked at by seagulls, and the hedge along the path left little to be seen of the houses beyond, its trimmed top interrupted by long spindles of yew. She realised that Viola had said something, and apologised for missing it. Her friend eyed her with concern.

'What's wrong? You seem off.'

'Off?' Gwenhwyfar questioned, suddenly feeling defensive.

'I mean distracted. You were out of it on Friday, too. Is everything all right?' For a moment Viola tried to figure out what to say. 'It's not Arthur, is it?'

She was insulted by the assumption. 'No, it's not Arthur. Arthur's fine.' Suddenly the words seemed to crawl up her throat, and before she knew it they were tumbling from her lips. 'I overheard my mam talking with my aunt on Thursday. She thinks my father is having an affair.'

Viola was shocked. 'She does?' Gwenhwyfar nodded. 'Does he know?'

'No,' she said, angrily. 'She doesn't know that I know, either. So they're both lying to me, acting like everything's normal when it's *not*. This weekend was a complete nightmare. I thought I was going to explode.'

Viola joined her on her side of the bench. 'What did your mum say? Does she have proof?'

Her tears were immediate. 'She found a bank account. Apparently he's been using it to buy that *whore* presents. He's always working late and staying up in London. I'd have never thought he was capable of such a thing, but now that she's said it, I feel stupid. It's obvious.'

'Nothing's obvious,' Viola contested, calmly. 'You may've heard wrong. And remember, your mum doesn't know for sure. She thinks he's having an affair. She could be mistaken.'

'She should talk to me about it, at least. I'm her *daughter*. I can't just go on, pretending like everything's normal. I can't!' She gasped, struggling for the breath to speak. 'Why else would he have a hidden bank account? What else could he be hiding?'

'I don't know. You can't assume anything.' Viola frowned. 'Maybe you can talk to one of them about it?'

'Oh yeah, that'll work,' Gwenhwyfar remarked. '"Hey, Mam, Dad; is it true Dad's having an affair?" Right.'

'What else can you do?' Viola huffed, removing her supporting arm as Gwenhwyfar sat up straight. 'Either that or you don't say anything: ignore it. Push it to the back of your mind until one of them sits you down and tells you that they're getting divorced. Plenty of couples stay together after affairs. Nothing may come of this.'

Gwenhwyfar sniffed up the mucus that clogged her nose, rubbed her eyes, and nodded.

'I know it sounds harsh, but if he *is* having an affair, and if they *do* break up, you'll have plenty of things to worry about later. Trust me.'

She huddled into herself to stave off a sudden chill. 'Why did your parents divorce? Was it because of your dad?'

'Partly. My mum also had an affair. I only found out when she'd already run off to Paris with her new squeeze.' She offered her an empty smile. 'My dad sat me down and said they'd decided I should stay with him because I was English. She's French, but I haven't spoken French since I was six.'

There was a moment's silence. Gwenhwyfar watched Viola closely.

'I don't blame her. I mean, I *did*, but after learning that my dad was gay I realised that it wasn't just on her. He never told her. He was afraid to. It's easier to have a wife and kids. In a way it's good of them to have held up the façade for so long, just for me.'

'But they lied to you,' Gwenhwyfar pointed out. 'You must be angry.'

'Why? They both love me, and they both loved each other once; that was real. At least if it happens for you, you'll be prepared. I'm sorry though. I know it sucks.'

'Don't be. It's not your fault my father's a sleazebag.' Gwenhwyfar laughed slightly, but it was false laughter and only made her feel worse. She bent her head to dry her eyes on her woollen gloves. Viola stood up.

'We should go. Bedivere's obviously missed us.'

Sniffing, Gwenhwyfar nodded and followed Viola back into Badbury, fanning her face in the hope that she could blow away all evidence of her tears.

No one seemed to notice that anything was wrong during registration, and when Gwenhwyfar and Bedivere came to their History room they found that Marvin was already sitting at his desk, letting his students wander in as they pleased. As they passed Gavin and Tom's empty seats Bedivere frowned, and looked back to the door.

'Marvin's raring to go,' Arthur remarked as they joined him. 'He's got us set for a lesson on the Tudors.'

'Makes a change from the World Wars,' Bedivere murmured. He leant towards the middle of their two tables anxiously. 'Is Gavin in today?'

'I think so,' Gwenhwyfar said. 'Why?'

'I need to ask him something. About Marvin's club.'

'What about it?'

'Marvin's said we can invite one person each,' interrupted

Arthur. He looked at her expectantly. 'I was going to invite you.'

'Oh.' He'd caught her off guard. 'So I don't have to ask Marvin if I can join, after all?'

'No. He's fine with it. I can pick you up, if you like.'

'Couldn't you have asked him earlier?'

'What do you mean?'

'I mean, if you really wanted me there you could have just asked him in the first place. It's not like he would've said no.'

'He did say no, actually,' Arthur frowned. 'I asked him two weeks ago but he was worried about expanding too quickly.'

'And before?'

'I told you; it was by invitation only. He only invited me, Bedivere and Morgan.'

She wasn't in the mood for something like this. Shrugging, she turned to Morgan, annoyed that it was her who had been chosen first. 'Who are you inviting?'

'Lance, but I haven't asked him yet.'

That surprised her. Thrown, Gwenhwyfar looked to Arthur.

'I still can't believe you're choosing him,' he grumbled darkly. Morgan rolled her eyes and returned to her work. He set his brown eyes on Gwenhwyfar. 'So are you coming?'

'I'll think about it. After all, I'm sure it's just looking at stuffy prose, right? Completely boring.'

'He was only being cautious,' Arthur said. 'He wasn't suggesting that you wouldn't find it interesting—'

She felt a flare of irritation. 'That's what he *said*, Arthur.'

'You know he didn't mean it like that. Once you're in the club it'll be different. He knows you'll find it interesting—I told him.'

Reluctant to give in when she had been excluded for so long, Gwenhwyfar glanced at their teacher. 'I don't know. Fridays are difficult for me,' she lied. 'Look, if you're sure he wants me there, I'll come. I just thought it was a bit *exclusive*. When is it?'

'Friday, at quarter to six,' Arthur said, clearly wounded.

She thought for a moment. Perhaps it would be good to get out of the house. 'I'll see if I'm free.'

'It's only an hour,' Bedivere pleaded. 'You have to come, if only to help keep Lance in check.'

'Will you stop talking about him like he's some unwanted mongrel?' Morgan snapped, her face flushing pink with anger.

'But he *is* unwanted,' Arthur remarked with a smirk.

Morgan wheeled on him. 'What, afraid he'll knock you off your perch? That you won't be Marvin's favourite anymore?'

'It's not about that,' Arthur objected, abashed.

'No—? Then what is it? You're behaving like a spoilt child.'

'Why is everyone suddenly having a go at me?' Arthur exclaimed. 'I'm not the one who wants to bring the village idiot to the table.'

Morgan's cheeks brightened to beetroot, and whether it was pain that flashed in her eyes or anger, Gwenhwyfar couldn't tell.

'Fine!' she hissed. 'Ridicule him if you want. I'm asking him, and that's that. If you've got a problem with it, don't turn up.'

Gwenhwyfar had never seen Morgan lose her temper before, but was glad of it. Suddenly the other girl seemed more human. 'He probably won't want to come anyway,' she said with confidence. 'If Arthur's going, and Marvin's there, he'll keep as far away as possible.'

'Right,' Bedivere agreed, looking at his friend. 'You're probably worrying over nothing.'

Morgan caught his eye sharply, but held her tongue, and buckled low over her exercise book to scrawl in the margins. Gavin and Tom arrived late, and soon Marvin was on his feet again, lecturing them on the triumphs and tragedies of the house of Tudor.

'Did you hear about the Mobilisation Centres?'

They were sitting in the canteen, enjoying the rarity of a nearly empty hall. The door at the end of the cafeteria was open, refreshing the building with a clean autumn breeze warmed by golden sunlight. Gavin crouched closer to the table. 'Someone's blown the whistle. They're not as great as the New Nationals make out.'

Tom and Lancelot were in the practice rooms, working on their music with The Oxymorons. Gwenhwyfar frowned.

'You mean those reintegration centres where they send the homeless?' she asked quietly. Gavin nodded. 'What have you heard?'

'That the residents are being systematically abused,' Gavin explained in an undertone. 'Some have even disappeared.'

'Disappeared?' Gwenhwyfar echoed. 'What does that mean?'

'It means vanished: gone. People recorded in one register but omitted from the next. Old records amended to erase their existence completely. Families asking about loved ones sent away with lies about them reintegrating into society. It's the people with physical disabilities that go first.'

'What's this?' Bedivere arrived at their table with a dinner tray in his hands; his usual serving of mashed potato, gravy and peas piled high.

'Mobilisation Centres. They're basically hard labour camps. I've seen the documents… pictures.' Gavin's mouth distorted with revulsion at the memory. 'The government knows.'

'I haven't seen anything about this in the news,' Viola

commented.

'Of course not. The main broadcasters won't cover this. It's just been released on the Dark Net. If anyone does try to report it—'

'They'll get *corrected*?'

Gavin looked at Bedivere curiously. 'Right.'

'Corrected?' Gwenhwyfar asked.

'The article is amended, or deleted. The sites that published have already been taken down. The guy who blew the whistle, *Meerkat6791*, has gone into hiding. He published the official documents: it's all in there. The people who go into these centres don't come out. Think about it, when have they ever? We've all seen the homeless disappear off our streets, but do we ever ask where they end up?'

'This can't be true,' Gwenhwyfar said. Her voice seemed separated from her own body. 'People wouldn't stand for it.'

'People either don't know, or don't want to know. The New Nationals won't admit to anything. "It's just one centre. We've launched an investigation." I can hear it now. I'm thinking about getting in contact with the people who helped *Meerkat* publish.'

'Gavin,' Viola warned, suddenly afraid. 'You shouldn't.'

'Why shouldn't I?'

'Because it's dangerous?'

'Viola's right,' Gwenhwyfar urged. 'If this is true, getting involved is the last thing you want to do.'

'I know what I'm doing.'

'Do you?'

'Yes,' he retorted. 'I'm not stupid, Vi.'

'And neither am I!' she exclaimed hotly. 'I know that you want to help people, but sticking your neck through the guillotine—?'

'So you'd rather me sit back and do nothing?' he hissed, his voice rising.

'We don't know yet—'

'We do—!'

'I haven't read anything.'

'Look it up, then,' Gavin exclaimed.

'It's bad enough that you hide your activities from the New Nationals,' Viola argued, 'but to get involved in something like this? In a world of open doors, it's the locked ones that get picked. As far as the New Nationals are concerned wish to conceal will be taken as guilt enough. Involving yourself with activists will only give them more reason to monitor you.'

He shook his head, rejecting her attitude out of hand.

'There may be another way to help. Contacting people online can be traced.'

'It can also be hidden.'

'And it can be meddled with. The New Nationals love planting illegal material and fabricating browser histories. They do it all the time.' Her eyes went glassy with anger, and she shook her head. 'If this is true, then it's *horrific*. But don't let your anger make you do something rash that won't help.'

The table fell silent. Bedivere seemed to have forgotten about his food, but after a moment pushed his fork through it, his mind detached from the action. Gwenhwyfar thought of the little boy who had gone missing. Had he been sent to a centre? She didn't even know what they looked like, and with an abruptness that made her feel cold, realised that she had never even seen one.

It was Tuesday, and first period was over. Arthur joined Morgan the moment she came out of their French room.

'Morgan—! I was wondering if we could talk.'

She didn't stop for him. 'Don't you have Science next?'

'I wanted to see if you've asked Lance about the club yet.' He followed her as she strode down the hall. 'Because I really think it's a bad idea.'

'You do, do you?' Morgan scowled. 'Who should I invite instead, then? Any suggestions?'

He tried to think of someone she might like, but drew a blank. 'Viola?'

'*Viola?*' she repeated. 'Viola's never even spoken to me before. Why should I ask her? Though I don't know, maybe *Gwen's* got a cousin,' she bit. 'What happened to us being friends?'

He was taken aback. 'We are friends, Morgan.'

'Oh really? Then why don't we sit together at lunch?'

'Because! I've been busy. I've been spending a lot of time with Marvin. Besides, aren't you sitting with Hattie now?'

'So what if I am?' she huffed. 'I'm not an idiot. I know that Gwen doesn't want you spending time with me. What happened to us going to London together again?'

'We will!' He studied her profile. 'And we can sit together tomorrow if you like. Are you doing anything?'

'Yes. Asking Lancelot if he wants to join our club,' she remarked sourly. Their pace quickened, and they hurried down the stairs at the end of the Languages corridor. 'I can't do then, anyway,' Morgan added. 'I'm meeting Percy. You know, in Year Twelve. He's a sixth former.'

Arthur felt a twinge of jealousy. He knew who Percy was. Everyone loved him. 'I didn't know you were interested in those types,' he said, suddenly distracted.

'What types?'

'Popular types.'

'He's not popular,' she contested.

'Yes he is. He's the most popular guy in school.'

There was a flicker of something in her eyes, and her face softened. 'I'm free Saturday. We could do something then? If Gwen doesn't mind, of course.'

'I could always see if she wants to come with us.'

'That's probably not a good idea.'

'Why not?' They passed the practice rooms. The closed doors leaked the sound of a piano and a wavering note sung by an unbroken voice.

'Because,' Morgan declared, 'she obviously doesn't like me. So I'm sorry if I don't think your plan to turn us into *best friends* will work. I have to get to class,' she stated sharply, 'and so should you.'

Arthur stopped at the doors to the courtyard of the Drama studios and held them open for a string of year sevens. 'But what about Lance?' he shouted. Morgan strode on, and didn't look back.

He was late to Science. Mrs Paxton called him out as he tried to sneak in unnoticed, and as punishment he was forced to sit next to the known goody-two-shoes of the class, Chris; a small freckled boy with blonde hair who rarely said a word to anyone.

'Why were you so late?' Gwenhwyfar asked him once the bell expelled them for break. Mrs Paxton shut and locked the door behind them, and then hurried off to the staff room. 'You're usually the first one here.'

'I was trying to convince Morgan not to invite Lance to the club,' he admitted. 'She's adamant, though.'

'It probably won't do as much harm as you think,' she said as they walked to the stairwell. 'Marvin wouldn't allow it if he thought Lance was a risk. Morgan can invite who she likes.'

'She's just doing it to annoy me.'

'What makes you say that?'

'Because she only said she wanted to invite Lance once she knew I was inviting you. She thinks you don't like her.'

Gwenhwyfar said nothing to this, but as Arthur followed her down the stairs she seemed to think over something. 'Does it annoy you? That Morgan's inviting him?'

'It annoys me that anyone's inviting him.'

'But I don't get why Morgan would invite Lance just to upset you,' she said. 'I mean—if she's just a friend, she shouldn't care who you invite.' They came into the old entrance hall by the medical room, and paused. 'She knows that you're not interested in her, right?'

'You think she's jealous?'

'Isn't she?'

He didn't know what to say to that. Gwenhwyfar looked towards the blue double doors that led out into the car park, and shifted from foot to foot.

'So have you thought any more about joining?'

'Do I have to decide now? It's not till Friday. I'm still thinking about it.'

'What's there to think about?'

She turned away from him, and together they pushed their way out into the car park. In daylight Arthur noticed her make-up seemed thicker than usual. Her eyes were heavily bruised with eyeliner. 'I just find it odd. An afterschool club at a teacher's house... is it even allowed?'

'Technically? No. But Ravioli wouldn't let him set one up

here. Not in a million years.'

'And it's just you, Marvin, Morgan and Bedivere?'

'And Gavin, I should imagine. Bedivere's supposed to be asking him.'

'And Lance.' She chewed her lip thoughtfully. 'I don't know. I mean, I'd like to, but I'm not sure if I'll have time at the moment.'

'Why not?'

'I've got a lot going on. My... my mum's going through something, and I feel I need to be there to support her.' She looked down at her feet and paused by the tennis courts. 'I don't suppose you can hold onto my invitation?'

'Is she all right?'

Gwenhwyfar nodded. 'She's fine, it's just stress. My dad's not in much—he's working.'

'Next week then, maybe,' he suggested. 'But if you change your mind, let me know.'

'Thanks, I will.' She turned to leave. 'You're seeing Marvin?'

'Yeah, I said I would.' He frowned. 'Do you want me to stay with you?'

She shook her head. 'It's fine. I'll see you later? You know where to find me.'

She left. The car park was emptying now as students moved on to inhabit the fields and cafeteria. Knowing that he would be thrown out if he got caught by the Prefects or staff on patrol, Arthur hurried into New Wormelow and headed to his tutor room, where he hoped to find Marvin waiting for him with his latest read.

Knights

Friday the eleventh of October was a grey day, with a heavy mist that broke into a thick curtain of drizzle. By the time Arthur made it to Marvin's house he was drenched, his hair hanging in flat locks and his wool coat beaded with rain.

'Arthur!' Marvin exclaimed, opening the door. 'Come in, come in! Dreadful weather, isn't it?'

Rudolph greeted him like an old friend as he was ushered into the hallway. The stag's glassy eyes followed him about the room. 'Good day?' he asked, shaking off his greatcoat and spraying the hallway with rainwater.

'Very,' Marvin said, excitedly. 'I'm looking forward to welcoming our new members. I've even got a bottle out. Shall we?' He took away his coat to hang it up, and then rejoined Arthur in the study. 'Did you determine if Gwen is coming?'

'She's having to miss it, this week. Her mum's not well. She's asked if we can hang on to her invite. Do you mind?'

'She's your invitee, so that's entirely up to you.' Uncorking the bottle of red, Marvin filled five of the six glasses already set on the table. 'I feel I should allocate seats, really. You've all been seat hopping too much. It unnerves me, being a teacher and all.' Grinning, he handed Arthur a glass, and then the two toasted each other briefly.

'I have to say, I'm feeling a little unsure about this,' Arthur admitted, taking a small sip. 'I hope we're not making a mistake.'

'This group was always going to expand. It may as well be sooner rather than later.' The doorbell sounded. 'That'll be them. Would you mind?'

Arthur set his glass down and moved into the hall. When he opened the door Morgan was standing before him, sodden. She hurried inside, shedding her coat immediately.

'Percy!' Marvin exclaimed, appearing behind Arthur with a merry smile. 'Glad you could join us. I trust Morgan's filled you in?'

He was of average height; slender, with a round handsome face framed by sable, curling hair. It was his eyes that all the girls at school went on about, however; his brilliant blue, twinkling eyes, and as he moved to shake Marvin's hand they glinted joyously.

'Mr Caledonensis! Still putting crazy ideas into your students' heads?' He turned to Morgan, and looked at her far too fondly for Arthur's liking. 'I used to be in his History class. I didn't do well. There's a reason I gave it a miss for my Level Fives.'

'Don't worry, your record of being my worst student has long since been surpassed,' Marvin chuckled, showing him into the study. 'But I *do* hear you've found your calling. Particularly good at Psychology, am I right?'

As Morgan went in after them, Arthur caught her by the arm.

'You brought him?'

She looked at him with confusion. 'Marvin said we could bring who we liked this week.'

'I thought you were bringing Lance?'

'He seemed to have a problem with it. I thought you'd be pleased. It's not like you wanted him here.'

'No, I didn't want him to know. I'd rather he didn't know about The Round Table and wasn't here, than him knowing and *not* being here. Him *not* being here means he has no reason to keep quiet.'

'You should give him more credit,' Morgan insisted, pulling her elbow away. She walked stiffly into the study, and pointedly sat next to Percy, who looked to Marvin in surprise.

'We're having wine?' he asked.

'If there are no objections.' Marvin handed them each a glass. When Morgan politely declined, Arthur took it for her. 'It's good to have you with us, Percy. We should probably wait with introductions until Bedivere—ah, there he is now.'

He put his glass down and went to answer the door, leaving the three of them in an awkward silence. Soon they were rejoined, and after a quick introduction Marvin announced a toast, his extravagant words celebrating their newfound camaraderie. Their glasses clinked and tastes were taken of the red. For Gavin the wine went down well, but Percy winced at the initial potency and laughed, coughing.

'I am glad you're all here,' Marvin said once they were gathered at the table. 'As it is, we're still missing a member, but she'll hopefully be joining us next week.'

'Gwen?' Gavin asked. Marvin nodded. 'Where is she now?'

'Her mum's not well,' Arthur excused. 'She's looking after her.'

'She hasn't said anything about her mum being ill,' Gavin remarked with concern. 'When did you hear this?'

'Tuesday.'

Percy eyed the group, eager to be included. 'Who's Gwen?'

'She's in our year,' Gavin said.

'You're all year elevens?'

'You're the odd one out,' Morgan told him with a smile.

'We would have all been year elevens, had Lancelot said yes,' Arthur remarked.

'You invited Lance?' Gavin asked, surprised.

'Morgan did, but apparently it's not his thing.'

'It's completely his thing,' Gavin contested. 'Maybe you'd know that, if you knew him better.'

'Boys! Let's not argue, hmm? I don't think any of us were expecting Lancelot to give up his Friday evenings to join us. Let's not worry over the *whys*. The important thing is we have Percy with us, who is very keen on world affairs—' Marvin glanced to Percy, '—*current* world affairs, at least,' he corrected.

Unruffled, Percy grinned.

'Now,' Marvin said, 'let's begin.'

The first fifteen minutes passed slowly for Arthur, as Marvin repeated much of what he already knew. Gavin and Percy said little to begin with, but listened to their host closely, neither one of them quite sure what to make of him. It was about forty minutes and one bottle of red into their session when the topic heated up. Marvin struck his hand against the polished table, making those nearest him jump.

'Do you think that the New Nationals won't come for you if you vote for them? Yes, at first they might not; but when they've come for your friends, your siblings and your parents, who will be left to save you? What makes you think you can complain about your loss of rights, if you fail to prevent injustice from happening to others?'

Arthur drew his eyes away from Marvin the moment that he looked at him. Bedivere was frowning, as if he wasn't quite sure whether or not to take him seriously, while Gavin watched Marvin's every move.

'Doing nothing about an injustice done to another can be as damaging as the injustice itself,' Morgan dared. Percy looked to her uncomfortably, his eyes stopping on Arthur in the process.

'Exactly!' Marvin declared loudly. 'Morgan has it! Why *would* an individual or an institution stop abusing their power unless people hold them to account?'

'But who would help you?' As Marvin's eyes fell hard on Percy, he shifted. 'I mean, if *one* person stands up for something they deem to be an injustice, and no one else stands with them, it's pointless. You can't stand against something alone.'

'True,' Marvin agreed. 'The old saying "United we stand, divided we fall" comes to mind. This is probably why the world is in such a state in the first place. At the first sign of hardship everyone turns insular. *My* country. *My* resources. *My* money. *Their* fault. Division like this can only end in one way. What happens when one person perceives another to have more than them?'

'They covet what the other person has,' Bedivere suggested, his wineglass half empty. 'They go to war.'

Marvin nodded violently. 'War, yes! The near-rebellion of 2033 is a good example of that. The poor becoming dissatisfied with how much the rich elite had. But who wins wars, I ask you?'

'The rich?' Arthur volunteered.

'The rich, yes: those with the most resources. Here, at home, instability is rife, even though the New Nationals don't want you to believe it. We have "enemies" abroad: we must *stand together*. It is a delicate lie ready to collapse. That is why the government is tightening its hold.'

There was a moment's breather. Marvin sat down, but hung on the table, his hands linked before him as if in prayer.

'Is this why surveillance is so prevalent now?' Bedivere inquired.

'I wouldn't say that it's any more prevalent than it was twenty years ago,' Gavin answered. 'More intelligent, however...? I would say it is.'

'What do you mean?'

He leant forwards into the round table, evoking a creak from the polished woodwork. 'Surveillance has long been in a new age. It's very clever of the government to let those being watched to do the recording for them; from smart glasses to texts and emails and cameras in phones, right down to your latest status update, where you are and how you're feeling. All you'd need to do is replace every social networking branding with that of the New Nationals. Who would post all of their personal information on NewNational-connect.com?'

Marvin pointed to Gavin with a strange light in his eyes, amusement perhaps, or pride; Arthur found it impossible to tell. 'Interesting point, Gavin! Bedivere was right to introduce you to us. *Very* interesting.'

'But how can the government get away with such a blatant invasion of privacy?' Morgan asked, her brow creased in distress. 'Surely everyone would be furious if they knew?'

'I am afraid, Morgan, that such knowledge is usually met with bemusement. Of course, one can see the humour in one's government trawling through an individual's private and often trivial emails; but these people are missing the point. No one should be reading what you're up to in an email meant only for the recipient; no one should be creating a file on you about your sexual orientation or political leanings. What these people don't understand, is that though *currently* their lives remain unaffected, there is nothing to stop this, or any government, from using activity collected from your computer as a means to prosecute or blackmail you, or from planting something that provides them with a good reason to ship you off to Halkirk. People who say if you've nothing to hide, you've nothing to fear are, quite frankly, idiots.'

'But how can they *justify* it?'

'In our society, surveillance of the collective is justified by the need to find terrorists. What terrorism consists of is entirely subjective to the government in power at the time,' Gavin interjected, gesticulating his point calmly. 'When a government begins to sift through the individual's private correspondence, however, that government openly declares that you, the individual, have something to hide, and that you, the individual, have something to fear.'

'I don't get it,' Bedivere complained.

'From this,' Gavin continued, 'we can conclude that ultimately, in the eyes of the government, *you* are the terrorist.'

'No,' Morgan objected, 'a terrorist is someone who causes mass harm and distress to civilians for an extreme cause.'

'And so it should be. But when you know that your own government also brands peaceful environmental campaigners and human rights watchmen as *extremists*, you begin to wonder where they draw their boundaries.' Marvin sucked his wine-stained lip. 'But this takes us back to the age-old question, doesn't it? Which is more important? Liberty, or safety? As Lincoln pointed out, those who do sacrifice freedom for security ultimately end up with neither.'

His grey irises settled on them each, and he waved his hand with indifference.

'According to the New Nationals, Arthur is a "terrorist". Arthur uses the Dark Net to investigate New National corrections applied to the local press. Percy is a "terrorist" because Percy supports—albeit secretly—*Rightswatch*. Still signing all those petitions, Percy?'

Percy nodded, but said nothing.

'I am a "terrorist" because I am sitting here, providing you all with extremist ideas. And you are here, willingly, listening to me. But what determines who is and who isn't? It's not some unilateral law. Language is very particular, but as far as the New Nationals are concerned, the term "terrorist" can, and has been, applied in the broadest of senses.'

Arthur glanced to the clock at Marvin's desk in the corner of the room. Their time was up, and the session was at an end.

'Gwen? What do you think of this?'

Her mother stopped by a very expensive-looking trench coat. Unhooking it, she held it up for her to see.

'Mam, it's hardly suitable for winter,' Gwenhwyfar complained. It was Sunday, and they were out on a spree at Hollow Way, a designer-shopping village that had come highly recommended by her aunt. Gwenhwyfar felt the fabric, and found that though it was soft, it was thin. She immediately hunted for the tag. 'What percentage is it? It's not even one hundred percent cotton. *Polyester*? Ugh.'

Shrugging, Eve put it back. 'Well, what *are* you looking for? You hardly need much more than what you already have. I hear it's going to be a mild winter.'

'I heard the opposite,' Gwenhwyfar remarked, stopping by a much warmer, much thicker coat with a fleece lining. She juggled with the bags she had already accumulated, five from three different stores, and hooked them over her forearm. 'Something like this is better. What do you think?'

'Try it on,' Eve encouraged, her face lighter than it had been all week. She held Gwenhwyfar's bags for her, clutching them tightly with her own. Gwenhwyfar took off her own jacket and put on the new one. It was warm, definitely, but too bulky.

'Maybe we should try somewhere else,' she said as she put it back on the rail. 'What time is it? I'm starving.'

'Two,' Eve said. 'Shall we get some lunch?'

Gwenhwyfar reclaimed the spoils of their shopping trip, which, like the spa yesterday, was her mother's treat. She had been afraid that their weekend together was a platform for Eve to tell her that she was filing for divorce, but so far nothing had been mentioned and they had only spoken of more trivial things.

When they were sitting in a café, on-site next to one of the smaller handbag boutiques, Eve asked Gwenhwyfar to remind her what she had chosen.

'The running shoes, remember?' she said, extracting the box and handing it to her to inspect. 'And that leather handbag you liked.' Pulling it out of its wrappings, she tried it on over her right shoulder. 'You don't think Dad will mind?'

'Why should he?' Eve said, giving the trainers back. 'It's my money. Which dress did you get again?'

'The black one.' She pushed the shoebox back into a bag, and rewrapped her new handbag. Her mother had bought her a bangle as well: a delicate silver band fashioned in the style of a torque. The whole café was packed with hungry shoppers, each one sitting next to their own hoard of expensive things. 'And those jeans. I've been needing new jeans for weeks.' As the barista brought them their hot drinks they cleared the table, and then sat in silence for a moment, recovering.

'Mam,' Gwenhwyfar said after a while, 'I was wondering... how do the finances work at home?'

Eve stiffened, and frowned at her. 'What do you mean?'

'I mean, do you and Dad have a joint account? Or separate?'

'Joint, of course, but we each have our own accounts, too.' She straightened up and fiddled with her favourite necklace, a silver chain with sterling beads that hung from her throat like raindrops. 'You should always have your own money Gwen, in any relationship. Always have something separate, that your partner can't touch.'

She wondered how contemporary the advice was, and if it was born of recent circumstances. Gazing down at the perfect swirl of whipped cream on her hot chocolate, she sighed.

'I know, Mam.'

'Know—?'

'I know about Dad. I know that you found a bank account he's been hiding.'

'How did you—?'

'I overheard you talking with aunt Melissa.'

'Darling, I—'

She looked up at her sharply. 'Don't lie to me! I heard

everything. He's been buying her things, hasn't he? That's why he's always *working*, that's why he's never home.' She shook her head, and suddenly she felt sick. 'Is that why we moved? So he could be closer to some squeeze?'

'I don't know, Gwen, really I don't,' Eve said quietly. 'I—I don't want to talk about it here, I don't even know if he *is*—'

'You said so yourself: you *know* something isn't right.' She sat back abruptly, her eyes stinging with the threat of tears. 'Don't you *defend* him, don't you dare do that. You're worth more than that, you hear me?'

'I'm not defending him, trust me,' Eve implored, her face ashen, her voice faint. 'I'm *not*—'

'Why didn't you tell me?' Gwenhwyfar hissed. 'You've been lying to me all week, pretending like everything's normal when it's *not*. How could you?'

'Gwenhwyfar Taliesin, don't you dare shift this onto me,' Eve snapped, her voice low. 'I didn't tell you because I don't want you to think badly of him. I don't even know if he *is* having an affair. What sort of mother would I be if I came running to you with this? This is something I need to work out. You shouldn't know. You shouldn't have heard.'

Shaking her head, Eve tried to lift her coffee, but when her hands trembled too much she set it back down.

'You shouldn't know. What am I supposed to do, now that I have you judging me?'

'I'm not judging you—'

'Well, it certainly feels like it. If you get off that high horse of yours for just one minute you might realise that I *don't* know anything but what I saw and that it was none of your business to go snooping around like you did. Why didn't you announce yourself when you heard us talking?'

'I didn't get the chance!' she snapped, her face burning. 'I heard it as soon as I came through the door. It's not like I closed it quietly. I wasn't *snooping*, if that's what you think.'

It seemed that Eve was no longer listening, for her head fell into her hands, and for a moment Gwenhwyfar feared she was crying.

'What am I supposed to do?'

She didn't know what to say. 'It's probably nothing,' she tried. 'It's like you say, you don't know... you can't be sure.' She watched her for a moment, forlorn. 'Can't you ask him about it?'

Eve rose from her palms, and shook her head. 'I went into his study. The door was locked, but I found the key. I was... I was just looking for some old documents. I thought they might have been put there during the move by accident. But I found all these files... a whole folder of receipts and transactions. An account, hotels... odd bookings, large withdrawals, restaurants...'

'Are you sure it's not just for work? He might have a separate account that they reimburse.'

'*Jewellers*,' she added, through a sudden sob. '*Florists*. I've never seen any flowers, not since my birthday last year.'

Gwenhwyfar jumped up and sat next to her mother, and wrapped her arms around her, furious to see her so heartbroken. 'I'll talk to him,' she decided. 'I'll ask him about it and see what he has to say for himself.'

'No, don't. I don't want you to.'

'Just let me talk to him. There'll be a logical explanation, just you see.'

'No Gwen, I'll do it. I want you to forget about this, do you hear me? I don't want you thinking that your father is some sleaze.' She took her by the hand, and squeezed it with her cold fingers. 'You're right, you're both right; it probably is nothing. I've just... let my imagination run away with me. It's that house; it's being at home all day with nothing to do. Mel's right. I need to start work again.'

Gwenhwyfar lingered next to her, reluctant to move.

'I'm fine, darling, really. I'll talk to your father when the time's right. I'll push Mel about the firm. George thinks they're doing well enough to take me on.'

The smile she gave her daughter wobbled, but as she dried her tears it became more concrete. The waiter reappeared with their lunch, so Gwenhwyfar moved back to her own place, and watched her mother anxiously as he set down their pasta and waltzed off.

'Are you sure you're all right?' she asked, picking up her fork.

'Yes, cariad,' she murmured in her awkward Welsh, 'I'm fine.'

'It's out, it's on the news.'

Gwenhwyfar looked up as Gavin joined them, his shoulders hunched and his head low. 'What is?'

'The Mobilisation Centres: it was on the six o' clock news this morning. Didn't you see it?' He pulled his phone out, tapped and swiped, and then slid it into the middle of the table. 'It's everywhere. As soon as the *Eyewatch* website published, the main news sites had to acknowledge the story. They're still playing it down as much as they can, but it's out. So much for Milton's great firewall.'

They were in the cafeteria for break. During registration that morning Gwenhwyfar had reassured Bedivere that her mother was fine, and that it was nothing to worry about, wishing she'd given Arthur another excuse for missing Friday. Viola reached for the phone first.

'*No*—' she said, still disbelieving.

'What did they say?' Bedivere asked.

Gavin sat back. 'The usual. *These reports are not yet confirmed, we are uncertain as to the source; it is likely to only be an isolated case.* That's what they'll go with, I reckon: that the abuse and disappearances have just been happening in one centre, and only a few heads will roll. Enough to convince us all that they think it's terrible too, and to show us that they're doing something about it.'

'Surely they can't get away with that now,' Viola said, handing the phone back to Gavin. Bedivere intercepted it, and Tom craned to read over his shoulder. 'They'll have to admit to everything if there are documents.'

'It's horrific,' Gavin admitted, 'but as far as they're concerned, there's too much at stake. They'll only admit to what they have to. They'll trim the weed and leave the roots.'

Tom's face darkened as he scanned the article. 'It says here it's just one centre.'

'Of course it does,' Gavin remarked.

Once again Gwenhwyfar thought of the boy that her mother had been worrying about, the one that she had given soup. 'How many?'

'All of them—it's what they're for. Obviously they weren't killing themselves quickly enough. The rehabilitation thing is a farce; it has to be.'

Gwenhwyfar waved for his attention. 'Wait, what? Killing themselves?'

'Cut funds, skeleton support from the state… there have been nearly a hundred suicides in relation to poverty this year alone, and that's not counting the deaths of those below the quality of life line. Though that's something else you won't hear about.'

'These people, these *disappearances*… where do they go?' Viola asked, her porcelain face paler. 'Do you think…?'

'I don't know what I think,' Gavin muttered. 'No one knows. There are theories, of course. All we can be sure of is that they're getting sent somewhere.' Scowling, he looked around. 'Where's Lance?'

'I haven't seen him,' Viola said quietly. 'Are you still thinking of… you know…'

Gavin shook his head. 'You were right—it's not smart and it won't help.' His blue eyes flitted left and right, and then he leant further into the table. 'I've heard there's a protest being organised for this weekend,' he murmured. 'It's in London. I'm going to that instead.'

There was a crash at the other end of the hall. All five of them looked up to see Lancelot shaking himself off as he disentangled himself from another boy in their year. Shouts were exchanged. Gwenhwyfar let her eyes linger on him as he loped towards them, shaking his head. She noticed Emily by one of the vending machines, sitting on her own.

'Clumsy idiot wasn't looking where he was going,' Lancelot said as he came upon them, twisting out of his bag and dropping it on the floor. 'Stupid phones.'

'That's still no reason to push him,' Viola scolded as he sat.

'I didn't touch him!' Lancelot elevated his hands. His dark eyes slunk around the group. 'What's the matter with you lot?'

'You haven't heard?' said Gavin.

'Heard what?'

'The Mobilisation Centres. It's on the news, the New National news. There's a protest about it on Saturday. We should go.'

Everyone exchanged a look.

'Hang on, Miles. You know what happens to protesters, right?'

Gavin remained still, and said nothing. Lancelot leant towards him.

'You *do* want to join the Marines after school, don't you? If you go on Saturday, and someone recognises you, that's your chance of a military career gone.'

'I know that, Lake,' he snapped, 'but I'm not going to sit back while they bury this in more lies and corrections. Are you?'

'When have you ever known a protest to work in this country?' Lancelot argued. Gavin shifted irritably and waved his arms. 'I suppose the organisers of this event have got permission to go marching through Central London, have they? If you go, you'll be breaking the law.'

'It's less than the New Nationals have been doing,' Bedivere remarked, still scrolling through Gavin's phone. 'I did a bit of research myself. These "centres" are essentially hard labour camps.'

'All right, then,' Lancelot retorted. 'What's your plan?'

'Masks, costumes: everyone will be wearing the same.'

'It sounds dangerous,' Viola remarked. 'If people are anonymous, it could attract criminals.'

'I heard there's a blacklist, and that marching gets you under heightened surveillance,' Gwenhwyfar added.

'Well, if all of you are too *afraid* to stand up for what's right, then we may as well be responsible for what they've been doing in those centres ourselves,' Gavin told them all, before wheeling on Bedivere. 'I'd have thought *you* would be willing to risk it at least, Bed.'

'Why?' Lancelot interrupted, 'because of Marvin's afterschool club? Don't tell me he's brainwashed you already.'

'What club?' Viola asked.

'Haven't you heard? *Marvin's* been inviting the cream of the crop to attend some fanatical cult on Fridays.'

'It's just an extracurricular History club,' Gwenhwyfar remarked, rolling her eyes. 'He's basically tutoring.'

Viola looked to Gwenhwyfar. 'You're going?'

'No, I haven't even been to it yet. I might not bother.' Gwenhwyfar fired a glance at Lancelot. 'It's supposed to be a secret. He'd get in trouble with Ravioli, if he knew.'

'Exactly. So no one's to go around telling anyone about it, you hear?' They all looked to Bedivere. His face was set. 'I'll march with you, Gav. If you're sure we won't be recognised.'

'I know what I'm doing,' Gavin promised. His eyes fell on Lancelot, who shrugged. He looked to Viola. 'Vi?'

She looked pained to deny him. 'You know I can't. I can't risk it, not with my father—'

'That's understandable.' Gavin's blue eyes moved on. 'Tom?'

Tom looked to Lancelot, and shrugged. 'Dunno,' he said helpfully. Gwenhwyfar felt the pressure of Gavin's eyes the moment they were upon her. Isolde's words about protesting flooded her mind.

'I'll think about it,' she told him. 'I don't know if I can.'

Gavin looked away with a dissatisfied shrug.

'We should ask Arthur,' Bedivere said in a low murmur. 'He'll want to be involved in this. Maybe he can talk to Marvin.'

'I'm definitely not going if Marvin *and* Arthur will be there,' Lancelot objected loudly. Immediately he was shushed.

'The more people who march, the better,' Gavin told them

solemnly. 'It'll make those out there who think that what the New Nationals have done is justifiable realise it's not the view of the rest of us. I can't just sit back while they label people *subhuman*. They don't even refer to them as people in their documents. They call them *Lessers*. I won't stand for it, and others won't either. We won't be alone. There will be thousands.'

'You're wasted on the Army, Miles,' Lancelot remarked again, but there was no spite in his words. He shook his head and leant into the table to join the others, offering them a resigned smile. 'Saturday, then.'

'Mam?'

She made sure she slammed the door hard again to avoid walking in unannounced. Llew appeared from the kitchen, slowly wagging his tail as he padded up to greet her. Gwenhwyfar bent down to fuss him for a moment, and then followed him into the living room where she removed her bag and coat. She could hear her mother thumping around upstairs, filling her afternoon with some needless chore.

'Mam!' she shouted again, shuffling through the post. There was the usual Monday leaflet; information sent to them by the New Nationals about how prosperous times were, including weekly statistics on immigration, employment and budgeting. She tossed it to one side, hoping to find something of interest— shopping vouchers, perhaps, or the points-card she had ordered from a fledgling cosmetics store. Left with the junk, she stopped on another flyer. Suddenly, her heart was racing. It was from *Free Countries*.

19.10.2052: The Mobilisation March

You may have heard that the Mobilisation Centres the New Nationals introduced to give vulnerable people a platform for reintegrating into society are, in fact, hard labour camps.

You may have heard that these institutions systematically abuse people whom society would class as addicts, disabled or homeless.

You may have heard that since the enrolment of loved ones, families have been told their relatives have reintegrated successfully, with no links for contact, and no proof.

What you have heard is true.

These lost people have not reintegrated. These people have been disappeared.

Those who have not been disappeared are locked into an institution that places a lower value on their lives, labelling them *Lessers*.

Our government believes that the most vulnerable in our society are "lesser people" and therefore deserving of such treatment. We at *Free Countries* think this is wrong.

We do not usually partake in protests, but in this we find that Milton has gone too far. March with us in London from Temple on Saturday the 19th of October.

Please see the following website for instructions on how to participate safely.

Rising against the regime.

'Gwen?'

She jumped, crumpling the flyer in her fist. Had her mother already seen it? Her head was pounding, and her blood felt thick. Isolde had made it explicit to her that *Free Countries* never included themselves in such methods: was this a direct order disguised as a rallying cry? Immediately she wanted to call her contact, but realised that she had never been given her number.

'I'm in the living room!' Hurrying through to the kitchen, she met her mother halfway. 'How was your day? Good?'

'Busy,' Eve told her. Gwenhwyfar continued on to the fridge. 'I've been on my feet all day, rearranging things in the attic. It's a mess up there.'

'Did you get it all done?'

'Nearly,' Eve said, sitting on one of the high chairs by the island. 'How was school?'

'OK I suppose.' Gwenhwyfar took a yoghurt pot from the fridge. 'Did you see the news? Apparently those Mobilisation Centres are pretty dodgy.' Her mind was stuck fast on the flyer. Did this mean she should go on Saturday? A running thought thumped through the back of her mind. Gavin had known about this before anyone: was he involved in *Free Countries*, too?

'I did hear about that,' Eve said, as Gwenhwyfar took a teaspoon from the cutlery drawer. 'Though so far the documents released haven't been verified. They think they might be fake.'

'Is that what they're saying?'

'I don't see why they would be real; you couldn't have something like that and get away with it. People would be outraged.'

'Actually, I think you'll find that most people don't care.'

Eve frowned at her. 'What makes you say that?'

Gwenhwyfar shrugged. 'It's obvious, isn't it? The only people who care, who *really* care, are going to be those who have family involved.' She paused for a moment, spooning yoghurt into her mouth. 'That boy you bought soup for. Do you think he got picked up and sent to one of those centres?'

'I don't know. He might still be on the street. I haven't been back to check on him. Not since...' she trailed off, and set her eyes on the windows by the back door.

'Have you spoken to Dad?'

'I haven't found the right moment. I'll do it soon, don't worry. You're probably right, it's probably just for work.'

'And the payment to the jewellers?'

'He could be picking up something for his boss,' she theorized. 'I don't know what his day consists of, but he's had to collect dry cleaning before when out on a job, so maybe it was something like that?'

'Probably.' Gwenhwyfar couldn't shake the feeling of doubt that was gnawing away at her. Something was wrong, but she couldn't place her finger on it.

'I still don't want you to say anything. It would kill him to know that you thought he was doing something like that, and if this all turns out to be one huge misunderstanding, he'd never forgive me.'

'I won't say anything,' she promised. She threw the empty yoghurt pot in the bin, and let the spoon clatter into the sink. 'I'll be in my room; I've got some homework to do. I'm thinking of going out on Saturday, just shopping with Viola. Is that all right?'

Eve nodded. 'It might be best if you're out, anyway. If your father is home, I was thinking of... you know.' She smiled, but the gesture was cold. 'This should all be sorted out by next week, love.'

'I hope so.'

Gwenhwyfar scaled the stairs to her bedroom, turned on her computer and sat at her desk. Llew padded in after her and lay stiffly at her side. The website provided on the flyer wasn't a *Free Countries* one, but it seemed secure, and it was there she found the details for Saturday. For a moment she sat still at her desk, gazing at her screen. This had to be an order, didn't it? And if it wasn't, it was certainly a push. Adrenaline coursed through her as she made her decision. She knew what she would do. She would march.

The March

Gwenhwyfar didn't see much of Gavin or Lancelot that week, but managed to spend some time alone with Arthur on occasions. By the time Friday came around she had agreed to attend The Round Table, promised by the others that Marvin would be helping them with the protest on Saturday. It was dark in their History teacher's study. The curtains were drawn, and the only light came from a desk lamp in the corner.

'I don't know what else we need,' Gavin was saying. 'I've got everyone's outfits already. You all owe me, by the way.' He emptied his rucksack onto the table and seven packages slopped out. Each one included something similar to a fencing mask. 'I had to pay for these. There was a guy distributing them last night by the old warehouses. There were a lot of people there.'

'How much were they?' Morgan asked as he passed them around.

'Five quid, so we'll call it fifteen each, yeah?'

'Fifteen?' Percy scowled. 'You just said it was five.'

'I went there, didn't I?' Gavin huffed. 'If any of us get caught, it'll be me, not you.' He threw one to Percy, who caught it quickly. 'I got a spare one, just in case. I wasn't sure if you'd need it or not, Marv.'

'I appreciate the thought, but no, I don't think I will. Masks and overalls won't be enough. We need to make sure there's no crossover.'

'Crossover?' Bedivere asked. He opened the plastic bag and turned the mask over in his hands. Gwenhwyfar felt uneasy the moment he tried it on. It was black, and hid his face completely.

'I need to make sure that none of you can be linked to your actions tomorrow,' Marvin explained. 'If you walk into an alleyway in that gear, then walk away without it, you may as well wear no disguise at all.'

'You mean the cameras?' Gavin said. Marvin nodded.

'But how?' Morgan asked, looking at her black overalls.

'Let me worry about that,' Marvin assured them. 'It's my responsibility to make sure you take part in this as safely as possible. I know Gavin was the one to organise it, but I feel that none of you would be marching were it not for what you've heard in our sessions.'

'Gwen hasn't been coming here,' Morgan pointed out curtly. 'And neither has Lance. He's marching tomorrow.'

'What does Lance care about this?' Arthur remarked.

'A lot,' Gavin interrupted. 'He's just aware of the risks involved. If any of us are identified, we'll be arrested for "disrupting democracy" and "disturbing the peace".'

'For taking a stand against the government's treatment of the vulnerable community?' Percy asked, appalled. 'I can't believe it.'

'There were rumours going around yesterday that we've got permission to protest from the Met, but for an entirely different cause,' Gavin told them all. 'So when we show up with the wrong banners, things might get nasty.'

'And that's the best case scenario, right?' Arthur asked.

'Worst case scenario is we don't have permission, and the police will arrest on sight.'

'They might do that anyway, if we're dressed like this,' Percy observed. Gwenhwyfar looked to Arthur, who was gazing at the black garments he held with unease.

'So what's the plan?'

'Dark spots.' Marvin said, standing. He brought a handful of maps over from his desk, and spread them across the table in no apparent order. 'These all indicate areas where there are gaps in the CCTV networks. Hard to find, these days, but they do still exist. The plan is to meet at these garages, change, and then pair up. I'll drive you up to London and drop you off here, here and here. We can avoid the main checkpoints if we drive in from Wimbledon. You'll then take these specific routes to Temple. You will have sole responsibility for your partner. It's on *you* that they get home safely. That said, I don't want to hear of two of you being arrested and going in for questioning together, understood?'

There were varying nods from the table. Gwenhwyfar felt her pulse quicken. The risk of attending suddenly seemed real.

'Now, as we don't know how this is going to go, I've drawn out three routes back to the rendezvous. I'll be waiting here from six o'clock.' He pointed to one of the smaller maps. 'I want you all back by eight at the latest, you hear me? From there, I'll drop you as close to home as I can manage.' He passed the directions he had arranged around the table. 'I think I can guess the pairs,' he said, looking to Arthur. 'The only question is, who's prepared to go as a three and watch out for Lancelot?'

'That'll be me and Bed,' Gavin volunteered. 'I've already spoken to him about it.'

Marvin nodded. 'Good.'

'Do we know who's organised this?' The table looked to Gwenhwyfar, and her palms began to sweat. 'I mean, is it an organisation, an individual, a family member…?'

'Why do you ask?'

She looked to Marvin. 'I got another flyer from *Free Countries* in the post on Monday. It was encouraging people to attend.'

'So that's why you changed your mind,' Bedivere grinned, and though she knew he was joking, she shook her head.

'Should we even go if we don't know who's behind it? I mean, if it's organised by a group like *Free Countries*… they're very anti-Milton. The New Nationals will be all over it.'

'It's a risk, yes,' Gavin told her, 'but that's what the disguises are for. If it's obvious that it's not safe, we can always just leave. As far as the New Nationals know, this march has nothing to do with the centres. They're expecting it to be small scale.'

'And what will they do if thousands of people turn up, hiding their faces, with banners about the centres?' Bedivere asked.

'Let's hope it is thousands,' Percy murmured. 'It lowers the risk of the hundreds who will be arrested being us.'

'They can't arrest anyone if the protest is peaceful,' Morgan argued.

'They can arrest whoever they like,' Arthur said. 'Once they see the banners and hear the chants…'

'Which is exactly why I want all of you to leave at the first sign of something going amiss,' Marvin said forcefully, his grey eyes bulging out from beneath his brows. 'No hanging around, you hear me? Keep away from the edges of the crowd, if you can. It'll be the stragglers they'll pick up. Remember, police officers have cameras with voice and facial recognition, so keep your mask on at all times.' He smiled ironically, and shook his head. 'Technically, the New Nationals have the right to arrest everyone for concealing their faces. But like Percy says, let's hope it's thousands that turn up, and not hundreds.'

'So who *is* behind all this?' Gwenhwyfar asked again.

'I don't know,' Gavin admitted, 'the guy who blew the whistle perhaps? Families of those vanished? It could be anyone.'

'We'll have to be careful.' Arthur leant into the table, his disguise before him with the blacked-out mask. 'Dressed like this, we might not even make it to Temple.'

'There's safety in numbers. If you see others, flock to them. Just as long as it's not each other,' Marvin added. 'I don't want all our eggs in one basket.'

Gwenhwyfar took hold of the veiled mask that sat with her protest uniform. She wondered who else might be going, whether there would be anyone from *Free Countries*, and if Isolde would be there. She took comfort in the anonymity of the event, yet at the same time it frightened her. Anyone could be there—the very best of humanity, and the very worst.

'Meet me here at twelve,' Marvin said, pointing at the local map. 'If you're late, you're not going.'

They each acknowledged his order, and then packed their outfits away into their rucksacks, ready for tomorrow.

They were dressed the part: their faces hidden by the full-head masks, their clothes cloaked by the anonymous overalls. They marched through London in ranks, beating drums, blowing whistles, their loudspeakers and placards all shouting in outrage. New National banners lined Whitehall and Parliament Square, crimson and angry. Metal fences mapped their way, manned by hundreds of armed police officers.

'The water cannons are waiting,' Arthur shouted to her, as they were carried with the crowd. He clutched her hand tightly, and bent his head to hers so he could be heard. 'I'm surprised they haven't used them already.'

'They're probably keeping an eye on the situation,' Gwenhwyfar called back, her voice muffled by the gauze. 'Think we're going to try for Parliament Square?'

'No,' he told her, 'Gavin said they're avoiding it.'

She nodded, but he couldn't see the gesture, and soon he was standing upright again, straining to peer over the heads of the crowd.

The noise was relentless. They stopped for a while in Trafalgar Square, where many remained, shouting facts and grievances through a megaphone half-drowned by the cries of solidarity thrown back at it. Despite the advice broadcast that morning not to march, tens of thousands had turned up and so far went unchallenged. Most wore the uniform black masks but others wore different faces, while a brave few wore no mask at all. The throng set off shortly after the megaphone changed hands. They were supposed to be marching along Pall Mall and up to Green Park, but the way was cordoned off and they were redirected down a different route.

'What's going on?' Gwenhwyfar elbowed Arthur in the side. He glanced down, and then up ahead, jumping to try and see.

'They're taking us down another road!' he called to her, concerned. 'I don't know which—I can't tell. There are too many people!'

They walked on over Charing Cross roundabout, and for a moment Gwenhwyfar thought they would be heading down The Mall to Buckingham Palace. Instead they went down Whitehall.

'Where are we going?' she called up to Arthur. He didn't answer. 'I thought we weren't allowed in Parliament Square?'

It was there, near Westminster, that the atmosphere changed. They came to a halt and the ruckus died a quick death.

'Cannons!' Someone yelled. The crowd surged backwards, spray raining down upon them as those caught in the jet were blown over. Protestors advanced angrily, shouting words made incomprehensible by the din. The sirens sounded again and water punched into them, hitting one man in the face. When the panic spread and people tried to escape through the cattle gates they were beaten back; and then suddenly the riot vans had descended, with dogs, tear gas and rubber bullets. Gwenhwyfar didn't know how it had happened but they were firing into the crowd.

She was knocked out of Arthur's grasp in a second, pushed aside by one scrambling body and then another, and suddenly she was being carried along with a stream of faceless figures, fighting against them, trying to get back.

'Arthur!'

A tear gas canister propelled past her, splitting the protestors. Someone pushed her hard in the back. Gwenhwyfar didn't realise she had fallen until she was on the tarmac. Instinctively her hands flew up to protect her head. Someone trod on her leg, another person tripped over her stomach. The shouting was frightening. Grabbing hands pulled her up, and then another protestor was asking if she was all right, helping her away from the scene. When she fought against them they abandoned her.

'Arthur!' she yelled again, cutting through the crush. He was tall; she should be able to find him, and at the same time she half-hunted for Gavin, who was tallest. She daren't jump to try and see better; if she did she would go down again, and this time she might not get back up.

She longed to take her mask off; it was hot and hard to breathe. They had been told to go to Marvin's meet-up spot if one of them got separated, but with her phone at home she was scared to leave when she knew that Arthur was here somewhere, just a few feet away.

The crowd struggled the only way it could—back into itself. Gwenhwyfar waited, alone and small as the road around her cleared, but when the police charged in with handcuffs and batons she shrank away, knowing she shouldn't linger. A sudden heat seemed to melt against her with the brightest of lights. Someone had thrown a Molotov cocktail.

The New National banner lit up in one great *woosh*, the flames licking the white stone of the building it hung from. The popping of plastic bullets clicked to the pop of metal, and the screaming was cut short; a dozen were down.

'Gwen!'

He grabbed her by the hand and yanked her away so hard she thought her arm might come off. He started to run, and she ran with him, looking back on the warzone; another Molotov burst and another banner lit up; rocks and stones bounced off riot shields, whilst the furious kin of the dead howled in handcuffs or were beaten to the ground.

She didn't realise she was crying until tears beaded on her lashes, blurring her vision. She stumbled, but Arthur dragged her up, and for a moment he was swinging her forwards with one arm until she found her feet again, and ran with him.

'We need to get out of here,' he urged, though the chaos was unfurling ahead of them now, too, and shots could be heard in Trafalgar. 'We need to get to Marvin.'

There was no way forwards, no way back. With determination Arthur pushed his way along the road, past Downing Street. It was packed here, as each street either side of Whitehall was gated shut, but there was some protection in numbers, and they were shielded.

'We've got to keep going!' Arthur shouted, dragging her, pulling her between other bodies and through gaps so small that she thought she might pop. 'A little further!'

They came to the next junction, blocked by cattle gating. The crowd was thinner at the side of the river. One of the gates had toppled and people crashed through it like water. Another gate near it was unguarded—an opening. Arthur turned Gwenhwyfar to face him, but she couldn't see his eyes.

'We've got to run for it! If I get caught, keep going, got it?'

She nodded, and then shouted when she remembered he couldn't see.

They ran at the fence together. Arthur was first over, Gwenhwyfar second. Someone grabbed at her overall and tripped her up mid flight. She landed on the gating with a painful crack, half over, and then it toppled, too. Immediately people were running around her, stepping on her, and she was pulled backwards, up and by the foot like a dead rabbit. Arthur grabbed her in the nick of time. She kicked herself free. Every inch of her throbbed as Arthur tugged her loose from the crowd, and suddenly she was running with him again out onto the Victoria Embankment.

'All right?'

Adrenaline coursed through her. 'What do we do?'

After a second's breath they were moving, sprinting with those who had managed to escape. The public stared. Others averted their eyes, as if looking at them was in itself a crime. Gwenhwyfar didn't like the attention they were attracting.

'We should change!'

'We can't change.'

'People are looking at us. What about the police?'

'We'll have to risk it,' Arthur said. 'We can't show our faces, not yet. Marvin said we should protect our identity at all costs.'

He hurried again, faster, and soon they had lost the other protestors and were running over Waterloo Bridge. Gwenhwyfar didn't think she could keep up the pace much longer. She was near to suffocating in the mask, each impact with the concrete sent painful shots up her shins, and she had a burning pain in her side; a stitch or a more serious injury, she couldn't tell.

They outran and hid from two more police officers before they made it to Marvin's rendezvous. He was waiting for them on the Southbank, parked in a back-alley out of sight of pedestrians and cameras. He got out of the driver's seat when he spotted them, slamming the door.

'Don't tell me what happened, I already know,' he barked, ushering them around to the rear of the transit van. Quickly he opened the doors, and they jumped inside. 'The others aren't back yet. If they're not here in half an hour, we're leaving.'

He shut them in before they could utter a word. The van was lit by torchlight. Gwenhwyfar took her mask off immediately, wishing she could have had at least one gulp of fresh air. Arthur did the same. His brow was glazed in sweat.

'Made it, then,' Bedivere smiled. He looked pale but seemed unscathed. 'Where were you when it happened?'

'Right by Parliament,' Arthur said, huffing. He drew in a sharp breath. Heaving, Gwenhwyfar sucked in as much air as she could. 'You?'

'Closer to Trafalgar,' Bedivere said. 'They almost got Gavin.'

Gavin lifted his right arm. It was cuffed. 'Don't suppose anyone's got the key?'

'What happened?'

'One guy got me in a lock, on his own. Lance rugby tackled him. Almost didn't make it, either. We got out just in time.'

'You assaulted a police officer?'

'He was bludgeoning unarmed protesters. He was no police officer,' Lancelot said in a low voice, looking to Arthur.

'You're lucky neither of you got shot,' Gwenhwyfar told him, still out of breath. 'They were shooting people where we were.'

'With rubber bullets, I know,' Gavin remarked.

'No. Not rubber.'

'Jesus,' he cursed. 'Are they—?'

'Dead? I think so.'

'Christ.'

The door opened, and they were blinded by the dwindling light of day. Two more people clambered into the van, joined by a third. Panting, Morgan took off her mask, and Percy struggled out of his. The doors were shut as the third figure removed her veil.

'*Emily*—?' She looked at them all sheepishly. 'What are you doing here?' Gwenhwyfar demanded. Suddenly all her pain seemed to have gone.

'What do you think?' she remarked, sitting down and crossing her legs. 'I ran into Morgan and Percy. They said they knew a safe way of getting home.'

'But how—?'

'We were looking for a way out, hoping to find some toilets or something. Emily was being harassed by some men,' Percy said, calmly. 'It was clear that the police weren't going to do anything, so we intervened.' He looked to Morgan proudly. 'Morgan walloped them with someone's drum.'

'You're the one who chased them off. One against three?' She smiled at him. His lip was bloodied. 'It was pretty impressive. It started a massive fight.'

Gwenhwyfar looked to Arthur, who frowned and said nothing.

'We didn't know it was Emily though, not until we spoke to her,' Morgan added. 'Talk about coincidence.'

'It's a small world,' Gwenhwyfar said, Emily's presence sitting uneasily with her. 'I didn't think you were the sort to go to this kind of thing.'

'Me neither,' Gavin admitted.

'Why not?' Emily dropped her mask on the floor, and scowled at them all. 'What they're doing is *terrible*.'

'Did you come by yourself?'

She set her blue, cat-like eyes on Gwenhwyfar. '*Yes*. I couldn't find anyone else who cared enough to bother. Though I don't want any of you talking about this to anyone, you hear? I didn't see you, if you didn't see me.'

'We didn't see you, if you didn't see us,' Gavin agreed. Emily sent him an unfriendly smile.

'Good.' She pulled off her gloves, and shook out her golden hair. Gwenhwyfar watched her suspiciously, and the dull ache returned, settling deep into her joints.

The engine started, and then they were moving. Percy sat down, nearly falling over, while Lancelot, Gavin and Bedivere were already wedged against the back wall of the van. Lancelot had a shallow head wound and the graze running down Gavin's left arm was long and angry. Gwenhwyfar settled next to Arthur, linking arms with him so that she wouldn't slide about, and Emily sat beside her. They were driven out of London in silence like cargo, until at last Marvin dropped them off one by one, and they each hobbled home.

It was dark by the time Gwenhwyfar got back. She was cold and shaken, but did her best to suppress the fear that was creeping within her as she took off her coat and prepared herself to lie to her parents. She came into the living room to find that they were sitting on the sofa watching the media station, a cushion apart.

'How was Viola's?' Eve asked, looking over her shoulder.

'OK. We went to the cinema.' The station was tuned into the period drama that they had been following last year. 'I'm starving.'

'Didn't you eat?'

Gwenhwyfar shook her head. 'Vi said she wasn't hungry. I think she's on some kind of diet.' She offered her mother a quick smile and went into the kitchen, mindful of her need to check herself for bruises. Getting up, Eve followed her.

'I hope that doesn't mean that you're on one, too. With all that running you do, you need to keep your calories up.'

'I know, Mam.' She opened the fridge, at the sound of which Llew clambered up from his chewed old bed.

'There's some leftovers on the top shelf. I'll warm them up. Are you in tomorrow?'

Nodding, Gwenhwyfar took out a glass and poured herself some orange juice. She could feel her back throb, but drew in a deep and long breath to expand her ribs, and was comforted to feel no sharp or stabbing pain. 'Have you spoken to Dad yet?'

Eve shook her head. 'Soon,' she murmured after a moment. 'He was busy today. He had a lot of work to do.'

'He always has a lot of work to do,' Gwenhwyfar complained.

'I'm a busy man.'

They both looked round as Garan came into the kitchen, offering them an oblivious grin. He pulled a beer from the fridge. 'Adverts. Horribly long. It's all drivel to brainwash you into buying this or buying that.'

'Isn't *Poplar Park* just brainwashing you into accepting the ongoing implementation of a class-driven society?' Gwenhwyfar teased, hurrying out of his way for fear he might sense what she had been up to.

'We're British,' Garan quipped, 'we're already conditioned to accept a class-driven society.'

As he exited the room Gwenhwyfar gave her mother an encouraging look, one that she ignored.

Later, she made her parents switch on the news, eager to see the full scale and impact of the march. The countdown to live broadcast began and then the headlines were rolling: a stern voice accompanied by the flashing, eye-catching images.

"Tonight:

Chaos in Central London as an illegal protest orchestrated by separatists turns violent. A police officer has died and several have been seriously injured after protestors opened fire during a march to demonstrate support of separatist dissidence. Eyewitness accounts describe how officers at the scene were forced to engage the offenders, killing two gunmen in the process. Four other protestors were wounded and are also in a critical condition. This was a bloody end to a day of violence sparked by the border row. Derek Peters reports."

The scene changed to Derek, who stood grim-faced before Parliament, his eyebrows twisted, his brow heavy, his shoulders drenched with rain.

"Earlier today this square was a scene of chaos and destruction. Arson attacks damaged iconic buildings and four New National banners. Water cannons helped to disperse protesters, most of whom were wearing full body suits and head masks to avoid identification by police. Several police officers have been injured, one has died. Police killed two gunmen at the scene and four rioters have been seriously injured. After dark, the rioters turned to looting shops and desecrating monuments. The Metropolitan Police announced earlier today that they have made over two hundred arrests, but that number is still rising."

'Do they think we're stupid?' Garan asked, pointing his beer bottle at the screen. 'We all know it was about those Mobilisation Centres, not the separatists.'

'Does it matter what it was about? They were armed,' Eve

pointed out, 'they shot at the police. They could have avoided this, if they'd picked people up on route.'

'There must have been at least five thousand people attending. They couldn't arrest them all.'

'They weren't *armed*,' Gwenhwyfar interrupted, upset. 'The police just fired into the crowd.' Both her parents looked at her with surprise. 'That's what Viola said,' she added quickly. 'She heard it on the radio.'

'Let me guess, on a local station?' Garan shook his head. 'They'll get done for that.'

'There were more than five thousand, too. I've seen photos on *Youconnect*. There were at least thirty thousand.'

'That many?' Eve asked.

Gwenhwyfar nodded. 'Probably more—it could have even been fifty.'

'I haven't seen anything online,' she frowned.

'The images have all been removed now,' Gwenhwyfar lied. 'No one's reporting it properly. The separatists had nothing to do with it.'

'It doesn't matter what it was about,' Garan said, looking back at the screen. The image changed, and suddenly the newsreader had moved onto the ongoing threat from the Slavic Union. 'Or how many people attended, or how many people died. This is why I don't protest. What's the point? If the news doesn't cover it, it never happened. If the news only shows ten percent of the crowd, only ten percent went. If the news says it turned violent and a police officer was killed, that's what the public will hear. That's it.'

The screen seemed to grow and brighten as Gwenhwyfar stared at it thoughtlessly, her vision blurring the garish colours.

Her father said nothing after that, and for a while the three of them sat in silence, watching as they were shown countless reels of how bad things were abroad. Gwenhwyfar always felt unsettled when she watched the news, as if someone was sitting next to her whispering in her ear that she should be very afraid.

'I'm going to bed,' she declared sometime after eleven, aching and utterly exhausted. She kissed both her parents goodnight and scratched Llew's head on her way up to her bedroom. She ended up checking if there were any varied reports about what had happened on the Internet, but all news websites were running the same angle. *Free Countries*' site hadn't been updated, either. She sent Arthur a quick text to see how he was, and after a final check to be sure that her injuries really were just scrapes and bruises, clambered into bed. It didn't take her long to drift off, and mercifully, her sleep was dreamless.

Casanova

The final weeks of October billowed with blustery winds and indecisive rain. Marked by limited celebrations, Halloween slipped by with small excitement. November appeared with a calmer front, though clear skies and pale sunshine sapped all warmth from the atmosphere; a cold briefly remedied by the blazing bonfires of Guy Fawkes. The Round Table had a week off for half term, and as school commenced Gwenhwyfar continued to divide her time between Arthur and her friends. She hadn't spoken to Emily since the protest, who, avoided by Charlotte, haunted the grounds like a lonely ghost.

It was the second Saturday in November, and they were gathered at Tom's house. Tom, Gavin and Lancelot were playing a shoot-out game on the media station. Now bare-skinned and convinced that make-up ruined her complexion, Viola was talking about her latest castings.

'They were horrible,' she told Gwenhwyfar, ignoring the spitting machine guns on screen. 'It took me an hour to get to each one, and there were at least a hundred other girls. They literally just flicked through my book and took a card. It felt like such a waste of time.'

Gwenhwyfar was thinking about Arthur. Despite the weekly experience of The Round Table and the social glue born of the Mobilisation March, he was still reluctant to spend time with her friends.

'And I had to walk for them, too. I mean, I don't know if I'm doing it right. How am I supposed to cross my feet in five-inch heels? Stick my hips forward and my shoulders back? No wonder so many girls trip up on the catwalk. Put a hole there and they wouldn't see it.'

'I'm sure you did better than you think,' Gwenhwyfar said, combing her fingers through her hair. 'You always say that you can never tell with such things. You just have to wait to hear from them.'

Viola huffed. 'So how did your date with Arthur go?'

'Good. We ate out.'

'Did he walk you home?'

Gwenhwyfar nodded. 'He always does.'

'And...?' Her eyebrows rose expectantly. 'Did anything happen?'

It was the same question she'd been getting for a while now. As she didn't really know what Viola meant by "anything", she shook her head and glanced to the shooting game. All three boys were absorbed.

'No,' she sighed.

'Well, that's probably good. It's only been a few weeks, after all.'

'More than a month, actually.' Gwenhwyfar glanced across to Lancelot's hard profile. He was sitting at the other end of the sofa. 'That's not the issue, really.' Her voice sunk to a murmur. 'I mean, we haven't even kissed yet.'

'You haven't?' Viola frowned at her. 'What, you mean at all?'

She shook her head. 'Well, I suppose I've kissed him on the cheek, but that's it. I'd have thought that if he wanted to kiss me, he would've tried it already. He's had plenty of opportunities.'

'Maybe he doesn't know that you want him to?' Viola tried, propping her chin in her palm.

'He must know that I want to,' she murmured, her cheeks colouring. 'It's not like it's not obvious. It's almost as if we're just friends.'

'Maybe he's gay?'

Both girls glared at Lancelot. Tom sniggered, and Gavin shot his avatar on screen.

'What? I'm only saying. It's not like he ever did anything with Ellie, and she was hot.'

'They kissed,' Viola argued, indignant.

'Yeah, but they never did anything else.' Additional sniggers emanated from Tom. Viola pushed him with her foot with a sound of disgust.

'That was in year seven, Lance. Don't be gross.'

'I would've,' he boasted, looking at Gwenhwyfar.

'I thought you did,' Tom said.

'Shut up,' he snapped. 'Besides, that's my point. He didn't touch Ellie and he hasn't had a proper girlfriend since. He must be gay.'

'Don't be ridiculous,' Viola remarked.

'I'm not saying there's anything wrong with it,' continued Lancelot, 'I'm just saying there's no point waiting for him to kiss you. It's unnatural to still be a virgin at his age.'

'I'm a bit worried by how much you seem to know about Arthur's sex life, Lance,' Gavin droned.

Lancelot turned a furious shade of red. 'How come you're defending him? Do you fancy him or something?'

Gavin snorted. The girls both rolled their eyes.

'It's not like you're any younger than him,' Gwenhwyfar pointed out.

'So?'

'It's not like you've had hundreds of women.'

'Who says I haven't?'

'You're telling me you've slept with someone before?' she asked sceptically.

'Yes, actually,' he snapped. 'Hundreds.'

'Hundreds?' She smiled. 'How many, exactly?'

His deliberation didn't last long enough. 'Five.'

'Five isn't hundreds, Lance,' Viola pointed out.

'I thought you meant times I've done it, which would be hundreds.'

'Who?' Gavin asked.

'What?'

'I said, who have you slept with?'

This approach seemed to throw him. 'He doesn't know! He's making it up,' Tom jeered.

'Of course he's making it up,' Viola agreed. 'All boys do.'

'Boys who feel they have to brag about such things, at least,' commented Gwenhwyfar. She hadn't thought her opinion of Lancelot could sink any lower; but once again he had surprised her.

'Emily,' he blurted, unthinking.

'What?'

'Emily. I did her, and Charlotte too. And that girl at that party we went to last year. Can't remember what her name was.'

'No *way* did you sleep with Emily and Charlotte,' Gavin scoffed.

'Why would anyone?' Tom remarked.

'Even if you did, that's only three. Who else?' Viola demanded.

'Juliet, in sixth form,' was his next boast. Gavin and Tom sounded impressed.

'Who's that?' Gwenhwyfar asked.

'Just some girl everyone fancies,' Viola remarked, voice sarcastic. 'There's no way. I know her. She wouldn't touch Lance in a million years.'

'Four,' Gavin prompted.

'And Morgan,' Lancelot finished, confidence boosted by his acclaim. 'We grew up together. I was her first.'

'This is ridiculous,' Gwenhwyfar muttered, suddenly upset. 'Claiming you've slept around just to make yourself sound cool. Well, it doesn't sound cool. Now I'm just worried about catching something off you.'

His sneer hurt her more than she expected. 'Don't worry, I'm not *that* desperate.'

'I think I'm going to check your story on Monday,' Viola commented, twisting a lock of her dark hair. 'I'm pretty sure Emily, Charlotte, Morgan and Juliet would love to be reminded of such an intimate moment.'

'Even if you do ask them they won't admit it.'

Gwenhwyfar felt she'd had enough. 'Why not?'

'Two of them had boyfriends. Why do you think?'

'Now I know why Arthur's convinced you betrayed him,'

Gwenhwyfar snapped. 'Your attempts to make yourself feel like more of a man in comparison to him are just sad.'

Her words seemed to stir a firestorm within him, and the look he gave her was cutting. Suddenly the conversation shifted. Tom's interest had dwindled.

'So what are we doing for your birthday?'

Lancelot relaxed into the sofa. 'Nothing: that's what.'

'Oh come on, we have to do something. You never celebrate your birthday.' Viola jumped up to retrieve her juice from the coffee table. 'It'll be fun.'

'How about we just drink ourselves silly?' Lancelot suggested.

'We should throw a party. Tom's found the perfect place. It's an abandoned warehouse that's not being demolished for at least another five weeks. The business went bust and they want to convert it into flats.' Viola explained. 'We could spruce it up with lights.'

'I know someone who could DJ,' Gavin suggested.

'We could turn it into a ball,' Viola ploughed on, enthused. 'Invite the whole year.'

'The electrics are all still working,' Tom added. 'All we'd have to do is sweep it out.'

'We should make it fancy dress,' gushed Viola.

Gwenhwyfar began to thaw from the preceding argument. 'Fancy dress sounds pretty cool,' she admitted. 'It'll be good to take our mind off things.'

'I dunno,' Lancelot fretted. 'What if no one turns up?'

'Of course people will turn up!' Tom chortled. 'And if they don't, we'll have all the solution to ourselves.'

'Is solution such a good idea after what happened last time?' Gwenhwyfar reminded him.

'It's not like Hector or the Furies will be there.'

'Can I bring a friend?'

'Who, Arty?' Once again Lancelot was observing her with that less than friendly look in his eyes. She returned it in kind.

'Well, he *is* my boyfriend,' she bragged.

Lancelot shook his head roughly. 'Sorry. My party, my rules.'

'If Arthur can't come, then I'm not coming either,' Gwenhwyfar threatened. Her tactic was less effective than she'd hoped. Lancelot merely shrugged.

'Gwen has to come,' Viola demanded. 'And she can bring whoever she likes. Just like you can bring whoever you like, whether it be Morgan, Emily, Charlotte or Juliet.'

Everyone laughed. The tension compressing the room suddenly lifted. Pleased she'd got her way, Gwenhwyfar leant her head back on her splayed palm.

'How about a masquerade?' she suggested. 'Everyone has to wear a mask. Then we won't know who's there.'

'Not like those horrible things we had to wear for that protest, I hope?'

'No,' Gwenhwyfar said, looking to Gavin. 'Cool ones. Halloween masks, that sort of stuff.'

The idea seemed to be well liked by all. There were murmurs of approval, even a nondescript shrug from Lancelot.

'What's the dress code?' Viola enquired.

'We could make it formal.' Gwenhwyfar pictured her prospective outfit. 'When's your birthday again?'

'Next weekend,' muttered Lancelot, as if she should already know.

'That's enough time for people to get organised. I've got a dress I can wear.'

'And I've got a Venetian mask you can borrow,' Viola offered.

'At least if the police make an appearance identifying people won't be easy,' grinned Gavin.

'Exactly,' Gwenhwyfar beamed, bubbling with excitement. It was settled. Lancelot's sixteenth birthday party was going to be a masquerade.

By the time she made it home the smell of supper was wafting throughout the house. It was already dark outside, a curse of the colder months, though thanks to this her father had given her a lift from Tom's. Llew greeted her enthusiastically and soon she was upstairs winding down in the confines of her bedroom. She hunted online for masks, and decided that she would definitely go for one that was Venetian. She was texting Arthur when her computer bleeped at her. As her eyes rose to meet the screen her heart froze. It was *Free Countries*.

Hello Omega Iota Eta.

Gwenhwyfar looked down to her phone, calmly finishing the message before pressing hard on *send*. She could hear her blood pulsating through her ears, and it throbbed in her head.

Did you receive our introductory pack?

Her eyes slunk sideways to the envelope sitting on her desk.

Omega Iota Eta, are you there?

She drew a steadying breath.

Yes, I'm here. I received the pack.

Good. Is it memorised?

Not yet.

You have to memorise it, and then you must destroy it. Understood?

What happens if someone else reads it?

Then we must inform the Alpha immediately.

Gwenhwyfar looked to the brown envelope. The sellotape she had used to reseal it remained intact.

Has someone read it?

No.

Make sure you keep it safe. Destroy it as soon as you can.

Gwenhwyfar wondered why she was being contacted now. It had been weeks since the march, and even longer since she'd spoken to Isolde. She didn't even know if this was Isolde she was speaking to.

Is this Omega Iota Zeta?

Yes.

What is it you want?

We've had interest from a potential member. They visited our site last week and have passed the security check. In five minutes you will be connected to their computer. They're online now.

Dread swamped her. She didn't want to do this, didn't want to meet up with a stranger. She wasn't ready. What if it was an undercover police officer? What then?

I can't, she tried.

You have to, was the response.

How?

Just use the pack, and remember how I did it. That should work.

Can't you help me explain it to them?

The window went blank, wiped from the bottom upwards, and then suddenly there was an empty conversation box with space for her to type. A small timer ticked in the corner. 30:00. She stared apprehensively at the screen. When she next glanced to the clock, it read 27:30. Quickly she opened the envelope, finding the four sheets of paper inside. She pulled them out.

The first was blank, but she knew it was not scrap because when she held it to the light it revealed a strange text comprised of dots and dashes. The second sheet was a numbered universal alphabet that she was still trying to decipher, and the third revealed two code names, *Omega Iota Eta* and *Omega Iota Theta*. She cast the unsolved paperwork to one side. The final sheet was a list of what *Free Countries* believed in. She looked to the ticking clock. Twenty-one minutes.

Fearing what might happen should she fail, Gwenhwyfar typed a rushed *hello* into the text field. She waited, dearly hoping that, unlike her, the potential recruit wouldn't switch off their machine. A few precious minutes slipped by, and then:

Hello? Who's this?

She sighed with relief. She began to type her name, but changed her mind at the last second.

Omega Iota Eta.

This took a while to absorb.

What?

I'm from Free Countries. *We said we'd contact you. You visited our website, right?*

That was ages ago.

I know, we're sorry. We had to run a security check to make sure it was safe to contact you.

She referred to the sheet again.

Would you like more information regarding Free Countries*?*

I suppose.

When can you meet?

Meet?

So we can discuss your interest in Free Countries.

The website never said anything about meeting someone, the potential member objected.

Gwenhwyfar frowned, wondering how she was going to convince them. She wasn't sure if she wanted to.

So you're not interested in joining Free Countries?

I never said that. What's your name?

Omega Iota Eta. How did you hear about Free Countries?

I saw the flyer.

She thought for a moment, considering.

Are you Irish?

What? No. Do I have to be?

What are you? Gwenhwyfar asked.

English. Is that a problem?

The clock was running down. Just eight minutes remained. Gwenhwyfar heard her father call her from the bottom of the stairwell. Supper was ready.

No. Do you want to meet to discuss Free Countries? *Don't have much time.*

A long silence followed. Six minutes.

Yes. When?

Tomorrow?

Sure.

At the park by Woodlands Road?

Where's that?

Logres. In Surrey, Gwenhwyfar explained.

Too far.

Is Southbank good for you?

No, I live in Cornwall.

Oh.

She looked to the other side of the text box. In small letters she noticed the location: Lostwithiel, Cornwall.

When are you next closest?

Time churned by. Her mother yelled for her. She tried again.

Hello?

I'll be going on a trip to the Natural History Museum in London in a couple of weeks.

Her panic lessened.

Perfect. What date?

Friday the 22nd of November.

What time?

One?

Great, I'll meet you in the main foyer under the T. Rex at one. I have long brown hair, and will be wearing—

She thought for a moment.

—a navy coat with a red hat.

You're a girl? What's your name?

Gwen.

See you there, Gwen.

The window vanished when the timer expired, leaving no evidence of their conversation. She suddenly realised that she had school that Friday. Her mother opened the door. The paperwork from *Free Countries* billowed across the desk.

'For the last time, supper is ready! So will you come downstairs and eat it, please!'

'I'm coming!' She whipped the secret code off the floor and stuffed it back with the other pages into the brown envelope. 'Sorry, I was in the middle of my Maths homework.'

Eve stormed off downstairs. Hurriedly Gwenhwyfar shoved the information pack into the first drawer of her desk, flipped the light switch and then slammed her bedroom door.

It was Thursday afternoon when she dared to broach the subject of Lancelot's birthday party again.

Her text to Arthur over the weekend had achieved nothing, and though she had tried to talk him into attending on and off throughout the week, he remained reluctant. It had helped Gwenhwyfar greatly to learn that she wasn't the only one disturbed by what had happened at the Mobilisation March, and for a while during History she and Morgan had something to whisper about. The rapport between them soon came to a natural end, however, and resulted in a mutual silence.

Marvin was marking papers noiselessly at his desk. When the hum of the class was at the right level, Gwenhwyfar leant forwards and prodded Bedivere in the back.

'Bedivere!' she tried with a loud whisper. 'Are you coming to the party on Saturday?'

His face brightened. 'Lance's party?' Gwenhwyfar nodded. 'I wasn't sure if I was really invited,' he frowned, keeping his voice low.

'Why wouldn't you be? It's a masquerade, remember, so it's smart dress with a mask of your choice.'

'I've only got a Halloween mask,' he fretted.

'That doesn't matter. It's going to be great. The others asked me to double-check that you were still up for it.'

Bedivere shrugged. 'Yeah, I suppose. Where?'

'The abandoned warehouse by Flint Park.'

He nodded and then, predictably, turned to Arthur. 'Are you coming?'

'I don't know yet.'

'It sounds like it could be fun. My mum can give you a lift, if you like.'

'I can pick you both up,' Gwenhwyfar offered.

Arthur glanced at Morgan, who quickly bent her head and pretended she wasn't listening. 'I'll have to talk to my grandmother about it first,' he said. 'I doubt it, though. Lance isn't going to want me there.'

'You think he wants me there?' Bedivere remarked, his voice a little louder. 'I'll go anyway, even if it's just to annoy him.' He set his gaze on Morgan. 'What about you? Are you going?'

'Of course I'm going. Lance and I grew up together.'

Gwenhwyfar couldn't help herself. 'Is it true the two of you used to go out?'

Morgan looked up at her, obviously surprised. 'Who on earth told you that?'

'Lance mentioned it at the weekend,' Gwenhwyfar said, her tone dismissive. 'He seemed to think you two dated.'

'Lance said that?' Morgan asked, dubiously. 'Well, it's not true. We've only ever been friends.'

'I thought so,' Gwenhwyfar shrugged, wondering why she felt so relieved.

Remembering his cause, Bedivere rounded on Arthur. 'So are you coming?'

'I don't know! Probably not.' Huffing, Arthur returned to his work. 'I'm sorry, but spending an evening celebrating the birth of

Lance Lake seems counter-intuitive to me.'

'But it'll be *fun*,' pursued Gwenhwyfar, longing for him to agree. 'It won't be any good without you, Arthur. If you're not going then I won't want to go, either.'

'Well, that means we can both do something else Saturday night, doesn't it?' he sulked.

'But I promised Viola I'd go. We won't have to hang out with Lance. We won't even see him.'

'It's his birthday; of course we'll see him,' Arthur muttered. 'You'll be hanging out with Viola, anyway. It's probably better if I don't go, it'll just cause a scene.'

'You're really going to miss it because of Lance.'

Arthur gave a rough shrug of his shoulders. 'Sorry.'

Gwenhwyfar felt a flash of anger. Everything always had to be about Lancelot with him. Why didn't he want to do this for her? Why wouldn't he kiss her? What was she doing wrong?

As Arthur hunched his shoulders and faced the front of the class, Gwenhwyfar returned to her work. If he didn't want to attend the party with her, that was fine. She would go anyway and have a fantastic time. No matter what reason he had for refusing her, Gwenhwyfar was not going to let Arthur ruin her fun.

Masquerade

So far the night had been a blur of colour, with sculpted faces that merged into one being, alien and unknown. There were porcelain masks, Venetian masks, Halloween masks and animal disguises, extravagant gowns and smart tailored suits. The old warehouse looked anything but abandoned with the fairy lights dressing the walls, and they twinkled in the dark like the Milky Way. Twisting quickly through the crowd, Gwenhwyfar attempted to catch a glimpse of someone she knew. A long-nosed demon whirled past, his eyebrows twisted and his nostrils flaring. She thought she spotted the hem of Viola's aubergine dress spin in the colour storm, but her eyes were deceived. Frankenstein's grimace grinned at her in the spotlight, whilst a long-dead American president sat saggy as someone's second skin. A burgundy figure tempted her into thinking she'd just seen Morgan, a patchwork cat mask hiding her features; while a candidate for Tom flashed through the crowd, with a long beak of green. Gavin's frame was perhaps the most recognisable of them all, though his head was the least decipherable; he for the night was half-man half-beast, a Minotaur in the making.

'Gwen!'

She spun around to face the unknown speaker, and suddenly she was tugged deeper into the throng, stumbling as the mischievous jester danced with her through the grotesques. Solution burned through her limbs, and as they halted she pulled her hand away from the whippet-like boy.

'I've been looking for you all over!' shouted the jester. It was Bedivere.

'Great mask!' she yelled, leaning towards him. 'Where'd you get it?'

'My sister picked it up when she went to Italy last year! Said I could use it!' he yelled back. 'Yours looks great too!'

'Thanks!'

'Where are the others?'

Her curls bounced as her head shook, framing the white and silver façade. 'I don't know!' she admitted, voice sore from shouting. 'I saw Viola earlier, but that's it!'

Bedivere began to search, his jester bells ringing with every movement he made. He pointed to the other end of the room. 'There!'

Gwenhwyfar couldn't see anything, but that didn't matter. Her jester was her guide. They passed a dame, a woeful amateur dramatics mask, another pointy-nosed demon and a darker feline. The Minotaur, the green demon and the porcelain-faced Viola were standing by the solution table, mixing and pouring drinks.

'Great party.' Bedivere lifted his mask as they joined them, revealing a face glazed in sweat. 'I've never seen anything like it.'

'Yeah, it's really amazing,' Gwenhwyfar enthused. 'How did you do it?'

'It's surprising what a good sweep and a few lights can do,' Viola grinned, her dark lips framed by the half mask.

The Minotaur removed his head as the long nosed demon handed him a drink. Gavin was suffering from the heat, and he hissed at the potency of the solution. 'So where's the birthday boy?'

'I was wondering that too,' Gwenhwyfar admitted. Viola and Gavin both exchanged a glance. Feeling the lure of the music, Gwenhwyfar decided to mix a drink. Four girls joined them. Cups were taken, cartons were exchanged, and as Gwenhwyfar lurched for the solution her hand collided with another bound for the same bottle. She looked up. 'Isolde?'

She stared at her wide-eyed, her mother's gold necklace hanging beneath her green mask. 'Gwen? What are you doing here?'

Her friends seemed surprised that she knew someone other than them. She glanced at Viola and then at her secret recruiter for a radical cause. 'I'm a friend of the guy whose party this is. You?'

'I know his cousin, Bobby. He's in my English class in college.'

'You live round here?'

Isolde nodded, as if it were the most obvious thing in the world. 'You?'

'Yeah, I go to Logres.'

'I used to go there!' Isolde exclaimed. 'Is Mr Caledonensis still teaching History?'

'Yep!' Gwenhwyfar replied. 'He's my teacher. He's pretty cool.'

'Everyone in my class used to love him,' the Irish girl revealed. On a whim, Gwenhwyfar decided to introduce Isolde to her friends.

'We go to the same pony club,' she lied, once names had been exchanged. 'We should go somewhere quieter to talk,' Gwenhwyfar gushed, enjoying her connection with Isolde through their association with the forbidden. 'I won't be two seconds.' She waved to Viola as they edged their way through the crowd. 'We're just going to get some air!'

This time her journey through the room was even less lucid. A foreign shadow seemed to stalk her movements, while the garish Frankenstein grinned at her from afar. Isolde hovered ahead of her, ever out of reach. She didn't realise how hot the premises were until she made it outside. The cold sharp air cleared her mind for a moment, and she inhaled it deeply, letting it harden the warm glow clouding her coordination.

'I can't believe we met here.' They found a low wall to sit on. 'It's so surreal.'

'It's a pretty surreal party,' observed Isolde. Neither one of them removed their masks, the colourful veils complementing their sense of secrecy. 'I've never been to anything like it. So how are you getting along with everything?'

'Good. I've arranged to meet with the new recruit, but he won't be in London until next Friday. I wanted to ask what I should do. I have no idea how to convince him to join *Free Countries*.'

'Just do what I did,' Isolde shrugged. 'Make sure that his interest is genuine, that he's not trying to bait you.'

'And how am I supposed to do that?'

'I'm not sure, really,' her superior admitted. 'You just have to listen to your gut. That's what I did with you.' There was a moment of silence. 'Oh, and exchange numbers. We should have done it before, but I forgot. You can have mine now, if you like.'

'Sure.' Gwenhwyfar opened her clutch and pulled out her phone. She handed it to Isolde, who traded their information. 'So you know Lance's cousin? Is he here?'

'He should be. I haven't seen him since I arrived.' She handed Gwenhwyfar's mobile back to her. 'His brother's not here, though. He's too young.'

'Lance has a brother?'

Isolde shook her head. 'Bobby's brother, Luke. Lance is their cousin. I only know about him because he lives with them.'

'He does? How come?'

'His parents died when he was young. Bobby's dad is Lance's mother's brother.' She shrugged. 'Lance said Bobby could invite people.'

She had thought that the hall seemed busy. Looking out into the dark, Gwenhwyfar's thoughts turned to Lancelot, and she suddenly wondered why she knew so little about him. 'How did his parents die?'

Isolde shrugged. 'Bobby never said.'

They were silent for a moment. 'Did you get that flyer from *Free Countries* telling us to go to the Mobilisation March?' Isolde nodded, and Gwenhwyfar frowned. 'I thought you said we didn't do marches?'

'We don't organise them. We don't usually attend others as a group, either. I don't think it was an order, I think it was a round-robin.' Her face darkened. 'I heard from my contact that the New Nationals are going to start restricting unapproved material sent through the post,' she muttered. 'So we might not be getting flyers for much longer.'

'But how will we recruit?'

'We'll find a way,' Isolde promised. 'Did you go?'

Gwenhwyfar's pulse quickened as she nodded. 'Didn't you?'

'No. It would've been too risky. I don't know why we were encouraged to go in the first place—it's completely against protocol.' She bent her head towards Gwenhwyfar's, her voice dropping to a dry whisper. 'Then again, I've heard that the Alpha and the Alpha Beta disagree on a lot of things. Apparently, even though the Alpha is in charge, the Alpha Beta is the brains behind the group. If they disagree something like this happens.'

Gwenhwyfar gazed at her, surprised. 'How do you know that?'

'My contact knows more than he should,' Isolde said. 'He does a lot of research. Don't worry, it's totally safe,' she added, sensing Gwenhwyfar's concern. 'He always trawls the archives for "little news" about underground groups. Sometimes things about *Free Countries* pop up. He's really smart.'

Gwenhwyfar felt anxiety resurface in the pit of her stomach. 'Do you think I shouldn't have gone?'

'If you kept your identity safe, I don't think it matters if you went to the march or not. Not as far as *Free Countries* is concerned, at least.'

They fell into another silence after that, and as time passed it became obvious Isolde was cold. Not quite ready to retreat back into the mad swirl of grotesques, Gwenhwyfar remained outside on her own, enjoying the crispness of the night. It was hard to hear the party from where she sat, and there was nothing to indicate its existence besides a few squares of light and the muffled sound of bass pounding the earth.

Her eyes had been closed for some time when she heard a bark of laughter. 'Gwen—?' an unfriendly voice bit. 'Is that you? It is, isn't it? What are you doing out here on your own?'

There was an element of sarcasm that belied concern. Frankenstein. Immediately she stood.

'Hector.' Another grotesque shadowed his footsteps: a smooth-skinned alien with bug-eyes. 'What do you want?'

'Saw you were alone. Thought I'd better come keep you company.'

She resisted the urge to shrink away from him as he stepped closer. 'I have nothing to say to you.'

'Who said anything about talking?' he jeered. 'You got me into a lot of trouble, with your tales. Running around, telling people I attacked you. I could have been expelled.'

'You did attack me,' she responded calmly.

'I didn't do anything you didn't want me to, and you know it.' He began to circle her.

'I pushed you away, remember?'

'And I get suspended just because you change your mind at the last minute?' The alien hung back and stood guard. Hector spiralled closer. 'I *know* you wanted it. You still want it.'

She snapped his hand away. 'Can't you take a hint? Everyone knows you're just some pathetic guy who has to leech around girls because no one likes him. Well, I've got news for you: no one does like you. The whole school knows what you did.'

She pushed past him, daring the alien to stop her. Hector grappled onto her wrist before he could.

'Pathetic?' He laughed. Gwenhwyfar picked at his fingers, reluctant to touch him, and tried to uncoil his grasp. He tugged her closer. 'You don't realise what you've done, do you? You've ruined everything. I can't apply to college now. Ravioli's already talking like I won't be able to stay here.'

She held his gaze. 'Your problem, not mine.'

He jerked her arm, hard. 'It's your problem if I make it your problem: you and your squealing friend. Now every school in the country will think I'm a rapist.'

'Why? Are you going to rape me?'

This threw him. Quickly he released her arm. Gwenhwyfar felt her heart pounding through her chest. Her phone was in her clutch. She prised it open with one hand.

'Rape you? Rape *implies* that I'd be giving you something you don't want.' He looked to the alien. 'Right?' He reached for her again. This time she flinched. He laughed with vindictive amusement. 'Jumpy, aren't we? Like a little rabbit.'

'Don't you touch me,' she hissed.

He expelled an exaggerated, wounded sound. 'I thought you liked me? No? That's a shame for you. Word is you're always moist.'

Disgust speared through her core. Frozen to the spot, Gwenhwyfar glanced to the warehouse. She could scream for help, but who would hear? Hector started at her again. She recoiled. Suddenly the alien came at her, too.

She ran. Hector was too close. He caught the back of her skirts and she tripped. Her clutch flew out her hand as she landed on her forearms and was winded by the earth. His clammy fingers scraped up her legs. She kicked at him, spearing him with her stilettos. His laughter broke and he swore. Pulled back, her torso scraped over the dirt. Gwenhwyfar lunged for her clutch. Phone. Keys. Anything. She only grabbed one before she was dragged out of reach. Hector was on top of her. She struck as quick as an adder. Her pocket deodorant hissed into his eyes. He howled.

She kicked him back, kicked his stomach, his shoulders, his

arms, his head. He toppled over. The silent alien was there the moment she stood. She pointed the deodorant at him like a gun. He held back.

'You do know I told the police about what you did, right?' She said, high on adrenaline. 'You know I'll tell them about this. They'll arrest you. They'll arrest you both. What you going to do in prison, Hector? Word is you're moist.'

She kicked him hard again, in the back. *Out, get out. Run while you still can.* Someone caught her eye at the door to the warehouse. Lancelot.

He came out quickly, sensing the danger. She fled and stopped the moment she was behind him. Hector got to his feet and staggered over, his mask abandoned.

'Crazy bitch blinded me!' he shouted, pointing a sharp finger her way. He growled, and then he was rubbing his eyelids, expelling the sounds of a wounded animal. 'Jesus! What is *wrong* with you? My eyes! She sprayed something in my eyes!'

'It's just deodorant, you idiot,' Gwenhwyfar told him. 'Go wash it out.' The alien stepped closer, vying for a fight, but Lancelot caught the movement and suddenly seemed taller. For a moment everything seemed to hang in the balance, but then Hector retreated and the alien followed.

'Crazy bitch,' he hissed again, stumbling away from the venue and into the dark. Lancelot looked as if he was going to start after them.

'Leave it, he's not worth it.' Gwenhwyfar touched his arm as she passed him to retrieve her clutch from the dirt.

He followed her. 'What happened?'

Carefully, she put her belongings back in her bag. 'Nothing. It was just Hector being an arsehole.'

'He did this to you?' Immediately he looked towards the wooded copse, but neither Hector nor the alien were in sight.

'I said leave it! Seriously, it's not worth the trouble.'

'Gwenhwyfar? What did he do?'

She was shaking, she realised. Calmly she drew a breath and fastened her clutch. 'Nothing, it's nothing. He was just harassing me, that's all. You know. Making... making threats.'

'Hector was making threats?' He looked over his shoulder, as if he could still see him. 'What kind of threats?'

She gave him a pointed look. His scowl blackened.

'What did he say?'

'You know, that I was asking for it, called me *moist*. Said it wasn't rape if I secretly wanted it. That kind of stuff.'

He was obviously furious, because in the seconds that followed, Lancelot was speechless.

'That... seriously...? He *seriously* did that. He *seriously* said those things.' He stepped about on the spot and ran a palm over his mouth. 'I should've... why didn't I? I *knew* something was up.' He turned from her, and was gazing into the copse again. 'Where the fuck is he? You should've said. I would've stopped him.'

'No, Lake. I didn't want you to do anything. It only would've made things worse.'

He turned to her, and took her by the arms. She surprised herself by being grateful for the contact. 'Are you hurt? Did he... did they...'

'Didn't you hear? I'm a *crazy bitch*. I sprayed deodorant in his eyes.' She offered him a quick smile. 'I just fell. He tripped me when I tried to leave. I don't think they were going to do anything. I think it was just talk.'

'So?'

'So I'm fine, really.'

'You're trembling,' he disputed.

'I'm fine. I just didn't know he would be here.' She looked at him critically. 'Why *was* he here? I thought we were checking.'

'We were checking—of course we were checking. He must have turned up when we weren't watching the door. I'm sorry.'

'It's not your fault,' she muttered, staring unseeingly into his chest. His hands migrated, and for a moment he was cupping her head.

'You should sit. You're in shock.' He looked to the wall. 'Can you make it?'

'I don't know. Wait, what are you doing?'

'I'm carrying you,' he insisted.

'No you're not. It's fine! I can make it.'

He scooped her up. Gwenhwyfar gasped as suddenly the world was tilted. Her long dress bunched up in his extended arms.

He huffed in surprise, his thick brow folding. 'Christ, what have you been eating?'

'It's the *dress*,' Gwenhwyfar said indignantly. She wrapped her arms around his strong neck. 'You've just got chicken arms.'

'Chickens don't have arms,' he contested. Carefully, he set her down. She hoisted herself up onto the wall. 'I think you've done my back in.'

'Shut up, Lancelot.'

He offered her a tentative smile. 'How are you feeling?'

'Don't ask me that.'

'Sorry. Should we call the police?'

She shook her head. 'Not yet.'

'How about your parents?'

She scowled at him, and turned her gaze out towards the dark. 'I don't want Hector to ruin my night.'

He eyed her grass-stained dress. Gwenhwyfar knew that her ankle was swollen; she could feel it. Her arms were grazed and Hector's hand had pressed blue finger marks into her skin.

'You might have to call them, unless you can think of a good way to explain this.'

'I won't go home,' Gwenhwyfar decided.

'No?'

'I'll stay at Viola's house. If I tell someone what happened, I'll just have to go through that whole thing with Ravioli again. The police won't care either. I told them about Tom's party. They said there was no point pressing charges.'

He seemed shocked. 'It might be different this time.'

'I doubt it.' She laughed harshly at herself. 'They're more likely to arrest me for blinding him. God, I shouldn't have done that. Do you think he will go blind?'

'So what if he does?' He shook his head and hunched his shoulders. 'I should do something. I should see what the hell he thinks he's playing at.'

'No Lance, don't.'

'Why the hell not? I should kill him for this.'

'I don't need you to. I can take care of myself.' He said nothing. 'Seriously Lance, just leave it. I don't want you provoking him, or anything. He's pissed enough as it is.'

'You should tell someone what happened.'

'I know.' She caught the concern in his dark gaze. She wanted to brush the night away, wanted to forget about it. 'Thanks, for being here.'

He shrugged. She edged closer to him on the wall, eager for the security he offered. He remained still.

'I don't know what would've happened if you hadn't shown up.'

'Are you kidding? You'd have blinded them both.' There was a heartbeat's silence. 'Who was that guy?'

'The alien? I don't know.'

'He looked too old to be from Logres. Something about him…'

'Maybe he's from Bobby's college?'

'Maybe. Or maybe he's just some friend of Hector's.'

'How were you ever friends with him?' Gwenhwyfar asked, suddenly piqued.

'I don't know.' He seemed troubled. The moonlight illuminated the white half of his monochrome mask. 'I guess you can know someone without ever really knowing them.' He shook his head, and sighed. 'I had no idea he would ever do something like this.'

Words escaped her. She felt a sharp pang from deep within, and suddenly she was thinking of her father. A roughened finger lifted her chin, and Lancelot's dark eyes filled her vision.

'Gwenhwyfar?'

She forced a swallow down her tear-swollen throat. As she turned her head, his hand fell away and her skin was left cold.

They sat in silence for some time. She leant into his side, her head falling against his shoulder. He was warm.

'I never had the chance to wish you a happy birthday,' she whispered through a wet sniff, staring into the ground.

'Now's a good a time as any.' He squeezed her arm, and she shifted to wedge her body against him. Looking up, she smiled.

'Happy birthday, Lance. Sorry for making your party so dramatic.'

'Thanks,' he grinned, teeth flashing in the gloom. 'And don't worry about it. I got to see Hector whiplashed by women's deodorant. It's been great.'

Sniffing, she tucked her arm around him and squeezed him tight. When she shivered Lancelot drew her closer.

She felt safe, she felt warm. A second thought made her hunt for Hector in the gloom, but she only found stillness. The sound from the party thumped on, and as she looked back to check the warehouse she thought she saw the patchwork cat lingering in the doorway. A second glance however, and the figure had gone.

A Proposal

Viola pulled her portfolio out of her school bag and placed it on the table. Immediately Gwenhwyfar snatched it up to hunt for new photos. Though she had spent Saturday night and most of Sunday at Viola's house, the pictures had arrived via courier that morning, and Viola had eagerly put them into her book so she could show them off.

'It's mostly because I've got an important casting after school,' she told them. 'It's for *Bare Make-up*. They're shooting a campaign for a new product.'

'Do you think you'll get it?' Gwenhwyfar asked, gazing wistfully at the latest photo.

Shrugging, Viola observed her pictures upside down. 'It'd be good if I did. The campaign's worth at least twenty thousand.'

'Twenty *thousand*?' Bedivere's mouth hung open. 'For a day's work?'

'It's a lot, isn't it? But that's the way it goes. You work for nothing, and then hope you'll get something like that once or twice a year.' Bedivere took the portfolio for a closer look. Viola turned her attention to Gwenhwyfar. 'How's your ankle?'

'Not bad.' She rolled her foot and felt little discomfort. 'I can walk on it now.'

'What did your mum say about the dress?'

'She hasn't seen it yet.' She glanced across to Charlotte's table. Emily was still sitting there during registration, but the other girls whispered to one another and ignored her completely. 'I'm going to take it to the dry-cleaners. She thinks I fell over. She'd freak, if she knew.'

'I still think you should report Hector. There was no misunderstanding this time.'

'He was just trying to scare me. You know, seeing how I *ruined his life*.'

'You should be scared. He's acting like a complete psycho. How can you be happy with him still in school?'

'Of course I'm not happy about it. Look, whether I go to the police or not, *he* thinks I'm talking to them. I told him I would.'

'That might just make him more desperate.'

She was temped to tell her how her last attempt to report Hector had gone, but she couldn't bring herself to relive it. 'And what am I supposed to say? Some drunk guy groped me so I half-blinded him? For all I know I *have* blinded him. I'm half expecting Mr Hall to appear and escort me to the principal's office.'

'All the more reason you should talk to Ravioli first,' Viola urged quietly.

'Ravioli will just want to bury it,' she argued, as Bedivere closed the portfolio and handed it back to Viola. 'He's hardly going to want Hector locked up. It'll disgrace the school.'

'And what about your parents?'

'They've got enough going on as it is. I'm still waiting for my mum to talk to my dad.'

'About what?' Bedivere asked.

'Nothing important.' She couldn't face telling her parents. If they heard she was in the same situation after having attended yet another party with solution, they would never let her go out again. 'Just marital troubles.'

Frowning, Bedivere looked to Viola. 'The police, then?'

'I don't want to tell anyone!' she snapped. 'I can handle it. If he so much as looks at me I'll say something. But for now I'd rather not have the hassle.' Her friends both eyed her as if they knew better, and it annoyed her. 'I don't want people knowing. *Especially* not Arthur. He'll do something silly, or insist that I tell, I know he will.'

'He'd be right to.'

'Please, just keep it quiet, would you? Bedivere?'

'I won't say anything!' he exclaimed, clearly insulted to be told twice.

'Just think about it,' Viola pressed. 'That's all I'm asking. None of us will forgive ourselves if something like this happens again.'

Defensively, Gwenhwyfar nodded. 'Fine,' she muttered, if only to please them. 'I'll think about it.'

The shrill bell sounded, and Mrs Ray released them all into the corridor.

By the time Bedivere and Gwenhwyfar made it to History, Morgan and Arthur were already in their seats. The old classroom was stale with dust, but it was too cold outside to open the windows. As Bedivere sat down he offered a cheerful greeting that was not reciprocated, and when Gwenhwyfar said hello to Arthur he gave her an upturned shoulder. She glowered. What had she done now?

'Good morning, class!' Marvin said brightly. He was in early again, and was hovering awkwardly while he waited for his students to sit. 'How is everyone today? I hope you're all ready for your first revision session?'

There were general groans of protest throughout the room, the most verbal from Tom. Marvin scribbled "Level Fours" across the board. Turning to face the class, he smacked his hands together.

'Page two-hundred-and-seventy-seven, please! Hurry up now, we don't have all day. I want to introduce you to the concept of *practice papers* in the second half of the lesson.'

Gwenhwyfar split open her thick, glossy History book and flicked through it, her eyes slinking across to Arthur. After a few moments she realised that Morgan was staring, and as their gazes crossed the other girl glanced away with a worried look in her eyes.

'What is it?' she whispered. Morgan said nothing and looked pointedly ahead, listening to Marvin. Apprehensively, Gwenhwyfar studied Arthur. Had he heard about what had happened? Feeling uneasy with the memory of what Hector had done, she ducked her head and set to work. Conversation swelled as Marvin failed to quieten his pupils, and the remaining hour left her with a niggling sickness that she couldn't shake.

Her heart leapt when the bell rang. Immediately the class jumped up, abandoning their test papers. Shouting above the din, Marvin endeavoured to control the outburst, waving his hands about as his words fell on deaf ears.

'Don't forget questions five and six for your homework! Bring your practice papers to the *front*! No pushing in the aisles!'

Gwenhwyfar bolted to her feet, her eyes fixed on Arthur. He packed swiftly, grabbed his paper and then attempted to squeeze past Bedivere. She stretched over her table and took his arm.

'Arthur?'

A look was all she received for her concern, a hard, ugly look that made her feel small. Marvin stared in surprise as his usually talkative student shot straight past him, with Gwenhwyfar close behind.

She could barely keep up. A group of Year Eights shouted as she elbowed past them. 'Arthur, please! Just tell me what's wrong!' Forced to break into a run, she pushed through the double doors that swung shut on her as he escaped out onto the strip between the Maths rooms and mobile classrooms. 'Arthur!' He stopped and glared at her mutely. She was on the verge of tears. 'Please, just tell me what the matter is!'

'You don't know what the matter is? How can you not? It's obvious, Gwen. Really obvious.'

His riddle threw her. As she tried to sense what might have upset him, she could only think of Saturday. 'I don't know. You'll have to tell me.'

He turned to leave. She hurried after him.

'Morgan told me. Of all people, I shouldn't have to hear it from her.'

'Hear what from her?' She reached forwards to stop him, but he shook her away. 'You *know* she doesn't like me.'

'So you're denying it then?'

Her heart pounded. 'Denying what? I don't know what it is you're talking about!'

They came under the annex between the girls' toilets and the back entrance to old Wormelow. He wheeled round on her.

'You and Lance! That's what I'm talking about. Morgan said she saw you at the party together. Don't deny it, Gwen. She said he had his arm around you.'

Relief, then panic, flooded through her. 'So?' she said, daring him to make the accusation. 'You think that because he had his arm around me, we're seeing one another? Is that it? Do you have any idea how ridiculous that sounds?'

'It wasn't just the arm, Gwen. Morgan said you had your head on his shoulder.'

Suddenly she was angry. 'So what? We're just friends! *Nothing happened.* Besides, it's not like you've got the right to care who I associate myself with.'

'I haven't?' The very air around him seemed to blacken. Gwenhwyfar's eyes flashed as his did, and she squared herself closer.

'No, you haven't!'

'I thought we were supposed to be going out?' he snapped.

'Are we? It's not like you ever actually *asked* me out, Arthur!'

'I thought it was obvious!'

'Obvious?' she flared, nostrils widening. 'After that stunt you pulled with Morgan, nothing was *obvious*!'

'How clearly do you need to hear it? I'm not interested in Morgan. And I don't see how you couldn't have known we were exclusive!' he added hotly.

'Exclusive?' she mocked. 'You're making it sound like something actually happened! It didn't! Lance is just a *friend*.'

'Oh, so now he's a friend? I thought you couldn't stand him?'

She growled in vexation. She didn't want to explain; she shouldn't have to explain.

'She said you were holding each other, Gwen!'

'I don't see why you're so wound up!'

'Don't you?' he fired.

'No!' her voice broke above his. 'Especially when you and I haven't even kissed yet!'

He fell silent, and so did she. Their anger leaked away and left them both cold.

'I'm sorry, I wasn't aware that I'm failing to meet your expectations,' he muttered, wounded.

'No, that's not what I meant,' she tried.

'No—you're right. It's none of my business who you sit with.' His broken sarcasm was biting, and it split straight through her chest.

'Arthur!' she called as he turned away. Angry tears launched into her eyes, but furiously she blinked through them. The doors to old Wormelow swung open and a flurry of pupils swarmed around her. She attempted to follow him, but was forced to give up. He was out of sight in less than ten seconds.

English was set to the tune of heavy rainfall, a sudden and unexpected outburst that beat down on the windowpanes and cut streams across the glass. Bedivere listened to Gwenhwyfar's news concerning Arthur's mood with interest, though he seemed to withhold his opinion and offered few solutions. Break time passed with no sign of either Arthur or Lancelot, and she spent most of General Studies longing for a resolution to their conflict. She walked with Gavin to the canteen through the lingering drizzle, but as they were about to slip through the double doors she was arrested by the sound of her name.

'Gwenhwyfar.'

She knew the voice before she turned. Lancelot. Gwenhwyfar

looked for sign of Arthur, but he was nowhere to be seen.

'Can I talk to you?'

She nodded, and started to follow Gavin into the depths of the canteen. He stopped her again.

'No, not in there—somewhere private.' He led her down the paved slope to the nearest tree, and soon they were stood under its partial shelter.

'What do you want?'

'Hector went to hospital. He's off school for a couple of days. I don't think he's said anything about what happened. Apparently he's telling people it was an accident.'

She gazed at him, and the attention seemed to make him nervous.

'I still don't know who the alien was, though. I thought it might be someone from Bobby's college, but he doesn't know anyone who went with that mask.'

'You told Bobby?'

'Only that a couple of guys had been making trouble. I didn't say what.'

The pressure she had been feeling over the weekend lifted slightly. 'Looks like I taught him a lesson after all,' she murmured. Lancelot looked a lot nicer when he smiled. For a moment they stood in silence, but then a large, cold droplet of water made it through the naked branches and landed directly on Gwenhwyfar's head. She wiped it off with a shiver. 'I think I'm going to head back.'

As she turned to leave he panicked. 'Wait!'

She halted. Now she was standing in direct contact with the rain. 'What?'

'I wanted to ask you something.'

'Can't you wait until we're inside? It's freezing out here.'

'It won't take a moment.'

'What is it?'

He struggled over his words. Gwenhwyfar realised she had never seen him so flustered before. Slowly, she began to understand what it was he wanted. It couldn't be, could it?

'I... I...'

Stammering was never a good sign. She was about to turn around again, but her attempt to escape only forced him to blurt it out.

'Will you go out with me?'

She froze, suddenly afraid. Why did he have to ask?

'Gwen?'

Reluctantly, she turned to face him. His hair was lank, his shoulders drenched. He stared at her earnestly and in his eyes she felt she witnessed something people rarely saw.

'I know you're supposed to be seeing Arthur—'

'*Am* seeing Arthur,' she corrected.

'I know, but... after Saturday... and I've liked you for some time now, but I didn't know what to do about it, or if you liked me... but after... I thought you might...'

A sharp emotion whipped through her stomach. What was it? Nerves... anxiety? Her heart was pounding and the sensation felt akin to fear. She laughed inwardly at herself. Now Arthur had something to be upset about. Though why should it reflect on her if Lancelot felt this way?

'Lance...' she began softly, 'I have a *boyfriend*. I can't just forget that.'

The disappointment on his face was heartbreaking. 'But Saturday...'

'I was afraid on Saturday. And I was drunk.' The drizzle turned to cold needles as a stronger wind cut between them. She winced. 'I'm sorry.'

'You're not even the slightest bit interested?' he asked hopelessly.

'I like Arthur.' She felt odd saying it to him, and folded her arms across her chest.

'But I like you,' he argued.

'Sorry, Lance. I don't know what you want me to say. I'm flattered, but no, I can't go out with you.'

He soon withdrew, and shrugged carelessly. 'Right,' he murmured. 'Whatever. Just thought I'd check. Guess I misunderstood.'

'We can still be friends though, right?' she probed in an effort to cheer him.

He shook his head, his shoulders drooping. 'Whatever, Gwen.' He expelled a rough sigh. 'Yeah, I guess we can still be friends.'

She tried to dispel the guilt creeping within her. 'Come on. Let's go and find the others. Gavin will be wondering where I got to.' She turned to briskly ascend the hill. Half-heartedly, Lancelot followed.

They both received strange looks when they returned together, drenched from the rain. Eager to put some distance between them, Gwenhwyfar positioned herself at the far end of the table, shedding her coat and dragging her fingers through her wet hair.

'Where have you two been?' Gavin asked. He eyed Lancelot with concern. 'Swimming?'

'Yes, actually,' Gwenhwyfar replied lightly. 'It's like walking around underwater out there, isn't it Lance?' Lancelot sat staring into the crowd. 'Freezing too,' Gwenhwyfar continued, 'I'll probably catch a cold.'

'You'd better not,' Viola remarked. 'Remember when you made me promise to take you to any modelling parties? Well, I just heard from my agency. I have to go to a preview party for that new make-up product. You know, *Bare Make-up*? It's next Saturday in London. You're my plus one, if you're up for it.'

'Of course I'm up for it!' Gwenhwyfar exclaimed. 'Where is it?'

'Some club in Mayfair. We'll have to catch the last train home, but it should be fun.'

'If it's in a club, how are you going to get in?' interrupted Gavin.

'It's a private party. I just have to take a calling card to show the bouncer.'

'Jealous,' remarked Tom.

'You can come to the next one,' Viola promised, grinning. 'I'll let you know if I see anyone famous.'

Gwenhwyfar's eyes slunk across the table to Lancelot. He looked back, and she averted her gaze as if scalded. As her friends changed the subject she retreated into her thoughts and mindlessly stared out of the water-stained windows. Silence surrounded her. Gwenhwyfar didn't see Arthur stride into the cafeteria, as wet as an otter; nor did she notice him hasten straight to the table he usually went to great lengths to avoid. She started in surprise when suddenly he was there, towering above her.

'Arthur?'

He deliberated for a moment, but then he held out his hand.

As soon as Gwenhwyfar grasped it she was tugged to her feet.

The tables erupted into a chorus of whooping as he stooped down and caught her firmly on her lips. Surprised, she relaxed into him, her chest expanding with joy. He broke away for a moment, lust darkening his eyes. Eagerly he kissed her again, deeper this time, holding her close.

The cheering died, and the jeering started. Bliss embraced her. His lips were soft and warm, just as she had expected, and they fit against hers perfectly. She welcomed his tongue with her own, touching, tasting. After a perpetuity, she was finally released. Gwenhwyfar felt a sudden rush of cold air. Abruptly, Arthur abandoned her.

The cafeteria erupted into roars of laughter.

'What?' She sat down quickly, her cheeks a furious shade of red. Tom was in hysterics.

'What was that about?' Viola asked, amused.

'I have no idea,' Gwenhwyfar remarked, still in shock.

'Well, at least he's kissed you now,' teased Gavin, pressing his chin into his knuckles. 'Ask and you shall receive.'

She tasted where Arthur's lips had touched. Had he been trying to make some sort of point? It hadn't felt like it. Warmth flooded her, and she smiled.

'It's quite cute, really,' Viola mused. 'When he left he was blushing and everything. I think he really likes you, Gwen.'

Gwenhwyfar thought so too. Euphoric, she surveyed the table. There was something missing, the lack of a biting comment that was expressed whenever someone mentioned the name Arthur. Her eyes fell to where Lancelot had been sitting, and her insides turned to frost.

'Where's Lance?'

'He left,' Gavin remarked.

'When?'

He shrugged. 'After Arthur showed up.'

Suddenly she felt terrible. Her eyes scanned the hall again and then slipped to the door. Blood seemed to pulse in her ears with each thud of her heart. He was nowhere in sight. Deflated from her moment with Arthur, she began to worry about how she could rectify the damage caused to Lancelot's feelings, and then fretted over the fact that she cared.

Tristan

Taking advantage of her impeccable attendance record, Gwenhwyfar had conned her parents into thinking she was unwell. She was only able to sneak out of the house by chance, as her mother had scheduled a last-minute shopping trip with a new acquaintance and would not be home for several hours. The trains were running late and the Underground was congested, but she managed to make it to South Kensington in good time. The museum's security nearly turned it into a wasted trip, however, and when she was finally let into the main exhibition hall she was desperately late.

She waited by the foot of the Tyrannosaurus Rex, trying not to look too suspicious. A boy soon approached her, eying her apprehensively. 'Omega Iota Eta?' She nodded. 'From *Free Countries*?' the boy continued. He looked similar in age to Isolde, and spoke with a Cornish lilt.

'Gwen,' she expelled, holding out a hand for him to shake. 'And you are?'

'Tristan,' the lanky boy replied. He had long, stalk-like limbs and a clear complexion with tawny brown skin. He wore his full curling hair loose, and was dressed in a grey jacket, old blue pullover and worn jeans. Gwenhwyfar smiled.

'Thanks for taking the time to meet me here. Sorry I'm late. The trains were a nightmare, and I'm supposed to be in school.' She looked to the displays, and then up at him. 'Have you eaten?' Tristan shook his head. 'We'll go to the café, then.'

They walked in silence, past the great panda now extinct in the wild for many years, and the polar bear, a species long absent from the Arctic. The food hall was still busy for lunch. They queued for hot drinks and found a small table in the corner. Once seated, Tristan produced a lunchbox and ripped it open, clearly ravenous.

'Do you mind?'

'No,' Gwenhwyfar said, removing her coat and hat. 'Go for it.'

He unwrapped a sandwich and took a healthy bite. 'So how does this work?' he asked, chewing.

'I see if you have any questions regarding *Free Countries*, and then you decide if you'd like to join.' Like Isolde, she had brought a notebook. She fished for it in her bag.

'Questions?' He frowned, his dark eyes watching her closely.

'And I ask you a few things, too.' She flipped open the book and produced her favourite pen. 'So,' Gwenhwyfar began, trying to sound authoritative, 'why do you want to join *Free Countries*?'

He shrugged unhelpfully, as she had done. 'I don't know. I just saw the flyer and found the website.' She scribbled it down. 'I think George Milton's an idiot, and you seem to be against him.'

'We're not just against Milton,' Gwenhwyfar remarked. She un-crumpled the short manifesto that she'd brought with her and held it as a point of reference. 'We have other policies, too.'

'Such as?'

She took him through the full list of what *Free Countries* was about, but it didn't seem as if he was really listening. He was too busy wolfing down his yoghurt. 'Does that all make sense?' Gwenhwyfar asked afterwards, taking a sip of her hot chocolate.

'I suppose,' he murmured.

'You don't have any questions?'

Tristan shrugged and rattled his spoon around in the emptied pot. 'It all sounds pretty straightforward. So what happens if I join?'

'I tell the person who recruited me, and they pass the message on to the guy in charge, the Alpha. I suppose you've already guessed that we have code names, indicating what rank we are. You'll get one too, and then when another member wants to join *Free Countries*, you'll be contacted by me and told to go and meet them, just like I came to meet you. You'll also get an information pack with further details. Most orders come through in code, though I *did* get an indirect one once in the form of a flyer. They sent it to everyone. You know, about the—' she leant forwards to whisper, '—Mobilisation March.'

He frowned at her. 'The what?'

She refrained from elaborating, fearing she had already said too much. 'Just something political *Free Countries* wanted me to get involved in. It doesn't matter. What *does* matter is that you'll be sent the translation for the code with your information pack. You'll have to decode it to learn it. I'm still trying to figure it out myself.'

'So you've been with *Free Countries* for how long?'

She shrugged. 'About two months.'

His brows knotted. 'Is that all?'

She didn't really know what to say to that. The noise from the café seemed to amplify. 'I know it's not been long, but so far I'm glad I joined. I feel like I'm a part of something, doing something worthwhile, you know?'

He bit into an apple. Gwenhwyfar glanced to the large clock displayed on the opposite wall.

'So what happens after I get the information pack?'

'You wait for the instructions to come through. I'm not sure about that part, really,' she admitted. 'All I know is they're waiting until they get enough people recruited, and then they'll make a move.'

'What kind of move?'

'I don't know. We have to wait until we get a message from the Alpha. He'll tell us what to do. We can still be politically active in our own time and go to things like protests,' Gwenhwyfar added, 'but that would be separate from *Free Countries*, unless they specify otherwise. Oh, and it's like a grapevine,' she suddenly remembered. 'You'll only be in contact with me, and the person you recruit. News travels from member to member, until the information reaches the person at the top, or the person at the bottom.'

He seemed to think this over for a while.

'The person who recruited me is very nice,' she added in an effort to convince him. 'I think it's legitimate. Obviously there's a risk involved, but as far as objectives go I think we're just gathering members until we have enough people to stand against Milton and the New Nationals,' she considered.

'How many members are there?' asked Tristan.

'I'm not sure. Isol—the girl who recruited me seemed to think it was at least five thousand.'

He dropped the apple core back into his lunch box. 'That many?'

'She thinks so,' Gwenhwyfar nodded. 'But I'm not so sure.'

'And that's not enough to "make a stand" with?'

All she could do was shrug. How was she supposed to know what it was that the Alpha intended? 'I think they're probably aiming for at least twice that.'

'That's a lot of people,' Tristan murmured.

'Most of them are citizens of Scotland, Wales or Ireland. Or like you,' she concocted, 'from Cornwall. They want independence from Milton.'

'Don't tell me you're in league with the *Celtic Rebels*?'

She smiled, and shook her head. 'I asked that, too. There may be things that *Free Countries* agree with, as far as the separatists go, but they definitely disagree with their methods. *Free Countries* has nothing to do with the border struggles in Ireland and Scotland.'

He propped his ankle on his knee and observed her closely. 'So what made a schoolgirl like you join? Do you want independence, too?'

'Like I said, it's good to be part of something. Independence from England can't be a bad thing: Scotland and Wales are perfectly capable of going it alone.' She flicked the ends of her hair over her shoulder with freshly painted nails.

'How old are you?' he queried.

'Seventeen,' she lied. He clearly didn't believe her. 'Why, how old are you?'

'Eighteen.'

'Are you going to university next year?'

'If I get a scholarship,' he said.

Their detour led to another drawn-out silence. Gwenhwyfar's

eyes returned to the clock.

'I have to go,' Tristan declared, rising.

She jumped up, and gathered her coat and hat. 'Are you interested, then?' She fell into step beside him. 'In joining *Free Countries*?'

He stuffed his lunch box back into his bag, and struggled to get the straps around his shoulders. 'I suppose. Yeah, why not? I'll join.'

She felt a strong sense of accomplishment. 'Great, that's perfect. You won't regret it.' The panda and polar bear passed them once again. Gwenhwyfar glanced at a poorly stuffed lion, snarling at them from beyond the glass. 'I'll give you your code name and let the Alpha know you're joining. An information pack should arrive shortly.' She pulled the sheet from her bag that revealed both their codenames, and followed him through to the main hall.

'How will they know where to send the pack?' he frowned.

She hadn't thought of that. They paused by one of the grand archways, and she handed him the crumpled paper.

'What's this?'

'Your code name, it's the one under mine. Hold it up to the light.'

He read *Omega Iota Theta*, and then returned it to her. He glanced to an older man who strode past them, bound for the Tyrannosaurus Rex.

'I have to go.'

'Wait! I should give you my number.' Gwenhwyfar ripped off a corner from the codenames, and scribbled it down against the wall. 'Text me yours so we can keep in touch.'

Nodding, he stuffed the note into his trouser pocket. 'I will. I really have to go.'

'No problem.' She followed him slowly, forging a route to the door. 'Thanks for meeting me here. We'll contact you in a few weeks.'

He offered a quick, discreet wave, and then joined the small group of college students gathering at the centre of the entrance hall. Feeling rather pleased with herself, Gwenhwyfar exited the building and fished for her mobile as she hurried down the museum road. She had to get home, and fast, before her mother returned. It didn't take long for her call to be answered. She ducked into a doorway to let the rushing Londoners past.

'Isolde? It's Gwen. I just met the new guy, and he's in.'

Her walks to school were twinned with Arthur's, but she could not convince him to share her break times, even though he seemed to get on well with Gavin at The Round Table. December was creeping up on them, showing no sign of a snowy reprieve from the constant drizzle. The miserable weather lingered on well into the fourth week of November, making times of recess humid and unpleasant in an overly crowded canteen.

Their Science room smelt of old sawdust. Wet shoes produced a chorus of squeaks on the metal bars supporting tables and chairs, a baritone of conversation turning it into a clamour. Gwenhwyfar pulled at the zip of her bag, opening the damp canvas to find her books still dry inside. Beside her, Arthur did the same. Students removed raincoats and shook out umbrellas. Mrs Paxton was shouting.

'Settle down, please!' she bellowed, snapping a wooden ruler against her desk. 'We'll be revising the syllabus today, given that your Level Fours are fast approaching. By the end of the term I want you *all* to have structured a revision plan for over the holidays, because January will be here faster than you know it!' She printed "Level Fours" across the board. They were the two words that now commenced every lesson.

'So I was thinking.' Arthur tugged the lid off his pen and neatly inscribed the date. 'How about you come over to my house this weekend? We might have to eat with my grandmother, but we could go out and see another film afterwards. What do you think?'

She recalled the last time she had been there. Though his cat, Lionel, had been more than welcoming, the atmosphere with his grandmother had been fraught, particularly as Arthur kept having to remind her who their guest was. 'There is another film out that looks quite good,' she agreed. 'But wait, I can't! I promised Viola I'd go to her modelling party with her. It's the first one she's been invited to. She's really nervous about it.'

Arthur frowned. 'Never mind, we can always do it some other time.'

'Sunday?' she suggested.

'Sunday's no good for me—I have to take my gran to visit my grandfather's grave and finish my homework for the week. Sorry.'

'Some other time then,' she agreed.

For a while they worked in a silence that was surprisingly comfortable. Towards the end of the lesson Gwenhwyfar felt Arthur's hand coil around hers beneath the table. She looked up and smiled. He returned her warmth in kind.

'So what are you doing at break?' she asked. The room was growing restless.

'I'm going to see Marvin. He says he has another book for me to read.'

'What is it?'

'Something called *The Lord of the Flies*. They don't teach it anymore: it's too shocking.'

She combed her right hand idly through her hair. It snagged, the ends still damp. 'You can always spend break with us, you know.'

As he shrugged, Gwenhwyfar repressed a surge of annoyance. 'I don't know,' he murmured. 'You know I can't stand Lance.'

'He's not that bad. You just have to ignore the irritating things he says, and then he stops. Surely you can put up with him for a little while?'

He scowled and dropped her hand. He always grew irritable whenever she said something that could, in a twisted way, be considered praise of Lancelot.

'You don't have to,' she huffed. 'I just thought it would be nice. He probably won't even be there—he'll be playing football.'

'Why don't you come and sit with me?' he challenged.

'Because! I don't feel like spending all my lunches with Marvin Caledonensis. We spend enough time with him as it is.'

Arthur dumped his chin in his upturned hand. Mrs Paxton looked up from her desk.

'Why do you dislike Lance so much, anyway?' Her arms folded across the table. 'What Emily and Charlotte said about him and Ellie is obviously *not* true.' Mrs Paxton made a harsh hushing sound. Gwenhwyfar lowered her voice. 'Gavin said that you were best friends, once.'

'So—? It doesn't matter if what they said is true or not. That's not the point.'

'Then what *is* the point?' she asked, incensed.

'Quiet!' They jerked upright at the snap of the ruler. Mrs

Paxton was glaring at them dangerously, daring them to continue. Gwenhwyfar had intended not to let this setback stop her, but Arthur quickly bent over his book and resumed their classwork. Realising that he was ignoring her again, Gwenhwyfar decided to return the favour. The lesson ended with the setting of homework and the shrill call of the bell.

Arthur walked with Gwenhwyfar to their History room, where they parted in the corridor with a lingering kiss. Once she was gone, he irritably pushed his way into the room to find Marvin reading a tattered book with a sickly chocolate bar in his hand.

'Arthur!' he exclaimed, mouth full, 'I wasn't sure if you'd be spending break with Gwenhwyfar or not. I trust it's going well?'

He dumped his bag on a desk and found a chair. 'You wanted to give me a book?'

'Yes: *The Lord of the Flies*. Quite disturbing. One of the many reasons why I decided never to have children.' Marvin pulled a copy from his satchel. The cover was old and plain; green, discoloured fabric with the title and author embossed in black. Arthur flicked through to find the synopsis. In places the language was hard to decipher.

'It's not quite banned,' Marvin remarked, swallowing down the last bite of chocolate, 'but it's controversial enough for a restriction to be in place for classrooms.'

Arthur looked back to the front page. Again, in the corner it read *Merlin Ambrosius Caledonensis*. He smiled. 'Thanks. I'll start reading it tonight.'

'I think I'll dig out some more copies and give it to the others as homework tomorrow,' Marvin mused.

'Good idea,' Arthur agreed. He put the book down on the

table and scowled. 'Do you think, Merlin, that it's unreasonable for me to not want to sit with Lance at break times? It's just that Gwen keeps asking me to spend lunch with her friends, with *him*, even though she knows I don't want to.'

'Why don't you want to sit with Lance?'

'Because he's an idiot?' Arthur suggested.

Marvin set a packet of crisps on his desk and smacked his hands together, drying the grease and chocolate into his skin. 'You're not still stuck on that Ellie circus, are you? The whole thing was a classic example of gossip gone wrong.'

'It's not just that,' Arthur muttered.

'You still think he did it? Isn't that a bit unfair on Ellie?'

'What do you mean?'

'I mean, if she never actually gave you reason to doubt her, you shouldn't have doubted her. You and Lancelot were good friends, too. Why would he betray you like that?'

'I know he probably didn't do it: that's not the point. It was the principle of things,' Arthur bristled.

Marvin's expression was not one of comprehension. 'The principle of what?'

'Of the way everyone always liked him more!' he exploded, kicking the chair on which his feet rested. 'Ellie was the first girl who didn't, and in the end even she ended up siding with him. Now Gwen is hanging around with him, too. I hate it, and I hate *him*.'

He got nowhere with his outburst, and as Marvin wiped the dust away from a disused textbook, his bitter words left him empty.

'It's not as if you actually have to *sit* with him,' Marvin pointed out mildly. 'You'll be sitting with Gwen, and if she keeps asking you to spend time with her so that you can get to know her friends, that implies that she likes you more than Lance, wouldn't you say?'

Arthur knew he couldn't argue, despite his urge to.

'How about a compromise?' Marvin suggested. 'You say you'll sit at her table one day, if she spends lunch away with you the other. I can't see the issue here, really.'

'But it's not that easy. Lance hates me.' His brown eyes followed Marvin back to his desk. The older man collapsed into his chair.

'If Lance doesn't like it, I rather think that Lance can move. It's been what, three years? And you're still letting him affect your life? Do what you want, Arthur; don't blame others for the way you act. Life is too short for such trivialities.' There was a moment's silence. 'Have you thought about joining that political party? With the elections coming up in May, now would be a particularly interesting time to jump in.' Marvin stuffed his mouth with a handful of crisps and crunched noisily as he ate. 'I'm sure the Eco Party would benefit from your involvement.'

'I'm sure they'd benefit from anyone's involvement,' Arthur remarked.

'Quite,' Marvin agreed. He opened his book, turning to the right page. There was a long silence. Arthur opened up *The Lord of the Flies* again and flicked through it for a bit, but then he abandoned it, rubbing his eyes.

'You seem distracted,' Marvin observed.

'I'm fine,' he insisted.

'You're not still thinking about Lancelot?'

'No.'

'No?' Marvin sounded sceptical.

'No.' Arthur turned his gaze out of the window.

'You know, I read your latest paper yesterday. It's not quite what I would expect.'

'What do you mean?'

'I mean, it wasn't exactly your best. It's completely fine for the syllabus, of course, but I rather felt you were *somewhere else* whilst writing it. I would just hate for you to suddenly lose your balance, especially when you've been doing so well.'

He'd had enough. 'I'm going to get some air,' Arthur declared darkly, swiping up his book and bag. He strode out into the corridor, hating that Marvin just nodded unperturbed and resumed his reading; hating that all would be forgotten later, that he would return to him, and they would talk as if they had never disagreed over anything. He ended up in the library, not out on the grounds, and as he settled down in an empty chair and opened up his new read the name Merlin gazed out at him forebodingly.

Emily Mary Rose

Had she not needed to pop into the girls' toilets, Gwenhwyfar would have been walking to lunch with Lancelot. Cold water spewed over her wrists as she washed her hands and massaged them with soap. The mirrors of old Wormelow were flaking with the graffiti of lipstick and gloss, written opaque with love hearts, initials and profanities. Scowling, Gwenhwyfar snatched a towel from the dispenser and smeared the professions into the glass to clear her own reflection. The letters lingered. Behind her a flush sounded from the only closed cubicle. Quickly she threw the stained towel into the bin.

Footsteps shuffled towards her. Checking herself in the mirror, Gwenhwyfar glanced sideways as she was joined at the sinks. It was Emily. Her eyes were swollen and her mascara was bleeding. As the flow from the tap dried out, she let out a loud sob. She was crying. Gwenhwyfar felt a spiteful satisfaction. Finally, the first of the Furies was getting what she deserved, and whatever it was, it was making her miserable.

Quickly she turned for the door. Emily swallowed down

another sob and sniffed pathetically. Unexpected pity pried its way into Gwenhwyfar's heart. Emily didn't even seem to care that she was there.

'Are you all right?' she asked, hovering awkwardly with her arms crossed.

Emily nodded, wiping her face with a fistful of tissue. 'I'm fine.'

'You don't look fine,' Gwenhwyfar disputed.

'Well, I *am* fine. So why don't you just leave me alone?' Emily bit, rubbing the mascara staining her cheeks. Tempted, Gwenhwyfar looked to the door.

'Let me guess—Charlotte?' Emily looked up, surprised. Gwenhwyfar expelled a sigh. 'What did she do?'

'It doesn't matter what she did, all that matters is she's *vile*. Hattie too. And Rhea and Rebecca.' She wiped her eyes again, twisting the tissue into a small brush. 'They're all *vile*.'

'I could have told you that.'

'As if *you* can say anything, after what you said about me.'

'What did I say?' she demanded.

'You said I was *ugly*.'

'No I didn't,' she objected, but Emily was insistent.

'Yes you did. How can you not remember?'

'I never said anything of the sort!'

'You're such a liar! *Charlotte* told me. You even called me *fat*. So don't you talk to me about bitching, because you *are* one.'

Resisting the pull of a fresh argument, Gwenhwyfar uncrossed her arms. 'I never said you were fat. I never said you were ugly either,' she replied, shortly. 'Charlotte was obviously lying. Don't *you* remember? She hates me. That's why she was always avoiding us when we were friends, and that's why she told you I said those things. So you'd hate me, too.' She shook her head. 'What does it matter? It doesn't change anything. Even if you did go to that protest, you still—'

'That was *Charlotte's* idea,' Emily said quickly, her eyes drying. 'I only went along with it because of what you said about me—'

'—What *Charlotte* told you I said about you,' Gwenhwyfar corrected.

'Whatever.' Emily shrugged, and stared down at the dirty basins. 'Look, I know it was out of order. I had no idea it would go so far.' She glanced at her momentarily through reddened eyes. 'It just *happened*. I'm sorry about that, really.'

'You already apologised,' Gwenhwyfar said curtly. She ought to leave, to let Emily wallow in the consequences of her ill-directed actions, but she didn't. 'And what about Arthur?'

Emily sniffed again, pinching wet mascara off of her lashes with her fingers. 'What about him?'

'You told him that Ellie kissed Lancelot. Why would you do such a thing?'

'But she *did* kiss Lancelot,' Emily contended. 'Hattie saw them together. And I didn't tell Arthur, *Charlotte* did. So I don't see what the problem is.'

'The problem is that *Charlotte* told him,' she huffed. 'Haven't you figured it out yet? Ellie never did anything with Lance. He says so, she said so, and so do his friends. It's only Arthur who still thinks she did.'

'So it's not true, then?'

'Its about as true as anything Charlotte's ever said about you,' Gwenhwyfar quipped.

'It's *horrible*,' Emily begun. 'She's been spreading all kinds of nasty rumours. She practically had an orgasm when she found out Bedivere said I was a crap kisser.'

'He never said that,' Gwenhwyfar lied, hoping to spare Bedivere some grief. 'I made it up. Sorry.'

'I'm sorry too,' Emily admitted, and Gwenhwyfar thought she heard relief in her words. 'I should never have listened to Charlotte.'

'It's not your fault she's a liar.' Swinging her bag around her shoulder, Gwenhwyfar fished out her make-up wipes. 'Here, use these.' Emily took one and handed the packet back. 'Keep them,' Gwenhwyfar insisted. 'There's only three left.'

'Are you sure?' She nodded. Emily clutched them gratefully. 'Thanks.'

'Will you be all right?'

'I'll be fine.' She scraped the wipes over her face, dirtying them with orange and black before tossing them into the bin.

'I'm going to the canteen. You can come and sit with us, if you like. With me and Vi?'

She couldn't tell if she was relieved or disappointed when Emily shook her head. She wouldn't have to explain the situation to her friends, yes; but at the same time she realised that Emily was still loyal to Charlotte, and that she would quickly return to her.

'I'm OK,' Emily said, fishing through her make-up bag. 'I'm going to stay here for a bit. But I'll… I'll see you around?'

Gwenhwyfar nodded. 'You know where to find me.'

Emily turned back to the mirror, pulled out her foundation, and began to reapply the mask that would hide all evidence of her tears.

That evening Gwenhwyfar was looking for something to

wear.

'Gwen? What about this?'

Her mother came into her bedroom holding up a dated dress. Eve pressed the gold fabric to herself, looking down at the loud garment before holding it out for her daughter. 'What do you think? Something like this would look wonderful on you.'

Gwenhwyfar looked at the offending item. 'Mam, it's got feathers.'

'So?' Eve surveyed the dress again. 'What's wrong with feathers?' Gwenhwyfar dove back into her closet, hunting around the bottom for shoes. 'You'll stand out in it. Besides, this was all the rage when I was younger. It's alternative.'

'It's ancient,' Gwenhwyfar remarked.

'No, it's vintage,' disputed Eve. 'Come on, just look at it for a moment. This dress, those shoes, with your hair up in a bun? To accentuate your cheekbones?'

'Isn't it a bit long?'

'I don't think so,' Eve replied, stretching the hem out.

'I don't think it's going to fit me.'

'We could have it taken up.'

'By Saturday?'

Eve shrugged. 'There's bound to be someone in town who can sort this out. Why don't you try it on and see how much needs doing to it?'

Gwenhwyfar deliberated for a moment, kneeling in a pile of her own clothes. 'Put it on the bed with the others. I'll try it in a bit,' she relented. 'But I *was* looking for something a little... smarter. You know, cleaner. More sophisticated?' She pulled three shoeboxes out and threw them across the floor.

Eve tossed the garment onto the bed. There were already

three other options strewn across it.

'How about these?' Gwenhwyfar asked, pulling out a pair of glittery five-inch heels.

'I thought you wanted something sophisticated?' Eve said, joining her on the floor.

'They'd work with jeans and a black top,' Gwenhwyfar debated.

'Oh no, you don't want to be in jeans. You want the people there to *notice* you. You shouldn't wear black, either. Isn't it in a club? You'll just blend in, in black. You need something brighter.'

'Brighter than these?'

'Do you want those bookers looking at your feet? Forget about the shoes for a moment.' Eve pulled the platforms off her and put them to one side. 'How about green? You always look fabulous in green. What happened to that dress I bought you for Christmas? You could wear that.'

'It's practically a gown. I don't want to overdo it.'

Eve stood up and started to hunt through the wardrobe. She found it quickly. Gwenhwyfar went to sit on her bed.

'But it's gorgeous,' Eve enthused. 'It goes so well with your eyes. Why not try it?'

Gwenhwyfar caught the hanger as it was thrown to her. She put it with the others and began to undress. 'Won't I get cold?'

'You'll be inside. You'll be too warm if you wear much else.' She pulled another dress out. 'How about we go for red? People always get noticed in red. But then, that's too obvious.'

'It's not like anything's going to come of this. It's just a party.'

'A models' party,' Eve corrected, her eyes gleaming. 'Besides, what harm is there in looking good? You're much prettier than that Viola girl. Those photos you had taken for your fourteenth birthday, for example. Any one of those is ten times better than anything on that website you showed me.' She pulled out another dress and put the other one back. 'What's the agency called again?'

'Quantum Models.' Gwenhwyfar slipped into the flowing silk and turned to face the mirror, observing herself in the green.

'If Viola can be a model, then you can too.' Eve threw her another dress. Gwenhwyfar missed it.

'I'm too short to be a model,' she disputed.

'That Gisela Wolf girl is only five foot seven, and she's the face of *Excellence*.'

'Mam!'

'What? You can wear heels.' She smiled at her. 'See? You look lovely in green. We should try something purple, too.'

'No, not purple,' she objected. 'Viola always wears purple.'

Gwenhwyfar took off the green dress and changed into the next outfit waiting for her. She gazed at her reflection, wondering. She knew she was too short, but the idea of joining Viola on Quantum's books was a seductive one.

'Oh darling, you look lovely!' Eve gushed, smiling at her proudly. 'I think that's definitely a strong option—we should make another pile.' She threw the new dress in her hands onto the ones on the bed, and then pushed them all to one side. Gwenhwyfar played with her hair, searching for the best way to wear it. Her mother appeared behind her and batted her hands away. She started to fashion her hair into a high bun.

'You know, if your father had his way you wouldn't be going to this party. He's a bit nervous after that whole Hector thing.'

'Still?' Gwenhwyfar asked.

'You will be careful, won't you? You must ring us if anything happens.'

Gwenhwyfar winced as her mother twisted and pulled at what was now a ponytail. 'It'll be fine, we won't be there long. We're getting the last train back. I'll text you.' She hesitated a moment, and drew in a calming breath. 'Have you spoken to Dad yet?'

Her mother fell silent, and concentrated on her hair.

'Mam?'

'I spoke to him,' she said with a quick smile. 'We talked about it all, everything. You were right: it was just something for work. The florists was for his boss' wife, and the jewellers... well, he said I'd find out about that at Christmas.'

'That's good.' Gwenhwyfar didn't know that there had been a weight pressing upon her until it lifted. 'Didn't I say it was nothing?'

'You were right; of course you were right. Your father still doesn't know that you know. I think it's best if you just forget about it, if you can.' She stepped back from her handiwork. Gwenhwyfar admired the makeshift up-do in the mirror. 'Something like that, but bigger,' Eve advised.

'Are you sure it's not too harsh?' Gwenhwyfar asked, tilting her face to observe it from each angle.

'No.' Eve caught her head with her hands, and turned it face-on to the mirror. 'It's perfect.'

Gwenhwyfar smiled. She was right, it was. Eve went to pick up her next outfit, and held it out in extended arms as Gwenhwyfar peeled away the chiffon dress and dropped it to the floor.

The club hosting the modelling party was one of those exclusive venues that housed celebrities and sold bottles of champagne for thousands, not hundreds. Models, however, got to drink for free, and though the priciest vintages were off limits, Viola supplied Gwenhwyfar well. She felt like a dwarf amongst all these giants, despite the five-inch heels adding to her height. Though Viola gushed about a certain model being the face of Kolburn or the fittest guy to walk the earth, Gwenhwyfar found most to be too perfect, like mannequins, and in comparing them to Arthur, pitched Arthur, and even Lancelot, higher.

It turned out that other than her booker Viola knew no one, and so for most of the evening they were pulled to and fro and introduced to various clients. Later, when it was the next New Faces' turn to be presented, Viola and Gwenhwyfar sought refuge in a corner to forage through their freebies.

'I've never tried this stuff before,' Viola said, as she unscrewed one of the mascaras. 'It's so expensive.'

'My mam always wears it. I remember stealing it from her dresser when I was five. She was furious.' Gwenhwyfar giggled, and Viola did too. She sipped at her fruit punch through a thin straw, high on the sugar. 'How long have we got?'

'About an hour,' Viola responded, glancing at her phone. 'We won't miss much. All the important people leave before then, anyway,' she shouted. For a meet and greet, the noise was insufferable.

'So how are things with you and Tom?'

'Good,' Viola said, after some consideration. 'How about with you and Arthur?'

'They're OK.' Gwenhwyfar's mind drifted to the issue with Lancelot, and she wondered why it still plagued her. 'Better, now we're official.'

'Have you stayed over at his yet?' Viola probed. When Gwenhwyfar shook her head, she frowned.

'It's not like we've been going out long,' Gwenhwyfar reasoned. 'Besides, he lives with his *grandmother*. It'd be a bit weird if I did stay the night.'

'I suppose. But you want to, right?'

She nodded. Viola seemed to find this fascinating.

'Really?'

'Yeah, of course, why wouldn't I?' She stirred the ice around in her drink. 'I like him. And he's nice. He hasn't pressured me into anything yet; he's not that sort of guy. He's really mature, you know? Unlike most boys his age.'

For a moment Viola seemed to think this was a dig at her boyfriend.

'You know, like Hector?' Gwenhwyfar corrected herself, and Viola's frown faded.

They soon took to the dance floor and spent the rest of their hour doing their best to attract attention from the too-perfect males milling arrogantly around the club. Once they'd given an exaggerated goodbye to Viola's booker, they left the venue, the cold night air pressing on their alcohol-numbed skin. The streets were not quiet. Gwenhwyfar leant into Viola as they walked together, each one grasping the other for support.

'God, we're going to miss our train, aren't we?' Gwenhwyfar said as their heels beat along the tarmac. They crossed to the opposite pavement, hurrying past the parked cars.

'I wish we could have stayed for longer,' Viola lamented. 'The face of Kolburn was definitely checking me out.'

'It was a pretty cool party. Thanks for letting me tag along. I know you could have taken Tom.'

'Are you kidding? He'd have spent the whole night keeping me in a corner, glaring at the guys while he drooled over the girls.' She laughed. 'Besides, he hates dancing. I always have to bully him into it and then he throws me around as if I'm some rag doll. Does Arthur dance?'

'You know, I have no idea.' They shouldered past a group of women and hurried on round a corner. 'It's not like I've ever had the chance to find out.'

The explosion was deafening. Punched in the back, Gwenhwyfar hit the ground and lay there in shock. Red cinders rained down on the street like confetti. Thick dust came aglow with a strange, orange light. One scream sounded, and then another. Soon a chorus of terror erupted in the streets.

As she tried to move she became aware of the blood on her arms, but a testing shift revealed the grazes to be superficial. Viola lay motionless, her head oozing a ruby stripe from beneath her hair. Gwenhwyfar hacked a cough as a sharp breath drew in brick dust. She gagged, and spat out the irritant.

'Vi—!' She tried to rouse her. Nothing. Looking around in panic, Gwenhwyfar forced herself to her feet. Squinting through the fog, she coughed again. A shrill noise was ringing in her ears.

A man rushed past her, sprinting away from the disaster zone. Car alarms squealed. Gwenhwyfar hobbled to the street corner to find her path blocked by rubble. Suddenly the air was hot. Flames belched out of an angry hole in the terraced buildings opposite. Sirens wailed closer. Trembling, she returned to Viola and checked for her pulse. She panicked when she felt nothing, but quickly realised she had been looking in the wrong place.

Paramedics found them. They were hurried to the back of an ambulance. Given a blanket and oxygen for shock, she watched as someone roused Viola, checked her for signs of concussion and then cleaned and inspected the wound on her head. Many people tried to leave the scene, but movement was restricted. It was in the nearest Accident and Emergency when Gwenhwyfar finally checked her mobile. She had thirty-seven missed calls.

It was well past one. With Viola lying on a cot in silence beside her, Gwenhwyfar scrolled through her phone. Two thirds of the missed calls were from home and the rest were all from Arthur. She settled on relieving the panic of her parents first.

It was her mother who answered, her distress level palpable. 'Gwen! Oh God, Gwen, where are you? Are you all right?'

'I'm fine.' She glanced sideways to Viola, who was also checking her phone.

'We saw there was an explosion on the news. You weren't near it, were you? Why aren't you home?'

'We missed our train. We're in Accident and Emergency. We're OK, but Viola hit her head and I scraped my knees.'

'You're hurt?' Eve said, her voice flooding with panic. Her father was shouting something in the background.

'Just my knees and my arms—I'm fine, really. I don't want you to freak or anything, but the explosion was on the street of the party. It knocked us over.'

There was a long interlude where a number of questions and sounds of horror muffled the receiver. Frowning, Gwenhwyfar struggled to make sense of her parents' demands. Her father commandeered the phone, and she heard a relieved sob from her mother in the background.

'Gwen, listen to me. Where are you? The trains are all down: there have been a number of explosions and they've shut the Tube. I'm going to drive up and get you—you'll need me there to sort out the insurance. Have you been seen yet?'

'They took a quick look at the blast. There's a nurse going

round tending to minor injuries.' She couldn't quite stand the sight of the more serious cases being wheeled through. Many had limbs missing, or horrible angular shapes protruding from their chest cavities. 'How many explosions…?' The strength she had shown for her mother wavered with her father. His voice always unravelled her.

'Three,' he stated. 'They think it was deliberate. They got a tip off and managed to stop the fourth. It was going to be on the Thames Water Barrier.'

'Do they know who did it?'

'Not yet. To be honest, I'm not entirely happy about you being there.'

'We should be fine now, though?' she asked, her voice cracking.

'Yes, of course. They've got it under control, cariad. Where are you?'

'Mayfair, at the Royal Mary…?'

'I know it,' confirmed Garan. 'I'm on my way now. Is Viola alright?'

'They've got her lying down in a neck brace, but they seem to think she'll be OK.'

'Has she called her parents?'

Gwenhwyfar nodded. 'She's calling them now.'

'Good. I'll see you soon. Be careful.'

There was a click. Gwenhwyfar pressed down on Arthur's name. The number dialled and he answered immediately.

'Gwen? Is that you? Are you all right?'

She explained everything, stressing the fact she was unharmed. He didn't seem convinced, and when she told him that her father was coming to get her, he wanted to come too.

'I should be there; I want to be there,' he argued. 'I have to know you're all right.'

'But I am all right,' Gwenhwyfar insisted. 'Besides, he's already left. I'm just a bit shaken. The blast was right behind us. Are you OK?'

He seemed surprised. 'Of course I'm OK, why wouldn't I be?'

'I just wanted to make sure.' She shifted in the uncomfortable plastic seat. Her limbs were aching terribly. 'My dad said there were three explosions, one failed. Do they think it's terrorists?'

'I don't know what they think,' Arthur admitted, 'I just heard there'd been explosions on the news. My grandmother's still up too, worried about you.'

'Tell her I'm fine,' she pled. 'Viola's the one with the gash on her head.'

His concern returned. 'Is she all right?'

'I think so.' She glanced over. Viola was still on the phone. 'They saw to her briefly in the ambulance. They just want to double-check her head injury now.'

'Right. That doesn't sound too bad. They'd be paying her more attention if it was something serious.' There was a short silence. 'What about money? Are you insured?'

'That's all fine—my dad's going to sort it.'

'What about your Biometric Identity Card? Have you got that?'

'I've got it—it's in my bag.'

'Are you sure you don't want me to come with him? I'd feel better if I did.'

'I'd rather you stayed out of London,' Gwenhwyfar told him firmly. 'It's not safe. My dad's worried about the hospitals; that's one of the reasons he's coming to get us.'

'You should probably leave, yes,' Arthur agreed. 'I wish I could do something. I hate not being able to help you.'

'You are helping me,' Gwenhwyfar countered. 'You're distracting me.'

'I am?'

'Yes.' She averted her eyes from the waiting room, and smiled. 'Keep doing it, if you like.'

For the best part of an hour Arthur recounted what he had been up to that day, including the homework he had done, an account of what he'd made for supper and the film he'd watched afterwards. Whenever he faltered Gwenhwyfar prompted him for more details, until at long last her father arrived, his face pale, his brow folded.

'My dad's here,' she murmured quickly into the receiver.

He sounded relieved. 'Good. Let me know when you get home. Be careful, Gwen.'

'I will,' she nodded.

'You'd better.'

She hung up and sprang to her feet. Her father hugged her fiercely. He held her by the shoulders and inspected her.

'Where's Viola?' he asked.

'Over there. Where's Mam?'

'I made her stay at home.' His eyes trailed around the roomful of casualties, observing the unpleasant scene with distaste. 'Are you all right?'

'I'm fine,' Gwenhwyfar assured. 'We're still waiting to be seen. I'm worried about Viola. She doesn't look well.'

'We'll ask someone,' he stated, hunting for a medic to snare. He caught a nurse just as she left a patient. He was told to wait and take a seat. Immediately Garan looked around for someone else. 'Where's the medical care I'm paying for?'

'Dad—' Gwenhwyfar cautioned. 'Let's just sit down and do what she says.'

'Have you got your B.I.D?' She nodded. 'Good. Give it here.'

Gwenhwyfar felt her face burn. People were looking at them, and in the muted atmosphere of the waiting room everyone could hear Garan's angry outbursts.

'There's got to be someone who knows what they're doing,' he growled. 'Go and sit down. I'm going to find a doctor.'

Mortified, Gwenhwyfar gazed after him as he strode to the reception desk. He exchanged strong words with the nurse there, and then with a doctor who seemed to have been called out at his particular request. The two went off to one side to talk. Her shame only increased when suddenly the young doctor was next to her, asking her to sit.

It didn't take long for him to deduce what she already knew, that her wounds were superficial, and soon he was snapping his fingers at the closest nurse. Despite the embarrassment of skipping the queue and the anger it caused among the other patients, Gwenhwyfar couldn't help but feel relieved as Viola underwent another examination, the doctor decreeing that she should be x-rayed. Her wounds now cleaned, Gwenhwyfar went to stand beside her.

'Did you get hold of your dad?'

'Yes. He should be here in a minute.'

'How are you feeling?'

'Not too bad,' Viola responded. 'Killer headache, though.' She smiled, and Gwenhwyfar did too. 'Did they sort you out at least?'

She nodded. 'I only cut my knees.'

'Viola!'

Gwenhwyfar looked behind her. It was Viola's father, Samuel. She had met him a few times before. He strode into the building, his tall, slight frame bent with worry. As Viola tried to greet him he hurried over and urged her back down. 'No, no, don't move—stay where you are. Are you all right? What did the doctors say?'

'They're taking her for x-ray,' Gwenhwyfar told him.

'I'm fine,' Viola murmured gently. 'Just tired, and headachy.'

'Gwen.' Her father leant between them. 'We should get going. Your mother will be worried.'

Gwenhwyfar nodded and looked to Viola, reluctant to leave. 'Will you be all right?'

'I'll be fine,' she said quietly. 'The doctor will be back in a moment.'

'Let me know when you get home. Call me if there are any problems.'

'I will.'

'It's all right; she'll be fine. You go home, Gwen. Get some rest,' Samuel urged. The doctor returned to the cot.

Gwenhwyfar squeezed Viola's hand, but then she was wheeled away and their fingers parted. 'I'll see you on Monday,' she promised, watching her vanish through the hospital doors.

She followed her father out of the emergency room into the night, which was noisy with the arrival of fresh casualties. She was relieved to finally be within the safety of the family car. Ring-fenced by concrete, a solitary tree stood before them in the car park: a lingering blood vessel to a mortal earth. Silently her father arranged himself in the driver's seat.

The drive home was long as the city was filled with diversions and temporary checkpoints. Her eyes played tricks with the shadows in the dark. It was almost sunrise when they pulled into their driveway, and a faint eastern light quelled the moon. Weary and aching, Gwenhwyfar stumbled out of the car. Despite being notified of their safety, Eve ran out of the house to greet them in a panic born of exhaustion.

Just before bed, Gwenhwyfar received a text from Viola stating she had been discharged and was on her way home. She then sent Arthur a message announcing her safe return, hoping he was still all right.

Old Friends

Sunday morning passed with Gwenhwyfar in bed, and had Arthur not called in around twelve she would have slept for the rest of the day. Her parents had never met Arthur before and were surprised to learn of her interest in him, but both were grateful for his ability to encourage her to spend a little time downstairs.

The media station was ablaze with the incident. Garan's account of the situation had been accurate. There had been three bombs: one in a club, one in a bar and one in a hospital, but the third had not detonated. The fourth attempt was on the Thames Barrier to coincide with the chaos of a congested city. The mystery, however, was not where, but why, and who.

The montage of images flashing across the screen halted, the broadcast interrupted by a speech from George Milton. He sheltered from the drizzle under a black umbrella, his grey suit still dry despite the rain. Camera bulbs flashed like strobe lighting. Milton was a man of average height, softening with middle age, his dark hair starkly receding at his temples.

Gwenhwyfar gazed at her Prime Minister, secure in the crook of Arthur's arm, with her mother's hand tightly clutching her own. The newsreader mentioned further developments in the government's response to the attacks, described the scene, and was then silenced by George Milton's opening words.

"Thank you all for being here with me. There are some people out there who are not going to like what I have to say today, but given the severity of the situation, I am going to give it to you straight. Last night, two hundred and seven British citizens were murdered in a set of mindless attacks that struck at the very heart of our great nation. Two hundred and seven men and women: fathers and mothers, brothers and sisters. My heart, and indeed the hearts of all of us here today, goes out to the relatives of the victims: the bereaved, the cheated. There is nothing that I can do that will bring those lost back to us, but as a father and a husband, I understand the pain that many of you will be going through today. I remember my own pain when I lost my beloved Macy, who died of leukaemia when she was only seven, and I remember that I, too, felt cheated. Cheated out of all those years, and days, that we never had.

Over the past few years the British way of life has repeatedly come under attack. It was only a few months ago when our cities were terrorised by riots, and more recently when London was assaulted again during a violent protest, which resulted in the death of a celebrated and much loved police officer. Our country is still in shock. The war on terror has been long.

As your Prime Minister I assure you: this terror will not be tolerated. This reign of fear will not last. Together we will fight these terror-mongers head on. To this purpose a new special force has been enlisted, dedicated to counter extremism on every level of society. These servicemen will ensure your safety and keep our loved ones from harm. They will target the beliefs that feed extremist ideas and, by wiping out terrorism for good, secure the future of our children.

Despite our losses, there is hope. We stand together as citizens under one banner with the rallying cry that we will not be bowed by terror. As Churchill said: 'It is no use saying, "We are doing our best." You have got to succeed in doing what is necessary.' Well, I, your Prime Minister, will do what is necessary. We will hunt down those responsible. We will dismantle those who would harm us. Together, we will see the rise of a New National Britain, through the hard iron fist and the justice of the New Moral Army."

A flurry of commotion commenced upon screen. Reporters fired out questions as George Milton edged sternly away and someone else took the stand. Garan hissed a sound of irritation.

'New Moral Army?' he growled, his thin frame hunched over. 'New morals: whose morals? Or does that not matter?'

'It can't be a bad thing,' her mother said. 'What would we have done if Gwen had been closer to the blast? We would have been desperate for something like this to be in place already. We have nothing to worry about.'

Arthur lingered close to Gwenhwyfar for the rest of the day.

A rigorous discussion on the news preceded a quiet afternoon in her bedroom, one during which both her parents hovered downstairs anxiously, calling up to see if anything was needed. When Gwenhwyfar had told her mother she was fine for the fourth time, she gently closed her bedroom door and went to join Arthur on the bed.

The sheets had been straightened, though it was not her doing. Silently she sat next to him, their sides touching. After a few moments Arthur wrapped his arm around her, pulling her into a close hug. The room smelt of sleep and perfume. Her dirtied dress lay over a chair.

'I'm glad you're all right, Gwen.' He drew his other arm about her. 'I don't know what I'd have done if something had happened to you.'

'I know.' She inhaled deeply, and his scent calmed her. 'Thanks for coming over. I know you were busy today.'

'It's nothing,' he told her. 'We went to see my grandfather this morning, and my grandmother insisted I come here afterwards.'

'Do you always visit your grandfather's grave on Sundays?' she asked.

'Yes.'

In the silence she stroked his side. 'Do you ever visit your father's?' Arthur nodded, and Gwenhwyfar looked up. 'How much do you remember of him?'

'Not much,' he admitted, trailing his fingers along her back. 'I was too young. He's buried next to my grandfather.'

'How did he die?'

'Car accident.' Arthur shrugged. 'He liked to drink. He always used to sit up late with bottles and cans around him. I saw my grandparents once, dragging him up the stairs in the morning. I think they moved him so I wouldn't see him like that when I woke up.'

They sat in silence. Idly, Gwenhwyfar's fingers worked under Arthur's shirt and caressed his skin. The result was instantaneous. As she looked up to him he firmly took her cheek, drawing her into an eager kiss.

'Arthur,' she murmured into his lips. His hands tugged her closer, drew her against him, and suddenly he was all over her; kissing, tasting, touching; though mindful in his passion of the wounds she bore. His large hands slipped beneath her top and slid along her spine, and as she collapsed into him they toppled onto the mattress, kissing furiously.

Arthur quickly became frustrated with her clothes. The barrier of fabric ground between them as he pulled away her top, his need consuming. He kissed and sucked at her skin, feeling the contours of her bra, and as Gwenhwyfar straddled him she found her thoughts go bounding into chaos.

They didn't explore one another further. Tongues wrestled and hands wandered, but as the hour wore on they found themselves lying half dressed across the bed with their limbs entwined. The nervous tension had not been dispelled, and as Gwenhwyfar lay in the nook of his arm her fingers played restlessly across his skin.

They said goodnight at six, on the front doorstep with another long exchange. They found their lips hard to separate, and they parted with a promise that they would see each other in school. Smiling up at him, with the ache of her knees still present, Gwenhwyfar thanked him again in earnest. She waited at the end of the driveway, gazing after him as he walked down the street, her longing eyes fixed upon him until he had vanished from sight.

News of the bombings was already common knowledge at Logres, and the moment she and Viola appeared in their tutor room on Monday morning they were hounded by their classmates. Charlotte, Hattie and Morgan all treated their dressings as if they were badges of honour, uttering words of horror at their account of events, but it was Emily who was the most sympathetic. As she arrived, late, she appeared at their table with wide, white eyes.

'How *horrible*!' she enthused, once she had caught up with the tale. 'Are you all right? How's your head?'

'It's OK,' Viola told her, clearly unsettled by her strident concern. 'It's just a bump. I've got stitches, though.'

'Four,' Gwenhwyfar added, eyeing her bandage. 'They were pretty worried. They had her in a neck brace, and *insisted* on doing an x-ray.'

Viola gave her a look, as if to say that she shouldn't encourage her.

'That's *awful*,' Emily exclaimed, grasping Viola by the arm and squeezing it. 'You will let me know if you need anything, won't you? Either of you. I can carry your bags, if you like.'

Bedivere was keeping his attention diverted in the hopes that Emily wouldn't engage him.

'Or if you feel unwell, let me know. I have a *ton* of painkillers in my bag.'

They expected her to return to her table, but with one seat spare she stayed at theirs, awkwardly sitting next to Viola throughout the register.

History passed, as did English, and as the morning wore on versions of their story circulated around the school and became more fantastical. Bedivere walked with her to the canteen, where she waited at the usual table for someone to rejoin her. The sun bleached the world outside, presenting to all the illusion of warmth, its foolish worshippers shivering in the frigid air. Lancelot's absence would have alarmed her had Gavin not assured her he had seen him on Sunday. A small number of students were absent due to the loss of a loved one.

'Gwen?' Her eyes drew back from the window. Arthur was standing beside her. Nervously, he offered a smile. 'How are you feeling?'

'Good, thank you.'

'And your knees?'

She looked down to the white dressing partially concealed beneath her tights. 'Getting better. My arms hurt more, really.'

He hovered uncertainly for a moment, but then to her great surprise sat down. 'And Viola?'

'She's fine,' Gwenhwyfar assured him. 'She's getting some lunch now. She's only got a bit of a headache.'

Arthur put his bag next to hers on the table. 'You know, I've been hearing all sorts of rumours about Saturday. I think my favourite version involves you carrying Viola out of a burning building.'

Her cheeks bloomed crimson. 'Not a rumour started by me, I can assure you.'

'I know.'

'In all honesty, I had no idea what to do. I completely panicked.'

'Most people would,' he pointed out.

'I didn't help with anything. And I definitely wasn't heroic.'

Arthur eyed her, and Gwenhwyfar had the feeling that he

thought she was being modest.

'There *were* people pulling other people from burning buildings, though.' She folded her sore arms, and unfolded them again. 'People keep talking about it like it's something from a movie, but it's not, it's real. People died and I didn't help anyone.'

'Sorry,' Arthur apologised, 'I didn't mean to annoy you.'

Gwenhwyfar detected irritation in his tone, and battled a flare of it herself. 'You're not annoying me,' she snapped. 'It's just that everything else is. *You* could never annoy me.' Forcing a smile, she flicked her hair, tossed her head and exuded confidence that everything would be all right. 'Lance isn't in today. So you can sit with us if you like.'

'I was going to anyway.' Unzipping his bag he produced his lunch and offered a lopsided smile. 'But I'm glad he's not in—it means I don't have to try to be civil, at least.'

She brightened at his words. 'But what about Marvin?'

'I'm sure he'll cope without me for a little while,' Arthur said. 'Lately he's just been trying to get me to join a political party. I'm not even sure if I want to.'

'You don't want to be a politician, then?' Gwenhwyfar teased.

'Who does?' Her friends began to regroup at the table. 'It's corrupt, anyway. The system's a poor excuse for democracy. They call it that, but it's not really. Once you elect someone, they can do anything they like, including the exact opposite of everything they promised in the first place.'

'What's this?' Gavin sat down, his face a picture of curiosity.

'Politics,' Gwenhwyfar stated, a smile playing her lips. 'Apparently Marv thinks Arthur should become a politician.'

'You feel like being Prime Minister? Good luck with that. Milton's probably immortal.'

'Or has access to the elixir of life,' Arthur added. 'No, I don't think it's for me. Not that job, at least.'

'You never know, you might enjoy politics,' Gwenhwyfar added.

'Or you can just do it for the money and the five bedroom house like everyone else,' suggested Gavin. The others joined the table. Bedivere was clearly pleased to see Arthur, and greeted him brightly.

'Money doesn't interest me,' Arthur shrugged, once everyone had settled. 'Not in that sense, at least.'

'In what sense?' Gwenhwyfar asked.

'In the sense of working merely to earn, living to work. If I had the choice, I'd rather work to live.'

Gavin unpacked the burger he'd bought himself and took a generous bite. 'So did you all see the speech? It's bloody scary, if you ask me.'

'What's wrong with it?' Gwenhwyfar asked.

'It's like your dad said,' Arthur commented. 'Whose morals? Milton's speech was vague for a reason. It's an anti-extremism cell, and that could mean anything.'

'Isn't it clear?' Tom interrupted. 'Anti-extremism means anti-extremism. They'll be chasing after the bombers of Saturday.'

'You're forgetting what they include in their definition of extremism,' Arthur pointed out. 'Had any of us been caught during the Mobilisation March we'd have been charged as terrorists. They linked it to the separatists; remember? Even though they could've just got us for disrupting the standard order of democracy, or for negatively affecting the economy.'

'Arthur's right,' Gavin murmured, his burger suspended in one hand. 'I've been following this for a while, it's no coincidence. Milton's been reorganising his pyramid. The New Morals will eventually replace the police.'

'The police?' Viola frowned at him. 'Why?'

'Because they're privatised, but not by him. Milton wants full control. He *is* in charge of the New Morals, though; or he will be. He's planning to replace police chiefs with his guys, reshuffling so the police will eventually fall under the New Morals' command. I wouldn't be surprised if the New Moral Army is somehow connected to the Army.'

'That's why I didn't march,' Viola pointed out. 'What did it achieve? They did exactly what you said they would, Gav. Blamed it on one institution and sacked everyone they claimed to be involved. *It doesn't happen anymore.* Problem solved.'

'Except it's not solved, is it?' Bedivere asked. 'People are still vanishing. We never even heard what became of those who disappeared from the centre that was penalised.'

'Who cares? They won't be missed; the New Nationals know it.' Gavin wheeled on Viola. 'And you're happy with them introducing a new power force to further implement their human rights violations?'

'What human rights?' Arthur looked to Gavin. 'We lost those when we lost the EU.'

'We have a bill of rights,' Tom contested.

'It's not the same,' Arthur argued. 'It's filled with loopholes. It's basically a document written to give us the illusion of rights, when in fact, when push comes to shove, we have none.'

Gwenhwyfar looked at them all, each one becoming more strident in their own view, and she found herself wondering what Isolde would think. The fear within her told her that the New Moral Army was a good thing, but everything she had witnessed over the past few months convinced her otherwise. She turned on Gavin.

'Would you still be saying what you are, had Viola and I died yesterday?'

He seemed taken aback by the question, but then his eyes hardened under a deep scowl. 'Sorry, but yes.'

The table erupted in outrage. Gavin struggled to be heard without raising his voice.

'Come on—all I mean is there are things in place *already* to prevent this sort of thing from happening! That's why we're all so watched. What good does introducing the New Morals do other than give Milton more leverage to keep everyone in line? It'll be *your morals* that he comes after next.'

'You say that,' Viola remarked, 'but maybe this *is* just to deal with the bombers on Saturday. Don't you think they would have stopped the attacks if existing surveillance was enough?'

'You're the one who was terrified about the idea of me giving the New Nationals reason to label me as a *cyber terrorist*,' Gavin retorted hotly.

'Everyone just calm down—!' Gwenhwyfar raised her hands, but to no avail, and had to shout louder. 'Come on! We can disagree on this. I *don't know* if this is a good thing or a bad thing. Given that I was nearly blown up yesterday, I can see where Viola's coming from. I can also see Gavin's side. With what's still going on with the Mobilisation Centres, it is worrying that Milton's suddenly grasping for even more power.'

'*Thank you!*'

'I said I saw both sides,' she remarked, looking sharply at Gavin. He sat back in his seat and looked to Arthur, the only one other than Bedivere clearly on his side. 'I do find it worrying.

Clearly the police aren't enough to prevent attacks. They weren't enough to prevent this.'

'Do we know who did it yet?' Tom asked.

'No,' Arthur said. Everyone looked at him again. 'I won't be surprised, however, if it turns out to be the *Celtic Rebels*. Separatists have tried to bomb London before.'

'You think?' Gavin asked, calmer again. Arthur nodded, and Gavin shrugged. 'I don't know, we can speculate all we like. At the end of the day, until someone claims responsibility for it, it could have been anyone.'

Gwenhwyfar recalled the noise of the explosion, the heat on her back and the grit in the air, and wondered why someone would want to cause such devastation, such absolute hurt. Each of the two hundred and seven fatalities of Saturday night were people and had been cherished by someone; be it grieving mothers and fathers, sisters and brothers, friends, or children.

To his great surprise, Arthur thoroughly enjoyed sitting with Gwenhwyfar's friends during break, and eagerly rejoined them on Tuesday. Though during lunch there had been much speculation among the group as to why Lancelot might be absent, Arthur had kept quiet and refused to offer his opinion. *He* knew why Lancelot was off sick, and judging by Gavin's silence on the matter, the other boy did too.

His absence lasted until Wednesday. They were sitting in a loose cluster at break when his boisterous laugh cut through the hall. Twisting in his seat, Arthur saw him enter the canteen with Gavin. 'Here he comes,' he muttered to Gwenhwyfar, who turned so suddenly he felt he had announced some sort of flying wonder.

'Just ignore him.' No sooner than the words had left her lips Lancelot was upon them.

'Hey Arty.' It was sarcastic, it was snide, and it was completely expected. 'How's your granny?'

'Good, thanks. How's your uncle?' He didn't get an answer. The canteen felt like an overcrowded bus, humid from the rain. Lancelot stalked around the table. 'Where've you been all week, Lake? We were worried about you.'

'None of your business,' he snapped, sitting.

'Were you poorly?' Arthur pried.

'Fuck off,' he scowled.

Gwenhwyfar glared at Lancelot. 'No, not poorly?' Arthur continued. 'Perhaps you were just scared?'

Lancelot sprang to his feet. Arthur rose to face him, his chair clattering to the floor. Amid loud protests the two entered a staring contest.

'Arthur!' Gwenhwyfar exclaimed. 'Just *leave* it, would you? He's not worth the hassle.' Gavin was already prying Lancelot away, encouraging him to take his seat at the opposite end of the table. Arthur couldn't hear what was murmured, but it sounded calm and seemed to work. Soon he was left standing feeling rather foolish, with anger to spare but nowhere to direct it.

'Sorry,' he muttered blackly, as Gwenhwyfar helped to right his chair. He flopped down and glared at the floor.

For a while, normality returned. They were all talking about their favourite musicians when Lancelot started up again. Arthur didn't know how it happened, because all he'd heard was something about some guitarist being a drug-addict, and then:

'Hey Arty, wasn't *your* dad a drunk?'

His jaw clenched. He refused to look up, though it was almost impossible not to. Gwenhwyfar squeezed his arm.

'Arty? God, are you deaf or something? Didn't he like *die* drink driving? I mean how stupid can you get?'

'Lancelot!' Gavin bellowed.

He jumped in his seat. 'What? I'm just *saying*.'

'Yeah, well, don't,' Bedivere snapped.

'Shut it, Beddy. No one asked you.' Lancelot turned his wolf-like smile on Arthur. 'Aww, is he going to cry? Poor Arty. I'd cry too if my mother was a whore.'

Arthur surged to his feet in a move so powerful it disrupted the whole table. 'That's a bit hypocritical, considering how your mother spawned one.' Silence fell. 'I wouldn't talk to me about *drunks* and *whores* if I were you Lancelot—if your father were still alive, your behaviour would have driven him to alcoholism, and your mother would have been determined to breed with every single man in sight in an effort to gain more tolerable offspring.'

Lancelot's face grew dark with anger.

'How about you go back to mad Marvin so he can molest you some more?' Tom sneered. Viola smacked him hard around the back of the head.

'Yeah, go get molested by that freak teacher of yours,' Lancelot barked, firmly planted in his chair. 'No one wants you here, anyway.'

'I don't have to listen to this,' Arthur muttered. Bedivere jumped up as he walked away, hurrying after his long, troubled strides. Gwenhwyfar sprang to her feet, fury in her eyes.

'You're *pathetic*,' she hissed.

She stormed off, snatching her bag roughly from the table. Viola bolted up and separated herself from Tom. Gavin lingered long enough to remind his friend that he was an idiot, but despite his best efforts Lancelot exuded the impression of total indifference.

Gwenhwyfar knew that she couldn't guarantee anything involving Lancelot, but with Viola and Bedivere both backing her she tried, insisting to Arthur that nothing like this would happen again. Their words fell on deaf ears, however, and Arthur was adamant it would be best if he no longer sat with them. It was third period. Still furious, Gwenhwyfar decided she would hunt Lancelot down. When his Maths class produced no trace, she tried the bike shed, and then hurried out to the strip of grass running behind the sports hall. Her suspicions were confirmed as she approached the thick bank. There he was, milling about with two other boys she didn't know.

'Gwenhwyfar,' he exclaimed with some astonishment. 'Don't you have Geography?'

She pushed him, hard.

'What the hell do you think you're playing at?' she demanded, feeling him stumble. 'Do you have any idea what you've done?' His dark brows twisted. She tried to shove him again, but this time he hardly moved. 'Why can't you just act *normal?*'

The two boys laughed. Gwenhwyfar wheeled round. 'What do you think you're staring at?' she said, stomping after them. 'Don't you have a lesson to get to? Go on, go!'

They rushed off down the back of the sports hall. 'I should kill you!' she declared, turning on Lancelot. 'I should! How dare you say those things! Do you have any idea how horrible that was? How would you like it if someone started calling your parents that?'

His scowl turned to bewilderment as she slapped at him again and he failed to block her.

'I *hate* you! I can't believe you *mocked* his father's death! When has he ever bullied you for being orphaned? He won't sit with us anymore, thanks to you. Are you happy?'

'Yes.'

Gwenhwyfar couldn't believe it. Any sympathy, any tenderness she thought she held for Lancelot vanished in that moment. 'Why do you do it? You used to be best friends! Why can't you just get along?' When he failed to respond she slammed her hand into his shoulder. 'What about me? What about what I want? I thought you were decent, but you're not! All you care about is yourself.'

'That's not true,' Lancelot stated, 'and it's not fair.'

'Fair?' She laughed at him. 'Fair! What do you know about fair? You're the most *un*fair, *un*kind, *un*attractive person I've ever met. I hate the way you always sulk and scowl at people, I hate the way you beat everyone up, I hate the way you talk about Arthur, and I hate you—!'

She'd had enough of his presence, enough of his face, enough of him. A sudden lump rose in her throat and she turned to hurry down the bank.

'Gwenhwyfar.' He reached for her arm, but she smacked him away. Lancelot tried to catch her flailing hands. He didn't know what to do when she abruptly collapsed into his arms. He supported her gingerly at first, but as she broke down in earnest, Gwenhwyfar felt him envelop her in a strong hug.

'Everything's just so messed up,' she sobbed, her words muffled in his chest. 'How could someone do that? Just murder all those people?'

'Gavin told me that you and Vi were in London, Saturday.'

Gwenhwyfar sniffed, and nodded. 'Just think of it like this: you're lucky everyone you know is still alive.'

His words weren't much comfort. For a long while she stood with him in silence, clutching tightly to his torso. Eventually, she prised herself away, and his arms fell uselessly to his sides.

'Why weren't you in yesterday?' she ventured, a horrifying thought penetrating her mind. 'Oh God, you didn't lose someone, did you?'

He drew his gaze away, and immediately she felt awful. 'Oh Lancelot, I'm so sorry. I didn't know.' She reached out to hug him again, her arms splayed. 'Who?'

'No one.' He turned his hard eyes upon her. 'I lost no one.'

She stopped, affronted by his severity. Of course, a recent death in the family would explain too much, would make things far too simple. Once again Gwenhwyfar found herself perplexed by Lancelot's bipolar behaviour. She wished she could retract her outburst, but could offer nothing more than an apology. When he responded with a silent shrug, she left him on his own, deciding it would be best to leave it at that.

She rubbed her raw eyes with her fingertips, looking to the sky to dry the last of her tears. Wondering if she and Lancelot would ever get along, she wished desperately that he and Arthur would make amends, and put what was past behind them.

Anarchism

Thursday arrived with milder weather. They were sitting in their tutor room, waiting for Miss Ray to appear and take the register. The morbid fascination with the victims of Saturday had passed like a rolling fog; and their fellow students were now concerning themselves with other matters, mostly what they were hoping to get for Christmas. Emily was sitting with them again, as she had been since Monday, frequently causing Bedivere to absent himself.

'Have you heard?' she whispered to them all, once the register was taken. 'The New Nationals have realised the New Morals scheme. The officers will be put in place today.'

She was trying, Gwenhwyfar thought, and because Emily acted as if they had always been best friends it was hard to treat her otherwise. Even Viola had said nothing to repel her, despite complaining about her in her still-frequent absence.

'Says who?' Bedivere asked.

'The news.' Emily inspected her cuticles. 'I saw it this morning. They've already stormed ten key properties; they did it last night. They arrested several cells working with the separatists. Already the New Morals are a big success.'

'Weren't you at that march with Gwen?' Viola suddenly asked.

'I thought you said you wouldn't tell anyone?' Emily snapped, shooting Gwenhwyfar a glare.

'Viola already knew,' she explained. 'She knew we were going. So did Tom.'

'Tom?' Emily asked, alarmed. 'But Tom's—'

'Tom's what—?' Viola interrupted. 'He won't tell anyone. He knows how dangerous it was.'

'Who else knows?'

'No one,' Gwenhwyfar insisted. 'Just Mr Caledonensis.'

Emily seemed wholly uncomfortable, but after she shifted in her seat and glanced nervously around the class her blue eyes settled on Viola. 'So why didn't you go?'

'I couldn't,' Viola told her. She glanced to Charlotte's table, keeping her voice low. 'I can't do anything that would jeopardise my father. Besides, I knew it wouldn't work, and it didn't. They just buried it.'

Gwenhwyfar leant into the table. Reports of rape had marred the otherwise peaceful protest, along with fatalities, petrol bombs and the chaos the police had caused. 'You never said why you were there,' she pointed out. 'How did you find out about it?'

'Someone pushed a flyer through my letterbox. I looked it up online. I think it was some kind of organisation.'

'*Free Countries*?' Bedivere asked. Gwenhwyfar's eyes skipped to him, her heart pounding.

'I think so,' Emily breezed. 'No one else seemed bothered about it, so I went on my own. I suppose it didn't do any good. Like you say, it's been buried.'

'Just like Gavin predicted,' Bedivere concluded, his manner still stiff.

There was a moment's silence, and then Emily brightened again. The blare of the classroom seemed to intensify as the bell marked the beginning of their lessons.

'So,' she asked, eyeing them hopefully. 'What are you guys doing for lunch?'

Break time was welcomed with bruised clouds that raced across the sky in an invigorating wind. Forgoing the canteen, Gavin headed for New Wormelow after an hour and a half of Spanish. Lancelot was waiting for him by the low wall along the path outside of Marvin's classroom, squinting in reaction to the on-off sunshine.

'Rupert's starting a game of rugby,' Lancelot said. The two made their way towards the sports field. 'Told him to save centre and flanker. That all right?'

'Yeah.' Gavin traced the grass as it passed beneath their feet. 'You get up to much last night?'

'Not really. You?'

Gavin shrugged. 'Just did a bit of reading. You know, on the forums. There's talk that Milton's planning to introduce a youth division for the New Moral Army. Word is it's going to be mandatory service.'

Lancelot seemed surprised. 'Mandatory?'

Gavin nodded. 'We'll miss the sign-up age. We could join voluntarily, hypothetically. It's worrying. It's like they're trying to get as much hold as possible, just in case these elections don't go their way.'

'Won't they?'

'I have no idea. I suppose... there's always the *risk*.'

'You shouldn't read such things.'

'Why not?'

'Look at you; it clearly messes with your head. What does it matter? Let the idiots sign up if they want to.'

'It matters because it's not right. Doesn't it *remind* you of anything?'

Lancelot eyed him, and then looked away with an irritated huff. 'All right, what's this young army going to be doing besides tying knots and composing camp songs?'

'I don't think it's going to be so harmless.' They climbed the shallow bank onto the first sparsely populated field. 'Perhaps they're just going to use it to drum up support for the party? Or it might be to flesh out the Watchmen, that seems to be a popular theory.'

'So this is just speculation,' Lancelot remarked. 'Someone might be stirring. You don't know who's posting or where they heard it. I heard they put spies on those things, to bait people into saying something they shouldn't.'

'I know the bullshitters from the truth-tellers,' Gavin insisted. 'The people who are saying this are the ones who helped spread the word about the Mobilisation March.'

'Makes me wonder, given what that achieved. Arrests, and not much else.'

'Wonder about what?'

Lancelot shrugged, not willing to elaborate. 'At least we're missing it. Thank God.'

'Maybe not. Word is they're going for the Cadets.'

This stopped him. 'What do you mean, *going for*?'

'Absorbing it. Funding it with money reserved for the New

Morals. It might well become their young army, or part of it, in the long run. It'll still be Cadets, but politicised.'

'As if it's not already?' He sighed roughly, and started walking at a quicker pace. Gavin kept up with ease. 'When is this happening?'

'It'll be done by February. It's being snuck through with the reshuffling of the police. They're going to merge us with their new youth recruits, I just know it.'

'February.' Lancelot thought for a moment. 'That gives us, what—a month? Maybe I can convince my uncle to let me do Tai Quan Do instead. What do you think?'

'You're leaving?'

'You're not?'

Gavin was silent.

'You want to stay there—? You want to be part of Milton's wet dream?'

'It's not that simple.'

'What's not simple about it?'

'You know that if I leave I'll practically ruin my chances of signing on as an officer with the Marines,' he snapped. 'You will too.'

'I don't want to join the sodding Marines,' Lancelot hissed. 'I don't want to be shipped from one country to the next for the sole purpose of shooting people.'

'That's not what it's like.'

'Oh, you know, do you? You've been to Ireland, Israel and Africa? What did you do there? Make all those separatists cups of tea?'

'You think I like the idea of Milton getting his claws on the Cadets? You think I want what we do to be drowned in New

National doctrine?'

'I don't know, you don't seem that opposed to the idea.'

'I can't just *leave*, not now. And you shouldn't either.'

'I'm leaving the moment the funding changes. It'll make a point.'

'It'll make no point.'

'They can't influence the Cadets if all the cadets leave.'

'And that'll happen?'

'No, because you'll still be there, wagging your tail when Georgie throws you a tit-bit.'

He wanted to push him, hard. Sometimes his quips got the better of him. It didn't help that Lancelot knew him well, better than most. 'It won't be like that.'

'No?'

'I'm only his *attack-dog* if I think like them. I don't think like them, I'm never going to think like them. Why should I let the sodding New Nationals prevent me from doing what I want?'

'What, shooting people?'

'You sound like Gideon.'

'Gideon makes sense. You want to help people? Be an engineer or a doctor.'

Gavin shook his head, thoroughly disagreeing. He knew he should leave if the New Morals started to fund the Cadets, but he had worked too long, too hard to give in now. His goal was in sight. He was nearly eighteen.

'Just two more years,' he said. 'We'll be in the upper squad next term. The change won't be so big there. They'll only shake things up for the new recruits, otherwise they wouldn't get away with it.'

Lancelot said nothing. The game of rugby had already started, with others filling their roles for them.

'Two years,' Gavin said again.

'Right,' Lancelot sneered. 'It's like you said: if you're not police or army, you're little people.'

He ran onto the field before Gavin could retaliate. Irritated with his lack of understanding, and also with himself, Gavin watched as Lancelot flagged down Rupert and negotiated his spot. Huffing, Gavin jogged onto the pitch to join them, no longer eager to partake in the game.

It was lunchtime, and they had decided to enjoy the rare bit of sunshine. Though it was icy, Gwenhwyfar and Emily were sitting outside on one of the picnic benches, waiting for the others to join them. She hadn't seen Lancelot all day. Whether it was her that he was avoiding or Emily, Gwenhwyfar couldn't be sure, but his eagerness to not spend more time with her than he had to suited her perfectly.

Emily was examining her nails, red and immaculate. 'So do you always sit with Bedivere?'

'Yeah, why?'

'Oh, I was just wondering,' she shrugged. 'He sat with Morgan for registration yesterday. Do you think he's got a problem with me or something?'

Gwenhwyfar didn't know how to put it without being rude. 'I think he's still a bit uncomfortable with what happened. You know, at Tom's party?'

'So he *has* got a problem with me. I don't know why. *He's* the one who said I was a crap kisser.'

'I made that up, remember?' Gwenhwyfar contested. 'You did apologise to him. I'm sure he'll get over it eventually.' She eyed

Emily closely, wondering. 'You don't have an issue with him, do you?'

'Not at all,' Emily insisted, sitting up straight. '*He's* the one who's being weird.'

'Aren't you just a little bit embarrassed about it, though? I mean; you *kissed* him. You kissed Bedivere.'

'So what? It was just a kiss, it means nothing.' Suddenly Emily shuddered, and made a sound of disgust. 'You know what? Maybe I *am* embarrassed about it. I mean, what was I *thinking*?'

Gwenhwyfar wanted to remind her it had been part of Charlotte's cruel plan, but thought about what Viola had said to her on the way to Wormelow that morning: that the Furies had all changed allegiance in the past. Emily's infatuation with them wouldn't last—soon she'd scurry back to Charlotte, and all would be forgotten.

'So we can't just ditch him, then? I mean, it's bad enough that I kissed him without having to sit at the same table as him.'

She was shocked that she would even ask. 'No, of course not.'

The serious expression across Emily's brow dissipated. 'I'm *joking*.' She laughed. 'I don't care if he sits with us, if he doesn't care either. So you're going out with Arthur, right? How's that going?'

'Oh, good,' Gwenhwyfar said, reluctant to discuss something so personal with someone so loose-tongued. 'You know: *Arthur and Gwen*, just like you said it would be.'

Emily was pleased to find they still had common ground. 'I *knew* it would work out,' she gushed. 'I'm glad for you, really I am.' Pausing, she looked down at the grain of the table and picked at her own fingernails. 'What about Lance?'

Gwenhwyfar's heart tightened. 'What about him?'

Emily propped her chin in her hand. 'Is *he* seeing anyone at the moment?'

Gwenhwyfar traced Emily's gaze to the cafeteria. Lancelot was waiting by the doors with Gavin, presumably for the others. She felt a surge of anger as she remembered the incident yesterday. She had offered to sit alone with Arthur today, but he had insisted he wanted to spend time with Marvin instead. 'I don't think so. Why?'

'No reason. I was just wondering.'

She felt her stomach twist into an uncomfortable knot. Emily couldn't, could she…? But then she remembered what Gavin had once said, *that blonde girl who's obsessed with Lance.* Suddenly Lancelot's own words resurfaced, and she felt sick.

'Lance—?' she said in disbelief. 'You like… *Lance*?'

'*Shh!*' she hissed at her. 'I never said that!' Despite the words, she smiled. 'But he *is* fit. Have you *seen* him playing rugby?' She released a sound that made Gwenhwyfar feel uncomfortable. 'I'd be surprised if he is single.'

Gwenhwyfar could barely speak.

'Do you know if he fancies anyone?'

Yes, me, she wanted to shout. *He fancies me.* But did he? That was nearly a month ago now, and a lot had happened since then. What if he liked Emily, too? 'I did hear that he had a thing for Juliet in sixth-form,' she lied, grasping at straws.

'Juliet?' Emily's nose wrinkled. 'Ugh. I don't know why all the boys like her: she's such a *hag.*'

'Emily, you've never dated Lance, have you?'

'What do you mean?'

'This is going to sound weird, but have you ever been *been* with him?'

She didn't get it. As Gwenhwyfar tried to convey her meaning through her gaze, Emily merely looked at her as if she were strange.

'You know,' Gwenhwyfar murmured, reluctant to say it. 'Have you... *slept* with him?'

Emily's sudden look of surprise turned to horror. 'What? No! Ugh, don't be so vile! Of course not! Who told you that?'

'Lance,' she revealed with some satisfaction. 'He said he'd had sex with you.'

'What? When?'

'Ages ago, months. He was obviously bragging. He said he'd had *hundreds* of women, and that you were one of them.' She offered her a false smile. 'Now I know he was lying.'

'Lance said he slept with me?' Emily scowled. 'Why would he do that? Unless... unless he actually *wanted* to. Gwen! Don't you see? It's obvious! He said that because he *fancies* me!'

She stared, slack-jawed. 'You think?'

Emily shushed her to silence as Lancelot loped over with the others. He sat down, pulling a stolen apple and chocolate bar out of his pocket. He soon realised that Emily was staring at him.

'What?'

Gwenhwyfar felt the jealousy within her explode. '*Emily* was wondering why you were telling everyone you slept with her,' she snapped. Emily smacked her arm, the part that was still sore.

'Lance made that up?' Tom hacked out a mocking laugh. Gavin and Viola looked about the table in surprise. Lancelot's knuckles whitened. He stood to leave.

'Who said he made it up?' Emily blurted out. 'We were just wondering why he's told everyone, when I specifically asked him *not* to.'

Gwenhwyfar couldn't believe it. Even Lancelot looked stunned. 'Right,' she said, her mouth dry.

'You slept with Lance?' Tom asked, his disappointment evident.

'It was ages ago,' Emily shrugged. 'It wasn't anything serious.'

Gwenhwyfar felt nauseous. What was Emily playing at? None of them had forgiven her for what she had done, and yet she was here, as if she had always been one of them, and she was ruining everything.

'Is this true, Lance?' Viola asked, as shocked as Gwenhwyfar. By this stage Lancelot had regained his composure and was sitting as he always did, smugly, with an unshakable air of confidence.

'Of course,' he claimed. 'I said we did, didn't I?'

The table fell into deliberation. Eventually the subject changed, the claim forgotten, but Bedivere seemed troubled and Gwenhwyfar found her feelings warring for the rest of recess.

She was hurrying into the girls' toilets when Viola caught up with her. The other girl slammed the door open, and Gwenhwyfar looked round in surprise.

'What the hell was that?' Viola demanded, striding into the bathroom. Gwenhwyfar pressed her hips into the ceramics as she adjusted her appearance in the dirtied mirrors.

'Gwen?'

'What was what about?' she snapped, irritated with herself.

'That!' Viola exclaimed. 'That whole charade with Lance! You getting stroppy with Emily!'

She sniffed, and pushed back her hair. 'What's it to you? I thought we hated her anyway.'

'I thought so too, and then you go and let her sit at our table!

Don't you remember what she did?'

'She apologised for what she did,' Gwenhwyfar bit. 'Besides, you've got a mouth, haven't you? You could've said no, but you just sat there and told her you *didn't mind*. Well, now look what happened! Bedivere's clearly upset about it.'

'So you're going to blame this on me, are you?'

'*No*. I just don't agree with Lance bragging about things that aren't true.'

'You didn't have a problem with it before.'

'What's that supposed to mean?'

'It only seems to bother you now that Emily's around.'

'Don't be such a hypocrite.'

'I'm not the one taking the moral high ground here,' she shouted. Gwenhwyfar decided she wasn't going to answer that. She didn't want to argue. 'You're not even listening to me,' claimed Viola.

'I *am* listening.'

'No, you're not. What the hell is up with you?'

'She had a right to know. She didn't sleep with him. She's only saying she did because she likes him. She wants to make him think she *understands* him.'

Viola stared.

'And she *doesn't* understand him,' continued Gwenhwyfar. 'She has no idea who he is. And Lancelot seems to have forgotten what she did to him. I mean, who does that? Claims they screwed the person who destroyed their life?'

Viola waved her arms in exasperation and brought her palms up to her forehead. 'I can't deal with this!' she expelled. 'I mean, God! Emily's only been with us for five minutes, and you're already acting like her.'

'Acting like what?' she dared.

'You know, like *her*. Like a complete bitch.'

She was stunned, hurt, but couldn't back-peddle now. 'Oh, so now I'm a bitch, am I?'

'No! You're acting like one, but it's not you. It's Emily, and it's driving me insane!'

Gwenhwyfar pulled out the grimy bottle of lip-gloss that often sat in her pencil case and, lost for words, applied it angrily.

'Look, I'm sorry. You're not a bitch. But I mean, do you fancy Lance or something?'

She turned to face her. 'What? No!'

'Are you sure? Because you're certainly acting like it.'

'Don't be ridiculous.'

'So you like Arthur, then?'

'You know I do,' she affirmed. 'Why wouldn't I? He's *perfect*.'

'Right! You like Arthur, and you don't fancy Lance. So you shouldn't care if Emily *does* fancy Lance.'

'Of course I care! I mean, he's my friend, isn't he? Of course I care that that harpy wants to dig her sharp little claws into him. It's just wrong.'

'Lance is a big boy, Gwen. He can take care of himself.'

'But she *lied*. She lied about sleeping with him, and she lied about Ellie. How does she think she even has a chance?' Gwenhwyfar began to doubt herself. She couldn't like Lancelot, not in that way. The possibility that she might terrified her. 'Lance and I are friends. I'm just looking out for him. You know what Emily's like.'

Viola's eyes narrowed to suspicious slits. 'Good, because I know him. Arthur believed what Charlotte said for a reason. Ellie and Lance were close, really close. Just friends, so they insisted, but it was a complete disaster.'

'What do you mean?'

'You know how things ended up, the division it caused.' She sighed. 'Lance is… volatile. Just trust me.'

The two girls stared at one another, considering. Gwenhwyfar bit her lip and found her eyes shifting to the tiled floor.

'I'm sorry. I'm sorry for acting weird. I'm just still a bit freaked from this weekend, you know?'

'I know. Just be careful. What would Arthur do if he found out you were jealous?'

'I'm not jealous,' she countered.

'*He* won't see it that way.' There was another silence between them. As always, the toilets of Old Wormelow smelt vaguely of cigarette smoke. A tap dripped into a clogged sink, which was half-flooded with stagnant water. 'Do you love Arthur?'

'I don't know.' Gwenhwyfar sighed, and wrapped her arms close to her chest. 'I don't even know if he loves me.'

'Arthur!'

He jolted, blinking. He was sitting in Marvin's study for another meeting with The Round Table, but at some point his mind had wandered off. Gwenhwyfar wasn't here tonight—she had commitments with her family—and as Marvin gazed at him expectantly Arthur shifted in embarrassment and tried to guess what he had missed.

Marvin sighed. 'Is something troubling you, by any chance?'

He looked about the room. Opposite him sat Morgan and Percy. Next to them, Gavin and Bedivere watched Marvin closely. Arthur felt his face heat up.

'Sorry, I was thinking about what the implications are for the introduction of the New Moral Army,' he adlibbed. 'What was the question again?'

Marvin huffed. 'An *interesting* distraction, I am sure, and it is one we will continue to cover; but right now we want to know what your opinion on the national lottery is. You know, the lottery that was called in 'twenty-one, to replenish military forces stationed in the Middle East? What do you think?'

Arthur looked to Bedivere for help, and then to Gavin, but the tall boy eyed him critically with a strident opinion that he didn't want to loan. 'I don't know,' he admitted. 'I wasn't really listening.'

Bedivere smirked. Marvin waved his hand in annoyance. 'Well, thank you for being honest, but please let me know when you *do* next decide to listen to me, hmm? Morgan?'

Morgan went into a long series of arguments that, though intended to upstage Arthur, only caused him to switch off again. Gavin contested her point of view until the discussion moved on to politics, and as Marvin refilled their glasses—Morgan's with squash, the boys' with English wine—Arthur was pulled back to those around him.

'It's terribly tragic of course,' Marvin was announcing, 'but I can't quite see how, in this day and age, when everything from what you eat in the morning to where you sleep at night is monitored, something like this could be organised. I mean, how could anyone evade all those surveillance methods undetected? I wish I knew.'

The wine bottle glugged as it poured into Arthur's glass. He held the stem steady, watching the crimson swirl. 'Gwen was on the street where one of the bars exploded,' he remarked.

'Yes, I was made aware of that at the start of the week. I do have one pupil whose sister died, and many others who were in some way involved, so by no means am I commending the attacks. I'm merely suggesting that they're odd.'

'It is odd,' Gavin agreed, 'but not impossible.'

'Not impossible, no, but unusual?' Marvin sighed. 'We were told that the last series of attacks in London happened because the government didn't have enough control over monitoring mechanisms. The odd blast since then was to be expected from lone wolves, but something as orchestrated as this? I just don't know how it happened.'

Morgan propped herself forwards on the table. 'Isn't that when Lance's parents died? I remember; it was in Year Seven. At Christmas.'

'They were on the Tube, going out for their anniversary.' Gavin looked up, and for a moment met Arthur's eye. 'They weren't supposed to be on that train, but the line they wanted was shut due to a jumper. They had to take the Central.'

There was a long silence. Marvin sucked his teeth and ruefully shook his head. 'We do live in such a violent world.'

'That's inevitable, considering we're essentially a violent, destructive species,' remarked Arthur, a hint of disgust in his tone. 'If we can't kill it off or drive it to extinction, we destroy it and exhaust it, and if we can't fulfil either of those ambitions we murder and rape one another instead.'

'That's very cynical of you, Arthur. Don't you think?' Marvin exclaimed.

'It is,' Morgan agreed.

'You would argue that we're not a parasitic life form?' Arthur challenged. Morgan seemed wounded.

'Do you think I'm parasitic, Arthur?' asked Bedivere, brows

raised.

'No, but—'

'How about Gwen?' he added, teasing.

'Of course not, I didn't say that the individual is parasitic, just our current way of life. Consumerism is destroying the planet. No, it *has* destroyed the planet. Why do you think half the world has starved to death? There's not enough left to support everyone.'

'Says who?' Morgan snapped.

'Says common sense.' He could feel the wine loosening his tongue. 'People are lying when they say things aren't that bad. What do you think all those wars were for? We were all just fighting over who got to eat the last éclair.'

Marvin's stomach growled, and he awkwardly cleared his throat. Morgan gazed at Arthur, her mouth downturned. Frustrated, Arthur leant into the table, gesticulating to emphasise his point.

'It's like farming. Once every few years, after you've worked the earth, grown your crops and ploughed the land, you have to let it rest. Otherwise nothing will grow the next time you try to plant something. Think of it like that. The Earth is one big field and we've farmed it for much too long, so all its nutrition and minerals have been sucked out. We've bled it dry.'

'Yes, but we can't just not eat,' she countered.

'Why not? The other half of the world isn't at the moment.'

'That's no argument,' Percy interrupted.

'What do you mean?' Arthur bristled.

'The "They're not eating, so let's not eat either" argument. That's like those people who use an example of a country in a worse state to invalidate the arguments and concerns of Western society. It gets neither side anywhere.'

'But Arthur's right to an extent,' Marvin butted in. 'If we weren't all so greedy about having the latest technology evenly distributed for our consumption, it wouldn't be such a problem. But then, consumerism suits our society. As long as we are diverted by owning the latest *toy*, we are kept infantile: passive, apathetic, and easily led to hatred of the vulnerable. In this world, a world where we are shielded from responsibility and are distracted by successes measured by how many trinkets we have, those who rule us can do as they please.'

'Noam Chomsky,' Percy pointed out, referencing Marvin's words. Marvin nodded.

'Recycling may be better than it was a hundred years ago, but we're all still encouraged to buy the latest things. Our use of plastics has not significantly declined, either. That, and nothing is built to last.'

The six of them fell to silence. Arthur sipped a little more of his wine.

'Oh!' exclaimed Bedivere, looking at his watch. 'The news!'

'The news!' echoed Marvin, waving his arms. He cursed as his drink slopped onto the table. 'Bedivere! Go and turn it on, immediately! Percy! A cloth! Gavin—Morgan! Come on! Arthur—!' He grinned. 'Let's go and see if we can't discover another clue to this little mystery, shall we?'

Soon they were all gathered around Marvin's ancient television—thick, box-like and badly pixelated—listening to the dramatic music underpinning the flashing headlines.

Arthur did his best to lean elegantly on the sofa arm, careful not to disrupt the artefacts pinned to the wall behind him. Morgan sat beside him, with Percy closely wedged against her, and Bedivere sat at the opposite end of the suite with Marvin in the middle. Gavin sat in the armchair. The introduction ended. They were greeted by a stern woman gazing out at them from her strangely two-dimensional studio. It had taken Arthur a while to get accustomed to Marvin's television set, and now he was used to the older technology.

> "Good evening,
>
> Tonight, the Prime Minister has announced that the security services have reason to believe the terror cell *Free Countries* bears responsibility for the bombings last weekend. Evidence has been found linking the group to this horrific attack through their communication records, provided by independent companies across the UK. The Prime Minister's Head of Security stated in an interview earlier today that such evidence was only discoverable due to George Milton's personal dealings with UK Telecom, with whom he has been working closely since the inhumane attacks on Saturday night."

Arthur frowned. Marvin let loose an exclamation that startled those nearest to him.

> "Linked to the separatist *New Celtic Rebels*, *Free Countries* is a terrorist organisation believed to have been involved in the riots of September and November this year. According to our sources, they stand for anarchism and an end to our current governmental system. The security services are still trying to locate the main leaders of *Free Countries*, but this group is the terror cell believed to be

responsible for the death of hundreds. The general public have been asked to stay vigilant against any hint of activity from this highly dangerous extremist group."

Arthur licked his lips, still able to taste the wine. The woman on screen blinked with every other word, and it annoyed him.

"The head of Milton's private security firm joins us in the studio now. Good evening, Sir Bennett. Tell me; is it true that, as yet, no real suspects have been detained?"

Morgan leant back in the sofa, her arm brushing against Arthur's thigh. He sat still for a moment, but then shifted away uncomfortably, the heat from her body seeping into his own.

'*Free Countries*?' Bedivere asked. 'I got a flyer in the post from them about the Mobilisation March.' He turned to face the others. 'We all went to it. Does that mean we're now involved with a "terror cell"?'

'I don't think so—I get flyers from them all the time,' Morgan said, curling her hair around one finger. 'And in terms of the march, no one knows we went, right?'

'Right,' Gavin assured them, his voice calm.

'What sort of *terror cell* advertises themselves using flyers and leaflets anyway?' Arthur mused, emptying his glass.

'I don't know,' responded Bedivere. 'Were they even involved in the September protest? I thought they blamed the separatists.'

'They did. But they'll blame them both if it suits them,' Gavin said.

'What if it was *Free Countries* that organised the bombings, though? How would we know?' Morgan looked up to Arthur.

'They could easily be telling the truth.'

'Right,' Bedivere fretted. 'For all we know *Free Countries* could be filled with psychos and extremists.'

'Maybe they are, maybe they aren't, but that doesn't affect us.' Arthur looked at Percy. The sixth former was gazing at the box-like screen, his eyes and ears fixed on Sir Bennett, straining to hear above their chatter. 'What should we do?'

Marvin was standing now, his fingers pressing into his lips as he gazed fixedly at the carpet. 'Do—? Why, we *do* nothing. The news has just given us a scapegoat for the atrocities committed on Saturday. Whether it is true or not, you never went to that march; you were never there. If you get any more flyers, burn them. We weren't involved in anything, no matter what happens.'

'You don't think it was *Free Countries*, then?' Percy asked suddenly.

'I don't know,' Marvin replied. 'If it was, you want to wash your hands of them, and if it wasn't, well; the need is the same. They're a fairly ambiguous group, small I imagine, and pose little to no threat to Milton himself… so what reason would the New Nationals have for falsifying their involvement? I know I never usually take the news at face value, but in this instance… I am inclined to.'

Nodding stiffly, Percy turned back to the screen. Gavin downed the last of his wine and stood up. Morgan shifted, and Bedivere seemed to think over everything in silence. Arthur detached himself from the sofa. It was late, and their hour was up.

The Warning

She didn't know what to do.

The terror that gripped her upon seeing the news had turned her blood to ice. How was this possible? Not once had Isolde mentioned anything to do with terrorist activity, and she hadn't heard of it through the grapevine, either. Gwenhwyfar paced back and forth, wearing an erratic line into the carpet from her bed to her door. She hadn't yet shut the curtains. The cold glass loomed in the night, a portal through which she came to stare for a moment, replaying the news anchor's words in her mind.

Free Countries is a terrorist organisation… they stand for anarchism… extremism…

Responsible for the death of hundreds, she thought, her head pounding. What was she going to do? What could she do? She could barely fathom the implications of what she'd become involved in, let alone comprehend the consequences. What if the police found out she was a part of the most wanted terror group in Britain? What if they found out she'd even recruited a member? The grapevine had to be traceable to her. It wouldn't be difficult to track her down, and it wasn't as if she'd ever been careful. Thickly, she swallowed down the bile that gathered in her throat.

How could *Free Countries* be responsible for this? Surely they would have known there'd be a chance of murdering their own members. Abruptly, another paralysing revelation hit her. She had been at one of the crime scenes—was on record for being treated at the nearest hospital—and had walked away just as the bar had exploded.

But no, she had been attending a party—was there all night—and there were hundreds of witnesses. For a few moments she calmed herself, swiftly running through all the solutions she had to hand. She would swap phones and destroy her old mobile. She would cut contact with Isolde. She almost leapt a mile when her phone rang. She didn't recognise the number, but on the fifth ring, she picked up. The voice wasn't familiar, and she felt a wave of panic. What if it was the police?

'Hello? Is that Gwen? It's... it's Tristan.'

Her relief was only momentary. 'Tristan! Are you insane?'

'I didn't know what else to do!' he hissed, voice urgent. Something that sounded like reinforced glass was beaten down upon by what had to be rain. 'I've been thinking.'

Gwenhwyfar was thinking, too. As far as anyone knew, Tristan could just be an acquaintance. They had only spoken once, she hadn't asked him to recruit anyone, and his involvement in the cause had been minimal. 'Did you get my letter?' she blurted, shaking.

He didn't get it. 'What letter?'

'The letter I sent you, explaining everything we *talked* about. I said I'd send you one, ages ago. Did you not get it?'

'I don't quite… you mean the thing?'

'Yes,' she affirmed. 'About the thing.'

He made a sound of comprehension. Gwenhwyfar hoped desperately that he understood she meant the information pack sent out by *Free Countries*.

'No,' he replied, 'I didn't get it.'

'Good.' Sighing, she turned about on the spot. 'I don't think we should speak to one another again, Trist. I mean I know I gave you my number and things, but I have a boyfriend now.'

'You do?'

'Yes, it's official. So I'm afraid I'm going to have to ask you to never call me again, understand? That's what the letter said, that it's over. I'm done.'

'I see,' he murmured. 'So it's over?'

'Yes.'

'I'm to never contact you again?'

'That's right, we're done.' There was a short silence. 'Where are you calling from?'

'A payphone.'

'Right, well, I have to go.'

'Gwen,' he hesitated. 'Did you know?'

'Know what?' she added, weary.

'You know.'

'No. I found out myself,' she remarked. He fell silent, and it seemed they understood one another.

'You're letting me go? Are you sure?'

She nodded, drawing up a thick sigh. 'I'm sure, Tristan. It's for the best. I'm with someone else.'

He hung up, and so did she. Her hand trembled as she examined the number on her phone. It wasn't from a mobile, and for some reason that comforted her. Tristan was safe at least, but what of her? She wanted an escape too, and wished she could wipe *Free Countries* from her mind.

She launched herself at her desk, ripped open the drawers and pulled out the brown envelope she had almost memorised. She shredded each document frantically. Still she didn't feel safe. Gwenhwyfar seized the scented candle and matches she kept on her dresser and hurried them back to her desk. She flung the candle away and threw the tatters of paper into the rounded dish, set them alight and rushed to open the window. When she returned she fed the final few shreds to the flame, and blew softly upon them, until it had all turned to ash.

She didn't know what to do with the remnants. Contemplating burying them or feeding them to Llew, she eventually flushed them down the toilet. At last, when she had destroyed her SIM card and taken her mind through every other eventuality, she tried sleeping, but found it impossible to switch off. Hundreds of scenarios raced through her head. What if *Free Countries* had been responsible? Did that make her a murderer? She didn't know what she had been thinking when she had considered joining them to be a good idea. She had been seduced by the secrecy, and it had led her blindly into danger.

She awoke several times during the night, something keeping her restless, but not until the early hours of Saturday morning did she realise what. She was chewing slowly on toast with a glass of orange juice, surfing the Internet, when the revelation descended. The unfortunate timing of things determined what she did next. A window popped up. It was *Free Countries*.

Her reflex was instantaneous. Angry sparks spat from her computer as the orange juice cascaded into it, frothing.

Gwenhwyfar squeaked as the glass shattered upon the table. A horrible, twisted noise crooned from the sagging machine. It cracked, a thunderous bellow, and then everything fell silent.

Cowering on the floor, she heard exclamations of surprise sound throughout the house.

'Gwen, what in God's name happened? Are you all right?'

She pushed herself up as her father rushed into her bedroom. Immediately he hurried over to the power outlet and snatched the plug out of the socket, swearing as he burnt his fingers.

'What the hell happened?'

'Nothing!'

'It doesn't look like nothing,' he contested, waving his arms through the smoke. He opened the bedroom window and tried to waft the fumes outside. 'Are you hurt?' He helped her off the floor and sat her on the bed.

Gwenhwyfar shook her head. 'I'm fine. I dropped my drink. My arm just... I lost my grip.'

'You lost your grip?' he repeated, sitting next to her. 'Which arm?'

She didn't know which one to choose.

'Was it the arm you fell on in London?' he asked. She nodded. 'Maybe we should get you to a doctor.'

'I'm fine. Just shaken, that's all.'

He frowned at her. 'You didn't shock yourself, did you?'

'No.'

'Try squeezing my hand,' he instructed sternly.

Gwenhwyfar did so without much effort. 'Really, I'm fine.'

'I don't know what we're going to do about this.' He inspected the computer. 'It's a mess, Gwen!'

'I know, Dad.'

'What on earth were you thinking?'

He wasn't usually this short with her. 'It was an accident! It's not my fault I dropped the drink.'

'No, but you shouldn't have had it at your desk to begin with,' he maintained.

'I know—I'm sorry.'

Garan sighed. 'I suppose we can get it fixed.'

'Fixed? But it almost killed me! Look at it; it's practically melted anyway. Can't we just get a new one?'

'Do you have any idea how expensive they are?' Garan exclaimed. 'I've told you hundreds of times not to have drinks at your desk, and now look!'

'But I don't need that one again, just any sort of thing will do. I don't care if it's old or cheap—I only use it for homework.'

'Oh, do you? And what happened to you wanting the upgrade to this model?'

'That was before,' she insisted. 'Now I know it's not that good. I mean it's *good*, but I don't need it, really. I'd rather just get something older, they're more reliable. You say so yourself.'

'Reliable, yes; waterproof, no.' He stood up. 'Look, I might be able to get something through work, but I'm not promising anything. First you'll have to learn not to keep liquids at your desk, understand?'

Gwenhwyfar nodded furiously.

'I think it flipped the fuse—the power's out.' He ambled stiffly to the door. 'Don't touch this,' he ordered, turning to Gwenhwyfar and pointing at the machine. 'The last thing I need is you getting electrocuted.'

Gwenhwyfar observed him with glassy eyes. She heard her mother call up the stairs. Garan went into the corridor and told

Eve to flip the fuse again. As she did, Gwenhwyfar's bedroom was once again illuminated.

Though *Free Countries* was mentioned often in the news, the further Gwenhwyfar made it into the second week of December the safer she felt. For many, the horrors of the attacks were forgotten as the festive season unfurled, with decorations going up and lessons passing with scores of old movies. Though Gwenhwyfar had successfully destroyed all evidence linking her to *Free Countries*, news had emerged of members coming forward and trading information in return for clemency. The "terror cell" was disbanding.

The dry winter air froze the earth solid. Any conversations she had with Lancelot were brief, and though Emily still flirted outrageously with him Gwenhwyfar did her best to ignore it. Emily, it seemed, was there to stay; and despite any initial frostiness caused by her presence relations were starting to thaw. Gwenhwyfar took solace in Lancelot's apparent indifference to the bubbly blonde girl, and even began to enjoy seeing her making a fool of herself.

She found Arthur waiting for her halfway between Badbury and Wormelow. She strode up to him and planted a firm kiss upon his lips. 'Hello.'

'Hello.' He kissed her again, and for a long while she forgot they were in school. When they finally parted, they strolled towards Wormelow. 'Did you get up to much last night?'

'Just a bit of Christmas shopping. I've decided what I'm getting my parents. My dad's needed a new coat for ages, and I'm going to treat my mum to a really nice dress I found.' She swung his hand with excitement. 'Have you figured out what you want yet?'

'You don't have to get me anything,' he told her again.

'But you're getting me something, you said so. Besides, I *want* to get you a present. I've already got a few ideas.'

'What are they?'

'Don't you trust me?'

He looked at her and smiled. 'No list, then?'

'If you think of one, but I like to buy early, and December is late enough for me.'

He lifted her hand to his lips, and then held open the door to New Wormelow.

'So what did you get up to? You never replied to my text.'

'Sorry. I had work, then Bedivere came round.'

'He did?'

Arthur nodded. 'It made me realise that the last time he came over was in the summer holidays. I hardly see him anymore.'

'Only because he's sitting with us,' Gwenhwyfar pointed out. They passed through the lobby and scaled the stairs to the upper corridors. 'You can still join him, you know. I mean, I understand if you don't want to, given what Lance did…'

'He still sits with you?'

'Barely. We see him, but usually he's out on the field with Gavin. I think he's avoiding me. I had a real go at him for what he said.'

This seemed to surprise Arthur. 'You did?'

Gwenhwyfar nodded. 'For all the good it did. He didn't even apologise—he still hasn't.' She shrugged. 'It doesn't matter, he's always been an idiot.' She could almost feel his approval shower over her. They pushed through a second set of double doors.

'Bed said that Emily's sitting with you now, too.'

'Unfortunately.' She hesitated, and then sighed. 'I suppose she *did* apologise, for everything actually. And I told you about the whole Ellie thing. According to her she only heard it from Charlotte and Hattie, and thought they were telling the truth.'

'And you believe that?'

'I don't know, mostly I just enjoy seeing her make an idiot of herself. Apparently she's got a thing for Lance. She won't leave him alone.'

'That doesn't surprise me,' Arthur remarked. 'They suit one another.'

They came to a stop. A thickset boy blocked them when they tried to pass through the Science corridor. He was stocky, of average height, and had short curly hair that was similar in colour to wet sand. 'You're Gwen, right?'

She eyed him suspiciously. 'Yeah.'

'Lance's friend,' the boy stated.

Arthur moved closer to her. 'Not really.'

'Wasn't talking to you,' the boy snapped. He set his gaze on Gwenhwyfar. 'Do you know him or what?'

She shrugged. 'Sort of, why?'

'Tell him to watch his back.'

'What? Why?'

He scrutinised her with beady eyes. 'Just tell him.'

Arthur stepped forward. 'Is that all?'

'No. Tell him to look after his friends, too.' His rounded cheeks split into a horrible grin. Gwenhwyfar felt a pang of cold fear in her stomach. The comment had to be directed at her. Arthur seemed to think so too, for he put his arm around her shoulders and immediately hurried her away.

'He said what?'

Lancelot was crouched in his chair, his elbows pressing into his knees and his hands cupped under his chin. Around him, Emily, Bedivere and Viola listened attentively. Gavin and Tom were playing football, something Lancelot had been eager to participate in. Gwenhwyfar repeated the words again. He stared intently at the floor.

'And who said it, exactly?'

'That guy you and Hector always used to fight with,' Arthur recalled. 'I thought I recognised him, but I wasn't sure. You know, the one with the fat neck that looks like a pig.'

Lancelot sat up, clearly surprised. 'What's he doing making threats? I haven't even spoken to him since last term.' His handsome face turned to a scowl of contemplation.

'Who's he hanging around with now?' Viola asked. She was sitting on the table with her feet on a chair. 'I doubt the threat would've come from him, not unless he had someone to back him up. He'll be the messenger.'

'The messenger for whom?' enquired Arthur.

'What's his name?'

Lancelot looked at Bedivere. 'Edward,' he responded, 'but everyone calls him Cooper.'

'Edward Cooper?' Bedivere brightened. 'I know him: he's in my Science class. He used to be friends with a guy called Jack, but the last few times I've seen him, he's been with Hector.'

'Hector?' Lancelot proclaimed. 'I thought Cooper hated him?'

'You *are* talking about Hector Browne, aren't you?' Emily's undiluted attention produced a ruby blush in Bedivere.

'Yes, it's definitely Browne. Cooper obviously can't hate him as much as he hates you, Lance, if he's willing to side with him just to get to you.'

'Not just Lance,' Arthur reminded them all. 'His friends, too.'

'Hector hangs around with a lot of people now,' Bedivere said. 'There's four of them—him, Cooper, Lucan Smith and Lyndon Grant. They're always down at Badbury, hanging by the courts.'

Arthur rubbed his jaw in concern. 'If Hector's involved, it's quite a serious threat.'

'Lance and his "friends"? That has to mean you, Gwen.' Viola looked to the group. 'We should tell someone. He's completely out of order.'

'Tell who? Ravioli? Don't you remember what happened last time? He practically made a joke out of me.'

'Yes, but this time it's different,' Viola contested.

'Why threaten Lance, anyway?' asked Arthur. 'Why not just threaten Gwen? What have you got to do with it?'

The two boys' eyes met, and Gwenhwyfar felt her heart contract. Suddenly she wished she had told Arthur what had happened.

'Hector and I used to fight with Cooper all the time,' Lancelot shrugged. 'Maybe it's that?'

'It's not that,' Gwenhwyfar volunteered, suddenly much too warm. 'Hector went for me at Lance's birthday party.' She looked to Arthur and swallowed. 'That's why he's making threats. He tried it on with me, and I sprayed deodorant in his eyes.'

The group went silent. Gwenhwyfar could tell that Arthur was hurt. He obviously understood that he was the only one, save Emily, who hadn't known. 'So that's why Hector was off for so long.' He frowned, and then his brown eyes rose to question hers. 'Why didn't you say anything?'

'I knew you'd be upset.' Now that she voiced it aloud, it

seemed a poor excuse. 'I didn't want to feel pressured into anything.'

'Pressured?'

'I thought you'd tell me to report it. I'm sorry.'

'Hector *attacked* you?' Emily butted in, scandalised.

'What happened?' Arthur eyed Gwenhwyfar with renewed concern. 'Was it just him…?'

'No, there was another guy,' Lancelot said. 'We couldn't figure out who he was. A friend of Hector's, we think. Possibly not from Logres.'

'And they attacked you?'

'It was mostly talk,' Gwenhwyfar dismissed.

'Not just talk,' Viola objected. 'Hector was on top of you, you said so.'

Gwenhwyfar felt her face heat up. 'Yeah, and I blinded him and kicked him in the head and told him I was going to the police. He hasn't bothered me since.'

'I still don't understand why he'd threaten Lance,' Arthur scowled.

'Lance was there after it happened,' Gwenhwyfar explained. 'I think he made them think twice about pursuing it.'

'He didn't hit them?'

'No,' Lancelot said sharply. 'Gwen didn't want me to.'

'And you've not said anything to them since?'

'I haven't *touched* Hector,' Lancelot hissed. 'Or said anything to him, Lucan, Lyndon or Edward. I haven't even seen them.'

'It doesn't matter,' Viola interjected. 'All that matters is that we tell someone. Before this escalates.'

'Tell who, exactly?' Gwenhwyfar asked. 'He's just trying to intimidate me. This is all this has ever been about. He's a bully.'

'I still think—'

'It's up to Gwen if she wants to tell the principal or not,' Arthur interjected. He looked to Gwenhwyfar, and she felt her heart expand. 'If you're worried about Ravioli believing you, I can always tell him myself. He might take it better, coming from me.'

'You would do that?' Gwenhwyfar asked, touched. She was suddenly sorry that she had underestimated his ability to understand.

'Of course—should I?'

'I don't know.' She looked across the cafeteria, hunting for a glimpse of Hector or Edward. 'If I do say something it should definitely come from me.'

'Not that it'll make much difference,' Lancelot grumbled. Suddenly all eyes were on him. 'Hector's dad is the principal's first cousin. They grew up together. Hector always used to brag about how he could do anything, because Ravioli wouldn't stop him. He could shoot someone, he said, and he wouldn't be expelled.'

'So they are related, then?' Arthur asked. 'I wasn't sure.'

Lancelot nodded, and Gwenhwyfar's heart sank.

With cheeks numbed by the bitter wind, Gwenhwyfar, Emily and Viola clustered together, hurrying through the icy grounds of Logres. The school seemed particularly dull in the absence of sunshine, though its bowels, at least, were warm and decorated excessively with tinsel. With arms interlinked, they discussed what should be done about Hector. Emily abandoned her post to kick open the door to old Wormelow, and Gwenhwyfar's fingers prickled against the sudden heat.

'I just feel like this is all my *fault*.' Emily pulled her hat away, combing her hands through her hair. 'I should have never listened to Charlotte. I mean, I know I'm partially responsible for what happened at Tom's party, Gwen, but if I hadn't trusted her, then maybe none of this would have happened.'

'We can't know that.' Viola plucked off her gloves and stuffed them into the pocket of her woollen coat. 'If Hector wanted to hurt Gwen, he would have done so anyway. Only it would've been worse, because we would've still trusted him.'

Their shoes clipped across the grey dappled stone. They were late.

'I wouldn't trust him.' Gwenhwyfar said. They ascended the old stairs that had a secret and disused feel to them. 'I remember the first time I saw him. He just stared at my chest. It was so creepy, you know? Like he was imagining me naked, that sort of look.'

'*Vile*,' contributed Emily.

'Well then, it's best he was shown to be a creep sooner rather than later.' Viola offered them a quick smile, and then they slipped into their lesson apologetically.

They were getting a practice paper back that day, and as they arrived their results were waiting on their desks. This led to a hurried exchange of grades among all students, leaving Viola, and Gwenhwyfar in particular, disappointed that they hadn't done better. As their classmates complained about the difficulty of the paper, Emily said nothing, and Gwenhwyfar assumed that she had done the worst. This assumption was dashed, however, the moment Viola asked Emily how she had done.

'Oh, not as well as I'd hoped,' said Emily, flicking her hair over her shoulder. 'I only got eighty-five percent. I was hoping for at least ninety. Geography's my worst subject. I'm so *behind*.'

It was halfway through the lesson when the lights went out again. Huffing and rising to check the corridor, Miss Barnes vanished for a moment to see that the failure wasn't just local.

'So what are you going to do about Hector?' Viola asked Gwen, as Emily twisted around in her seat to face them. 'Are you going to talk to Ravioli?'

'I need to think about it,' Gwenhwyfar frowned. 'I haven't seen him since Lance's party. This could be nothing. Going to Rav might just give him the satisfaction of getting what he wants—of knowing I'm afraid.'

'What's his problem with you, anyway?' Emily asked.

'He's annoyed that Bedivere told the principal what happened at Tom's, and that I spoke to Ravioli about it. Apparently it's *my fault* that he can't go to college.'

'Boys can be such beasts, can't they?' Emily said. Her blue eyes wandered off to some unseen point.

'I still think you should tell someone,' Viola murmured. She bent her head low, and Gwenhwyfar moved closer. 'That's not the only thing worrying me. It's the New Moral Army. What if someone catches on to the fact you all went to that march?'

'You don't think…?'

'I won't tell, Marvin won't, and neither will Tom. But what if someone *does* find out? You heard what Milton said. I mean, after the explosions, I thought it might be a good thing, but now that I've had time to think about it… Gavin's right. Whose morals? The New Nationals are hardly ones for freedom of expression. I'm worried that in looking for members of *Free Countries*, they'll find out who went to the protest, too.'

'What can they do? We wore disguises. We were careful. I don't know about Gwen but I made sure no one could link me to that march. I even made sure I had an alibi.'

'*Free Countries* wasn't actually involved,' Gwenhwyfar told them quietly. She glanced to the door, but Miss Barnes was still absent, and the noise of their classmates blanketed their whispering.

Viola frowned at her. 'How do you know?'

'Gavin told me,' she lied. 'He read it on one of those encrypted websites of his. Besides, they blamed it on the separatists first, remember? It's only now they're saying it was *Free Countries*. All they did was raise awareness for the event through flyers.' She hesitated, and glanced over her shoulder. Miss Barnes returned to quieten the buzz. The lights were still out. 'As far as I know, *Free Countries* don't even take part in protests. They're too concerned about keeping themselves off the heightened surveillance list.'

'But if the New Morals think they are…'

'They can think all they want,' Gwenhwyfar insisted, 'but if it's not true, and if there's no physical link between the two, we're safe.'

Safe. Her heart began to race at the thought. The others were safe, but she wasn't. For a moment she wanted to confess to everything, as if that might make the fear go away, but the words stuck like thorns in her throat.

She couldn't tell anyone, not ever. She thought perhaps if she changed the events in her mind, they would change in reality, too. *It never happened.* She had never heard of *Free Countries*. As Miss Barnes settled the class she repeated the thought until she fooled herself into believing it was true.

The day had been long, but at last it was over. Eager to get home as quickly as possible, Arthur hurried through the outskirts of Logres, his lips stinging with each cold breath. It was dark now, but the streetlights were lit, staring gloomily down at the pavement with their yellow eyes. He stopped off at the kiosk on his way through town and bought what was left from the day's lunch run: a chicken salad with a wrap and, feeling generous, a chocolate sundae with a packaged spoon. Absently Arthur wondered if the homeless woman had somewhere to sleep, one of those shelters perhaps that were struggling to stay open.

Should he bring an extra blanket next time? He wasn't sure if his grandmother had one that wouldn't be missed. Perhaps he should just ask the woman if there was anything he could do to help, but he was weary of the risk. The police patrolled these streets on a regular basis, and after work the Watchmen were usually out in anticipation of their late-night shift.

He was walking down a quieter side road on his way to his drop when he saw them, a group of boys a few years older than him, clustered together on the pavement. A quick survey counted five. They were jeering.

Instinctively Arthur crossed the street. It was best not to get too close. Even if such groups weren't looking for trouble, they were often aware of their presence and took delight in intimidating others. The laughing greatened. One of the lads pushed at something with his foot.

'Illegal scum,' the youth said unashamedly. 'What you doing sitting on our doorstep? We own this doorstep, it belongs to the British.' He bent down and reached for something. Quickly he retracted. 'God, she *stinks*.'

'Stinks of piss,' said another.

'Did you piss yourself? Probably did. Old bag.'

'Show us your tits—come on,' demanded the third. He reached for something. The others laughed.

'She's an illegal,' said the first again. He kicked something, hard. 'Shouldn't be here. Lazy cockroach. Ugh, she smells more when you kick her. *Disgusting.*'

There was a person huddled at their feet, wrapped up in an old blanket. Arthur stopped, stayed by shock, and then anger. He stood planted to the spot as the boys laughed again. One had an umbrella and was poking at the unfortunate human as if it were already a corpse.

He crossed the road without looking. 'Hey!' They didn't hear. '*Hey!*'

Two police officers appeared at the end of the street. Arthur flagged them. They hurried over, flanking him as he brought them to the scene. The boys split, but stood their ground. Arthur's heart dropped the moment he saw the terrified woman's face. It was the woman he'd been helping.

She probably looked older than she was. She was weathered from excessive wind, sun and rain, and her wiry hair had greyed before its time. Her chin was square, and she had a tired, gaunt face that stared up at them all with yellowed eyeballs.

The two officers left no room for intervention. The first stepped into the circle and eyed the teenagers.

'What's going on here?'

'Rough-sleeper,' one of the boys said, matter-of-factly. 'Probably an illegal.'

'No,' Arthur objected. 'They were kicking this woman, and spitting on her.'

'We were not,' the first boy said.

'What were you doing, then?' the officer asked.

He shrugged. 'She's an illegal.'

The police officer looked from the boy to Arthur. His colleague helped the woman to her feet. She dropped the few belongings that she had been clutching onto the concrete.

'She might be an illegal,' the second officer said. He took a sniff near the woman's head and drew back sharply. 'Definitely homeless.'

The first officer stepped closer, his manner stiff. 'You got an address?' The woman eyed him without comprehension. 'Proof of address—you got proof of your address? B.I.D.? Where's your B.I.D. card?'

This produced no results. The officer turned to the rest of them.

'B.I.D.s, now.'

Arthur fumbled for his identity card as the other boys made sounds of protest. The officer pulled out a reader hooked in his belt and scanned each one. When he was done, he waved Arthur and the teenagers away.

'You can go.'

'But wait—they were kicking her. I saw it.'

'Were they kicking you?'

'No, but—'

'Did they spit on *you*?'

'No, they—'

Shaking his head, the officer waved the group onwards. Emboldened, they sauntered down the street. One or two of them made crude gestures for Arthur's benefit. The officers gathered about the woman like crows, one tapping on his scanner, the other holding her arm so that she couldn't leave.

'What's your name?'

Silence.

'Where are you from? Do you speak English?'

'She's retarded,' claimed the second officer. 'Doesn't understand a thing.'

'Probably just not speaking so we don't hear her accent,' the first officer drawled. He sighed, as if he had been put at great inconvenience. 'Definitely an illegal. Come on then, you're coming with us.'

They manhandled her away from the step. Her blanket fell to the floor and was stepped on. Suddenly the woman caught Arthur's gaze and her eyes were filled with panic.

'Wait!' Arthur trailed them as they marched up the street. 'She's not an illegal—she has an address. She has my address. She lives with me.'

The officers ignored him. They were taking the woman to their patrol car. She stumbled with each forced step.

'She lives with me! She just can't talk because she's mute. We have the papers for her and everything. She's on medication—'

'You're willing to vouch for this woman?' The first officer turned to him. His partner opened the back seat passenger door.

Arthur nodded fervently. 'Yes, I know her.'

'You know her?' The first officer pointed a clean finger at the grimy woman. 'You live with her, you have papers for her.'

He wanted to say yes, but words failed him. Instead, Arthur nodded.

'You understand that attempting to prevent the arrest of an illegal is a felony.'

He said nothing. Suddenly his heart was racing and his palms were sweating. The officer squared closer.

'You understand that giving false information to a police

officer is cause enough for us to take you in with her.'

Arthur felt powerless. He couldn't get arrested, what would he do? Who would bail him out? Who would look after his grandmother? There was a thick silence. Both officers eyed him critically.

'You're just a young lad, so I'm going to ask you again.' The door was shut; the woman was jerked away from his partner and presented for Arthur to inspect like some ad-hoc line up. 'Do you know this woman?'

Her eyes were deep-set, ringed in hollowed sockets that made her seem sadder. She was appealing to him, appealing for help; though clearly not sure of the finer workings of the situation; only that she was in trouble, that she was in the hands of those who she should avoid; that she was there because someone had called the police and flagged them over. That someone was staring right back at her.

'Well?'

'No,' he said, so quietly that he had to clear his throat and repeat it. 'No, I don't know this woman.'

They didn't say anything as they bundled her into the back of the car. Arthur stepped away from the vehicle as both police officers got in the front, screwing their faces up with distaste the moment they were but half in.

'Fucking *stinks*,' they muttered, as they slammed the doors shut. Arthur lingered to watch as the car pulled away from the kerb. How had this happened? But he knew what they were like—of course they would take her in. He was an idiot. He should have intervened himself, got into a fight—perhaps then she would have had time to slip away while the police broke up the ruckus. Perhaps he should have done nothing at all.

He would think of this many times in the years to come, his failure, his cowardice and self-interest. He should have made more of a fuss. He should have been outraged. He should have done *something*.

THE CAMPAIGN

'To me, to me!'

Gavin huffed as the ball shot straight at him, and with a kick he sent it flying past the goalkeeper. An eruption of victory cries sounded from his team. Not quite able to mimic Lancelot's somersault, he ran about screaming. Lancelot met him mid-pitch, hooked his neck and violently ruffled his hair.

'Gav, that was brilliant!'

'Cheers,' he laughed.

They shoved one another and staggered apart. Lancelot surveyed the field. 'Where the hell is Tom?'

'Taking a break.' Gavin brushed off his uniform. 'Oi, Tommy! Get back on the pitch and stop being such a pansy!'

Their friend waved at them, then held his hand to his ear, taunting.

'I said, "Stop being such a pansy!"' Gavin bellowed, his words booming across the sparsely populated field. The gesture was replicated and, scowling, Gavin cast out a profanity that Tom also claimed not to hear.

They jogged briskly to join him at the other end of the pitch. Overhead, a military aircraft thundered past. Tom sat huffing, his arms draped over his knees.

'It's the New Morals, Gav. Coming to get you.'

'Don't even joke,' Gavin remarked, watching the jet get smaller and smaller as it passed over the horizon. 'It might well be.'

'Told you we shouldn't have gone,' Lancelot muttered, crouching down to the compact earth. 'It was idiotic.'

'It was necessary. What else were we supposed to do?'

'Do? It *did* nothing. Just got some scapegoats fired.' He shrugged, and pushed at Tom. 'Come on, the game's not over yet. We're winning, for once.'

'I'm fine here!' Tom insisted. 'I'm an artist, not an athlete.'

'You're a slob, that's what,' Lancelot countered. 'You should at least try. Just run around a bit.'

'Or stand still on the pitch, if you prefer.' Gavin sat and sucked in a deep breath. Despite the biting chill, his back was glazed in sweat and his shirt stuck uncomfortably to his skin. Lancelot sprang up, as controlled in his movements as a wild cat.

'Don't you want to keep in shape? You know, so you can hold on to your model girlfriend.'

'Yeah, you can't protect her like this,' Gavin bantered.

'Protect her?' Tom's voice filled with concern. 'From what?'

'From better-looking men, of course,' Lancelot mocked. 'The guys have been going on about her all week.'

'Who told them?' he barked.

'Rupert, I think,' Gavin remarked, still following the game.

'I *told* him not to say anything!'

'The whole school probably knows by now,' said Gavin. 'Well

done.'

'I didn't think it would be an issue if *one* person knew,' Tom countered. 'He shouldn't have told anyone.'

'Well then, go and chase Rupert down instead,' Lancelot added. 'That'll sort you out. He's even on the other team.'

'I can't, I have to rehearse for tomorrow. This is an important gig. I've booked the practice rooms for tonight. Can we do another run-through?'

Lancelot shrugged. 'Sure.'

There was a moment's silence. Gavin looked up at Lancelot as he half-danced about on his feet. 'So what are we going to do about Hector?'

'Nothing. It's up to Gwen if she wants to report it or not.'

'Except the threat was directed at you.'

'Yeah, but it was obviously meant for her,' Lancelot disputed.

'I kind of feel like this whole thing just got blown wildly out of proportion.'

Lancelot and Gavin both looked to Tom. Gavin frowned. 'What do you mean?'

'Hector. I mean, as far as he knew Gwen was up for it. Seems unfair he should be suspended over something he didn't go through with.'

Gavin looked at Lancelot. He was still now, completely still, and he watched Tom intently.

'He went for her at Lance's party—remember? There was no misunderstanding then. Lance said he had another boy with him.'

'I know *that*,' Tom added, 'and I'm not saying what he did was right, not at all. It's just… this is the second time this has happened. She must have done something to encourage it.'

'What, you mean that she was *asking for it*?' Gavin said,

appalled.

'No! Of course not, but—'

'Then what?'

'All I'm saying is that she should be more careful. There are things women can do to avoid it.'

Lancelot shook his head in disbelief. 'I'm sorry, do you walk around wearing a Kevlar vest?' he asked, his voice laced with anger. 'No? Well, I guess by your logic, it's *your* fault if you get murdered, then.'

'Tom?'

Scowling, Tom looked up. 'What?'

'You're an idiot.' Gavin pushed him, and Tom shoved him back. Gavin pushed him again, and this time Tom fell over. As they sat in silence, Lancelot stalked about with hunched shoulders. Eventually Gavin stood up to rejoin the game, and stretching, glanced towards Logres, which stood bruised under the hanging clouds. 'Who's that?'

Hawk-like, Lancelot studied the approaching figures. Tom twisted round in an effort to see, though his frown only thickened. 'Is it the girls?'

'Emily,' Lancelot breathed, his voice filled with dread.

'Maybe she's come for a snog?' Tom's eyebrows curved up sardonically.

'Who else?' Gavin asked.

'Viola,' Lancelot added. His voice wavered. 'And Gwen.'

'Should I be worried?' Tom asked as he stood next to Gavin. The three girls began to run.

'Something must have happened,' Lancelot said. 'Do you think it could be Hector?'

Exchanging glances, they set off. The girls tore towards them, and soon Viola was flying ahead. Tom only had a second to brace himself before she jumped into his arms. Laughing, she let go as Emily and Gwenhwyfar caught up.

'I can't believe it,' she gasped, 'I just had to tell you!'

'Tell me what? Is everything OK?'

'Everything's fine. It's brilliant! You'll never guess.'

'Guess what?'

'Do you remember that casting for *Bare Make-up*? Well, I got it! I got the job! It's a campaign! They'll be paying me twenty-eight *thousand*; can you believe it? Oh, but you mustn't tell anyone, you hear me? I'm serious Tom, no one can know. I don't want everyone thinking I'm rich now.'

'But you *are* rich,' Emily pointed out. 'What if this is just the first job of many? You'll be *loaded*, Vi.'

'I just wish I had that much!' Gwenhwyfar exclaimed. 'You're so lucky!'

'Twenty-eight thousand?' Gavin repeated, astonished. He looked to Lancelot, who frowned, but said nothing.

Grinning, Tom snaked his arm around her waist. 'That's brilliant, Vi. I'm proud of you. Well done.'

Viola smiled, and pressed into him with a happy kiss.

'Out, out, brief candle! Life's but a walking shadow, a poor player that struts and frets his hour upon the stage and then is heard no more: it is a tale told by an idiot, full of sound and fury, signifying nothing.'

Tom glanced, agitated, at the clock. Julie studied him expectantly, waiting for him to continue. The eyes of her other students were settled upon him.

'Thou comest to use thy tongue; thy story quickly.'

The other reader, red and sweating in anticipation of her turn, blurted out her line so quickly that no one understood it.

'Slower please, Charlie,' Julie interrupted. Charlie took a wavering breath and started again.

'*Gracious my lord, I should report—*'

The bell rang. Immediately Charlie sat down.

'Aww—!' Tom exclaimed, lowering his book with impatience. 'I didn't even get to the good bit!'

'Time's up!' Julie declared. 'I don't know about everyone else, but I'd quite like to get to lunch sometime soon, wouldn't you?'

'Can I read next lesson?'

She marked the page of her copy and set it to one side. 'It's Jack's turn to read for Macbeth, next. You've already done it twice.'

Grumbling, Tom sat amongst his packing classmates. Julie eyeballed those already standing.

'Did I say you were dismissed yet? Homework! I want you all to examine and translate Tom's—*Macbeth's*—last speech. No minimum word count, just as long as it takes for you to feel you've done all you can. Understood?'

With a few nods and with most students craning in their seats towards the door, Julie finally let them go. Viola followed Tom into the corridor, but then turned back towards her as she gathered her belongings at the front of the class.

'Miss?' she asked, once the room was empty. 'I was wondering if I could talk to you for a moment.'

Julie hoisted her over-packed satchel onto her shoulder and gathered up the other papers that wouldn't fit. 'Of course. What can I help you with?'

'Well, I have news.'

She could sense her excitement, and immediately knew what it was that she was talking about. 'Do you mind if we walk and talk?'

'Not at all,' Viola said casually. She hung her coat over her crossed arms. 'It's nothing important.'

Julie walked her out of the classroom and locked the door in silence, conscious of the camera looming above their heads. They were usually positioned at the end of each corridor to cover every corner, but Marvin had told her that because of this they often failed to catch quiet conversations held in the long stretches between them—particularly when there were other students still bustling in the halls.

'So tell me,' Julie murmured when it was safe. 'Is this to do with your modelling?'

Viola nodded, keeping close to her side. 'I got a job,' she whispered, looking straight ahead. 'A campaign. It pays a lot, more than you can imagine.'

'Oh, brilliant! Well done, I am pleased. What is it for?'

'Have you heard of *Bare Make-up*?' Julie nodded. 'It's a new product that they're launching. I completely wasn't expecting to get it, but my agency said they were keen on me because I'm unknown. I know it's really last minute, but the shoot's tomorrow. I only just found out.'

'You'll miss class?'

'Sorry. It's annoying it's not over the weekend, but if I don't do it, another girl will.'

Julie nudged her as they approached the end of the corridor. They walked in silence again, until they were a suitable distance away from the spying black sphere.

'It is short notice, but you can't not do it; it sounds like a great opportunity.' She offered her a smile. 'Honestly Viola, I have no problem with it so long as you keep up with your class work. And it's only a one-off, right?'

She nodded. 'My agency knows that I'm still in school. Fashion week might be a problem, but I don't think my dad will let me do it with my exams so close.'

'He's right. You can put off a degree until later in life, but you only really get one chance at your Levels. You should be careful. It's great that you're doing the whole modelling thing, but I hear girls feel pressured to smoke to stay thin, and worse. I don't want you getting sucked into any of that, or for you to rack up some huge debt with some agency that you can't pay off.'

'I know, miss,' Viola said dutifully. 'The money shouldn't be a problem though, especially not since I've got a job already.'

'And that's great, but I wouldn't go spending any of it until it's clear you're going to get something else. And you remember what I said—the moment you don't feel good about yourself because of the modelling—'

'I'll stop, I know.'

Julie looked to her imploringly. 'You promise?'

'Yes. You've said all this before.'

'I know.' Julie hesitated as they passed into the main foyer outside the assembly hall. 'I just worry about you. How is your dad?'

'He's good.'

'And Bert?'

'Still making his fortune selling at the London markets,' she said fondly. 'My dad's coming to the shoot, I have to have a guardian with me.'

Julie frowned. 'Do your other teachers know about it yet?'

Viola shook her head. 'No one else knows that I'm modelling.'

'And the principal?'

'I was going to speak to him, but the earliest appointment I could get was for next week. I was wondering if I should mention it to him tonight, rather than going off sick.'

'No, I wouldn't do that,' Julie murmured. 'If you tell him now, you could find yourself in a very difficult situation. Just pay for a sick note.'

Viola seemed surprised. 'You're saying I should skive?'

'If you can't miss it. How much did you say it was again?'

'A lot.'

'Well, if you're getting paid *a lot*, do you really want to run the risk of the principal saying no? If you call in sick when he knows about the shoot, you'll be looking at suspension faster than you can say *cheese*.'

Viola sniggered. 'Miss, that was terrible.'

'I know, it was, wasn't it?'

They came to a halt outside the Wormelow staff room. The door was shut, but already several of her colleagues were inside. The building had begun to empty, leaving only a few avid studiers to gather at the doors to the small library down the hall.

'Pop by after lunch,' she said, secretly pleased that she had been chosen as Viola's confidant. 'I'll give you your homework for Friday.'

'So I shouldn't talk to the principal?'

'I would still go and see him next week. Part of me thinks that he'll like the prestige of having a model boosting the achievements of the school, but I do know how strict he is with attendance. It might be a case of no exceptions.'

'Right. He did get twitchy with Tom's record when he had glandular fever last year.'

Julie offered an encouraging smile. 'Don't worry about it yet. You just go to this thing and have a fantastic time. Let me know when you get the pictures. I can't wait to see them.'

Viola's face lit up once again and she nodded fervently. 'I will.'

They parted just in time. Mr Slow came trundling down the corridor and the staff room door was opened by Andrew Graham, who, delighted to see her, let Julie in with an exclamation and an immediate reference to one of the New National's latest policies.

History was Gwenhwyfar's last lesson of the day. They were each given a practice paper to complete, though as the holidays were approaching Marvin let them discuss their answers with one another while he read with his feet up. Gwenhwyfar spent most of the lesson whispering to either Bedivere or Arthur. Despite making her usual effort with Morgan, the other girl seemed happy to be left alone.

The sky was darkening as the school day ended. Gwenhwyfar had just passed through the main gates when a tight hand grasped her wrist. She wheeled round. Isolde.

'Get off me!' She smacked her on the forearm. Retreating, Isolde reached for her again.

'Gwen, wait! I need to talk to you.'

'Leave me *alone*.' Gwenhwyfar backed away. 'I don't want to talk to you ever again. I'm done; do you hear me? I'm *out*.'

'I'm not here to make you stay, I swear. I just wanted to talk—please?'

'We have nothing to talk about,' she snapped, walking away as quickly as she could without running.

'But we do,' Isolde argued, dogging her steps. 'It won't take long.'

'How did you even find me?' she hissed. 'Have you been following me?'

'Of course not—I used to go here, remember? I didn't know what else to do. Your phone goes straight to answer machine and when I tried contacting you online I got disconnected.'

'I changed my number,' she stated. 'Specifically so you wouldn't try and contact me. What if someone finds out? Tracks you down and then discovers me?'

'They won't,' she insisted.

'How can you say that?' Gwenhwyfar demanded, irate.

'If they could, don't you think they would have done it already? If they knew who was responsible for the bombings, they would have caught them by now.'

She wheeled round on her. 'Haven't you been watching the news? They *know* it was us.'

Isolde rubbed her eyes. She looked ill. 'I know. I swear though—if you let me explain now, I'll never bother you again. I had nothing to do with any of this.'

'And why should I believe you?' she flared. 'What's to say you're not one of the ones who have gone to the New Morals already? Who's to say you're not baiting me?'

'I'm taking a risk here, too. There's every chance you could turn me in,' she argued.

Gwenhwyfar hunted their surroundings for signs of anything suspicious. 'If I talk to you, you'll leave me alone?'

'If that's what you want.'

'Fine. Where's safe? A coffee house?'

'There might be people watching,' Isolde disagreed. 'Here?'

Gwenhwyfar nodded towards a camera gazing at them from

the street corner.

Isolde frowned. 'My house—?'

'No. We'll go to mine.' Gwenhwyfar turned on her heel and resumed her walk home.

The entire journey was made in silence. Thankfully, her mother wasn't in and so difficult questions were avoided. Only Llew was present to witness affairs. He shoved his nose under Isolde's hand, vying for attention. Betrayed by his willingness to trust anyone, Gwenhwyfar dragged him away to sit by her instead, pushing his rear end down to the carpet.

'Well?'

Isolde sat uncomfortably at the far end of the room. 'Firstly, I just want to say that I had no idea about any of this until I saw it on the news,' she began. Gwenhwyfar experienced a flare of irritation that she felt privileged to, as one who had actually been there. 'And that since then I've met other members who are just as scared as us.'

'I thought this was all highly confidential?' Gwenhwyfar frowned, clutching Llew's collar. 'How did you find them?'

'By going up through the grapevine,' she explained. 'Everyone I spoke to found each other the same way.'

Gwenhwyfar felt her veins contract. 'You didn't mention me to any of them, did you?'

'I wouldn't do that without asking you first. I didn't tell anyone, I swear.'

'Well, that's something at least.' Gwenhwyfar glanced at the clock with agitation. She didn't want Isolde to still be here when her mother came home.

'The people I met... none of them had a clue what was going on. We tried to get higher up the vine, but the numbers we had weren't recognised.'

'They probably destroyed their phones. I can't say I'm surprised.'

'They must have deserted us. The chain's broken. Now there's no way of us ever knowing what it was the Alpha intended.'

Gwenhwyfar couldn't say she was deeply upset by this idea. Isolde, however, seemed distressed.

'It's funny, you know. Most of the people I met were under thirty. They were all clueless. There's no way a group with members like that—no matter how large—could have ever organised something as brutal as this.'

Gwenhwyfar held her tongue, scraping her nails into Llew's fur. Her mind entertained the notion of calling the New Moral Army to let them know she had a wanted member of *Free Countries* in her living room. Perhaps then she too could be granted clemency.

'I'm sorry I got you dragged into this.'

'I chose to join,' Gwenhwyfar snapped. 'You didn't make me.'

'I'm still sorry,' Isolde said. 'I should have known it was suspicious. I mean, how long have I been a member? Nine months? And not once have I heard anything from anyone other than the odd update concerning codenames, the occasional checks and possible recruits. We've done nothing to protest Milton's policies. It's been such a waste, and in the end, what did all this secrecy produce? Fear.'

'And what would you have done in protest, exactly?' Gwenhwyfar asked, holding the accusation on the tip of her tongue.

'*Anything.* We could have campaigned, we could have created our own political party with the members we had, but now it's gone to waste. We're being blamed for something we didn't do.'

'How do you know we didn't do it? We might in some way be responsible merely by supporting such ideals. The government seems to think so.'

'As far as I remember, that list I read you didn't involve us blowing things up. If *Free Countries* was responsible, we would have heard of it when it was in the stages of being planned.'

'I doubt it,' Gwenhwyfar snorted. 'And anyway, is this the sort of plan you'd expect to hear about? A terrorist attack?' She pulled Llew closer to her as he whined. It was completely dark now, and he was pining for a trip into the garden.

'Of course not, but don't you think it's a little odd? Why would the Alpha spend all those years gathering members to risk losing them to panic like this? The news said people are coming forward with information. Maybe they knew nothing about *Free Countries* to begin with. Maybe they just wanted to know who, what, and how many.'

'So? For all we know the Alpha is just a psycho who likes blowing people up for fun,' she bit, hackles raised. 'I don't care about your stupid little conspiracy theories, and I don't care who's responsible. All I know is that I'm *not*.'

Isolde sat tight-lipped.

'Don't tell me you're thinking of staying involved. You can't!'

'Why can't I?' she disputed.

'Because it's crazy?'

'I'm not giving up. The New Nationals are just trying to scare us. There's no way we were responsible for those attacks.'

'And I suppose the Alpha himself told you this? When? Or was it in a dream?' Gwenhwyfar sneered. 'Don't you go thinking he won't give everyone up the moment they catch him,' she warned. 'He's obviously a coward if he's been keeping quiet for this long. What do you think will happen when they get him? He'll give up every number, every address he ever received.'

'Well, he won't give up yours,' Isolde said. 'I never passed on your number. I should've got it when we first met, but I forgot, remember? After that party I didn't get the chance to send it to him.'

For a few brief moments Gwenhwyfar felt gratitude flood her system. 'You mean he never got it?' Isolde affirmed this with a shake of her head. 'He'll have yours, though?'

'Yes.'

'Then I suggest you get rid of it, if you don't want to get caught.'

She shrugged, an air of resignation about her. 'It won't make a difference. You'll be all right, that guy you recruited too—because the Alpha never got your numbers. Everyone else is done for. They'll know whose names were listed to what number, along with where they live and where they were for all those years.' She gave a strained smile. 'You're lucky.'

'But what about addresses?' Gwenhwyfar frowned. 'You must have my house listed somewhere for an information pack to have been sent here.'

'We send flyers to every house in the South,' Isolde shrugged. 'How will they ever know what we posted? Besides, I was talking with a contact involved with the technical team. Apparently, if he knew an IP address, he knew where that computer was stationed. Every time someone visited the site the corresponding address was put onto an encrypted hard-drive. The Alpha had no copy. That's why it was entrusted to those involved in the communication, so that if the Alpha was ever discovered the drives could be destroyed. He wrecked his in a microwave.'

'Surely he can't have been the only one with addresses?' Gwenhwyfar let Llew go, and he trotted into the kitchen. She heard him whine.

'There were several people with his role, some in different counties. He said that the best we can hope for is that everyone else thought to destroy their drive, too.'

Gwenhwyfar's head swam with everything that had gone wrong, but her nerves were beginning to calm under the belief that she would be safe.

'Maybe the Alpha has some way of wiping his records,' she tried, becoming aware of the terror Isolde must be suffering. 'If he was smart enough to organise all this, he must have taken precautions. There might not even be a hard copy of the numbers.' Her suggestion was unlikely, but it seemed to offer Isolde some comfort. 'What about the people coming forward? What if they give away the contacts they have?'

'I don't think there's much we can do about that. All I know is that the people I've spoken to are lying low. As far as our details go, assuming that the Alpha never gets caught, we should—hopefully—be safe.'

Gwenhwyfar nodded in silence.

'I put my computer's drive in the microwave last night along with my phone. My parents went crazy. I had to make up some excuse about a Science project.'

Suddenly Gwenhwyfar felt an urgency to do the same, but it was too late. 'It doesn't matter. I'm out, Isolde. That guy I met is gone too. We're both escaping while we still have the chance.'

'I suppose it's best. I'm thinking of starting something new with those other contacts, but we're going to wait until this has all settled down.'

Gwenhwyfar thought she was insane.

'In the meantime we'll just have to lay low, pretend that we're not afraid, act as if nothing's happened.' Her fingers toyed with the gold necklace around her throat. 'Then they won't suspect us.'

'I don't need you to tell me what to do,' Gwenhwyfar said stiffly, rising to her feet. Llew barked by the back door.

'I wanted to ask if you'd be a part of it,' she dared.

'I think you should leave.'

'We can't let them win, Gwen. Doesn't it make you angry that they can just lie like this?'

'You can't prove they're lying,' she countered, ushering her towards the door.

'No, but they can't prove that they're not.' Llew yapped again and then proceeded to expel a long series of whines.

'You should go—I have to let Llew out.'

'You won't even consider it?'

'I'm not interested.'

'But—'

'Go, would you? It's too dangerous. You need to leave before my parents get home. I don't want to lie to them again.' Gwenhwyfar pushed past Isolde and opened the door.

'Just think about it, that's all I'm asking,' she said, clutching her bag.

'Leave, now.'

She slammed the door shut the moment Isolde was through it. As Llew whimpered again from the kitchen Gwenhwyfar let out a cry of vexation. Striding to the back door with hard stomps, she ripped it open and let him loose into the murk.

The Oxymorons

The winter air nipped at his lips. Hanging within a pale sky, the sun bled meekly through the thick fog that sat heavy on the ground. Arthur sucked in a deep breath, feeling the bitter moisture chill his lungs. He was glad to be outside. As he blew on his hands for warmth, his thoughts turned to the holidays ahead, anticipating a quiet Christmas with his grandmother. He eyed the old entrance to Wormelow, hoping to catch Gwenhwyfar on her way out from class.

'Arthur?' Morgan appeared through the double doors. She was wearing a thick woollen hat that folded over her ears, and her chestnut hair was neatly plaited in a single braid. 'Marvin's looking for you. He wants to know if you've joined that political party.'

He didn't appreciate being pressured. 'Not yet, I was going to do it this weekend. I'll let him know tonight.'

'But I told him I'd come and get you,' Morgan objected.

'Well, he'll just have to wait, won't he? I'm meeting Gwen for break. I promised I'd sit with her.'

'Oh.' Morgan's thick eyebrows met in a frown, and she looked back to the building. 'Well, you might have just missed her. I saw her with Viola. They were talking about meeting Lance in the canteen.'

'I hear you're taking life drawing classes?' Arthur smiled politely.

'Actually, I'm meeting Percy for break. I usually sit with him now.' She sent him a brief smile. 'And his friends. They're really nice.'

'I'm sure they are.'

'I think you'd like them.'

'You do?' Morgan nodded. Arthur searched past the cars and bikes, hoping to catch a glimpse of Gwenhwyfar.

'Percy's taking me to Lance's gig tonight,' Morgan said, her breath clouding about her lips. Her squared face brightened. 'You know, the one in the warehouse?'

Arthur frowned, turning to her suddenly. 'What about the club?'

'I've already asked Marvin if we can miss it. He doesn't mind.'

There was an awkward silence. 'So how's it going with Percy?'

Morgan coloured. 'Good. He's really nice, don't you think?'

Despite himself, Arthur nodded. 'Marvin seems to like him.' He stuffed his hands in his pockets. 'So you won't be at the club? That's fine. I'm sure Gwen, Bed and I will cope without you for one week.'

'Actually, Bedivere's not going either.' She smiled up at him apologetically. 'Neither is Gavin. We're all going to see Lance play.'

'Don't tell me it's cancelled?'

'Not if Gwenhwyfar's still going.' She gave him a look, and

Arthur wasn't entirely sure what it meant.

'Well, does Marvin know that we'll be there, at least?'

'Ask him,' Morgan shrugged, turning her head away to gaze across the car park. The second bell rang. 'I'd better go; Percy will be waiting for me. I'll see you on Monday?'

Arthur nodded, but said nothing. His mouth had gone dry.

'Want to walk with me?'

'Actually, I think I'll go and see Marvin,' he excused, offering an empty smile. 'Have fun tonight.'

'I will.' Grinning, Morgan left him on his own and joined the crowd of students streaming out of Wormelow. Arthur waited for a few moments before walking on behind her, mindful to keep out of sight.

Determined that she shouldn't be left on her own, Arthur managed to meet with Gwenhwyfar, but only just. Lancelot annoyed him with every word he uttered, but wasn't unpleasant enough to warrant getting into an argument. Throughout Psychology he found himself wondering why Morgan's attachment to Percy bothered him, eventually settling on the theory that he merely felt she could do better. When he arrived at the benches by the mobile classrooms for lunch to find Lancelot and Gwenhwyfar talking amicably, his irritation increased.

'Hey,' Gwenhwyfar beamed. Arthur dropped his bag and sat down opposite them. 'We were just talking about Vi. I got a text from her—apparently the shoot's going really well.'

'Good.' Arthur unpacked his lunch. The air was bitter, but now that the fog had cleared the sun warmed him slightly. 'Have you decided if you're going to speak to Ravioli yet?'

Gwenhwyfar shook her head. 'I'm not sure if I should.'

Arthur frowned. 'Why not?'

'I don't think it'll do any good. Even if Ravioli does take it seriously, Hector's not going to admit to threatening me. We can't prove it was him. It's just speculation.'

'Well-founded speculation,' Arthur argued.

'I know. But Lance thinks it's all just talk.'

'Does he, now?'

'Yeah,' Lancelot confirmed. 'They used to say this sort of thing all the time, Edward and that lot. Nothing ever came from it then, either.'

Arthur appealed to Gwenhwyfar. 'I still think it would be worth mentioning it to a member of staff. Even if you just tell them what he did at Lance's party.'

'She'll be fine,' Lancelot dismissed. 'We'll make sure that Hector doesn't get anywhere near her. Won't we?'

Arthur struggled to keep his temper in check. 'And how are *we* going to do that, exactly?'

'It's not hard. We just make sure Gwen's never alone.'

He didn't know why, but this upset him. 'What—here, there and everywhere? What about when she's walking home? With all his friends involved?'

Lancelot shrugged. 'I can handle them.'

'What's your plan?' Arthur bit. 'Violence?'

'It's worked for me so far.'

Arthur looked to Gwenhwyfar. 'Can you believe this? It's that sort of attitude that made Hector threaten you all in the first place.'

'What sort of attitude?' Gwenhwyfar asked, already scowling.

'The kind where people gallivant around smashing each other's teeth in!'

'I'm still here,' Lancelot growled.

'Unfortunately,' snapped Arthur.

'I said I'd handle it.'

'So I heard.'

'I can protect her.'

Arthur rose abruptly. 'She's not yours to protect!'

Lancelot sprung up to match him. 'Well, *someone* has to do it. You seem to be clueless.'

'Clueless about what—? Beating people to a pulp?'

His mouth distorted to bare his teeth. 'In a way.'

'If you're offering yourself as practice, Lake, I'd be more than happy to learn.'

Gwenhwyfar snapped. 'Stop it! Just sit down, the both of you! You're behaving like children.'

Arthur stared stubbornly at Lancelot. It seemed as if he didn't want to sit first, either.

'*Sit!*'

'You should probably listen to him, Gwen,' Lancelot remarked, snidely. He sat down after Arthur did. 'Arty knows best.'

'I don't want to tell the principal, all right? This is *my* choice. It doesn't mean I'm never going to tell someone. If I see Hector again, or if he comes even the slightest bit near me, I'm going straight to Ravioli—and the police—immediately. I'm not *stupid*.'

Huffing, she picked up her bag and separated herself from the table. When Arthur rose to follow her, he realised that Lancelot did too.

'No,' she scolded. 'I need some time to think by myself. The last thing I want is you two bickering around me. It's insufferable.'

They sank back down as she stormed off to Badbury. Arthur

glared at Lancelot. 'Idiot,' he muttered.

'Berk,' Lancelot retorted, gathering up his bag. Determined not to be the one left on his own, Arthur grabbed his belongings and jumped up as Lancelot did, striding back up to Wormelow. Gwenhwyfar would want to tell if it weren't for Lancelot, he thought blackly. What was she afraid of? Abruptly he resolved to talk to her about it over the weekend. If she still refused he would tell the principal himself first thing on Monday, before Hector made good on his word.

The gathering dusk had sucked all light from the sky. It was colder now, cold and dark, but the streetlights half-lit the way home with their weak homage to the stars. She caught him just outside the school gates; his dark curls restlessly twisting in the wind.

'Lance!' Gwenhwyfar hurried towards him as he waited, the cold stealing her breath. 'I was hoping I'd run into you.'

Her enthusiasm threw him. 'You were? Why?'

'Want to walk home together?'

'Where's home?'

'Near Potters Park. Do you know it?'

'Of course I know it,' snorted Lancelot. 'Let me guess, you live on Upper Well Street? In one of those massive houses?'

'No,' she smiled, 'on High Oak Lane. It's a few streets away.' The two walked together. 'Actually, compared to High Oak, Upper Well is a bit of a dive.'

'All right, all right, I get it. You're a rich snob,' Lancelot smiled. 'At least it's kind of on the way to mine. I'll drop you off.'

Gwenhwyfar pulled her hat down to better cover her ears. 'Where do you live?'

'Like I'm telling you, Miss High Society. My house is probably a shed compared to yours. I'll bet your bedroom is as big as the whole of our downstairs.'

'It is not,' Gwenhwyfar gasped, pushing him on the arm.

'How do you know?' He maintained his balance effortlessly. 'God, you're not still stalking me, are you?'

'Yes. That's exactly what I'm doing now. I'm stalking you.'

'Lucky me.'

'Shut up, Lake.'

His lips curled up into half a grin. 'So how's Arty?'

'Arthur,' she corrected, gazing at him. 'You know how he is. He's fine.'

'Still having a wobbly over telling someone about Hector?' he teased.

'He's just worried. To him it would make sense.' She huddled further into her coat. They were quite far from the school now, and turned another corner on the approach to Potters Park. 'It's a shock to him, that's all. He didn't know.'

'You probably should have told him,' Lancelot agreed. 'But I can see why you didn't. He had a proper hissy fit when you said you didn't want to tell the Nutcracker.'

'That's because you wound him up,' she huffed.

'He wound himself up,' Lancelot dismissed. 'Besides, he's right. You probably should listen to him. He is your *boyfriend*, after all.'

Gwenhwyfar scowled. For a long while they walked in silence. They passed the park and came into the smarter neighbourhoods, with cleaner streets and tidier buildings, and tree-lined avenues that were naked for the winter. She found herself thinking about the day that Lancelot had asked her out, and wondered if he still had feelings for her.

He knew that she was looking at him, she could tell. There was a hint of self-awareness in his countenance. 'What?'

She tugged her eyes away. Now he was staring at her. His arms were bare, with his sleeves rolled up to his elbows. She wondered how he could endure the cold. 'Nothing.'

'No, what?'

'Nothing!' she expelled. Frowning, he looked away. 'It's nothing, really. I was just wondering.'

'Wondering what?' he asked. 'Gwenhwyfar?'

She couldn't get out of it now. 'I probably shouldn't say.' She bit her lip. 'Do you like Emily?'

She almost wished she had gone with what was on her mind. Lancelot surveyed her as if he were a wolf assessing a kill, but his eyes held amusement, as if he suddenly knew her deepest secret.

'Do I fancy Emily?' he repeated. His eyes cut through her. 'Why?'

His question was much too loaded. 'No reason.'

'No?' he asked.

Gwenhwyfar flushed. 'No.'

'Are you sure?'

'Yes,' she replied, strengthening. She looked him in the eye. 'So you do like her.'

His eyebrows only arched. 'Jealous?'

She shot him a sarcastic smile and ploughed ahead. 'Don't be ridiculous.'

They were approaching her street now. Lancelot was looking around. 'So this is your neighbourhood? It's nice.'

'I hate it,' Gwenhwyfar remarked.

'Hate it? Why?'

She shrugged, coming to a drawn out halt. 'I just do.' They stood for a moment in an awkward silence.

'So I guess you're not inviting me in, then.'

'I can't,' she smiled. 'I have to get ready.'

For a moment he seemed to brighten. 'For the gig?'

She shook her head. 'For Arthur. We're going to Marvin's club.'

His eyes darkened at this. Turning his head away, he exposed the line of his neck. Gwenhwyfar's eyes trailed his throat, slinking down to the collar of his shirt. 'Sorry.'

'For what?' he muttered, bored.

'For not coming tonight. I really would have loved to see you play.' She didn't know what to say next. 'Lancelot?'

He turned to look at her. Biting her lip, she stepped towards him. He was still, his whole body taut. She could smell his shower gel from P.E., could detect his muskier undertone masked beneath. He was frowning. He was always frowning.

'Thanks. For walking me.'

He stared at her.

'And good luck. For tonight.'

She left first, and glancing over her shoulder offered a wave too casual for the way she felt. Lancelot lingered for a while, but when she looked again he had turned away, and soon vanished onto the adjoining street.

The venue was a large hall in an estate connected to larger warehouses, with a temporary bar that wouldn't sell to those under twenty-five. The Oxymorons weren't headlining, but their set was in the perfect hour when the crowd was at its freshest. The air was thick, and Tom and Lancelot's foreheads glistened under the spotlights. The crowd lapped up the unusual music, dancing to it nonsensically. Lyrics were sparse but interlinked so expertly that they became one with the sound.

Bedivere couldn't admit to liking the style, but he did appreciate that, musically, they were skilled. Gavin stood next to him, his huge hands clapping out a booming applause, while Emily was on his right, screaming and whooping between each number and the next.

'Did you see that?' she shouted breathlessly, eyes wild. 'Oh my God, they're *amazing*.'

He caught her as she fell into him, helping her find her feet. Someone had been selling solution on the sly.

'What do you think? Do you like them?' she asked, brushing her hair away from her flushed face.

Bedivere nodded and said he did.

'Sorry?' she yelled.

'I said, yes—they're good!'

'Great!'

Gavin bent down towards him and shouted in his ear. 'I'm going to the bar! Want anything?'

He shook his head, already dizzy. Gavin leaned across him.

'Em—?'

'No thanks!' Nodding, Gavin moved off to the bar. 'It's a shame Gwen couldn't make it!' Emily said, as the next song started. 'Where did you say she was again?'

'Out with Arthur!' His throat hurt. Shouting over the sound of the bass was too much. 'On a date!' he lied.

'I'm sorry!'

'What?'

'I said I'm sorry! For what I did!'

He felt his face heat up rapidly, and he was suddenly grateful that it was dark. He didn't like being reminded of Tom's party; still felt like an idiot for falling for what had ultimately been a practical joke. 'Don't worry about it!'

She smiled up at him and nodded, and then waved her arms as she danced to the beat. Bedivere, however, found that he could not move on.

'Why did you do it?' he yelled.

'Do what?'

'Kiss me!'

She looked at him as if he were violating some social norm. 'It was just a kiss,' she shrugged. 'Didn't you like it?'

'Of course, but—'

'Then what's the problem?' She sent him a pink smile. 'I said I was sorry about all that.' She applauded mid-song and then turned, searching. 'Where's Gavin? He's taking ages!'

'Still queuing at the bar,' Bedivere said, unsatisfied. He caught sight of Charlotte some way off in the crowd. Edward Cooper pushed past them, his sleeves rolled up to his elbows. 'So you like Lance?'

She ignored him and looked to the stage.

'Did you really sleep with him?'

'I said I did, didn't I?' she remarked. 'Anyway, what's it to you?'

'I'm going to get some air,' he told her, deafened by the speakers.

'You're going?'

'I'll be back in a bit.'

'You can't leave me on my own,' she protested.

'Come with me, then!'

She frowned at him. 'But they're not done yet!'

'Gavin's over there. Go and find him!'

Bedivere pointed, and Emily turned, looking for the tall boy. He shouldered his way through the tightly packed audience and heard an eruption of cheers as he made it through the door.

It was cooler in the hallway. How could she be so callous? *Just a kiss.* It had been more than that. Bedivere didn't understand how she could have done something so intimate if her heart wasn't in it. But it had just been a joke. *She had slept with Lance.*

The music started up again as the applause faded, and mindlessly he collected his coat from the cloakroom. He came out into the night, scrolling through his contacts. Maybe he should just call his mother and get her to pick him up now. He halted in the middle of the road. He would text Arthur. He and Gwenhwyfar should have left The Round Table by now. They should go out and do something. They hadn't been out in ages.

The lot was almost deserted, filled with empty alleys and storage houses locked up for the night. He waited for a response from Arthur, but there was none. He checked the time. Gavin, he would go back and get Gavin. They could go out, they could leave Emily with Lancelot. She would be happy with that, he thought. He turned around to head back into the venue. A fist to his stomach: a knife through butter. The masked figure held him upright, whispered coldly in his ear.

'Pop goes the weasel.'

NEW MORAL ARMY

Blood. A raw taste: beaten copper across his tongue. Hector held his shoulder, pinching. The knife came out: the hand was gone. A voice barked. Not Hector's. He fell forwards. The barbed fist struck again.

In, out. His phone slipped from his fingers and cracked on the concrete. Another hand, pushed. Folding on yielding knees.

He didn't catch himself. Yelling, and Hector was gone. Backwards he fell, backwards and over, and for a moment he was falling eternally. Is this death? A trip, the trap below. Creeping darkness. A warm blanket on a cold night. A mother's kiss. He saw the sky, but no stars. Blackness: above and below. Hitting the ground, falling through it. A crack. The back of his head on the concrete.

The Round Table was quite relaxed, and as it was just with the three of them, Marvin's topic choices were much less political. They still touched on the New Moral Army and listened to Marvin remark on the press' handling of the Mobilisation Centre scandal, but much of the session was spent discussing their futures and listening to tales of events before their time.

They were encouraged to leave early, gifting them extra time alone. As soon as the door was closed and they were shut out into the night, Gwenhwyfar felt Arthur snake his arm about her waist.

'Do you think Marvin's right about medical school?' she mused. 'I mean, I was thinking about it, but I have no idea if I'll do well enough in my Level Fives and Sixes for that.'

'You should try,' encouraged Arthur. 'How long does it take in total? Seven years?'

'Something like that,' Gwenhwyfar said. 'It can even be twelve or thirteen, depending on what it is you want to do.'

'And what is it that you want to do?' he queried, walking beside her with mismatched steps.

'I don't know. I'm looking at taking a first aid course. They do them at school as an extracurricular module. It would be brilliant to go to medical school,' Gwenhwyfar enthused, bubbling with alcohol-induced excitement. 'I've been doing some research, and they all recommend getting experience as early as possible. Going to study in London would be fantastic.'

'You'll have to start with the work experience right away, then. Most people who want to become medics are already storming ahead by the time they're fourteen.'

'But that's just ridiculous. How can anyone know what they want to do for the rest of their life when they're fourteen?'

For a while they walked in silence, passing through the quieter streets and onto the busier roads.

'Do you want to go to university?'

'If I can afford it.' Arthur squeezed her middle and then let go. They held hands instead. 'I'll apply for a scholarship next year. There are other bursaries as well. The problem is, Bedivere wants them too. The competition is going to be tough.'

'You'll get one,' Gwenhwyfar encouraged. She found herself wondering if Tristan had ever heard about his scholarship. Now that she seemed to be safe from arrest, she wished she had asked. 'Where do you want to go?'

'Oxbridge: whichever will have me. The people who go there have the best prospects.' They turned onto the end of Gwenhwyfar's street, a quiet cul-de-sac with grand townhouses that seemed imposing in the moonlight. 'I'm not even sure what I want to study yet.'

Gwenhwyfar kissed him. She drew him closer and tasted his tongue until they both pulled away, smiling in the streetlight.

'That was unexpected,' Arthur breathed.

She bit her lip, eying him mischievously. 'I couldn't help myself.'

He stooped to kiss her again. Her heart drummed as his fingers pressed gently over her cheeks. 'I have something to give you,' he murmured, holding his head near hers. 'An early Christmas present—I hope you don't mind.'

He produced a small packet from his coat pocket. It was simply wrapped, a rectangle of some sort, and as he handed it to her Gwenhwyfar felt a pang of guilt.

'But I haven't got you yours yet.'

'That's why it's early,' he grinned.

She peeled the paper apart carefully, finding that it separated with little persuasion. Another small packet was revealed, still wrapped. She turned it about in her hands. 'Chocolate?'

'Not just any chocolate,' Arthur stressed, 'real chocolate. The kind you can't get. It's seventy percent. That means that seventy percent of it is made up of the cocoa bean.'

Gwenhwyfar's eyes rose to meet his, comprehending.

'I know it's a bit of a strange present,' Arthur continued, 'but I thought you might like to try some.'

She moved to press their bodies closer. 'It's perfect. Thank you.'

He smiled with relief. 'I was going to give you some of ours, but it seems my grandmother's been nibbling it away over the years. There's not much left.'

'How did you get it?' She hunted for the ingredients and sure enough, in place of *cocoa substitute* was printed *cocoa beans*.

'Marvin,' he boasted. 'The guy he usually buys his wine off had a contact that just intercepted a shipment of chocolate. He mentioned it in passing a few weeks back, and I asked if he could get me some.'

Gwenhwyfar was stunned. Surely she wasn't worthy of this. 'You won't get into trouble, will you?'

'That's the wonderful thing about chocolate.' Arthur took her hands. 'Once you eat it, it's gone.'

'Here.' Smiling, she carefully opened the paper wrapping and pulled back the silver foil. She snapped off a piece and handed it to him delicately.

'Are you sure?'

Gwenhwyfar nodded. Arthur placed it on his tongue, and she did the same. Packing the chocolate away and clutching the bar in her hands, she began to stroll thoughtfully down the street.

'It's best if you let it melt,' Arthur advised.

She found it hard not to chew. It was very bitter, and at first she wasn't sure if she liked it, but eventually her tastebuds adjusted and she began to savour the rarity of the flavour.

'What do you think?'

'Delicious.' Gwenhwyfar rubbed it around her mouth and then swallowed, pleased to find a sweeter taste lingering. They stopped by the foot of her drive. She gazed up at him tenderly. 'Thank you.'

'You're welcome.' He kissed her again.

'I suppose supper's nearly ready,' Gwenhwyfar said after a while.

'I hope the chocolate hasn't ruined your appetite,' he murmured.

'Not at all.' Their lips connected again and then once more, before eventually they resigned themselves to being parted.

The rattle of the door reverberated around the house.

All the lights were off, casting the furniture into a gloom interrupted only by the distant glow from the street. The curtains were partially drawn and the clock by the mantelpiece announced the time with its own tune.

Unsure how she was going to top Arthur's Christmas present, Gwenhwyfar slipped the bar of chocolate into her pocket and draped her coat over the nearest chair. She called out to see who was in. There was no answer. She found a note from her mother on the kitchen table. She had gone to the supermarket nearly two hours ago.

With the house deserted and her father probably working late, Gwenhwyfar wished she had invited Arthur in. She opened the fridge to hunt for a snack, but with the taste of chocolate still strong in her mouth, soon reconsidered. It was then she heard a high whimper.

Llew snuffled and snorted at her feet through the crack in the bottom of the back door. It was locked. Fumbling, she found the key. Soon he was upon her, panting and shaking his rear end about gratefully. When Gwenhwyfar asked him why he had been outside, the old dog whined, and there was a sound of movement upstairs. His ears pricked.

'Mam? Dad?'

There was someone upstairs. Suddenly the thought came to her that there might have been a break-in. Llew could easily have been tempted into the garden with a slice of cooked meat. The feeling that she was in danger grew as she ascended the stairs. Her heart pulsed, and she strained to hear above the sound of her own breathing.

Another thud. For a while she froze. The disturbance seemed to be coming from her parents' bedroom. When she came to a stop outside the closed door, her suspicions were aroused. Llew whined, and gazed up at her with concerned eyes. The lights were off.

She took a breath and flung the door open. The imposter froze.

'*Dad?*'

Her father stared back at her, his hands filled with clothes and her mother's jewellery. 'Cariad,' he breathed, swiftly resuming what he was doing. Llew padded into the room, wagging his tail. When Gwenhwyfar's eyes fell upon the large suitcase on the bed her stomach folded.

'What are you doing?'

'Packing,' he remarked, briskly stuffing the bundles into the case. He shoved them down.

'In the dark?'

'The power's out,' he excused.

'Where are you going?'

'Just away for a few days.' He hurried to the wardrobe and flung it open. Splitting the clothes on the rail, Garan bent to a safe concealed at the back. Gwenhwyfar hadn't known it was there.

'How long is a few days?'

The safe clicked open. He pulled out five thick rolls of money. Most of it went into his briefcase, but then he hesitated, crushing two packets into Gwenhwyfar's hands. 'Be a darling, would you, and go put that under the stairs? There's a hatch under the floorboards. Tell your mother it's there when she gets home. It's for emergencies.'

Alarmed, she clutched the heavy bundles to her chest. 'Why are you going?'

'Business trip.'

'At a weekend?'

'A colleague's been taken sick,' he explained. 'I'm already late—my plane is leaving in a few hours.'

'You're going abroad? Does Mam know about this?'

'I've tried calling her. I'll be back soon, don't worry.' He zipped the case up and closed his briefcase. He was taking more than he needed for just a few days. Garan pulled his bags off the bed, kneed Llew to one side and then attempted to get past her. They were at the bottom of the stairs when he put his cases down again. Thinking they were going somewhere, Llew cantered past them, ready for adventure.

'I'm sorry Gwen—I know this is a bit of a shock, but it can't be helped.' He closed his hands around the money she held, nervously striding to hide it himself. 'Remember, under the stairs in the hatch. Llew needs feeding too. Tell your mother I'm sorry, that I love her, and that I'll speak to her soon.'

She watched as her father vanished into the cupboard beneath the stairs and then emerged to grab his coat. Her suspicion of his extramarital affair immediately resurfaced. She expelled a terrified sob.

'Are you leaving us?'

'No, of course not.' He came to her briefly, offering a short hug that gave her little comfort. 'Don't be silly. And don't cry, either. I'll be back. I'll call you when I get there. I promise.'

'Where are you going?'

'I love you, cariad.'

A firm kiss on the forehead was all he left her with. She stood tear-stricken as he struggled with his case to the front door. She barely heard the tyres crackle over the driveway. Suddenly he flew back past her with his briefcase, through the kitchen and out the back door.

The sound of splintering wood crashed through the house.

'New Morals!' Torch beams lanced through the dark. 'New Morals!' they roared again, their camouflage turning them to shadows. They swarmed through the house, stripping curtains and upturning cabinets. A gunman marked her. She raised her hands to the ceiling. He shouted and jerked his gun, and she knelt in the middle of the kitchen floor, trembling.

Her father reappeared, bound and blindfolded. Llew yelped, his howls silenced with the butt of a gun. Gwenhwyfar cried for her father from the floor. He shouted back, his voice frantic through his shroud.

The gunman left her. Scrambling, Gwenhwyfar ran after Garan. A white van stood in the drive, its back doors gaping and hungry. A bound, oversized Alsatian snapped at her legs as she hurried past the threshold. They threw her father into the van. She tried to follow, pleading, but she was pushed back. There was a woman in there too, her hair sticking out like straw from the bottom of her hood.

'Gwen? Gwenhwyfar? Is that you?'

'Mami!' she howled, tears running from her nose. Someone hauled her away and suddenly she was crumpled on the front doorstep, knees aching. Neighbours who had emerged to watch the scene vanished behind their curtains. Doors were slammed shut, engines roared. She wasn't aware whose hands she pushed at as she tore after the van, only of the pain in her shins and the burning in her heart. She made it to the end of the street and halfway down the next road, but finally the unmarked vehicles turned out of sight. Gasping for breath, Gwenhwyfar fell sobbing to the concrete. They were gone.

ACKNOWLEDGEMENTS

Going it alone on a project like this is not possible without the help and support of others. Thank you to Kristof, Madlen, Mark and Martin for being involved in the final proofread before publication; and to Cat and Holly for putting the idea of self-publishing in my head. Special thanks again to Madlen for answering my questions about the Welsh language and for your invaluable advice and encouragement. Thank you also to my sample readers and to everyone who offered to help out during this process—your kindness will not be forgotten.

Kristof, thank you always for your continued investment and support in this and in everything I do, for your advice and patience, and for providing the platform I needed to write this book. Most especially thanks to Anna, who read through every draft and helped make this novel what it is—I could not have done it without you. Last but not least, to my family and friends—for your support and interest in *The Future King: Logres* and for not getting too bored with my most recent obsession: thank you.

Printed in Great Britain
by Amazon